PRINT EDITION

Crimson Winter Vol. 1 Ruins of Sapphire ©
2020 by Mirror World Publishing
Edited by: Robert Dowsett

Cover by: Justine Dowsett

Published by Mirror World Publishing in June 2020

Mirror World Publishing
Windsor, Ontario
www.mirrorworldpublishing.com
info@mirrorworldpublishing.com

ISBN: 978-1-987976-71-7

For Adam, Sabrina, Robert and Christine.
For all the memories.

Also by Justine Alley Dowsett:

Crimson Winter

Lands of Jade
City of Ruby

Neo Central

With Murandy Damodred:

Mirror Worlds

Mirror's Hope
Mirror's Heart
Mirror's Deceit
Mirror's Despair

Ismera

Unintended
Uncharted

And Coming Soon...

Uncommon

CRIMSON WINTER

Vol. 1:
Ruins of Sapphire

J.A. Dowsett

"When it seems you have everything, you probably have nothing worth appreciating, but if you have next to nothing...well, what you do have is really important.

My name is Yukari Namikoya and this is a lesson I learned the hard way. When this all began it was a Tuesday like any other. I was fifteen years old and attending Shinjuku High. I lived comfortably with my parents in an apartment complex in Tokyo, Japan. However, by the time that Tuesday ended, my life was irrevocably altered in ways I could have never dreamed possible...

Ruins of Sapphire

Prologue

The night was silent and the only light came from nearby apartment buildings as the four of us walked abreast past the park near our apartment complex. Kaji, Hotaru, Yue, and I – all residents of Hyuski Heights and friends since childhood – were heading home together following our school's swim meet victory celebration. It was before midnight and the four of us were together, satisfying both of my father's requirements for my late night excursion.

I had enjoyed myself, but my friend Kaji, usually so self-assured, hadn't enjoyed his evening much. Even now, he still seemed distraught over the fact that his girlfriend, Shuzhue, hadn't shown up for the swim meet today. In fact, she had been conspicuously absent since that morning without explanation.

I let Hotaru's empty words wash over me as my excitable best friend chirped incessantly about her day and the success of the swimmers in the competition, while Yue, with her long chestnut hair draped over her shoulder and hiding her face from view, kept quiet.

She had her earphones in, presumably listening to music. After a while Hotaru trailed off, realizing no one was really listening to her, and I quickened my pace, noting we were almost home and that it must be drawing close to midnight.

A ringtone broke the relative silence. The dancing notes sounded vaguely familiar, but that still didn't account for the way Kaji stiffened beside me and stopped moving forward. I looked toward him in surprise; the ringtone wasn't coming from him or any of us – it was coming from the park.

"Shuzhue…" The expression on Kaji's face was strange – I couldn't place it.

"It's a common enough ringtone," I stated, a little taken aback by his behaviour. "I doubt it's hers."

"Let's go see," Hotaru suggested promptly, her dark ponytail bouncing behind her as she headed toward the park's darkened entranceway.

I frowned. Shuzhue was missing, yes, but I didn't see how or why she would be in the park near our apartment building, especially not this late at night. Also, who would be calling her if she were?

But Kaji seemed to take Hotaru's suggestion with the utmost seriousness and he veered off toward the park's entrance. Yue, with her earphones still in, had not noticed the change in conversation or that we had stopped, so she continued on ahead.

I looked from her to the others and I couldn't help but feel some responsibility for them all. I couldn't let Yue continue on home alone, but I also couldn't let Hotaru and Kaji explore the dark park by themselves. We lived in a relatively safe district, but Tokyo was still Tokyo and it was nearly midnight.

Making a split-second decision, I ran a few steps and grabbed hold of Yue, steering her into the park with me. Yue made no protest, and I thanked her silently for being the kind of person who didn't mind an unexpected detour. Kaji and Hotaru's confidence ebbed somewhat as the dark silence of the park surrounded them, allowing Yue and I to catch up as they reached the playground in the center of the park.

I could still hear the cell phone's eerie music; it hadn't stopped ringing, though by now it should have gone to voicemail. Yue, unconcerned, wandered over to the swing set. I watched as she started swinging higher and higher, her exceptionally long hair fanning out around her, and the other two converged on the lonely sandbox on the edge of the playground area.

The ringing continued.

I saw Kaji bend down to pick something up and the ringing finally stopped. It was darker here, with only one nearby streetlight to light the park. I headed over. Kaji did in fact have two cell phones in his hands and Hotaru had hers out as well, so the extra one must have been the one that had been ringing. It said conspicuously, 'Property of Shuzhue Chi,' down the one side of it, confirming Kaji's initial suspicions.

Kaji was busy checking the call history. The last answered call was just now and it had the same listing as the one before it: Unknown Name, Unknown Number.

"Well, you've found it. She's not here," I stated.

For some reason, Hotaru had decided to squat down in the sand and start digging. Instead of answering me, Kaji began doing the same. Surely they didn't think Shuzhue was hiding in the sandbox?

I furrowed my brow, then checked the time on my cell phone; quarter to midnight. We were no more than a few minutes from home – you could see our building from the park's entrance – so we could easily make it in time.

"Kaji – you have ten minutes, then we're leaving," I stated authoritatively.

Kaji and Hotaru ignored me and continued to dig, their motions oddly frantic. I turned to head back to Yue, when I noticed we weren't alone in the park anymore.

He was perhaps a little older than the group of us, but he was still a teenager. In the light of the single lamp I could see his blond hair was fashionably spiked. He looked vaguely familiar to me, and I might have been able to place where I knew him from if it wasn't for the red contacts in his eyes and his stark black clothing. Was he some sort of Goth? Besides his all black attire, he also wore a long chain around his neck that ended in a diamond-shaped ruby red crystal. He also wore a scabbard on his hip, which fit him comfortably, as strange as that seemed.

I'll admit he intimidated me, but I took a few steps forward to confront him anyway. I didn't like his sly expression and I would have felt better if I could have put a finger on just why he felt so familiar, or at the very least figure out why he was there, watching us so intently. Before I reached him, however, Yue was in his face.

"What are you doing here?" she demanded.

The strange teen did not bother to reply, though the corner of his mouth twisted up a little in an obvious smirk.

Behind us, Hotaru called out, "Yukari! I think we found Shuzhue's skirt!"

Hotaru's sudden outburst caught me off guard and I turned to look toward her and Kaji, thankful I had Yue to keep an eye on the stranger. In fact, I began to feel glad all four of us were here and it wasn't just me, though likely I wouldn't have come into the park on my own under similar circumstances.

Though what if Shuzhue had come here alone...and this guy had come in after her? Hotaru just said they had found Shuzhue's skirt in the sandbox?

Shaking my head to clear it, I tried to think rationally. I didn't know why the Goth had followed us into the park, or if Shuzhue had ever been here, but it was highly unlikely he had anything to do with her or that any material Hotaru found in the sand was Shuzhue's, let alone a piece of a skirt at all.

I turned back to consider the Goth once more. He was definitely smirking and there was no mistaking his expression this time. It was also clear he was beginning to piss Yue off.

"Answer me, you," she demanded of him, "why are you just standing there?"

Ignoring Yue, the teenager straightened, his red eyes and red jewel seeming to take on an unnatural glow I hoped was just a trick of the light. He looked out beyond Yue, which was driving my friend crazy if her expression was any indication. She looked poised for a fight, though what Yue was actually intending to do, I had no idea.

I followed his gaze and I thought at first he might be staring at Kaji and Hotaru where they were bent over in the sandbox, still frantically digging, but his gaze seemed to go over them and it was then I noticed the rest of them.

Directly across the playground from where the teenager stood there was a girl about his age and dressed just as strangely as he was. She was wearing all black as well, but in her case that meant a tight-fitting dress that flared out from her waist and belled at her ankles. That was strange enough, but she also had a glowing, red-jeweled necklace around her neck that matched her companion's exactly. Her hair, which framed her face and fell almost to her waist, was the same fiery red as the contacts in her eyes.

There were two more as well, one to each side, and the four of them had the four of us surrounded. My fear spiked – this wasn't normal.

Rash, fiery Yue again did the unexpected and she leapt for the gothic teenager nearest us. Oddly, he did not react, nor seem to care in the least. Then, somehow, her outstretched arms passed through him as if he wasn't even there at all.

I didn't waste the time or effort trying to reason out how that could be possible. I simply did the only thing I could think of; I lifted my phone and called the police.

"What is your emergency?"

"My friends and I are being accosted by a gang in Hyuski Heights Park, Shinjuku district." If I sounded panicked now, I had the police on the phone and did not care. I clung to my cell phone like a lifeline.

The Goths all stepped forward, and in unison they each lifted their crystal necklaces in what I assumed to be a ritual motion. This was it. Whatever they had come here for, it was going to happen now.

At the request of the dispatch lady, I described the four people around us. They continued to ignore us – even Yue, who had taken several swings at the blonde one with no results. Amazingly, red lights shot upwards like laser beams from their upheld crystals to connect in the air above us. I didn't bother to explain this to the woman on the phone – she wouldn't have believed me and I was beyond shock at this point – the police would see it when they arrived.

"The police are on their way," she informed me. "Did you need me to contact your parents?"

"No," I answered a little too quickly, stricken, "but can you please stay on the line with me?" I thought I might lose what grip on reality I had if I lost this woman's voice – that was how scared I was.

The glowing beams cast a red hue onto the park and us. The point where they connected to each other pulsed brightly above our heads. Surely someone would see this and come looking? Hotaru and Kaji had stopped digging by now and were staring about in surprise. They had been too preoccupied to notice our predicament before and I had not thought to warn them. The center point continued to pulse and we, in the midst of it all, stood almost riveted, watching as it grew and lengthened inexplicably until it formed a column of red light reaching to the ground.

Yue was the first to snap out of the trance the odd phenomenon had caused in us. She changed her tactics abruptly on the gang member she was facing, and weaved to dodge past him, making a break for the exit. I could hear sirens in the distance now and I thanked providence the local police station was not far away. There was a sharp crackling sound as Yue struck an invisible wall, seemingly created by the joining of the red beams of light. She cried out in pain and was flung backwards by the impact. The blonde teenager laughed and I ran forward to make sure Yue was okay, all the while dictating what was happening to the dispatch woman, no longer worrying how crazy or delusional I sounded.

"Hello? Hello, are you hearing me?" I demanded into the receiver. "Yue is hurt! You have to hurry."

Yue was in pain, I could tell, but she climbed to her feet regardless, wincing as she did so.

"Um, Yukari, Yue…" Hotaru called in an uncertain voice and we turned to look over at her.

The pulsing light in the center of the red dome they had created was now in the shape of a pillar – no, a gateway – and something was coming out of it.

I knew in that instant I didn't want to know what that something was.

A clawed metal foot stepped out from the pillar of light and I stood riveted by this strange new horror, unable to react as more of the creature revealed itself. Shaped vaguely like a man, it was covered in armour so deeply purple it might have appeared black except for the otherworldly red light bathing everything in the park. The armour was pointed, with spikes on the arms, knees, and shoulders. The helmet was the most grotesque and frightening of all, with great curving metal tusks and an alien cast to what features there were. Not an inch of what might lie beneath the armour showed, not even in the eyes, which glowed a sinister red, exactly like the crimson rubies used by its followers to trap us here.

"This is impossible…" I breathed. "Impossible…"

The police sirens snapped me back to reality as nothing else could have. The police were here! They would see this, and we would be believed and saved – possibly. I had hope the police could drive off at least the four that surrounded us – if not the armoured monstrosity – so we could run and maybe break free of this horror.

I turned to let Yue know the police were coming – I hadn't yet told her about the call I had made – but I hadn't counted on her temper. She was already riled up from being unable to lay a finger on the blonde guy behind us, and now something was in the ring with us – so to speak – so she was gearing herself up to face it head on.

"Yue, no!" I screamed as I watched my friend charge the armoured menace.

It watched her approach impassively and I wondered if it truly saw her. Yue leapt full force at the last moment, and tried to grab hold of the armoured suit, not nearly careful enough to avoid the spikes. It was as if she didn't care if she got hurt; she only wanted to stand in the creature's way so it would fight her and leave the rest of us alone.

My heart went out to her for her bravery, even though her actions were foolish and dangerous. Yue managed to wrap herself around one of its armoured arms with only a minimal amount of scratches and bruises, and she was screaming at the thing to get its attention.

Suddenly the arm of the suit of armour lifted; Yue had not been expecting this, so her hold slipped. She scrabbled for purchase, but that smooth metal must have been fairly slick. Her leg flailed, catching on a knee spike, and she screamed, but miraculously she managed to hold on for whatever good it would do her.

I couldn't watch Yue throw her life away. I knew this thing, whatever it was, wasn't yet trying to hurt or kill her. It was doing her body damage just by being what it was and if it decided to get serious, I knew that Yue – and possibly the rest of us – wouldn't stand a chance.

I turned away and was almost surprised to see that the police had indeed arrived. To my dismay, however, the police were not paying any attention to us or the metal monster in the playground; they were talking – seemingly calmly – to the blonde teenager.

They were asking him questions and he was answering them in a very open and non-threatening way. Could they not see us here? I realized then I couldn't hear them. The invisible barrier…I remembered Yue throwing herself against it. It must have been concealing us, somehow.

My theory made about as much sense as any of this did. I tried yelling, to no avail. I thought about trying to get through to the woman on the phone, but I had to admit I had known I hadn't actually been speaking to anyone in a while – perhaps even since the barrier had been erected.

We were well and truly trapped.

I heard Yue cry out again, and despite myself, I turned to see what had happened. Yue was lying on her back, her leg bleeding profusely, about ten feet away from where that thing was. It seemed as if it had managed to throw her off and now it was raising his arm again, as if it was aiming at Hotaru and Kaji. Yue was taken care of…were they to be next?

I looked down at the cell phone in my hand. It was useless now. I had called for help and there the police stood, not ten feet away from me. They didn't even know we were here, about to die.

A flash of insight crossed my mind. I snapped my phone shut and hefted it in my fist – then I reconsidered and bent slightly to remove my left shoe instead. Calling forth all the rage I could muster at the futility of our situation, I lobbed my shoe with deadly accuracy at the blonde teenager, knowing full well it would stop at the barrier.

It did, but it also did what I expected, creating a surge of power and a flash of light where my shoe struck. The Goth shot me a look of pure malice, but the cop looked a little surprised. Since I was focusing on his reaction so closely I was able to read his lips as he said, What was that?

I smiled, but it was a grimace more than anything else. They had heard – or saw – that. The two policemen standing outside the barrier now had matching curious expressions on their faces as they examined the air beyond my blonde adversary.

I removed my other shoe and threw that too. Then I began throwing anything I had on my person – my purse, my keys, and even my swimsuit. The only thing I kept out of sheer perversion was my cell phone – it would cost too much to replace and hitting that force field would no doubt short it out. Enough objects hitting the force field would alert the police to the fact that something strange was going on here, and with any luck they might at least arrest the blonde one who I believed had started all of this.

I could tell the policemen were really intrigued now. They were looking at the space where the barrier began intently. The blonde teenager had backed up from them and now he was standing behind the policemen, glaring at me. It seemed he, at least, could see me, and knew what I was trying to do.

Without warning he unsheathed two slightly curved blades, longer than his forearms. They glinted in the glow of the barrier as he raised them high and then drove them without hesitation into the necks of the two unsuspecting policemen. They never got the chance to raise an alarm. The dead men crumpled to the ground and the Goth wiped his blades clean on their backs with a sickening nonchalance.

I froze. My fear of this gothic stranger had finally been proven to be correct – he was as dangerous as they come and had no compunction whatsoever about killing.

While I stood there, oblivious to my friends' plight and the real danger behind me, I almost gave up hope entirely. In my mind's eye, all I could see was the sudden death of the two policemen over and over again. I was the only witness to how they had fallen and I couldn't even scream for help.

My cell phone rang.

I stared at it stupidly. The familiar beep was so normal I couldn't relate to it now. The screen lit up to reveal the identity of the caller: Unknown Name, Unknown Number.

Instinct, or maybe just social programming, kicked in. I flipped open the phone and stuck it to my ear. "Hello?"

"I can help you," a tranquil female voice said enigmatically on the other end of the line, "if you'll let me."

"What?"

"Just say the word…and Sapphiros will aid you," she continued in the same tone.

I didn't know who this woman was or what was going on. Maybe this was the person Shuzhue had talked to before she disappeared and maybe it wasn't. I immediately felt bad for Shuzhue, having possibly gone through something like this on her own, but she was likely dead already and there was nothing I could do for her now.

I looked up at my friends; Hotaru had helped Yue to her feet and they now stood side by side, facing the threat head on. Kaji stood a little further back, still confused, if his stance was any indication.

The creature was no longer advancing. It looked instead as if it was gathering power, intent on striking us all down, perhaps in one blow. A red lava-like substance – it might have actually been lava for all I knew – formed from its hands and began to grow between them. I could see the heat rippling from it in the still air. If it unleashed this power on us, would there be anything left to save?

"Yes!" I said into the phone, not knowing what I was agreeing to, only that it was my only hope. "Help us! If there is a way to get us out of here – do it!"

"All of you must stand together and be ready," the voice responded coolly, but with more urgency. "There is not much time."

I forced my body to obey her commands. I didn't know who she was or what she could do, but I was not going to throw away this new lifeline my cell phone had provided me. I raced up to stand beside Kaji. I didn't have it in me to get any closer.

"Yue! Hotaru! Fall back!" I yelled to them, unsure if they would listen.

"In Rubia's name – Die."

The voice was the deepest I had ever heard and it rumbled malevolently through the monstrous helmet the creature wore. I had no doubt the man or beast beneath the armour meant the threat exactly as uttered – no matter who this Rubia it spoke of was.

The lava between the thing's hands grew until it erupted from them in a wave of heat and destruction, directed towards us by the armoured creature's will. Remarkably, we all stood our ground, though I supposed with the barrier in place we truly had no choice.

A blue light began to glow. At first it was just a pinprick, only slightly visible over the shoulder spike of the monster before us, but as it grew it became more noticeable and it seemed to be coming through the center of the red pillar of light where the suit of armour had emerged.

A reflection of blue bounced off of something on Hotaru. No, wait – it was coming from Hotaru herself. There was a glowing spot of blue on her chest, from about the same place a necklace like the ruby ones our captors were wearing would have hung. I looked to Yue and saw the same glow coming from her. They were both glowing now, their points of light pulsing in time to the blue light in the center of the pillar.

The lava surged forward to meet us. Yue formed her outstretched hands into a Shinto priestess hand sign she had no doubt learned from her mother and Hotaru tried her best to copy the motions. What they thought they were doing was beyond me, but to my surprise it seemed to work.

Blue light erupted from their hands, washing over the flow of lava and freezing it in place. It struck the suit of armour full on and had much the same effect, then it continued on to join with the blue light behind the creature and the pillar of light changed completely from red to blue.

"Go now!" the voice from the cell phone spoke suddenly, urgently, startling me into action before I was fully conscious of the decision to obey.

I took Kaji's hand; I didn't have time to explain and he was the nearest to me. Together we ran around the frozen lava, which released from its stasis as we passed to continue its deadly course. Yue and Hotaru were following my lead; I could hear their footsteps in the otherwise eerie silence of the scene. I dove past the suit of armour's spikes – in a fit of courage I didn't know I had – and I dragged Kaji with me every step of the way.

When I struck the light, time stopped, and I knew no more.

Chapter 1 – Tuesday… Again?

I woke up to the alarm on my cell phone – a utilitarian sound, as I've never bothered with the more colourful ringtones. As I came to, I wondered about the vivid terror of my nightmare, but it was quarter after eight and time to get ready for school, so I didn't dwell on it.

School wasn't too far away. As I crossed the threshold of the school gates I noted my friend, Hotaru Hatsumuya, accosting another Hyuski Heights resident, Kaji Zukatoro, as he stood with his girlfriend, the red-headed Shuzhue Chi. Despite being my best friend, Hotaru could be a bit much at times – she had near limitless energy and not enough brains to put it to good use – so I avoided her wave of greeting in favour of continuing into the massive stone structure instead.

Shinjuku High greeted me with its usual hustle and bustle in the early morning, and though I never took part in the conversations or activity that buzzed around me, I took comfort in the sense of sameness. Home was a quiet place where I was often under scrutiny by my overbearing mother and my father was most often absent. Here, I could occupy my time by watching others or keeping up with – which usually meant working ahead of – my studies.

"Here comes the Ice Queen," a voice whispered urgently to my right, followed by a whistle.

My blue eyes did not betray any reaction behind the square frames of my glasses. It was never in the same place, but undoubtedly at least once a day I would encounter someone – usually male – who wanted to stare at 'Ice Queen' Yukari.

I was tall for a Japanese girl and long-limbed, but that wasn't what made them stare. It was my pale blue, curly hair - the likes of which I had never seen on anyone else - and my intense, bright blue eyes.

I supposed that was enough to draw attention my way, but I also studied really hard, wore glasses, and my hair was often tied up into a tight bun atop my head to try and control my unruly curls, which would become a ball of frizz if I let them. I was by no means conventionally attractive and I never did anything to encourage the attention. I kept hoping one day people would let my odd appearance fade into the background, although well into highschool it still seemed as if that wasn't to be the case.

Other than the usual annoyances, the morning was calm and relatively quiet. I carried my books in my arms and was quite looking forward to my daily routine as I passed through the halls. On Wednesdays, I had Phys Ed first thing in the morning, so I headed to the change room, eager to get into the pool.

The change room was empty when I reached it, which was no surprise with how early I was. I dug through my bag and then my locker, but I couldn't seem to find my swimsuit. I recalled putting it in my bag after the swim meet last night…

…then I threw it at the red force field to get the attention of the police.

The other students began filing in, interrupting my thoughts. I looked up to ask if any of them had seen my swimsuit, thinking maybe I had managed to misplace it, but these students weren't the ones from my class. I stared open-mouthed for a moment, and then gathered the presence of mind to check my cell phone.

Tuesday – 8:55AM

It was Tuesday, not Wednesday at all…did the swim meet really happen? What about the Karaoke café? The walk home through the park afterwards? Had it all just been a part of that strange dream?

I didn't know, but on Tuesday I was supposed to be in Science class on the other end of the school, so I picked up my books and ran.

I skidded into the classroom, the latest I had ever been. The class stared at me in shock and so did my teacher, Sonoma-sensei, until he recovered himself enough to say, "Nice of you to join us, Namikoya-san. As I was saying," he continued as I crossed sheepishly to my seat, "we're having a pop quiz."

Another one? I distinctly recalled having written a surprise science test yesterday…

"Form into groups and I will hand out the test booklets. They must be fully completed…"

As Sonoma-sensei continued I found myself unable to focus on his words. It was the same. The same as my dream, or the same as the last 'Tuesday', I wasn't sure.

"Yukari!" Hotaru exclaimed as if she had only just noticed me there, giving me an even sharper sense of déjà-vu. "You're smart, so you'd be the best person to have on our team. We've already got Harford-san and Mizu-chan," she continued, indicating the smart and personable foreign exchange student from England and one of her other friends.

Kaji was also there, without Shuzhue, as she wasn't in this class, and Yue Noh, another person I had known for years – our fathers had both been in the military together when we were younger. She was included, I assumed, because of her proximity to the group, though she seemed preoccupied by taking a nap on her desk, her impossibly long chestnut hair fanning out around her like a blanket.

My suspicions about this day having happened before were confirmed when I received my test booklet – I knew all the answers.

"Phosphorous," I began reciting as I sat, not looking at the test booklet as I did so. "Bone. An Egg. Gasoline."

Tim Harford looked at me like I had grown horns.

I didn't make any excuses for my behavior. "Kaji-san, I think we should send Hotaru and Yue for the things we need, while you and Harford-san write out the responses in the booklets. I will handle the phosphorous and Yue," I said as I woke her up with a poke to the ribs with my pencil – she was only pretending to sleep anyway, if my knowledge of 'last Tuesday' was correct – "will find the bone and the egg in the cafeteria."

Kaji opened and closed his mouth for a moment, much like a fish, but then he seemed to shake himself before getting down to business. I headed over to the chemistry supply cupboard to fetch what I needed to make phosphorus, then returned and began to recite the next group of answers as I worked to set everything up.

This science class went much more smoothly than the one from my memory. When we finished more than fifteen minutes early, I was confident we had managed a perfect score. Even grumpy old Sonoma-sensei looked impressed.

Instead of being pleased, I was pensive. It was scientifically impossible for the same day to happen twice – I didn't know what was going on.

◊

Lunchtime was another routine for me. I brought my own bento I made for myself in the morning and I always sat at the big empty table by the floor to ceiling window overlooking the school grounds.

I had no reason to act differently than I had before, so I headed unerringly to my usual spot at lunch, leaving an open textbook within easy view, so people would think I was studying. In the Tuesday I remembered, I had been caught off guard by a new student who'd stumbled over to my table looking to introduce herself. Only this time, when the transfer student approached me, I was ready.

"Is this seat taken?" a higher-pitched girl's voice spoke timidly from behind me exactly as expected.

She looked too young to be in high school, but I remembered from our conversation the other day that she had skipped a few grades. She was in reality maybe thirteen or fourteen, but looked twelve, with a short bob of white-blonde hair and a friendly expression. I welcomed her and asked her to sit with me. As she did so, she waved unexpectedly to someone outside, in view of the window – that was new.

I turned to see who she was waving at. There, by the tree. He was meeting me stare for stare, as if he were watching me and not the other way around. He was of medium build and dressed as we all were in a Shinjuku High school uniform. His face was angular with strong lines, which made him appear a little older than my fifteen years. His blond hair was fashionably spiked and he met my gaze with unwavering brown eyes. I stiffened, for his expression was filled with an inexplicably familiar anger.

A group of four at a nearby table caught my eye, two boys and two girls. One of the girls with them was Shuzhue, oddly enough. She was looking down as if she didn't want to be there but she didn't have it in her to leave. As I watched her, I realized that in the Tuesday I remembered Shuzhue was missing by the time the swim meet began after school. She looked up and met my eyes, seeming to smile sadly in my direction. I couldn't help but feel she was imploring me to understand something – or maybe she was just asking me silently for help.

"My name's Reiki," the young girl's voice startled me into turning to face her once more. "I've just transferred here. It's my first day," she stated with a hopeful expression.

I ignored her, turning back to discover why that student under the tree had seemed so familiar. His eyes met mine once more and they flashed red. In my vision his clothes changed too – they flickered from his school uniform to his Goth blacks, with the red jewel prominently displayed.

"Is something the matter?" Reiki spoke, but I didn't turn to look at her. My gaze was riveted on the three people at the table with Shuzhue. They were all dressed the same now – black clothes, red jewels. They were the ones who had accosted us and now they were surrounding Shuzhue.

"I'm fine." I forced myself to break their gaze and turn to face Reiki, though I felt uneasy having them at my back, even if they were a floor away. "If you'll excuse me," I said as calmly as possible before standing and walking away from her.

As I exited the cafeteria, I heard the student council president of Shinjuku High, Goji Nakamura's, voice ring out behind me, "I hope everyone is ready for the swim meet after school!"

I couldn't think of what to do. The only thing that came to mind was to go down there and confront them, but I didn't know if I had the courage. I could continue to let this play out, and now, being forewarned, I could avoid the park and its deadly trap...

But there was still Kaji, Yue, and Hotaru. If I didn't go with them, would they still go? And what about Shuzhue – would she still meet her mysterious fate? If I wanted to change this, I would have to do things differently. Forewarned is forearmed, as they say.

I gathered myself and headed purposefully outside to face those goths and demand some answers, but by the time I got down there they were gone, and only the spiky blond-haired one remained.

As I came within view of the tree and picnic table, I saw him coming towards me. I ducked out of sight and used the corner of the building to conceal myself for the moment. He went past, his walk a confident swagger, but never looked back to see me. I tried not to stare at him with too much intensity, lest he feel me watching him as he had before.

I followed him out of Shinjuku High's grounds. He never hesitated nor slowed. It didn't seem to me he knew I was there. I followed him across the street at a careful distance. He was heading away from the school and perpendicular to Hyuski Heights. I couldn't fathom where he was headed. Did he intend to miss his afternoon classes, or would he come back for them? I didn't know him well enough to judge.

On the other side of the street someone was waiting for him. I recognized her at once. She had long, vibrant red hair and she was dressed in a school uniform, but I remembered her bell-shaped black dress.

She was looking about, as if searching for someone, and I had an instant of dread as her eyes found mine. A look of triumph crossed her face; she had found what she had been searching for – me.

Chapter 1 – Tuesday… Again?!

I awoke to the sound of the alarm on my cell phone.

Confused and muddled by sleep, I reached for it and put my glasses on to read the display.

Tuesday – 8:15AM

Something told me today was going to be much the same as the last. I snapped the phone shut in disgust, silencing it. It rang again as soon as I had done so.

I stared at it astounded for a moment, then I read the screen. *Hotaru-chan's residence.*

This, at least, hadn't happened before. I answered it. "Hotaru?"

"Uh huh," she answered in an uncertain tone. I marveled that she didn't sound sleepy this early in the morning. "Um, Yukari-san, you haven't noticed anything weird, have you?"

I was cautious in revealing my insanity, even to Hotaru who might be the only person to believe me – my friend had a very active imagination.

"Hotaru, I just woke up," I informed her steadily.

"Yeah, well me too…it's just that…well…" She floundered. "Are you sure you haven't noticed anything strange…" She took an audible breath. "Over the last couple of Tuesdays, maybe?"

"Um," I hesitated, which is rare for me, "you mean the way that Tuesday just seems to keep repeating itself?"

"So it's true then…what should we do, Yukari?"

So I wasn't the only crazy person. Hotaru, someone I had known my entire life, was here with me. Somehow, knowing Hotaru, that was only a small comfort. Growing up together, anytime something had occurred that Hotaru couldn't grasp or keep up with, she would turn to me. I was smart, she said, so I would know what to do. Well, generally she was right – I just wished this time could be that simple.

"Meet me outside the gates at school," I said, sounding more confident than I felt. "We'll figure this out."

"Do you think anyone else realizes this is happening?" Hotaru asked and I realized she had a good point. Was everyone affected, or were certain people just reliving this day over and over again to some purpose? There was only one way to find out.

"We'll look into that too. I'll see you at school."

I finished getting ready and I hurried to the gates. Hotaru looked worried. I greeted her in what I hoped was a reassuring fashion.

"Look," I said, gesturing, "there's Kaji and Shuzhue over there. Let's go and talk to them, and see if they know anything. I'm almost certain Shuzhue is at the heart of this."

Hotaru nodded, trying to look determined, and together we approached Kaji and his girlfriend as they milled about school grounds, waiting for the bell.

"Kaji-san, Chi-san, do you have a minute?" I asked.

"Sure," Kaji replied easily as Shuzhue seemed shocked I was addressing them. I guess I don't have much of a reputation for being social.

Hotaru jumped right in without any of the sensible hesitation she had shown earlier when broaching this subject with me. "Have either of you noticed the odd way this Tuesday seems to be looping? It's like that anime, *'The Girl Who Leapt Through Time'*."

Shuzhue grew even more confused, but Kaji seemed to be waiting patiently for me. I made a few calculations in my head. Corroborating Hotaru's claim would only make whatever I had to say seem implausible and I would run the risk of not being taken seriously. "Chi-san, did you have any plans for after school today?"

This, I could tell, was even more surprising to her. "Um, well, yes actually," she answered tentatively and Kaji looked at her in surprise. This was evidently something he didn't know either. Good – I might be getting closer to the circumstances under which she went missing.

"I'm supposed to go with my mom to visit my grandmother." I frowned, that didn't seem a likely possibility for a kidnapping.

"Oh," Kaji said. "How is your grandmother? I don't think I've seen her since last Christmas."

Shuzhue did not look pleased the subject had come up and truthfully neither was I. Kaji was veering the conversation away from where I was likely to get information about Shuzhue's disappearance.

"Actually, she's not well," Shuzhue admitted reluctantly. "We're going to visit her in the hospital tonight."

I opened my mouth to ask her more questions about her plans. If I had the details, maybe I could accompany her there or follow her to see what happened, but as soon as I even thought it –

Reset the program.

The words were in my head, spoken by a strange voice. It was unlike anything I had ever heard before or experienced before. The voice may have been robotic, that was the closest descriptor I could think of.

Again? A different voice responded. This one was more guttural and less clearly defined. It was harder to make out.

I shook my head, trying to clear it.

Reset the program. The robotic command was repeated and Hotaru in front of me met my gaze with a shocked expression of her own – she had heard it too.

Chapter 1 – Still Tuesday…?

Tuesday – 8:15AM

  I stared at my phone – silenced now – and I thought long and hard about all I had seen and heard over the past few 'Tuesdays'.

Hotaru called. I answered it automatically, knowing almost the exact second when it would ring. "So, Tuesday again, huh?"

"Yes," I responded. "It seems it still is. This time we're going to try something a little different, though."

"Oh? What do you have in mind?"

"Meet me at school again. Same place."

We went through our day as normally as we could and did nothing to upset the balance of events. We passed our science test, I met Reiki at lunch, and I took the blonde stranger's hatred as naturally as I could. I even signed up for the swim meet, though I didn't know if I would ever make it to the end of the day again.

After school, Hotaru and I met up and broke the pattern by taking the bus to the hospital. We figured Shuzhue's grandmother would have been admitted to the nearest hospital to their home, so that was where we went. I picked a few flowers from rows outside the hospital to make our story seem plausible.

"Excuse me," I addressed the nurse behind the glass in the main lobby, "would you be able to direct me to Chi-sama's room?"

"Are you friends or family?"

"Friends," Hotaru supplied.

"I'm sorry," he replied. "I can only give out room numbers to immediate family."

"I understand," I replied, containing my frustration. Of course they would have to control who was allowed to visit the patients.

In a flash of insight I looked down. There on the desk was a sign-in sheet for visitors. The last two people to arrive were *Chi Shuzhue* and *Chi Junae* and next to their names was labeled *6ᵗʰ Floor.*

"Thanks anyway," I said to the nurse before taking Hotaru's arm to lead her away.

"That's it?" Hotaru demanded in a hushed whisper. "We're just going to walk away?"

"Not exactly," I replied, steering her toward the elevator while checking over my shoulder to ensure the nurse wasn't watching where we went. "I checked the sign-in sheet. They're on the sixth floor. We just have to go up there and check the charts by the doors."

The elevator door opened and the blonde Goth stepped out. I was so startled I almost let out a yelp, but I kept it together and hauled Hotaru to the side. There was nothing normal about his appearance. He was not in school clothes, but in his black goth outfit. The red jewel hung limply around his neck with no hint of a glow, but to me he still seemed otherworldly.

He didn't seem to notice us or care and he continued walking right on by. Though I was not exactly relieved, I pulled Hotaru into the elevator and pressed the button for the sixth floor with a near frantic haste.

"Yukari, what was that all about?" Hotaru demanded once we were safely in the elevator. "You acted like you saw a ghost."

"That person we just passed," I said as I tried to calm my nerves enough to explain, "he was one of the four in the park. The ones that surrounded us and trapped us in there with...him." I couldn't bring myself to relive that night any further and Hotaru didn't ask me to. She just looked thoughtful, but I could tell she knew who and what I meant.

The elevator stopped and opened onto the sixth floor. "Come on," I instructed Hotaru and we split up to check each of the charts along the walls. We were lucky this hall was a quiet one and no one came to stop us.

Finally we found the room we were looking for. "This is it," I said to Hotaru as I stood in front of a door. It was open just a crack and I put my ear to it to listen for Shuzhue and her mother's voices.

I was mildly alarmed not to hear anything at all. A creeping suspicion dawning on me, I gently pushed the hospital door open. It was silent on its hinges, so I pushed it the rest of the way open and entered cautiously.

There were two beds in the room, separated by a curtain that billowed loosely in the wind from – I assumed – an open window. The bed nearest the door was neatly made up. The far one appeared rumpled, but even past the moving curtain I could see that it, too, was empty.

There was no one there. No sick grandmother, no visitors, and most importantly no Shuzhue.

I entered the room fully and I could feel Hotaru behind me. Moving the curtain out of the way, I made to inspect the room – they had been here, of that I was certain. What I didn't know was what had happened to them and where they were now. Did the doctors move the grandmother to another room or take her somewhere for some kind of treatment? Would they not have taken her chart with them?

The window was indeed open – wide open. And on the sill was the strangest thing, a single red sneaker with its laces undone.

Comprehension dawning, I approached the sneaker with mounting dread. This shoe could not have belonged to Shuzhue's mother or grandmother. If I was correct about the occupants of this room before we entered it, then this shoe likely belonged to Shuzhue herself. My hand closed around the sneaker, almost surprised to feel it was real. Size five. Shuzhue had small feet.

Gripping the mysterious sneaker to my chest, I leaned out the window, the evening wind whipping about my face and I looked down first – nothing down there – then up.

We were six stories up. Two floors away from the roof.

Reset the program. The metallic voice spoke again in my mind.

No! the other voice responded. *This has gone on too long...there isn't enough time.*

Reset the program.

Chapter 1 – This Was Getting Ridiculous

The alarm sounded on my cell phone. I reached over immediately and shut it off, thumbing through the menu by memory to find Hotaru's cell phone number. At the last moment I put on my glasses to double check I had it right and pressed send.

It rang and rang, but there was no answer.

Frustrated, I hung up and called her house line. Hotaru's mother answered immediately.

"Hatsumuya-san, good morning," I said politely, even though the delay grated on me. "Would Hotaru-san be available to talk to me? I'd like to meet her to walk to school this morning."

"Sure thing, Yukari-chan," Hotaru's mother responded happily. "I'll just go get her."

I waited much longer than I expected for Hotaru to finally come to the phone. When she did, her demeanor was completely different than it had been on the previous Tuesday mornings.

"Yukari," she said, sounding panicked, "there's something really wrong here!"

"Hotaru," I responded authoritatively – I wasn't in the mood for nonsense this morning, "calm down. What is going on?"

"Well," she said, as she forced herself to breathe as normally as possible, "I haven't been able to find my cell phone. It was ringing just now. I could hear it, but it's not where the sound is coming from."

Okay. That was weird, but it didn't call for the level of panic Hotaru was displaying.

"So I reached for it," Hotaru continued, still sounding shaky, "and my hand grabbed hold of a metal pipe instead."

"What?"

"There is a metal pipe in the center of my room," she repeated as calmly as she could. "I'm still holding it, I haven't let go. It comes up out of the floor on a strange angle and then goes across the room a ways before bending down and disappearing through my bed. I've hidden it with a blanket so my mom didn't see it, but Yukari, what is it?"

I tried to consider this rationally – and failed. "I don't know, Hotaru. The only thing I can think is there is something seriously wrong about this whole circumstance. We need to see what happened if we are to make any sense of this. Let go of the pipe, Hotaru. Let's try something different today. We'll go straight to the hospital."

"And skip school?" Hotaru sounded scandalized at the suggestion.

"Why not?" I answered, somewhat uncharacteristically. "It's not like it'll matter by next Tuesday."

The hospital was quiet during the day and infinitely less ominous than it would be later – closer to the mysterious disappearance of Shuzhue and her entire family. Hotaru and I walked the grounds of the hospital as I searched for something specific.

"There." I pointed for Hotaru's benefit.

"The fire escape ladder?"

"That window there is on the second floor. If we find that room, we can lower the fire escape ladder," I explained. "Then if we need an alternate route to the rooftop, we'll have one ready."

"The rooftop?" Hotaru asked, not following my logical leaps. "Isn't Shuzhue's grandma on the sixth floor? What's on the roof?"

"When I found that sneaker on the windowsill I figured they had to have taken Shuzhue either up or down. There was no trace of her down here. No prints in the moist ground," I said, nudging the dirt with my foot so Hotaru could see how soft it was, "and no indication someone had fallen or landed there. So I looked up, and that's when the day reset, remember?"

"Yeah, so?"

I shook my head. Hotaru was so dense sometimes. "Every time we've changed something that brings us closer to the truth – essentially every time we break the pattern completely – the day resets. We've been pushing the limits, but now we're into completely new territory. None of this," I said, indicating the hospital around us, "happened on the original Tuesday, so we must be getting closer."

Hotaru nodded, deep in thought. "If we want to find out what happened to Shuzhue in that room, we shouldn't go to the roof. That would be too late. We should be in the room."

"There's not really a place to hide in there," I pointed out, "and these people are dangerous, Hotaru. How about a compromise? We wait nearby and try to hear what's going on, and step in if necessary. Shuzhue had to have been taken between the time she signed into the hospital and the time we reached the room, so if we get to that time, we should head to the roof."

Hotaru agreed, so that was what we did. We spent the rest of the day staking out the hospital. We located the stairwell that led to the rooftop, found a nearby public washroom to hole up in while we waited for Shuzhue and her mother to come, and we lowered the fire escape ladder as a backup plan.

We were as prepared as we could be and the day still hadn't reset – I thought we were doing rather well.

We shared our bento in the restroom – which thankfully was fairly clean and did not seem often used – and we waited out the afternoon companionably, discussing our theories on this strange phenomenon we found ourselves in. We didn't come to any sensible conclusions, but we did agree that with the day as likely to reset as it was, any rules we needed to break to see this thing through would be forgotten by tomorrow, so there was no use hesitating if something needed to be done.

The public washroom door was directly across the hall from Chi-sama's door and a short run to the stairwell. I watched my cell phone clock with anticipation when the time indicated on the sign-in sheet drew near. Hotaru and I kept our ears glued to the door.

"You are her family, yes?" a deep, accented male voice said clearly in the hall – he sounded European of some sort. "Please come inside, so we can review her condition together."

There was the sound of a door opening and footsteps, but curiously no sound of the door shutting.

"This is it," I whispered to Hotaru.

Hotaru nodded and together we opened the bathroom door, peered out to make sure no one was watching, and then hurried across the hall to stand outside Chi-sama's partially open door to listen in.

"She's very ill," the accented voice was saying. "I'm afraid she does not have a long time left."

Through the crack in the door I could just make him out. I almost let out a gasp of horror, but that would have given us away, so I stifled it as best I could. It was one of them. He was dressed as a doctor now, but I remembered him from the park. Long black hair, pointed chin, dressed in a long black coat, and wearing a black eye patch over his left eye. He still had the eye patch now and it didn't look comical on him, it looked…intimidating.

The time on my cell phone was getting nearer to when Hotaru and I had come here yesterday, but they were all still in the room. Had something changed?

Just then there was a crashing sound and the room went dark and silent. I couldn't see into the darkness. I met Hotaru's gaze and we nodded in mutual understanding. It was time to go to the next phase of our plan. We ran for the stairwell.

The two flights took us no time at all. Still, however they had gotten up two stories from Chi-sama's window with several people in tow, I had no doubt it would be faster than us. At the top of the stairs was the rooftop door. It had a large red handle clearly marked: *Alarm Will Sound.*

No hesitation. Hotaru and I had promised. I lunged at the door and pressed the handle down to open it, bursting onto the rooftop with Hotaru on my heels.

The alarm sounded frantically and filled my head with noise.

Chapter 1 – Enough

The sound of the alarm buzzing in my head turned into the ringing of my cell phone. I already knew what it was trying to tell me; it was Tuesday morning, eight fifteen A.M. I got up, grabbed my clothes, and left the room, the cell phone ringing insistently behind me.

I met Hotaru outside my apartment door. Our determined expressions were identical. We didn't waste time with greetings. The two of us left Hyuski Heights immediately, picked up some lunch at a convenience store for later, and headed straight to the hospital. We knew now where the answers lay.

Once at the hospital, we split up. Hotaru, in an effort to follow her plan through, went up to Chi-sama's room to lie in the second bed and pretend to be another patient. I wished her luck, told her to be careful, and then headed to the second floor to lower the fire escape ladder for myself.

It was a long and careful climb up eight stories to the roof. I was immensely glad for the rudimentary climbing skills I had acquired in Phys Ed this year as I finally made it to the top. I had lunch on the windswept rooftop with its beautiful view of the Shinjuku district of Tokyo and then I hunched behind an air duct to wait out the day.

If I had hoped to end this on the rooftop, I wasn't disappointed. However, the conclusion of this strange series of events was if anything more puzzling than enlightening.

Just before the time when Shuzhue and her mother would sign in to the hospital's guest registry, the door to the roof opened without the alarm sounding. I hoped I wouldn't be spotted, but I was beyond caution at this point – I needed to know what happened up here – so I leaned out of my hiding place to see who had joined me.

It was one of the four from the park – I could tell by his clothes – but it was the one I least recognized. He was of medium build and height with short black hair in an average male cut. His clothes were black, of course, but plain. The only thing about him that stood out was the katana sheathed on his back and the telltale ruby necklace they all seemed to wear. He appeared bored as if, like me, he was waiting for something to happen. Behind him, the sun was beginning to set.

It would be full dusk when the others would arrive.

The wind picked up right on cue. Here, high above Tokyo, I saw the storm that was gathering above us, which was strange, as I didn't recall rain on the Tuesday night I had actually lived through.

He's coming. I heard a familiar, yet undeniably strange voice come from behind me. It wasn't in my mind this time, it was coming from the air duct. Without moving the rest of my body, I pressed my ear to the duct to better make out what the voice was saying. *He will ruin everything.*

Reset the program. The metallic voice echoed off the air duct vent in a predictable fashion. It sounded clearer now than it had before, though no less strange. It was almost certainly a robot or a computer speaking.

There is not enough time. The Vile Emperor is almost here. If we do not get them out, they will die.

I took in a sharp breath. It was too windy for anyone to hear me. Die? I had the sinking suspicion they meant us – as in Hotaru and I – not my companion on the roof, or the false doctor, or even Shuzhue and her family, though that was also a possibility.

Turning myself ever so slightly, I tried to peer down into the vent. Were they just voices or were they actually down there?

What I saw didn't match with the reality of the building at all, but it was undeniably as real as anything else was. I was instantly reminded of Hotaru's pipe as I gazed down upon two beings standing in a metal room, bending over a pool of still water held in a large basin. The one on the left was a robot as I had surmised, but he was man-shaped, so I assumed the correct term was android. On the right was what appeared to be some sort of frog-man; he was as large, if not larger, than the robot and dun-coloured – so a toad-man then.

In the pool was a reflection. I recognized the scene displayed, though it was from an aerial view. There I was, behind a duct on the roof of the hospital building and behind me was a man approaching with a katana held threateningly in his hand.

Agreed, the metal voice decided finally. *Terminating the program.*

I, unfortunately, had more important things to worry about than the state of the robot and the toad's program. Using the knowledge I had gained from gazing into that pool, I managed to roll out of the way before the katana sliced into the air duct where my head had been only a moment before.

Once I was clear, I looked up to face my assailant and noted the rage and hatred on his face, before the air duct exploded and filled my vision with a searingly intense blue light.

Chapter 2 – Rough Lands

I drifted to consciousness slowly this time as there was no alarm, save for the ringing in my head. I was lying uncomfortably on a hard surface and my skin felt battered and raw everywhere. My head ached and a harsh light filtered through my closed eyelids, making me see a haze of red. With effort I forced my eyes open – they felt gritty.

Sand – I was lying on sand – and it was everywhere, stretching all around me as far as I could see. My right leg was trapped in it, almost up to the knee. The harsh noon sun beamed down without a cloud in sight, and I could feel my skin baking in the intense heat.

I sat up a little too quickly in surprise and shock – I was naked and in the middle of a desert. I felt around myself instinctively for my glasses, which of course would not be in this place, but my hand did brush up against something – another human hand.

I screamed and looked down. My scream cut off abruptly when I realized I was looking at Hotaru, who was in no better condition than I was, and seemed to be struggling to sit up. Her arm up to the shoulder and part of her left side were stuck in the sand. I was close enough to help pull her out, so I did, but as I did so I noticed a bit of blue on her skin. I didn't want to stare at her – she was as uncovered as I was – but in the spot just above her heart there was a tattoo of two blue diamonds stacked on top of one another, the uppermost one three times larger than the lower.

I didn't figure Hotaru as a tattoo sort of person – then the memory struck me.

Hotaru facing the suit of armour...the strange cell phone call...and the blue light that emanated from her chest to join with the pillar of light in the center of the park.

"Yukari?" Hotaru questioned, blinking to clear her vision.

"Yes," I answered, somewhat surprised my voice wasn't hoarse from the dry heat – it probably would be soon, but it wasn't yet.

"Is that Kaji over there?" Hotaru continued, looking about. "And I think that's Yue's hair..." She then stared in shock with the same realization I had come to. "Why are we naked and what is this place?"

I ignored her questions as I didn't have any answers and turned to look behind me. Without my glasses I had to squint to make out his features, but Kaji Zukatoro was indeed behind me, his backside bare in the sand, and he, too, was waking up. Any moment he would see Hotaru and I – completely exposed.

I leaned over my trapped leg and dug somewhat hurriedly at it. The sand came away easily, and within moments I was free. I brought my knees up to my chest and wrapped my arms around them to conceal myself as best I could, as Kaji sat up, rubbing sand out of his eyes.

Kaji's realization and gradual acceptance of our predicament occurred in silence, but his expressions as he worked it all out spoke volumes. When he was through, he met my eyes. I was proud of him for not even trying to look where he shouldn't, but then, I supposed, Kaji had a girlfriend.

Shuzhue. Some pity must have shown in my eyes because Kaji looked away, the realization her whereabouts were still unaccounted for hitting him again.

The mound of hair beyond Kaji shifted and a low moan of pain split the silence of the desert – Yue!

I recalled abruptly how her leg had been sliced open on a deep purple spike of armour. But that was...when? The first Tuesday? So was it in fact the repeating Tuesdays that hadn't actually happened? Or was this, now, not real? But Hotaru had that blue mark, which didn't exactly look drawn on by a tattoo artist. It looked more like it originated from someplace under her skin. Despite the surreal sense of dislocation I felt, I also knew the pain and discomfort were real. Had school in Tokyo felt this convincing, this brutally vivid? I wasn't sure, and that scared me.

I cut my rationalizing short. Whatever the cause or true nature of our circumstance was, Yue was hurt, and right now that was more important.

"Kaji-san, look away. Hotaru can you help me get Yue out of the sand?"

Hotaru and I made quick work of freeing Yue and it was a good thing we did. Yue had at least been protected from the sun by being almost completely buried in sand, but she hadn't had much air with her immensely long hair in her face, and the ghastly wound on her leg and foot was caked with sand. At least the caked on sand slowed the bleeding, because we sure didn't have anything we could use as a bandage.

As we got her completely free, I noted that she also had the blue diamond mark. Hotaru also could not help but notice it and I saw her look quickly from Yue to me, and then she craned her neck to look down at her own chest. I must have also had it, then, I deciphered from her expression, and no doubt Kaji did as well.

Hotaru exclaimed over it with the others; mainly with Kaji as Yue was not very responsive. I ignored her, lost in my own thoughts.

Our situation was as inexplicable as it was dire, and I saw no reason in dwelling on what I couldn't affect or what I didn't understand. We could only hope there would be someone or something else besides us in this desolate place. Yue needed help, and soon enough in these harsh conditions without any clothing, supplies, or shelter – we all would.

I scanned the area around us. Without my glasses, my eyes were nearly useless for reading, but conversely I could see very well far away. I locked onto the only landmark in sight. There was a mountain range in the distance. It was a long ways off and I didn't know if we could make it that far – especially on foot and with Yue injured – but we had to try, having no other options.

"Kaji, keep your eyes on the ground," I directed him in a no-nonsense tone. "Someone needs to help Yue walk. We can't stay here."

I stood up once I was assured he wasn't looking. Despite my circumstance I was trying to retain some sense of modesty. I fixed my gaze on the distant mountains. "We've got a ways to go. I'll go on ahead and see if I can bring back anything to help us. Just walk in a straight line toward those mountains," I said as I pointed them out, though I didn't turn around to see if they were paying attention, "so we don't lose each other out here, or walk uselessly in circles."

"You shouldn't go alone, Yukari," Hotaru protested. "I'll come with you and Kaji can help Yue."

I nodded and started moving – we had a long hard walk ahead of us. Hotaru caught up to me quickly and for once she had nothing to say.

We had lost sight of Kaji and Yue behind us when we first saw a disturbance in the landscape ahead. It appeared as a dust cloud that grew steadily larger; whatever was creating it was coming toward us – and quickly.

"Hotaru, look," I prompted her, as she was clearly focused on doggedly putting one foot in front of the other instead of keeping an eye on the surroundings as I was.

"Wha–?" She stared ahead, dumbfounded.

"Something is coming toward us," I explained what she was seeing. "There is practically no wind, and so whatever it is has to be moving very quickly to kick up that much sand."

"Oh…" Hotaru absorbed this. "Is that good?"

"Well, it means there is more in this desert than just sand," I said, stating the obvious. "As to whether that's a good thing, I suppose we're about to find out."

The dust cloud was nearing us rapidly and there was nowhere to hide out here. I was apprehensive as it approached, but soon I could make out two figures in the dust and without waiting for more information than that I frantically began to wave my arms and shout, desperate to get their attention. I didn't want to die out here anymore than I had wanted to die back in the park in Tokyo.

The figures noticed us immediately – there wasn't much else to see out here – and slowed as they approached us. As the dust began to settle, I determined our potential saviours consisted of a man and a woman mounted on horses, of all things. Upon closer inspection the horses glinted strangely in the sun and I realized belatedly they were made up almost entirely of metal. Were they armoured horses, then, or something more?

The woman, scantily clad in a leather halter with miscellaneous belts and straps intricately tooled with pointed metal bits, had short orange hair like flames dancing around her head. She wore goggles to keep the sun out of her eyes, but other than that and her deep tan, she was relatively unprotected from the unrelenting sun.

She carried a strange device shaped like a golden mallet with a long handle, and she put this over her shoulder in a practiced motion before addressing us authoritatively. "And what would the two of you be doin' all the way out here in the middle of the Sand Lake, all undressed as ye are?" She had an odd lilting way of speaking, reminiscent of a native of Ireland or Scotland, though I was fairly certain there were no deserts like this one on that side of Europe.

It was clear enough she was in charge, but I inspected the man quickly before I replied, wondering how far we could trust these strangers with the truth, as inconceivable as it would sound.

He appeared to be much younger than the woman who, while beautiful, gave off a grizzled quality, as if she had led a tough life but had survived it by gritting her teeth and plodding onward. He had well tanned skin, naturally, but his hair was a fair blonde, and he had it held back from flopping in his face with a black bandana.

He wore an open white shirt that had seen better days over well-developed muscles, and yet more belts adorned his waist and sturdy rough hide pants. As my inspection reached the proud lines of his face and my blue eyes met his brown ones, I realized that as I had been giving him a once-over he had been doing the same to me, only I had significantly more of me showing.

I blushed immediately and tried to fight my urge to run and hide. I opened my mouth to speak, but Hotaru beat me to it. "There are two more of us following behind and one of our friends is hurt. Please, can you help us?"

"Masaru," the woman addressed her companion, a hint of command in her tone, "why don't ye go on ahead and find their friends? I can handle these two."

Masaru heeded her directions immediately and rode forward without a word. I tried not to look at him as he passed, as I was mortified by my circumstance, but I couldn't help but notice that his cheeks seemed reddened also, though it could have just been the sun on his face.

"Ye still haven't answered my question," the woman pointed out after Masaru had gone. "What brings ye to the center of the Sand Lake?"

Unfortunately we didn't have an answer for her, so I did my best to be honest as I didn't know enough about where we were to make anything up. After all, there was no rational explanation for our predicament.

"We're sorry to impose on you," I began, speaking as clearly as possible, concerned that perhaps my accent would sound as strange to her as hers did to me, "but none of us know how, exactly, we came to be here and we could really use some clothing and shelter, or at the very least directions to the nearest…civilization from here?"

She seemed a little taken aback by this, though I wasn't sure what else she was expecting. "Help doesn't come for free, ye know," she stated bluntly, "but I can see that as ye don't have much to offer, I can probably take that into consideration just this once."

I was at a loss. She was right; she would gain nothing by helping us except four very confused teenagers who, in this rough land, would be nothing more than a liability. The woman turned her torso around toward the back of her armoured horse and felt around on its flanks. Having obviously found the spot she wanted, she gave her horse's rump a sharp whack with her fist and astoundingly a panel opened to reveal a hidden compartment. She pulled out two large empty potato sacks and ripped a hole in the top of each with her boot knife. Then she made a smaller pair of armholes on each side.

Threading the newly made potato sack garments onto the butt end of her hammer she thrust them out toward us without dismounting. "My name's Corporal Dahlia, and yours?"

"Hotaru," Hotaru supplied, and when it looked like this Corporal Dahlia wasn't satisfied by that she added, "Hatsumuya."

"I'm Yukari Namikoya. And…thank you. For what it is worth, we are indebted to you."

"It won't be comfortable, but climb on," Dahlia instructed. "We'll see how Masaru is faring with your friends, aye?"

Once properly covered, I mounted onto the hot metal frame of the horse behind Dahlia and helped Hotaru up to perch precariously behind me on the horse's metal rump. It was indeed uncomfortable, but with a slight roaring sound the 'horse' came to life beneath us, and we flew along the sand back the way we had come so laboriously on foot.

The scene we came across when we reached the others would have been entertaining had our circumstances not been so desperate. As it was, I think only Dahlia may have found it amusing. Masaru had gotten down off of his horse, presumably to have a look at Yue's injured foot. By the time we reached them, Yue was crying and cradling her leg, and Kaji had tackled Masaru to the ground bodily.

"Kaji!" I called out. "They're trying to help us!"

"Aye, I am," Masaru affirmed, his voice accented like Dahlia's, but a little rougher around the edges. "If ye'd only let me."

Kaji wisely backed off and Dahlia threw him an identical potato sack to put on. "Ye should know better than to let your guard down, Masaru," Dahlia commented by way of reprimand.

"Aye," Masaru replied simply, before addressing Yue. "Are ye going to let me help you, then?"

Yue sniffled audibly then nodded, offering her foot to him. Meanwhile, Kaji had donned the potato sack and accepted another from Dahlia for Yue, before heading over to observe Masaru.

Masaru lifted an oddly shaped device to inspect it. It appeared to be a metal tube with a handle attached and a pointed end. I was at a loss as to what it was, personally, and I could see why perhaps Kaji had thought it was a weapon of some kind.

"This is going to hurt," Masaru warned Yue as she tugged the potato sack over her head. She almost needn't have bothered, her long hair was more than adequate cover. "But I promise ye'll be able to walk much better in a bit."

Yue nodded once more and Masaru drove the pointed end of the device into the heel of her foot without further hesitation. She screamed and I might have protested, but it was over in a second and Yue's scream quickly quieted to panting.

"What was that?" Kaji asked.

"Flaqqer. Have ye never seen a Flaqqer before, then? Where'd ye say ye were from again?"

Kaji could do nothing more than shake his head at this line of questioning and thankfully Masaru let it drop.

With a nod to Dahlia, Masaru hoisted Yue up and placed her on his mount. He climbed up behind her and threaded the reins around her before turning to offer Kaji a hand up.

"So we can take ye as far as the nearest Roughlander outpost, but after that ye'll be on yer own," Dahlia informed us all. "We're not in the habit of takin' in strangers, and you folk are stranger than most we encounter."

"Anything you can do to help us get our bearings would be most welcome," I told her. "We don't want to make ourselves a burden to you, but as you can see we have little choice."

"Aye," she commented, and just like that we were off, racing across the sands perpendicular to the direction we had been heading previously. It quickly became evident that by walking forward as we had been, we might never have found our way, and the mountains were still impossibly far.

The hot metal of the armoured horse chafed unbearably against my bare legs and I found myself feeling sorry for Hotaru and Kaji who were forced to hold on as best they could while they bounced around on the horse's rear. Hotaru, however, had a death grip around my middle to keep from falling off and that kept my sympathy for her to a minimum.

Thankfully it wasn't too long before we reached what Dahlia called the 'Roughlander outpost', a massive single tower, made of rock the exact colour of the sand around it. I suspect that if we hadn't been guided to it, we would not have spotted it from out in the desert, so uniform was its colour.

Around the base of the massive tapered structure was a penned in space where similar creatures – or robots – to the ones we rode were stationed. Dahlia led our horse forward, and Masaru and the others followed as we slowed down to a walking pace.

Ahead, there were people milling about. This 'outpost' was a lively place. With all the people it looked more like a refugee camp than a military station. As I watched, a figure exited the shadow of the vast arched doorway and stepped into the light. I had to blink a few times to be sure I wasn't inventing what I was seeing.

The man was an amphibian. He had dull, brownish-green skin, with lighter spots under his frog-like neck and on his belly. He was easily seven, maybe even eight feet tall, and his massive legs were clearly designed for jumping great distances. I was reminded abruptly of the toad-man I had seen in the hospital roof's air duct – but that had been on one of the Tuesdays…had they been real after all?

The toad man lumbered towards us carrying a scythe-like blade on a long staff over his shoulder in a menacing fashion. The creature was intimidating enough by himself and the impossibility of his very existence only increased my apprehension, but he also had armoured parts to him just like the horses, only he was not as completely covered. It seemed as if his right leg had been replaced entirely with a bionic one and his lumbering walk showed it.

Hotaru and I cowered under his intense alien gaze as he inspected us. Yue, already distraught, only whimpered. I didn't look back to see how Kaji was taking this.

"What is this you have brought us, Dahlia?" the toad man demanded in a guttural voice much deeper than the one I had heard during the Tuesdays, but similar in quality.

"We found these out in the Sand Lake," Dahlia answered conversationally. "They were lost out there if you can believe it and with no clothes to speak of."

"Are you going to vouch for them, then?" the toad man asked her inexplicably.

Our rescuer sighed reluctantly. "I suppose I am at that."

He turned to the rest of us then, raising his scythe up into the air. "I am Krox, Head-taker of the First Spawn! I warn you now, should you cause trouble for us I will take your heads myself."

His message was clear enough.

"You may take them to the loyalty test now," Krox, Head-taker of the First Spawn, instructed Dahlia and Masaru. Our unwilling sponsors dismounted and indicated we should do the same. In Hotaru's case that meant hooking her with the hammer and pulling her off the horse, as she was too frightened to pry herself loose.

"What is this about a loyalty test?" I heard Kaji ask Masaru behind me.

"Ye'll see soon enough," he answered ambiguously, and the group of us entered into the outpost with a mounting sense of unease.

We were led high enough up in the tower that the room – no larger than a classroom – was semi-circle in shape. There were no stairs in the outpost; each floor was reached by continuing up a spiraling ramp that hugged the inside of the outer wall. Along the wall were arrow-slit style open windows with mirrors placed at intervals, which cleverly reflected the light into the building. There was no electricity here and no adornments along the walls. At each 'floor' more people and these strange toad-like men could be seen going about their daily lives; the two species intermingled, though there were clearly more humans than toads.

Inside the smaller arched doorway there was a metal desk and a relatively tiny – when compared to Krox, anyways – green toad-person seated behind it on a low stool. Somewhat comically, the toad had a pair of slit-shaped reading glasses perched low on his face.

"Come in, come in," the toad-man spoke, his voice much higher in pitch than Krox's had been and with a hint of a lisp. "Don't be shy."

We filed into the room with dubious expressions.

"What are you?" Hotaru asked the frog creature directly with her usual lack of tact.

He eyed her strangely over his glasses, as if trying to understand her question. "I'm Ticket," he answered shortly. "Take a seat, all of you."

"What's a ticket?" Hotaru wondered aloud as we looked about the room for places to sit.

There were rows of metal chairs set up like an auditorium and at the front of the room was what appeared to be a screen, though I couldn't fathom how and if it ran, having already determined the lack of electricity in this place. We took spots in the first couple of rows, Kaji and I in the front, and Yue and Hotaru a row behind.

"Croatin. That's what I am," the toad spoke again, presumably belatedly answering Hotaru, before straightening up in his chair. "Let's begin."

"Begin what?" Hotaru voiced what we had all been wondering.

"The loyalty test, of course," Ticket, the Croatin, answered factually. "What do you see?"

He was clearly speaking to Hotaru, but we all looked to the screen before us regardless. On it was a panoramic view of Tokyo at night as seen from the water. The view was breathtaking and so unexpected here in this place and after all that had happened, it was a relief to see it.

"Tokyo, Japan," Hotaru responded, just as caught up in the image as I was. "That's where we're from."

It hit me then just how far we must be from home, which was something even the sight of the desert and the strange frog creatures hadn't been fully capable of doing. This place we found ourselves in now couldn't exist in the world we knew and here these 'Roughlanders' thought we were the strange ones.

"And you," Ticket addressed me. "What do you see?"

I had turned my attention to the toad as he spoke again, and now I directed it at the screen once more. I could not help but gasp in surprise; there on the screen was the blond teenager who had stalked me around Tokyo before. I was surprised to hear my gasp echoed from somewhere near the door. I turned my head sharply to see who had reacted and I met Dahlia's eyes. She was standing just inside the open doorway beside Masaru, and she looked a little panicked, but she was obviously trying to control her reaction so as not to disrupt the test.

I tried to bring myself to answer the Croatin's question. "I don't know who he is, but I have seen him before. He…" I faltered. "He hates me – I don't know why."

"Ah." Ticket made a knowing sound before turning to Kaji. "What do you see?"

Our school student council president filled the screen and I began to wonder just where exactly they were getting these images. If we were no longer in Japan and our ways were so foreign to these Roughlanders, then they shouldn't possibly know about where we came from or who we went to school with. I mulled this over as Kaji answered.

"Goji Nakamura, Shinjuku High's school student council president."

No reaction from Ticket this time, he simply addressed the same question to Yue as yet another image filled the screen. This time it was Yue's father, Noh-san. This was an easy question, but after a moment of silence I looked back to Yue and noticed she had no intention of answering. She had a decidedly mulish expression on her face.

I heard Dahlia gasp again and I looked at her in surprise – surely she didn't have any way of knowing Yue's father. She and

Masaru both were staring at the screen with matched expressions of disbelief.

"Who's that?" Hotaru asked suddenly.

My eyes darted once more to the screen. Noh-san wasn't featured there any longer. The image had flickered instead to someone I had never seen before. The young woman had a short bob of pale white hair with a bluish cast to it. Her eyes were an uncommon red and glowed with a dim inner light, while her proud features faced us challengingly on a background of a deep blue field of stars.

Her clothes were even stranger. Flowing fabrics draped her form and were cinched to her here and there with star-shaped ornaments. The star-themed pattern was repeated on a necklace and earrings that dangled from her ears. The strangest part was between her outstretched hands, where she held a swirling ball of radiant energy the same colour as the diamond markings we all bore.

At the silence in the room and the obvious reactions of both Masaru and Dahlia, Ticket slowly turned around to look at what the screen showed.

"Do you know this person?" Ticket asked, but before any of us could respond the image on the screen changed again.

Now the image was a room filled with monitors and computer parts; some were broken, some apparently still operative. In the corner of the small room sat an obvious android. She appeared female in design and in a sad state of disrepair. Her red paint was faded and one of her legs was barely holding on, even with a generous application of a sort of tape.

Next to her seemed to be a coffee maker, of all things, but it too appeared to be robotic and was designed to walk. It even had arms with which to serve the coffee it produced. The coffee-bot appeared operative, at least from the picture.

"Binaris?" Ticket questioned. "They've never been here before, why would they see Binaris?"

"Masaru," Dahlia spoke, taking charge, "I think ye'd better go see Ark and tell him of this. I'm taking them to see Binaris."

Masaru looked doubtful, but to his credit he did not protest or hesitate in doing as he was commanded. Meanwhile, with our loyalty test – or whatever it was – having come to such an abrupt halt, we were all getting out of chairs and heading over to Dahlia and Ticket.

"I think before you take us to see anyone, you should tell us what is going on here," I demanded of Dahlia, reaching her first. "What is the reason for all this? What is the loyalty test for?"

Dahlia faced me head on, seemingly prepared to explain everything. "We needed to know if ye were sent by the Vile Emperor. It was a risk just taking ye here and the Roughlanders can't afford any mistakes. I think ye proved ye're the furthest thing from his agents – to me, at least. I'll leave the rest to Binaris to decide."

"The rest?" Kaji asked, but Dahlia shook her head, her lips pursed.

The Vile Emperor – where had I heard that before?

"Come. I'll take ye to Binaris," Dahlia instructed. "If I'm right, she'll answer all the questions ye have. That's what she's here for."

We followed Dahlia down the hall to the first actual door we had seen in the outpost. The metal of the door was sealed into the stone of the wall. It looked airtight, and remarkably it had a touch keypad on its face. Dahlia accessed the keypad and entered in a quick code, which caused the door to open, sliding it to one side. I supposed I had been wrong about the lack of electricity, but it was certainly a hidden feature of this outpost.

The metal door revealed the room we had seen on the last screen of the loyalty test, complete with the run-down android and the coffee serving robot. The room beeped and blipped softly in a familiar way and the metallic tang to the air reminded me forcefully of Tokyo.

"Binaris," Dahlia called into the room, "I've some people here to see ye."

The four of us filed into the room at Dahlia's direction and – the room being small – she remained at the door. Binaris was, I assumed, the android sitting on the floor, her upper half propped up against the wall. As we formed in a semi-circle around the android, her angular shaped eyes lit up with a blue light, like she was coming online after being inactive for a long period of time.

I was impressed at the level of technology in this room – the android most of all – as run-down as everything seemed to be. How long would they have had to have this technology for it to get this way? The people here didn't seem to be scientists or robotics experts, though I supposed someone had to have built the bionic components on Krox and the horses.

"Chosen," Binaris spoke, her metallic voice sounding as feminine as she appeared. "Sapphiros welcomes you."

"Sapphiros?" Hotaru questioned immediately.

"Password required for authentication," Binaris stated suddenly in a computer-voice monotone. I was immediately reminded of the *'reset the program'* voice from Tuesday and my confusion mounted.

"Sapphiros," she intoned, "one of the five gem gods. He represents balance and the understanding of all cultures."

Binaris, being a program, was no doubt just answering Hotaru's inadvertent question, but the name was familiar to me. The female voice from the mysterious cell phone call I had received in the park that night had said Sapphiros would aid me if I asked for help.

"What are the gem gods?" Hotaru continued to question.

"There are five gem gods represented on this world: Sapphiros, Rubia, Jedeite, Machalite and Damos," Binaris responded in the same fashion.

This was all well and good, but if Binaris was supposedly here to give us information, then we needed to start making use of her.

"Binaris," I addressed her and her head turned slightly to lock on to me. "Why are we here?"

"The Chosen of Sapphiros were summoned here from Earth in order to face the Vile Emperor and restore balance to this world."

"So it's true, then," Masaru said from behind us. We all turned to face him and Dahlia, who still stood in the doorway.

"What's true?" I demanded. "We don't understand any of this."

"Well," he answered, sounding a little uncertain and maybe even awed, "the Roughlanders hold that a long time ago, they made a pact with Yuko Seig to await the Chosen of Sapphiros. They – ah, you – were supposed to come and fight the Vile Emperor. But it's been about…eight hundred years or so now, and ye never came."

"Who's Yuko Seig?" Kaji questioned from behind me.

"Yuko Seig, High Priestess of Sapphiros," Binaris supplied. "Accessing message file…"

We all turned again as a whirring sound filled the room. A monitor came to life to show the same image of the woman with blue-tinged hair and proud features.

"That would be Yuko Seig," Masaru offered helpfully.

A recorded message filled the room: "Chosen of Sapphiros. Welcome to our world. We have been waiting for you. I regret we could not have met under better circumstances, but this world needs your help." I knew the voice instantly, of course. So Yuko Seig was the mysterious caller. It seemed now as if she wanted something in return for the help she had offered.

"The Vile Emperor's forces grow ever stronger and I am afraid I don't know how long we will be able to hold out. I have made a pact with the Roughlanders, so when you arrive you will have them as allies to help you against the Vile Emperor and the forces of Rubia.

"Come to the Temple of Sapphire. I don't know how long it will take you to arrive, but I will be waiting for you there and I will answer any questions you may have."

At the conclusion of the recording another image took the place of Yuko Seig. The image was of a city filled with snow. It had towers and spires here and there, though the city itself was not large, and beyond the buildings a mountain range could be seen.

"Well, we have a destination now at least," I commented. "Yuko Seig brought us here and maybe she can take us home again."

"Uh," Masaru interrupted, "like I said, Yuko Seig made this pact with the Roughlanders over eight hundred years ago. I hardly think she'd still be alive."

"Binaris," Kaji addressed the android, "how long ago was this message sent?"

"Eight hundred and fifteen years ago," Binaris responded in her computer monotone. "There is another message. Accessing message file..."

Yuko Seig's image appeared once more. "Chosen. The Vile Emperor is here." Sounds of fighting and the tearing of metal could be heard in the background. "We do not have much time. We have been waiting for you for almost three years, but if he breaks through our defenses now, I will not be able to do much more to help you.

"Please. Come to the Temple of Sapphire. I will leave–" The sound cut out abruptly with an awful finality.

There was an awkward silence while we all tried to process this information.

"So we're not on Earth anymore, are we?" Hotaru broke the silence by stating what I thought had become obvious.

"I don't know where this Earth of yours is, but no, ye're not," Masaru responded.

"We have to go to the Temple of Sapphire," I spoke suddenly and noted the surprised expressions of my friends. "It's our only lead on a way to go home, even if this Yuko Seig person is dead. And I…" I hesitated to reveal this, but I owed it to them to explain why we were here "I made a deal with Yuko Seig, to save us from the Vile Emperor – the armoured man in the park? I asked for Sapphiros' aid and she gave it."

Hotaru looked surprised. Yue had not yet spoken a word and she didn't do so now, but her eyes were wide trying to take all of it in. Kaji, on the other hand, was nodding.

"I spoke to her too," he said, "in the park, on Shuzhue's cell phone. She mentioned Sapphiros then, but I didn't know what she meant." He took a deep breath. "Yukari's right. We have to see this through. Shuzhue might also be here somewhere.

"Binaris," Kaji continued without pause, turning to the android once more. "What are we up against? What can you tell us about the Vile Emperor?"

"The Vile Emperor. Accessing…" The deep purple armoured being was displayed on the screen. I shuddered involuntarily – he was real, then. The first Tuesday, at least, had happened. "The Vile Emperor is the Chosen of Rubia. He has four Talons whom he has chosen from the planet Earth. The Talons are: Kai-een." The monitor showed the angry blond stranger, dressed all in black with his two katana blades held high. "Fuzen." The European doctor, but wearing a black coat, with his sinister eye-patch and a long, thin blade at his back. "Zai-Aku." The red-headed woman with the black dress whom I had crossed paths with more than once. "And Arocoth." The monitor showed the one who had attacked me on the roof of the hospital.

Was it all real? All the strange events and the repeating Tuesdays? I almost had to assume it was.

"Binaris, you've said we are the Chosen of Sapphiros and the Vile Emperor is the Chosen of Rubia. Do the other three gods you mentioned have Chosen also?" I asked.

"Negative," Binaris responded to my question immediately. "Of the five gem gods only Sapphiros and Rubia have Chosen. Damos has never chosen and Jedeite is missing."

Another image appeared on the monitor. This one I had never seen before. It was of a dangerous looking man. He was tall and handsome in a roguish sort of way, but he carried himself like a fighter and his left hand was no more than a metallic claw. The image showed him in a fighting stance, with his tattered cloak swirling about him and blood dripping from his outstretched clawed hand.

"Fuun," Binaris supplied, "is the self-proclaimed Chosen of Machalite."

"Okay," Kaji said, taking this new information in. "Now, Binaris, what allies do we have?"

"The Roughlander pact with Yuko Seig promises the Roughlanders' allegiance to the Chosen of Sapphiros," Binaris intoned. "Last recorded number indicates there are approximately forty thousand Roughlanders spread across twenty-six outposts.

"The Roughlanders are to be reminded of this pact when the Chosen arrive," the android continued. "Transmitting notification of the Chosen's arrival to all Roughlander outposts…"

"Binaris, no! Stop!" I exclaimed.

"Canceling transmission request. Should the command be terminated?"

"Yes," I answered Binaris decisively. Hotaru and Kaji looked as if they wanted to ask if I knew what I was doing, so I forestalled them. "It's been eight hundred years since this pact. A lot can happen in eight hundred years. There is no way to know whether the pact still holds with all the Roughlanders. Right now no one knows we're here, and if that armoured Vile Emperor and his Talons or whatever they are called are still looking to kill us, I would rest easier knowing our presence and location has not been transmitted across twenty-six outposts, some of which could have been compromised."

Kaji nodded. "You're probably right."

"So what do we do, then?" Hotaru asked, looking to me for further direction.

I sighed and then looked for Dahlia. She was beyond Masaru now in the hallway, deep in discussion with someone else out there. He looked ancient, with his hair completely white and his hands gnarled from age, but he was dressed in more colour than I had seen since arriving here. His pants were green and his jacket was red; I was reminded briefly of the western Santa Clause, though this person wore a more serious expression.

Since Dahlia was occupied, I addressed Masaru instead, "Masaru, does the pact with the Roughlanders still hold in this outpost?"

"Yes, it does," Masaru answered carefully, unsure of my direction. "Ye'll have to speak with Ark, o'course," he said with a gesture to the colourful man behind him. "He runs the outpost and all, but seein' as ye're here now, you four are officially the leaders of the Roughlanders."

"Well then," I replied, a little overwhelmed, "surely we'd be able to get some real clothes? And perhaps a map to look over and a place to rest for a little while?"

Masaru smiled. "Aye. I'm sure something can be arranged for ye."

We were introduced to Ark, the leader of the outpost, and then led up onto the flat rooftop of the structure, where four cots had been set up to give us some privacy and a place to rest. By now the sun was low in the sky, and even though my sense of time had been thrown out of whack by the repeating Tuesdays and this whirlwind trip to another world, I felt it was appropriate the sun would soon set on this momentous day.

Ark supplied us with a map and Masaru brought us some melons to eat, as we hadn't had any food or water all day and were starting to feel the effects. We changed into similar clothing to what we had seen so far on the Roughlanders; undyed rough fabric cinched on and decorated with extraneous leather belts. We sat in a tight circle in between the cots with the map between us, poring over it with the last light of day.

The Roughlander outpost sat in the center of a vast desert labeled simply as '*Sand Lake*'. There were four such Sand Lakes, equally as sizeable as this one, spread out on the map, and most of them had an outpost or two in or near them indicated by a little red dot. Most of the map was coloured with browns, including the tan of the Sand Lakes, and we were appalled to learn that according to the map there was only one real fertile area in the northwestern corner of the map, a city and region labeled as Taiyou. The only body of water depicted on the map encircled Taiyou.

"Chosen of Sapphiros," an unforgettable guttural voice spoke from the entrance to this level behind us, "I have brought you weapons. When do we ride?"

We turned as one to face Krox, Head-taker of the First Spawn. He had his scythe-staff at his back, and a lumpy bag hanging from his right hand and dragging on the ground.

"Krox, I know you are eager to face the Vile Emperor," Kaji stood and addressed the large Croatin diplomatically, "but we must journey to the Temple of Sapphire at the request of Yuko Seig before we are able to commit ourselves to battle."

I wasn't sure if Kaji's words were wise, but I was proud of him for meeting Krox as an equal and not being cowed by his overwhelming presence. I was also glad Krox, at least, as frightening as he was, was on our side.

"I understand," Krox said respectfully with a nod. "I will leave you to rest and prepare."

Krox left the bag of weapons on the roof and we turned our attention back to the map.

"The Temple of Sapphire is to the south." I stated, putting my finger on it. "We don't know what sort of scale this is, but it looks fairly far away. We'd have to either cross those mountains there," I said as I indicated a central mountain range, "or go around them here. This other side of them looks like a steep ravine. There may be a way through there, but it doesn't look likely."

"So it is going to take us a while to get to where we're going," Yue spoke, the first thing she'd said in my hearing since our arrival. I nodded. "Then we should get some rest now, while we can."

We took Yue's advice, and retired to our cots. We were all tired, and with a long and possibly difficult journey ahead of us into the unknowns of this world, we would need what comforts we could get now.

I lay on my cot, my mind whirling with all the information we had been given and all the new questions that were born from that information, and I watched the sun dip below the edge of the outpost where my view was cut off. As I tried to sleep, I kept expecting it to get dark, but it never did, and I watched in disbelief as the sun rose in the sky once more from the same side that it had set.

My eyes snapped opened wide in disbelief. Were there two suns for this world? I got up from my cot and scurried over to the edge to look out. There was only one sun to be seen and it was as bright as it had ever been with no clouds to cover it. With so little water on this world and constant sun, it was little wonder it was largely desert. I found myself wondering if it ever rained here.

As I stared out over the Sand Lake, however, I noticed a shimmer of heat out in the desert. The motion drew my attention and I soon realized I was staring at something infinitely more dangerous than a solar flare; there were troops out there, marching towards the outpost. The heat was glancing off of their black armour. I couldn't make out numbers or individuals, but there must have been a large concentration of them for me to make them out at all at this distance.

Panicked, I turned to wake my friends. I hurried to Yue first. "Yue, wake up! All of you! We can't stay here, either."

As my voice startled them each out of their dreams, I stood to run and tell someone what was going on, to warn the Roughlanders of this outpost what was coming. I almost bumped into Krox as he came up the ramp and an alarm sounded throughout the outpost in the form of a gong as I came to a stop before him.

"There are Deathsquad soldiers coming this way," Krox stated. "Do we fight or flee?"

"Flee," I responded, regardless of the consequences. "We need a guide to take us to the Temple of Sapphire. We need to live to reach it."

Kaji, not having seen the threat, was a little more in control of himself as he asked, "How many soldiers, Krox? Can we defend this place from them?"

"There are several squads, perhaps five thousand soldiers in all," Krox replied. "If they are coming here to destroy us or if they know you are here, then we can only stand in their path. They will destroy the outpost."

"Then we flee." Kaji stated. "Get everyone ready to leave. We may still need the warriors to buy us time to get away, but we're leaving this outpost before they get here."

Krox saluted with his fist in assent and lumbered back down the ramp, presumably to follow Kaji's direction. Meanwhile, Hotaru had upturned the bag of weapons Krox had left us previously and now she and Yue were rifling through it. I didn't think any of us would live two minutes facing an armoured soldier, but I was in an archery club and I spotted a quality longbow with a quiver of arrows in the pile, so I reached for it.

Hotaru had armed herself with a katana, though I wasn't sure if she intended on using it or not. Kaji, a member of the Karate club back at Shinjuku, followed our lead and selected a pair of brass knuckles and Yue, looking disgusted, scooped the remaining weapons back up in the bag and hefted them onto her shoulder.

"You never know what we might need." She shrugged and set off down the ramp. We followed her – we couldn't stay up here and wait for death to come to us.

"I'm going to go see Binaris," Yue announced unexpectedly.

"I'll come with you," Kaji offered. "She may have more information we need. If her program is downloadable, we should take her with us. The other outposts or the Temple of Sapphire might have another computer we can hook her up to."

"Hotaru and I will see about getting an escort to the Temple together," I informed them. "We can't just flee with nothing. We'll need supplies, some Roughlanders to protect us, and someone who knows the way."

With at least that much decided we separated on the level that contained Binaris' room, and Hotaru and I continued to the ground level. Outside the main entranceway we found Krox and Dahlia locked in an embrace. I blinked to clear my vision as Hotaru and I waited awkwardly for them to finish – I certainly hadn't been expecting that.

"The Croatins will meet the advance and head them off here at the outpost," Krox informed me gruffly.

Dahlia looked unabashed. "The rest of the Roughlanders are preparing to depart and flee in different directions for the nearest outposts. My crew and I will take ye to where ye need to be goin'. There's no crew better suited to help ye cross the Sand Lakes."

"Masaru's a part of your crew then, Dahlia?" Hotaru asked.

"Aye," Dahlia responded. "He's with the rest of them gathering what supplies we'll need. Come with me and I'll show ye how to work the mounts."

Meanwhile, Krox lifted his scythe-blade high above his head and filled his toad-like neck pouch with air to roar, "Croatins to me!"

Dahlia led us over to a line of stationed metal horses – mounts, I supposed they were called – and climbed onto hers. "Hurry up and get on," she instructed. "I'll show ye how to use them, but ye'll likely have to explain it to Kaji and Yue."

By the time we had it mostly figured out, the Deathsquads were a clear threat on the horizon and the Croatins had formed their own ranks, ready to face them. Yue had come out of the outpost and she now clambered onto her own mount. "Kaji's still up there, downloading Binaris. He shouldn't be too much longer. I sent some Roughlanders to help him carry her down.

"It seems as if this outpost has some defenses of its own," Yue continued, as Dahlia flicked a switch to make Yue's mount rumble to life. "As a security measure, Binaris activated landmines around the perimeter."

The Croatins, much varied in size and shape, let out a roar of challenge and surged forward as one to face the Deathsquads, even though they were more than outnumbered. Dahlia's face fell at Yue's words and she looked up to scan the Croatin force for Krox's lumbering form. He was there at the front, leaping ahead of the others. He barely touched the ground with his bionic leg when a shocking explosion split the ground at his feet and threw up sand in all directions.

Dahlia let out a moan of distress and the rest of us held our breath to see what the dust settling would reveal. Krox, however, wasn't to be slowed by this event. He surged out of the dust cloud on his good leg, flinging himself upon the first row of Deathsquad soldiers. The Croatins behind him cheered and their charge never faltered as the limber toad-people collided with the rigid ranks of black-armoured soldiers.

Dahlia turned her face away from the battle as Kaji and three Roughlanders carrying a heavy burden wrapped up in a tarp reached us. The other Roughlander groups were already leaving; some with caravans drawn by mounts, some on foot or more metal horses.

"Let's go." Dahlia gave the command and Kaji mounted up along with us.

I leaned over to start up his mount and we moved out at a walk, so the Roughlanders with Binaris could keep up. None of us could bear to look over our shoulders to watch the Croatins sacrifice themselves to protect us.

Beyond the outpost itself we met up with Masaru leading a team of Roughlanders and a mount-drawn caravan filled with supplies and refugees. The carriers of Binaris sought shelter in the Caravan, which was piloted by the Croatin, Ticket, and without another word we were off.

For a long time we could hear the sounds of battle and the dying behind us, until abruptly it all stopped and we turned back to look, surprised by the sudden absence of sound.

The outpost itself lit up the sky in an explosion that could be heard for miles across the open expanse of the Sand Lake. Smoke, fire, and debris exploded outward, wreaking destruction even we could see from this distance.

"We have to continue," Dahlia ordered, her voice grim and controlled. "We have no other choice, now. The Deathsquad that survive will no doubt be coming after us."

Chapter 3 – The Evil You Know

Dahlia had been gone awhile, leaving Masaru in charge as she took a few Roughlanders with her to scout ahead, and we were beginning to worry. Masaru, in an attempt to make us aware of the dangers of the Sand Lakes, was describing what sort of ferocious beasts could be waiting out here for the unwary and what to do if you encountered one. The lesson wasn't helping anyone's sense of unease.

With everyone so alert to danger, it was hard to say who noticed the riders approaching first, but Masaru and I came to the same conclusion, "Dahlia."

She was riding hard, as was her companion a little ways behind her. She had taken three Roughlanders with her, but the other two were nowhere to be seen.

We sped up to meet her and she reined in next to Masaru. "There's another Deathsquad ahead. There's not nearly so many of them, but there are still more than we can handle." I noted she was a little more disheveled than she had been when she left us and blood was seeping slowly from a scrape on her arm. She grimaced in distaste before continuing, "They spotted us, and they have a Skyraider with them. Gorfin and I lost them, but the others weren't so lucky. Unfortunately, they're blocking the way out of the Sand Lake."

"Where do we go then? Where is the nearest outpost?" I asked.

"The outpost we were headed for is beyond the Deathsquad," Dahlia responded unhappily. "They may have destroyed that too, but either way we have no hope of reachin' it."

"So what options do we have, then?" I pressed.

"Not many," Dahlia admitted. "There is a sharp ravine with no way down along the edge of the Sand Lake beside where the Deathsquad is guarding. It continues until the mountain range. We could go around the mountains, o' course, but that is a longer journey than we have supplies for, and we have no way of knowing if the Deathsquads would be blocking that path either."

"You mentioned mountains, though," I said, "could we not take shelter there? It would be easier to find shade there, at least."

Dahlia looked startled. "There is a pass through the mountains from what I've heard, but Roughlanders usually avoid the place. It's got a bad reputation."

"Well then it's perfect. The Deathsquads won't expect us to go there, we could buy ourselves some time," Kaji piped in.

Masaru shook his head disapprovingly. "It's got a bad reputation because no one ever comes back. There is something evil about those mountains."

"Well, I'd rather the evil I don't know to the certain death waiting for us just south of here," I stated boldly, the superstition of the Roughlanders not enough to deter me in this time of need.

"On to the evil we don't know!" Yue seconded. "It can't be worse than one of those Deathsquads."

Masaru and Dahlia remained subdued, but they could also see the mountains were the only feasible choice. Putting the mounts into a faster gear, our caravan surged forward and we were off, racing toward the foreboding mountain range visible on our left.

It was much cooler in the relative shade of the mountain pass and within moments of reaching it I was glad of our choice. The downside was that the covered wagon had to be left behind, so all of us were carrying what we could on our mounts and three Roughlanders had been permanently assigned to hauling Binaris along after us.

Soon enough, even our mounts had to be left behind. They were running dangerously low on water – apparently steam power was enough to keep them going, as they were partly organic – and the pass itself was too narrow. Before abandoning them, however, we were unfortunate enough to see what state they were driven to when they ran out of steam completely.

I was riding sedately behind Dahlia as we climbed the narrowing mountain pass when my mount shuddered and rocked suddenly in the middle of the path, stopping dead in its tracks.

"Yukari! Jump!" I heard Dahlia scream from ahead of me on the path and I instantly obeyed her command.

As I threw myself from the saddle of the mount, Dahlia raced up on her own mount and reached over daringly with her hammer to knock my horse into another gear. The failing mount made a sort of ear-splitting whine and took off ahead at full speed, wavering and crashing into the ravine walls drunkenly, until it exploded forcefully in a shower of metal, fleshy bits, and a pinkish fluid.

The path ahead was still narrowing, and after that display there was little complaint about leaving the mounts behind to continue on foot. Dahlia drained what little water remained in the mounts before she sent them all back down the path, so they would not all explode in the same place and cause a rockslide to bar the pass. She hesitated only slightly over abandoning her own mount, as it had likely kept her alive more than once in the past.

We continued, reduced to the use of our legs and our backs, only to come to an abrupt halt before a gaping chasm.

"We can't go back," Kaji stated.

Unfortunately, it seemed we couldn't go forward either. The chasm was too wide to jump, and looking left and right did not reveal any place where the gap was narrower or even a path to follow along either side.

I approached the edge cautiously, thinking perhaps we could climb down, but to my dismay the ravine floor was littered with the corpses of those who had come this way before. Ahead of us, however, on the other side of the sheer drop, the path through the mountains appeared to continue.

I looked back to the others. Dahlia was eyeing our prospects with distaste and Hotaru was leaning over the edge to look down as I had been, but with markedly less caution.

"Hey, Dahlia!" Hotaru exclaimed after a moment. "I think there is someone moving down there!"

Hard-bitten Dahlia shuddered visibly at this news.

"Hotaru," I addressed her on Dahlia's behalf, "I hardly think anyone could have survived that fall."

"Aye," Dahlia agreed, "but if they have, then it would be a mercy to put them out of their misery."

"Well," I said, getting back to business, "it looks like we have no choice but to figure a way across. Did we think to bring along any rope?"

The Roughlanders conferred for a moment before Masaru was able to present me with a thick bundle of sturdy rope.

"How d'ye intend to fasten it on the other end?" Masaru questioned, fathoming a part of my idea.

"Ticket?" I looked back for the Croatin.

"Yeah?" Ticket replied, scrambling over toward Masaru and I.

"Do you think you might be able to jump it?" I asked him, examining his powerful frog-legs.

Ticket considered the question very seriously for a moment, eyeing the chasm appreciatively. "I might be able to clear it with enough of a running start," he concluded.

"If you can get across," I patted my bow, "I'll send you the rope."

Ticket nodded and gestured for everyone to make way for him as he backed away from the edge, rubbing his webbed hands together in anticipation. He stood for a moment, preparing himself and rocking back and forth on the balls of his feet.

"Come on, chasm!" Ticket muttered. "Let's see what you got." He lifted his fists in challenge. "Just you and me now," he exclaimed and then he was off – only to stop dead at the edge. "Whoo!" He let out a relieved sounding breath. "Almost got me there, chasm!"

Ticket backed up and repeated the process while we all waited anxiously. This time he ran with all his might, putting on quite a bit of speed before he pushed off into the air and hurtled across the gap.

Ticket's midsection collided forcefully with the far chasm wall, knocking the breath out of the Croatin, but he held on, his webbed fingers allowing him better purchase on the sheer rock than a human could have managed. He tried to pull himself up, but it was all he could do just to hang there, his powerful hind legs dangling uselessly beneath him. I found I was holding my breath just watching him – there had to be something more helpful I could do.

I drew an arrow from the quiver on my back and quickly frayed the end of the rope to knot it securely on the fletching of the arrow. The shaft, I noticed quickly, was made of a light metal instead of wood like I was used to, but it would be stronger for it. The rope would drag heavily on the arrow, but with enough force, I hoped it would still fly true.

I stood once again and lifted my bow, pausing for a moment – this Roughlander bow wasn't what I was used to, either. Where the notch for the arrow should be was a mechanized device and the string appeared doubled in a sort of pulley system. I fumbled with it for a moment, praying Ticket could continue to hold on. In due course, I got the arrow situated properly. I took a deep breath to focus myself before adjusting my aim for the added weight and the drag of the wind, then let the arrow fly.

The arrow surged forward, powerfully propelled by the mechanism in the Roughlander bow, then thudded satisfactorily in a cleft in a rock on the other side of the chasm. The roped draped from there back to me, passing closely by Ticket.

The Croatin lifted one hand to cautiously transfer his grip onto the rope. Thankfully, it was wedged in tightly enough to allow him to pull himself up. The Roughlanders let out a cheer and Ticket preened under the attention. I couldn't help but smile in relief.

Ticket gave a solid tug on the rope, then as an added security measure, he looped the rope a few times around the rock it was attached to and tied it again to itself. On our end, Masaru made quick work of securing our half of the rope; soon it was done and ready to test.

"I'll go," I volunteered. It was my idea after all and I felt I owed it to Ticket, whom I had almost sent plummeting to his death.

"Let me go across first," Masaru suggested, "and you can follow after me."

I nodded in assent – I was not as eager to defy death as I made it seem – and Masaru attached the excess rope around his waist, and then made his way over to the edge of the chasm. He removed one of the shorter belts from around his leg and looped it around the rope before threading it through the belt on his waist and fastening it there. He let himself down until he was dangling into the mouth of the chasm.

My heart fluttered with tension just watching him pull himself along the taut rope hand over hand with his legs wrapped around the slender lifeline. All too soon it was my turn.

My heart was pounding and my hands shaking as I allowed Dahlia to help me fasten my belts as Masaru had done. I did my best to copy Masaru's motions and took comfort in the fact that on the other side, Masaru held the second rope attached to my waist – he would not let me fall.

It was a painstaking process, but eventually we were all across – even Binaris, whose inert form had to be hauled across with the second rope and whose metal bulk was a great strain on the whole system. Dahlia was the last one to make it over, but as soon as she had there was a collective sigh of relief – the Deathsquad would have a difficult time following us now.

A little ways past the chasm, the path curved suddenly and sunk into the mountain in the form of a tunnel no wider than two abreast. With some trepidation, but with no real alternative, we filed into the darkness and began a rapid descent into the core of the mountain.

After we had travelled a ways, the ground beneath us began to level out.

"We'll rest here," Dahlia announced, her voice echoing in the pitch-black cavern. "There is shelter enough. I'll go on back and make sure we're not bein' followed."

"And I'll check the way ahead," Masaru ventured.

"Can I come with you?" Hotaru asked.

"I don't see why not," he replied.

"I'll go with you then, Dahlia," Kaji offered.

The four of them set off in opposite directions, leaving Yue and I with the rest of the Roughlanders to make a sort of camp. Soon we had a couple of small fires going at either end of our procession. They seemed to burn a type of peat, as I had already noticed wood was extremely rare on this world.

As the flickering light of the fires took hold, I noticed a glistening on the wall near where I had situated myself. I brushed my hand along the wall and was pleased to find my hand come away cool and wet – water!

In the frantic journey across the Sand Lake we had fed most of our water to our failing mounts and our own supplies were now dangerously low. Dahlia had had the foresight to keep the water drained from the mounts, but I had seen the pinkish colour of the liquid she'd salvaged and I didn't relish having to drink it.

I felt along the cavern wall and traced the water to where it seeped the most. It was no more than a trickle, but since we were making camp here, we should have enough time to collect some – and the desert had taught me some water was infinitely better than none. I used another one of my arrows to allow the water to drip down its shaft into my canteen.

I was setting up Yue's canteen when we first started to think something might be wrong.

"Someone should have come back by now," Yue noted fretfully. "It's not far back to the chasm. I'm going to go check on them."

"I'd come with you," I told Yue seriously. I was a little worried too; after all we had been through I felt safety was too much to ask for. "But someone should stay here for when Masaru and Hotaru get back to tell us what's ahead. They've been gone a while too, but we don't know how far they intended to go."

Yue nodded and scooped up the bag of weapons she had been carrying since we had left the outpost.

"Do you think you are going to need all of that?"

"You never know what you might need," Yue repeated her cryptic words from earlier and set off without further explanation.

She had not been gone long when I heard a commotion from the direction she had gone. Wordless yelling – at this distanc,e anyway – followed by the sounds of a weapon firing and several bolts ricocheting off the cavern walls. All of this was superseded by the ear-splitting sound of something grating forcefully along the cavern walls.

The Roughlanders began to stir, panic rising at the sounds coming at them in the darkness. I stood quickly – no less afraid, but feeling I was in charge now since Dahlia and Masaru had left.

"No one panic!" I called out over the din. "Gather your belongings and get ready to move, but keep the fires lit so we can see." Unsure of what danger awaited me, I picked up my bow and quiver and followed after Yue to see what I could do to help. "Gorfin," I addressed one of the Roughlanders on my way by, "can you go on ahead and see if you can find Masaru, to see if we have somewhere to flee to?"

Gorfin nodded and set off. I continued forward, running now on the steep incline, though I dreaded to see what lay ahead. The faint light from the fires followed me for quite a ways as there were no bends in the tunnel and I soon bumped into Kaji, who was running full tilt towards me.

"We have to get everyone moving. We can't stop that thing!" Kaji exclaimed. "Dahlia's trying to hold it off, but it's not working. We have to fall back!"

"Go tell the others, then," I instructed him, trying to remain calm in the face of his panic. "They are ready to move. Have them head further into the tunnel."

Kaji raced past me and didn't think to wonder that I wasn't following him. I strode resolutely forward, the jarring sound of tearing rock growing increasingly louder and more threatening.

"Load!" I heard Dahlia's voice and after a brief moment the command was followed by the sound of another bolt firing. "Load!"

"That's it!" Yue replied, her voice sounding frantic as they came into my view.

I saw the clawed hand first as the faint light of the fire behind me gave me enough dark vision to make out the white bone of it. It dug right into the rock of the cavern floor with ferocious strength. The arm it was attached to was clean white bone also, but the face – if it could be called that – was half smooth skull and the other half rotting dead flesh. It had wickedly pointed teeth, stained darkly, and no eyes to speak of, save for gaping holes where they might once have been. As the other arm sunk into the cavern wall – this one also covered in decaying skin – the creature pulled itself all the way forward and revealed that its ghastly form ended abruptly and impossibly at the torso.

"That's it?" Dahlia questioned, her voice rising to a worried pitch.

Yue lifted the empty bag to show it to Dahlia and in that moment I realized they had fired or thrown every weapon they had at the creature. By the look of things, they hadn't even managed to slow it down.

"Run!" Dahlia screamed at Yue, and as one they turned to retreat back down the tunnel.

I watched the creature with vacant horror. I had my bow and in my hands with an arrow fitted to it, but I was incapable of moving. The creature's empty gaze seemed locked on me and I could not look away from its disfigured visage. As Dahlia and Yue reached me, I hardly realized it meant I would soon be within the creature's grasp.

Dahlia grabbed me by the arm in a vice-like grip. "Run, Yukari!" she commanded and gave me a solid push back down the path.

Allowing her command to sink in, I forced my legs to operate enough to let her tug me along. The torso was fast, but it had to pull itself along at a crawl, digging its claws into the wall, floor, and ceiling of the tunnel as it went forward, but without a real sense of direction. As soon as I got my legs working under me again, Yue, Dahlia, and I were flying down the tunnel, picking up speed on the downward slope.

We reached the place where our camp had been only moments before to find it deserted with only one peat fire remaining. Dahlia resourcefully snatched the arrow I had clutched in my left hand and stabbed it into the block of lit peat to use as a torch, without slowing her long stride.

We ran and ran, our legs pumping with adrenaline and fear, heedless of our lack of breath, until eventually the downward slope levelled out entirely and the tunnel opened out into a cavernous space. The light of the impromptu torch revealed a grisly scene. There was dried blood here and there on the walls, and on the floor ahead of us was a sticky pool of it, seeping freshly from the corpse of a man dressed in familiar Roughlander clothes.

At a glance it was hard to tell who it was. Where the body's head should have been there was a large boulder instead. My heart lodged in my throat, knowing it was likely someone I knew. I hoped it wasn't Masaru, as he had been a solid presence since our arrival here and losing him would be a massive blow to all of us, especially Dahlia.

We didn't have a chance to investigate further, however. We could hear the grating of the creature growing closer behind us, and after a moment of hesitation Kaji appeared to our left, gesturing for us to follow him. "This way!"

Silently making up our minds, we adjusted our course to follow Kaji, who ran on ahead to lead the way along the wall, before making a sharp left into another small tunnel. This curved right briefly before opening out into sudden, dazzling sunlight.

My clearing vision revealed the Roughlanders who had made it out safely, along with Hotaru, hunching over Masaru, who appeared to be trying to hold himself together. He had a gaping wound with ragged edges – like the skin had been torn – on his right shoulder, which was leaking blood at an alarming rate, and a purpling bruise from a bad blow to the head. He was in rough shape, but he was still alive.

I looked around at everyone else, and other than scrapes on Dahlia and an ugly scratch from the creature's claw down Yue's back, the Roughlanders were, as a whole, uninjured. Who was missing? I scanned the crowd of us – Gorfin. I had sent him after Masaru and Hotaru, but…he hadn't made it out of the cave. I shuddered. I wasn't sure I wanted to know who or what had killed him.

A harsh cry broke the air, followed by a pained hissing. I whipped my gaze around back toward the tunnel entrance to see the creature we had been fleeing was hovering at the tunnel mouth, just out of reach of the light. Alongside it was a Roughlander looking feral and not quite human any longer. I didn't recognize him as having come with us, but he had fatal wounds in his chest in the form of deep gouges, and he also shied away from the light of the sun as an ominous and inhuman hissing came from this throat.

It seemed the light stopped whatever that creature was and whatever that Roughlander had become, but we were too close to the dark cave and its dangers for my comfort.

I looked ahead to see where we had come and I was astounded by what I saw. We were standing on a rocky outcropping low on the mountainside overlooking a lusciously treed valley, encompassed as far as I could see by the mountain range we had been trying to cross. The air here was humid and very moist, a drastic change from the dry heat of the desert and the damp chill of the tunnels we had just come from. The foliage – so different from anything I had seen before – was a vivid green, with coloured vegetation and flora spattered here and there. I had never seen a rainforest before, but I assumed this would be a close comparison, although it was on another world and therefore still alien.

The outcropping we were standing on ended abruptly ahead of us, so I looked side to side for a way down into the valley below. Along the mountain's side, cut smooth away from the rough stone walls, was a narrow ledge curving from either side of the platform we were on and descending gently to ground level below.

The ledges looked too sleek to be a natural formation, but nothing about this place had made any sense yet, and yet again we had so little in the way of options. I could see Ticket was already halfway down the ledge on our right, eager to explore the wonder of the valley below.

"We should head down as well and try to find shelter from those things," I said, watching Ticket's descent to see how feasible it would be for us humans to make it down – it didn't look nearly as daunting as the chasm had been.

"Masaru, give me the Flaqqer!" I heard Dahlia demand. "Ye're in no condition to do it yerself."

I looked over to where Hotaru and Dahlia had propped Masaru up against a rock and were trying to administer to his wounds the only way they knew how. Masaru looked faint; he had lost a lot of blood and fighting over the manner of his healing was only weakening him.

As I watched, Hotaru easily plucked the Flaqqer out of Masaru's weak grip and handed it over to Dahlia. She checked the Flaqqer and prepped it before jabbing it into the base of Masaru's neck, just above the wound.

"Aaahh!" Masaru cried out, his body wracked with pain.

I winced in sympathy and I wondered about the effectiveness of this Flaqqer device. "Dahlia," I addressed her as she looked down at Masaru's writhing form with concern in her eyes, "I can bandage his wound. I've had first aid training. You should see about getting everyone to a safer place than this."

It was a measure of Dahlia's distress that she left me to take care of Masaru and did as I told her to without question. I turned my attention to Masaru with a frown. I didn't know what the Flaqqer was supposed to do, but I was appalled that neither Dahlia nor Hotaru had thought to clean the wound out before attempting to treat it.

"Hey," I addressed Masaru, as his panting quieted some and he looked like he was going to lose consciousness on me. "Look at me. I need you to stay with me. You won't do yourself any good if you give up now." He tried to focus his gaze on me, but I could see the effort it cost him and his eyes were glazed. "Tell me about the Flaqqer," I seized on a related topic to keep him distracted. "What is it and how does it work?"

"Sand crawler larvae."

I almost dropped the water skin in my hand – they had injected him with bug larvae? To what purpose?

"It's not as strange as ye might think," Masaru continued, seeing my appalled expression. "They're kept in a sort of stasis inside the Flaqqer. They're real small, but when they're released in a person they dig holes into ye then seal them up behind them. They mend yer skin and bones up faster than anything else. Hurts like hell, though," he finished with a hint of humour.

"I can see that," I commiserated, being as gentle as possible in applying water to flush out his wound. Indeed, I could see the flesh was beginning to knit itself up right before my eyes. As disgusting as the thought of larvae injected into a person might be, it seemed the Flaqqer was a medical miracle on this world. I moved on to removing his shirt to use it as a bandage, as it was warm and humid enough here that he wouldn't need it.

I needed to keep him talking, however, so I searched for another question to ask. "So they just stay in there? The larvae don't try to hatch?"

"No," Masaru answered with effort, "they can't live for long in us. They die within a few hours after they're done their work. In the Sand Lake, the sand crawlers hatch out of rock, so it's not the same."

I was thoroughly disgusted. How many of these Roughlanders had dead bug larvae in their systems? It kept them alive, I supposed, but still…

I finished wrapping Masaru up tightly. I was assured he would not lose any more blood and if this Flaqqer device did as promised, his wound should seal up quickly. I stood and asked, "Masaru, I need you to do one last thing and then you can rest, okay?" He nodded his assent, and together with Hotaru and a few of the Roughlanders, we managed to get him down the ledge to where Dahlia and the others had already begun setting up camp.

It was sheltered by the rocky outcropping and out of view of the horrific creatures in the tunnels above. The ground was level and perfectly flat where we had situated ourselves and before us it sloped down for a ways to the forest floor, which appeared to be covered in a dense layer of fog. In short, it was the perfect place to rest. The sun kept us safe from the horrors we had just fled and I sincerely doubted the Deathsquad would track us here.

I had a stroke of genius while eyeing the mist. We needed water – I hadn't been able to collect as much as I would have liked from the cavern wall, and most of that I had used on Masaru. I found Kaji over by Binaris, talking to the Roughlanders who had been assigned to carry her.

"Can I borrow Binaris' tarp?" I asked as I approached them. "I'll need your help as well, Kaji."

"Sure, Yukari," Kaji replied, unwrapping Binaris to gather the tarp for me. "What is it?"

I had Kaji follow me down to the edge of the fog. We stretched the tarp out between us and held it in the moist air, waving it slightly to dampen it. This process would take as much time as the dripping water in the tunnel had taken, but we had the potential of gathering much more moisture to squeeze into canteens.

"Good plan, Yukari," Kaji acknowledged.

"Moop?" An animal chattered strangely at us from the trees. I spotted it by following the strange sounds it made and saw it was like no creature I had ever seen before. If I needed more proof I was not on Earth any longer, I had it now.

It was likely a mammal; that much I could tell by its gray-brown fur. It had rounded ears like a koala while being the rough size and shape of a raccoon, with a long prehensile tail reminiscent of a monkey, but with a tuft of fur on the end. Its luminescent green eyes were large and round.

"Meep-moooop," a feminine-sounding voice – possibly the female of this species – called from lower in the fog and over to our left. My eyes moved to follow the sound and all I could see was a teardrop-shaped, vibrantly yellow fruit suspended in the fog.

"Kaji!" I whispered sharply. "I never thought. This is a forest; there are probably fruits and other edible things we can gather. Look at that one there." I gestured to the yellow fruit and as one we watched the koala-monkey-thing leap for the branch where it hung.

As the creature jumped it spread its arms much like a flying squirrel would to glide on the air toward its target. Landing gracefully, it grabbed hold of the fruit and opened its mouth to take a bite. Suddenly the creature jerked in pain and a crackling noise like electricity filled the air. Within seconds the animal was dead and slightly charred, and it dropped like a rock as it lost its grip on the yellow fruit.

The fog cleared underneath the falling animal with a sudden motion, revealing a writhing fleshy pink creature as it opened a gaping maw filled with rows of pointed teeth to swallow its prey in two quick snapping motions.

Kaji and I backed up, shuddering. "I think this will be enough for now," Kaji said, indicating the tarp. "We should tell the others about what awaits us in the forest."

We did just that. No one was pleased at our news, though they accepted the water gratefully. We did our best to try to relax and rest, sharing our rations. I slept a little, but my eyes kept opening, remembering where we were and the danger we were in. The images behind my closed eyelids weren't pleasant either; images of the horrible torso of rotting flesh, Masaru's severe wounds, and the fate of the koala-monkey in the fog stuck with me, cycling incessantly through my mind.

It soon became evident the valley was darkening. The strangeness of this struck me immediately – I hadn't seen night or even cloud cover since our arrival here. I stood and moved out to where I could see the sky.

The mountain cast a long shadow over the treed valley. The sun was still just visible over the mountaintop, but it was lowering and soon enough it would descend below the height of the mountain, leaving us completely in shadow. I swallowed apprehensively. When the sun went down we would no longer have its protection from the tunnel's undead creatures.

"Dahlia – the sun," I began, but she had already seen it and realized the implications.

"Weapons out and packs on," Dahlia ordered.

"They fear light, right?" Yue said from beside me and I realized she had also been looking out at the lowering sun. "Do you think fire would work just as well?"

We spent some of the little time we had left gathering some of the drier wood just out of the fog's reach. Some of the branches we kept for torches and to double as weapons against the creatures if they got too close. The rest of the wood we assembled into a pile as close as we dared to the tunnel entranceway. The creatures eyed us hungrily from the shadow's edge, as if they could tell their freedom was coming soon.

When the hasty barrier was erected, we lit it with our makeshift torches and fled back down to the forest floor. Masaru, I noted, floated in and out of consciousness. He had lost all colour to his face, but although he needed to be carried by two other Roughlanders, he seemed to be holding on.

With our torches held forward, we fanned out in a line to scan the valley and search for a possible exit. I hoped the torches would be enough to scare the meep-mooping pink predators as well as the undead corpses. In case that wasn't accurate, I left Yue to my right holding our torch and I had my bow drawn with an arrow notched. I noted Hotaru and Kaji had paired themselves similarly – Kaji with the torch and Hotaru with her katana.

The valley darkened quickly and completely. Within the tree line the darkness was absolute. Behind us we could hear the frustrated screams of the undead horrors and the crash of the wooden barricade when it fell to their efforts.

We veered left and tried to keep to the wall for guidance, and in case we should spot an escape route, but no tunnels or openings in the sheer rock face provided themselves. We were well and truly trapped in this false paradise.

"Meep-moop." We heard the call and the light of our torches revealed yellow rippling flesh ahead of us through the trees.

This creature did not appear to be as large as the one Kaji and I had seen, but it was still much larger than a horse. It kept its undulating body close to the ground, all except for its green tail with a lime-coloured fruit trap dangling from it. With the mouth closed and the wicked teeth not showing, the creature did not appear as intimidating, but I had seen it kill and I knew how dangerous it was.

"Is that the thing you saw?" Yue asked me and I nodded. "I wonder if it's friendly."

"What?!" I exclaimed, as Yue shoved the torch into my hands and practically flounced off toward the beast. Was she crazy?

As much as I would regret it, I couldn't leave Yue alone out there. We could hear the undead creatures tearing through the trees, trying to find us. I ran forward after her, and I could hear Kaji and Hotaru crashing behind me to follow.

By the time we had reached Yue, she was mounting onto the thing's back, if it could be called that, as it didn't appear to have bones, much less a spine. She had evidently tossed some dried meat into its mouth to get its attention and as I watched, she tossed it another piece from atop it, which it snapped up gratefully.

"Come on, Snuffles!" Yue called to it. "We've got some zombies to fight!"

Remarkably, Yue managed to turn the creature about with the promise of more meat from her supply pack. I wondered briefly how sentient this creature was. It evidently had enough instinct to patiently lure the koala-monkeys into its trap before feeding; maybe the thing was more intelligent than it looked.

Yue tossed a small hunk of meat in the direction she wanted to go and the beast took off quickly after it, moving sinuously through the trees. I wished her luck, though I worried about her safety. I knew she was buying all of us precious time to continue the search for a way out.

Unfortunately, Yue's success sparked an inexplicable desire in Hotaru. Spotting the pink meep-mooping creature from before through the trees, Hotaru sheathed her sword and ran toward it.

"Hotaru!" Kaji called out, appalled at her sudden flight, and chased after her.

I couldn't spare any more attention for them after that because a zombie had just crashed out of the trees to my left and it was coming straight for me. I let my arrow fly and quickly drew another. Unlike the torso in the tunnel, this zombie appeared to have 'died' more recently, so my arrow had more effect in slowing it down.

More zombies crashed through the trees and more Roughlanders formed up around me. Together we defended ourselves as best we could, shooting arrows and bolts and waving flaming torches to deter the creatures from getting too close. I knew we hadn't stopped all of them and that there were some casualties falling to the ground around me, but I just kept firing, fighting to stay alive.

Yue, on her yellow creature, crashed through the trees behind the corpses that had us surrounded and with one smooth motion, the meep-mooping beast opened its jaw wide and bit off the top of one of the undead. Moments later, it had electrocuted another. Yue was cheering it on as she rolled with the beast to keep her seat.

The yellow beast did a lot of damage. However, there seemed to be many more of these things than we had originally anticipated and they kept coming, centering in on the violence and death of our position. It wasn't long before the undead took the yellow beast down and began feasting on it, taking it apart piece by piece.

Yue had no choice but to abandon her mount and flee over to us before the zombies could get her too. Thankfully they were distracted enough from the meat of the corpse before them to be too concerned that Yue was escaping them.

As she reached us, I caught a glance of pink to my right.

"Over here!" Kaji called desperately.

The remaining Roughlanders, including Dahlia and a now thoroughly unconscious Masaru, regrouped, and we used the distraction of the dead yellow Meep-moop to retreat to where Kaji and Hotaru inexpertly rode the pink Meep-moop. Kaji looked like the motion of the Meep-moop was making him sick. He held onto Hotaru, who seemed to be faring better, though she was having no luck convincing this Meep-moop to go where she wanted. The meat she threw it was having no effect.

As we reached them, the meep-moop surged forward, away from where its kin had fallen, with Hotaru and Kaji clinging desperately to its back. Yue and I followed them and the Roughlanders followed us. The pink Meep-moop eventually slowed, but did not stop its forward motion, and we were able to keep up easily as it led us deeper and deeper into the valley. Soon the ground began to slope and we started to descend, the trees getting thinner and thinner until there was no more tree cover. The fog around us was ever present, but it was lightening – the sun must have begun to rise above the ridge of the mountains once more.

Around us we heard a cacophony of 'meep-moops' of varying pitches and volumes and we realized abruptly this beast was taking us back to its home. There were even little baby Meep-moops at our feet now, flowing eerily with their vibrant colours.

As the sun continued to rise, Kaji and Hotaru dismounted from the pink Meep-moop, and we collectively backed up slowly until we were no longer intruding on the Meep-moop nest, but still well enough out of the tree line so the rising sun would meet us.

The Roughlanders supporting Masaru were in front of me as we rose above the clearing fog into the weak sunlight. As the sun filtered onto Masaru's ashen face I saw his cheek muscles flinch, as if the light hurt him.

I felt my breath leave my body in a horrified gasp. He had looked…dead, until that motion distorted his face.

Some of the zombies I had shot at had been wearing Roughlander clothes. I abruptly remembered Gorfin's mutilated corpse back in the tunnel and how these creatures were walking corpses now. Were they the bodies of those that had died here in this place? Was Masaru one of them now?

I couldn't face the thought. It was too awful a fate.

"Dahlia!" I cried out, turning to the one person who generally knew what needed to be done.

Dahlia was by my side in an instant, but she didn't look at me for an explanation of why I had cried out. She was staring at Masaru's limp form and she watched it twitch once or twice, recoiling instinctively from the sunlight.

"No," Dahlia breathed. "No! I won't let it happen."

Without hesitation, she pulled the Flaqqer out of her belt pouch and drove it into Masaru's chest with enough force to break one of his ribs. I winced in sympathy for them both, but I knew it was too late. The Flaqqer couldn't work miracles – he was already dead.

"No, Masaru!" Dahlia cried out pitifully as she hovered over Masaru's form. The Flaqqer had produced less of a reaction than the sun's rays.

I addressed the Roughlanders holding him up, "You'll have to put him down. There's no hope and he will soon turn on us like the others."

The Roughlanders gently lowered Masaru's body to the ground and grabbed hold of Dahlia to pull her away from him instead. She fought them, tears streaming down the powerful lines of her face. "No! He can't be dead, somebody help him!"

"Help who?" A cheerful female voice rang out from the top of the slope. It was so discordant with the scene of grief before me that I couldn't help but turn to look.

There, at the edge of the trees, fully in the sun's rays, stood a strange little girl with vibrant red hair and a perplexed expression on her open features. She wore a red and white striped shirt under a black jumper, which ended in belled shorts, and high matching striped socks. She was pristinely clean, which stood out to me in this place of savage violence and uncontrolled wildlife, and she stood with her hands clasped innocently before her.

"Masaru is hurt. He may be dying," Hotaru answered, understating the matter in my opinion – I didn't know if she didn't know the truth or was just being optimistic. "Who are you?"

"I'm Lilyth. And you are?"

"Hotaru. Can you help our friend?"

I don't know what Hotaru thought this mysterious stranger could do, but I was so subdued with grief and sympathy for Dahlia that I couldn't rouse myself to interfere or question the newcomer's sudden presence.

"I can," Lilyth answered in a hesitant tone, "but he's not a human, is he? Father said I shouldn't help humans because they will just come and destroy everything in my valley. I'm supposed to get my guardians to kill humans for me."

"Um, no, we're not humans," Hotaru lied. "I'm Hotaru and this is Kaji," she said, introducing the nearest person to her, "we're...friends."

"Oh, okay then," Lilyth responded, betraying how innocent she was, and then looked beyond Hotaru and Kaji to where Masaru's body lay twitching more violently now. He would be upon us like the others any second now, but I was loath to draw my bow to fire my remaining arrows at a friend. "Is that him there?" Lilyth asked.

"Yes, can you help him?" Hotaru pleaded.

"Yup," the strange girl responded confidently, walking over toward Masaru. We made way for her, unable to do anything else. "Let's see...um..." The girl seemed to consider the problem for a moment before raising her arms to the sun above her. From her small form a ghostly image seemed to rise up above her. It swirled and rotated in the air insubstantially, and the shadowy shape of it was so alien I couldn't put words to it.

Lilyth seemed to be concentrating on bringing this power of hers forth and the rest of us watched mesmerized as the lines of pain washed from Masaru's face. The sunlight that had been so painful to him only moments before seemed to soften his features, breathing some colour and life back into him. The nasty purple-black bruise on his forehead also vanished completely, gently fading away from his skin.

When the extraordinary process was complete, Masaru opened his eyes slowly and Dahlia rushed toward him, sobbing with relief.

"Hey, there now, what's all this for?" Masaru asked, holding her tenderly. "I'm okay, there's no need for that, Dahlia."

Dahlia held Masaru gratefully and Lilyth smiled at them both. "Well that's better. Now," Lilyth turned to address the rest of us, "how did you all get into my valley? I don't get many visitors. The guardians aren't supposed to let anyone in, but if you're friends and not humans, then I can tell my guardians to let you in if you want to come visit me."

"We were just trying to get through the mountains," Hotaru explained. "We're trying to get to the Temple of Sapphire before the Vile Emperor can stop us. Is there a way out of your valley?"

Lilyth thought for a moment and then shook her head. "I don't know. I don't leave the valley. It's safe here and I have all my friends," she said with a gesture toward the Meep-moop nest behind us.

"Ohh, the Meep-moops," Hotaru concluded, using the name I had come to refer to them as because of the sounds they make.

"That's a good name for them!" Lilyth exclaimed. "Why didn't I think of that?"

"Lilyth, may I ask you something?" Kaji ventured.

"Sure," she answered agreeably.

"How is it that this place stays safe? Why hasn't the Vile Emperor come to destroy it yet?"

"Oh," Lilyth said, startled by the question. "Well, I have my guardians to protect me – you probably saw them on your way in – and the Vile Emperor is my uncle. My father says the only thing I have to worry about is humans, otherwise I get to stay here and my valley is protected."

This information did not sit well with any of us. Worried expressions crossed each of our faces.

"Well, I probably don't mean uncle the same way you might mean uncle," Lilyth conceded after a moment. "It's just that I'm a comet and my father's a comet and the Vile Emperor is one too, so we're like family. What are you?" She looked to Kaji.

"I'm Kaji." Kaji answered uncertainly, introducing himself without actually answering her question to avoid calling himself human in her presence.

"Ohhh," she said, knowingly. "Well, I'll just tell my guardians that when friend-Kaji's come to the valley, to let them in to see me. Then you can come and visit whenever you want to."

"But we can't come visit if we can't leave," Hotaru pointed out.

"Oh, that's true." Lilyth looked crestfallen. "Well, I'll just have to give you a lift to…where'd you say you were going again? The

Temple of Sapphire? I'll take you there and then you can come back whenever you want, okay?"

"That would be amazing!" Hotaru exclaimed, believing wholeheartedly this girl could do anything after her miracle healing of Masaru.

"I don't know why you would want to leave, but I'll take you wherever you want to go," Lilyth promised. "As long as you promise you'll come back again. It gets lonely here."

Kaji, ever practical, tried to get more out of this deal. "Would it be possible to get some water and food to take with us?"

"Sure," Lilyth answered congenially. "I have lots."

Ticket, who was remarkably still with us through all of this, spoke up suddenly, "I'm staying – if you'll let me," he addressed Lilyth. "This place is awesome. There's nothing like it. I finally know what these are for!" He held up his webbed hands with his suction cup fingers. I abruptly realized he was almost certainly some kind of tree frog, and not a toad at all. His green colour had improved drastically here in the moist air, so different from the dry desert.

"Of course you can stay!" Lilyth exclaimed happily.

With the deal made, the rest of us used this rare opportunity of safety to rest while Lilyth and her Meep-moops gathered some fruit to replenish our supplies. Lilyth used her inexplicable magic to fill our canteens, water pouring remarkably from her outstretched hands. We slept in relative peace for once and when we were all well rested we agreed it was time to move on.

"Okay!" Lilyth responded when we told her. "Here goes!" She copied her motion from before and raised her hands to summon her incorporeal spirit, or whatever it was she did. The sun grew impossibly bright for a moment, enveloping us all in its brilliance, and when the solar flare cleared we were looking out past a drooping Lilyth over an immeasurable Sand Lake vista.

"Oh dear," Lilyth said, swaying a little. "It's hot here…I better go. Good luck…" and with no further ado, she disappeared once more.

Chapter 4 – Temple of Sapphire

We found ourselves high upon the battlements of an ancient ruined city. The view from there, looking inside the walls, was vaguely reminiscent of the image Binaris had showed us of the Temple of Sapphire, but in her picture the compound had been intact and covered in snow. What we saw, instead, was a desiccated ruin bordered on one side by bleak mountains and on the other by an endless Sand Lake.

The buildings were crumbling here and there, and there was not a single sign of life below us. Not even after we had found a way to the ground and had a chance to look around in a few of the buildings did we find anyone there to greet us. Directly across the ancient cobblestone town square was a daunting flight of steps up to a massive, arched iron door. We inspected it, but it didn't seem to have a latch or any method of opening.

"This must be the temple itself," Kaji stated. "It's the central building in this place, anyway. Maybe it was sealed for its own protection, or to keep whatever Yuko Seig left behind for us safe?"

"Maybe," I responded dubiously, inspecting the archway with a frown. The surface was weathered, but it appeared there had been writing along the doorframe at one time. It looked suspiciously like Japanese, but I still couldn't make it out.

I could have spent all day wishing I could fly up and examine the writing on the top of the arch, but from what I could see from the ground, the top was even more faded, having been more exposed to the elements than the bottom.

I hadn't been expecting to find Japanese writing here or anywhere on this world now that I knew this wasn't Earth – but there it was. The one symbol I could make out right near the bottom was the kanji for 'death'.

I shuddered at the foreboding message and decided to take it as a warning not to take this seemingly abandoned place lightly.

"Well this is getting us nowhere," I stated. "What else have we got?"

"Yue's inspecting the gazebo-style building in the centre of the square," Kaji replied. "Maybe it can tell us something?"

I shrugged – it was worth a try. Leaving Hotaru to continue to examine the faded writing – I think she was happy to see some evidence of home – Kaji and I joined Yue in the circular building. It wasn't large, but the shape and build of it reminded me instantly of the conservatory at the museum back in Shinjuku.

My intuition proved accurate as I looked up at the ceiling. It was decorated with a field of stars, and though I had no way of confirming it– what with there being no night on this world – I assumed the constellation patterns to be those as viewed from here.

In the center of the room was a table depicting the same view, only the table seemed to rotate as Yue pushed it from side to side.

"Yue," I cautioned her, the faded message on the temple doorway still fresh in my mind, "do you think you should be playing with that?"

"It moves the ceiling," Yue informed me, "but in the opposite direction. See?" She wheeled the table around and I watched the ceiling. It was subtle, but some stars winked out and others formed, changing the scene.

When she had the table rotated all the way to the left, I could swear I recognized something. "Stop!"

She obeyed and I examined the ceiling more thoroughly. It looked like Earth's constellations, only flipped around. I looked quickly down at the table. It was a mirror image – before me the constellations were accurate.

"Yue, look," I said, pointing to the table. "There's Orion, and that one is Leo."

Yue glanced at what had me so fascinated, but she clearly wasn't interested.

"Constellations, huh?"

"Earth's constellations," I affirmed. "No matter where this planet is, their constellations wouldn't appear the exact same as ours. The positioning would at least be different."

"Oh, well..." Yue struggled for something to say. "I probably won't be too much help with that, so I think I'll go take another look around. Yell if you need me."

"Sure," I responded dismissively, my attention now completely focused on the mental puzzle before me. Earth's constellations didn't really belong in this place, unless someone from Earth was expected to be here to see it and recognize it for what it was.

I could only assume that if this Yuko Seig had tried to leave something here, then we were those people – or in this case me, as I was likely the only one with a significant knowledge of astrology.

Was it a message of some sort? A code, or some kind of puzzle? There was really only one way to find out.

"Kaji? Are you any good with astrology?"

"Um…" Kaji hesitated. "I know the basics, I suppose."

"Well, good then," I told him. "I'm going to need help with this. I'll turn the table slowly and you can watch the ceiling and tell me when one of the known constellations changes."

It was a lengthy process, made lengthier by lacking the means to make notes, but Kaji and I soon developed a system wherein we could remember each pattern's formation and know to which degree the table had to be turned to reach it. Through trial and error, we began to piece together what it all might mean.

"So if all the way to the left represents Earth's constellation pattern, then this pattern," I said as I swung the table all the way to the right, "which is the most different from Earth's, should represent the other end of the spectrum – this planet's star patterns," I concluded with a measure of pride.

"So maybe this is some sort of elaborate combination lock," Kaji suggested. "If we can figure out what order to place the patterns in, maybe the temple doors will open?"

"It's possible. Certainly the message would be clearer if we had the right order," I agreed. "Okay, well. Earth to here, or here to Earth?"

"Try the first and if that doesn't work, we'll do it in reverse."

We mapped the changes and spun out the patterns, so they shifted from Earth's constellations to this world's one by one. The shifting ceiling with its multitude of stars was beautiful to watch, and when we were finally done, the pattern abruptly changed.

I gasped at the sudden revelation of what must have been the solution, though I didn't immediately understand it. There were now only five stars lit and now they were in different colours. One was a greenish light, another blue, and then red. The last two were white, but one was a bright orb and the other merely an outline where a star should have been. They were placed equidistant from each other across the conservatory ceiling.

I had no more than a second to puzzle over this new development, however, when the floor beneath our feet suddenly began to shake. Worriedly, we backed up toward the exit. The table in the center spun under its own power, as if unwinding, and then it rose into the air, revealing a pillar and a platform beneath. The platform settled to a stop and five levers folded out of it. Kaji and I stared at them blankly.

"Another puzzle?" Kaji questioned and I shrugged.

The levers were colour-coded, which would have been helpful if I knew what the colours represented. They were like the stars: green, blue, red, white, and black.

Kaji approached the pillar cautiously until he stood at the edge of the raised platform. "They have symbols on them, too," he noted. "The blue one here matches the ones on our chests."

"It does?" I headed closer to inspect it over his shoulder, and sure enough the two-diamond symbol was present. "So that means Sapphiros, right?"

"Yeah," Kaji agreed. "This is the Temple of Sapphire, so should I pull this one, do you think?"

"That seems too simple," I said, "but go ahead and try if you think it might work. We've gotten this far with it."

Kaji took a deep breath and grabbed hold of the lever with both hands. It was bigger than it looked. He pulled it back toward himself and I stepped aside to give him some room.

I felt a blast of cold air and heard Kaji cry out in pain before I fully realized what had happened. I looked at him in alarm – he had gotten his left hand out of the way in time, but his right arm was covered in ice almost up to the elbow.

The platform began to rumble again and the levers folded themselves away before the whole thing lowered itself back into the ground.

"Kaji!" I reached for him, thankful he had reacted quickly and the damage wasn't any worse. I ushered him out of the conservatory into the hot desert sun. "Are you all right?"

He was wincing and cradling his frozen arm. "I think so," he chattered through clenched teeth. "I hope the sun melts it quickly, though – it hurts like hell."

Hotaru was back from the temple doors and she was talking with Yue. When they saw us emerge, they headed over.

"Oh no, Kaji!" Hotaru exclaimed upon seeing Kaji's arm, which was melting efficiently in the sun. "What happened?"

"We think we've figured out the puzzle in the conservatory," I informed them. "We may be close to opening the doors, or whatever it does, but I'll need help to try it again."

Hotaru eyed Kaji's arm dubiously, but Yue was obviously looking for something to do. "I'll help you."

Kaji stayed outside, but Yue and Hotaru followed me back in. Kaji helped by calling out the combinations and I spun the table to the correct points. Soon I had the platform rising again to reveal the five levers.

"Don't touch that one," I instructed. "That's what happened to Kaji. Each represents one of those gem gods Binaris told us about. See the symbols?" I showed them the diamond patterns. "Green for Jedeite, white for Damos, black for Machalite and red for Rubia, if I am remembering them correctly."

"This temple is here to fight Rubia, right?" Yue questioned. "Maybe pulling this one is the next step?" Yue reached up for the lever.

"Be careful, Yue," I cautioned.

She nodded to indicate she had heard me before she pulled the lever down. A burst of flame hit her full in the chest and she was flung back through the doorway, her back having been to the exit.

"Yue!" I turned to run after her, but stopped as I realized something was wrong. I didn't hear the sound of Hotaru's footsteps following me out of the conservatory, but instead I heard the distinct sound of another lever being pulled down. "Hotaru – no!" I whirled around, but it was too late.

I watched Hotaru try to dive out of the way as some sort of crystalline substance shot out at her in a spray. She wasn't fast enough. The strange substance encased her and immediately hardened, freezing her in place. The platform completed lowering itself again as I made it to her side and touched the crystal experimentally. It wasn't cold like the ice that had gotten Kaji, but it was as hard as a rock and covered Hotaru like a shell. It also covered her open mouth – there was no way she could breathe.

"Dahlia!" I called, running out into the sunny courtyard in a panic.

"Hey, hold on there," Masaru replied, "is something the matter? Dahlia headed back to the rooftop to scout."

"It's Hotaru–" I struggled with the words to describe her predicament. "Come." I took hold of his wrist and pulled him after me into the conservatory.

If Masaru was caught off guard by the peculiar nature of the problem, he didn't let it show – he simply got down to business.

"How long has she been this way?" he asked, indicating the crystal prison.

"It just happened now," I answered. "I thought maybe Dahlia's hammer–"

"There's no time," Masaru responded and drew a long-bladed knife from a sheathe on his forearm that I'd never paid much attention to before. It seemed he had one on each arm but the other was already empty. "I lost the other one in those damned tunnels," he commented bitterly, hefting the knife's handle in his right hand, "but one should do well enough for this."

He raised his arm, the knife hilt down toward the crystal encasing Hotaru, and then drove the hilt toward her shoulder with as much force as he could muster.

The crystal cracked, and with another sharp rap it began to break away. Hotaru was soon mostly free and gasping for air. I hugged her in relief and Masaru carried her outside to where the others were nursing their wounds.

"It hurts all over," Hotaru informed us and I found myself laughing in relief that she was well enough to complain.

"What happened here?" Dahlia demanded as she approached us, her voice ringing out in the empty courtyard.

"You have to try again," Kaji insisted. "Sapphiros – Binaris said he represents balance in all things."

"You're saying we have to pull all of them together?" I asked Kaji as Dahlia joined us, giving us all a questioning look.

He nodded and I took a deep breath. After what had happened to each of them, I wondered why I was even considering this. "If that's not the answer, we're going to be in a sorry state," I stated to Kaji before addressing Dahlia and Masaru. "I need you two and two more volunteers. Kaji, Yue, and Hotaru are in no state to help." I silenced them before they had the chance to suggest they try again. "We may have found either the message from Yuko Seig or a way into the temple. There's nothing else for us here in these ruins, so we have to try."

"All right," Dahlia agreed as Masaru eyed me strangely. "I'll get a few of the others."

Dahlia, Masaru, two of the Roughlanders who had been assigned to Binaris, and myself all filed into the conservatory and took up positions around the table. As the others watched with some confusion, I spun out the patterns from Earth to this world one last time and the pillar rose once again as predicted, revealing the dangerous levers.

I reached for the handle before me – Sapphiros. I winced as I remembered Kaji's arm and braced myself. My eyes met Masaru's across from me. He had the white handle, Damos – the one that had crystallized Hotaru. At least Dahlia, next to him at Rubia's lever, could smash him free with her hammer if it came to that.

"Okay, on the count of three," I announced. "And get ready to let go and dive out of the way. One, two, three–"

We pulled the levers and nothing happened.

"Yukari!" Kaji shouted my name from outside. "The door is opening!"

The five of us raced outside, leaving the dangers of the conservatory puzzle behind, and sure enough the temple door stood open. Kaji, Yue, and Hotaru were on their feet.

"Let's go," Kaji said, and together we raced up the stairs and through the now open archway.

The hallway revealed by the doors was long and the walls were vast sheets of metal. After the harsh sun outside, the darkness of being indoors took some getting used to. Before our eyes had a chance to adjust, however, the door closed behind us, leaving us in nearly complete darkness.

"The evil we don't know?" Yue ventured, a weak attempt at humour.

Binaris, who had been carried in by the two Roughlanders who hadn't thought to leave her behind, and the eight of us were stuck inside and our supplies were still outside with the rest of the Roughlanders. I had no reason to believe the ones we had left behind would have any hope of completing the constellation puzzle to be able to free us.

"Come on," I said aloud to the group. "We have to figure this place out if we want to get that door open again. There's bound to be a mechanism in here somewhere."

As if some silent command had triggered them, lights sputtered into existence somewhere further along the metal corridor. They had a decidedly fluorescent quality, and flickered on and off like strobe lights, but they were better than being in this foreboding place in the dark.

We headed forward cautiously and as a group, but nothing untoward accosted us. The flickering ceiling lights illuminated a point where the hallway branched. Before us was an oversized metal door operated by a panel lock on the right side of it. The symbols on the panel were not ones I recognized, but if I had to guess, I would have said they represented a number pad.

To the left, the hall was brightly lit and somewhat comforting for it, but to the right was complete darkness. Having had enough of combination locks for the time being, I suggested we go left.

"I'll stay here and guard, just in case," Dahlia offered, so we left her with the two Roughlanders and Binaris, who didn't need to be lugged around to no purpose.

We entered the lit area gratefully and made our way along the corridor. This hallway was a series of closed doors: three on the left, four on the right, and another large one at the end. All seemed to have those panel locks, including the one on the end that had two – one on either side.

I watched Yue head over to inspect one of the doors on the left, then she traced the indented symbol on the panel with her finger. To our surprise, the symbol lit up and with a whooshing noise the door slid to the side, expelling a gust of stale air.

"It looks like a dorm room," Yue observed, and I peered past her to get a look inside.

The room appeared untouched by time. The navy blankets on the bed even appeared still useable. The space had a standard-issue feel to it that implied this had been some sort of facility where people had lived and worked at one time. Curiously, I did not get any indication that this had ever been any sort of temple, to Sapphiros or otherwise.

"I'm going to try the door at the end," I told Yue. "Search the rooms and see if you can salvage anything useful."

The others split up to inspect the other rooms as Yue had done. Masaru stayed in the hall, presumably to continue to act as a look out, or simply because this place did not hold as much interest for him as it did for us. I paid him no mind and approached the larger door at the end of the hall.

I ran my finger over the symbol on the left hand panel as Yue had done, but nothing happened. Was the power faulty on this door? I took a step back and inspected the door – of course, the second panel. It would take two people to open this one.

"Masaru," I called him over as he was within view. "Can you help me with this?"

"Sure, Yukari."

I instructed him on what I wanted him to do. Together, line by line, we traced the symbol on either side as if we were reading it from left to right, though I had no way of knowing if it actually said anything.

The doors parted in the middle and slid away to each side, cold air suddenly wafting out of the large chamber they revealed, and I cautiously entered the frigid room. The power here was obviously operational if the sudden drop in temperature was anything to go by. I could also hear the faint whirring noise I associated with many computers, and I was delighted to see a computer monitor ahead of me, blinking slightly.

The room was a literal icebox and the walls were lined with great, round pillars of ice, causing the space to appear vaguely circular. The monitor, built with a clear glass or plastic, was straight ahead, and it had a stool beneath it in front of a variety of keyboards.

My face lit into a smile when I saw one of the keyboards was in Japanese. I hurried over to it excitedly, but stopped when I noticed a dark, looming shadow within the nearest ice pillar to the door.

I approached it apprehensively, wondering once more what this place was truly here for. As close to the pillar as I was willing to get, I stopped and reached out with a sleeve to wipe away the condensation, so I could more clearly see what lay inside.

To my surprise, the pillars weren't made of ice as I had originally surmised, but were actually tubes of thick glass. Within the one I stood before there was a strange-looking man. He was completely nude and had wiry muscles on his lean frame. He had a flop of brown hair that hid his eyes, but the strangest part about him – other than his presence here – was that his left arm and part of his chest were not normal at all. They were covered in red skin that seemed scaly, like a lizard's might be, and the arm ended in a wicked looking set of claws.

Cryogenics? Was that what was going on here? Perhaps this facility had been a laboratory and not a temple at all.

When I was able to tear myself away from the odd sight, I found Kaji and Masaru were behind me, looking at the man as well. I left them to it, figuring the frozen man wasn't going anywhere for the time being, and I resumed my course to the monitor.

I took a seat on the cool top of the stool, which thankfully warmed instantly to my form. Taking a deep breath in anticipation of what I would find, I lifted my hand a little exaggeratedly and pressed 'Enter'.

Welcome. Japanese writing flashed across the screen in green glowing font. *Pass code?*

Of course, there had to be a pass code. I was getting a little tired of having to crack ancient codes.

Sapphiros. I opted for the obvious answer.

Accepted.

1. System Operation

2. *Defenses*

3. *Cryogenics*

I was of course very curious about option three, but I decided the other two options were more immediately important. I selected option one first.

Current status: 32% operative. Shut down system? Y/N

This computer, though no doubt powerful, was elegant in its simplicity. I selected no and was taken back to the main menu, so I tried the second option.

Defense mode is currently active. View defense schematics? Y/N

I selected yes, hoping this would lead me to getting the main door back open. Luckily it did show me an outlined map of the facility, which was larger than it appeared to be and more than we had seen thus far, and all the doors were labeled as 'active'.

Deactivate? Y/N

I thought I'd better for now and let the other Roughlanders know we were okay. After I made my selection, I was returned to the main menu once again. Okay, here goes nothing – I selected option three, cryogenics.

System operating at 32% capacity. Cannot perform function. Diagnose the problem? Y/N

I selected yes without hesitation.

Main server disconnected. The map of the facility appeared once more with a room highlighted and blinking.

"Yukari!" I heard Hotaru call my name from out in the hall.

There being nothing more I could accomplish there, I got off the stool, feeling a little disheartened. I had expected to find a bit more of use here, even if only in the form of information. There had to be a way home.

"What is it?" I called back, heading toward the door.

Hotaru was visible in the doorway. "There's a body in one of the rooms. He was killed here!"

"Recently?"

"Well, no…I think he's been in there a really long time," Hotaru answered, scrunching up her face in distaste. "The smell when we opened the door was awful!"

I sighed in relief. Hotaru was just being overdramatic; there was no murderer here, waiting for us. I walked out past Hotaru in the hall and I realized that the room behind me – other than its mysterious frozen occupants – was empty. I could hear Masaru's distinctive voice coming from a room on the far side of the hall, talking to Yue, but Kaji was nowhere to be seen.

"We found stuff from Japan here, too," Hotaru said from behind me.

"Really?" I asked. "Like what?"

Hotaru handed me a ten-yen coin. "There's pencils and paper that were sealed up inside a desk, and there are military uniforms."

I held the coin tightly in my hand, holding on to the evidence home still existed.

"I'll be right back," I informed Hotaru, and headed off down the hall back to where Dahlia waited with the Binaris crew.

There, I found Kaji. He was eyeing the dark – now slightly flickering in spots – corridor with curiosity. "We didn't find too much of interest down that hall," he was saying.

"If you're interesting in seeing the rest of the facility," I interrupted, joining them, "I have to make a trip down that way to see if I can do anything to repair the main server."

Dahlia looked at me blankly, but Kaji nodded. "Sure, Yukari, I'll go with you."

"Be careful, both of ye," Dahlia advised, and with a nod in her direction, we set off cautiously into the darkness.

We had to navigate blindly down the darkened hallway, having no method of illuminating the blackness. The smooth metal floor soon became uneven, and if the crunching under my Roughlander boots was any indication, it was littered with debris. Out of deep curiosity I reached down to find out what I was stepping on and my fingers closed around a bullet casing. I dropped it quickly and stood once more.

"Ahh!" I heard Kaji cry out ahead.

"Are you all right?" I asked, putting my arms out ahead of me to feel the way and trying to step up my pace to rejoin him.

"There's something like barbed wire here. My leg got caught in it," Kaji informed me. "I'm free now, though."

"Watch your step, Kaji," I warned him. "I think this was a battlefield once."

Together we picked our way slowly through the treacherous corridor, going around, over, and under debris, discarded weaponry, and unfortunately decimated remains. I struggled to keep my stomach and my fear under control, but it was nearly the hardest thing I had done yet.

After what felt like an eternity of scrabbling through death and destruction, Kaji and I came to what felt like a wall. I could tell by its texture it was not metal like nearly everything else here had been. It felt more like a thick plastic.

"There should be a series of rooms on the left hand side," I told Kaji. "We want the last one."

We felt along the wall, heading to the left, when all of a sudden Kaji froze and I bumped into him. "What is it?"

"Nothing," Kaji replied, the fear in his voice barely controlled.

Beyond him the lights flickered again slightly and I caught Kaji's silhouette. He was standing shocked to stillness in front of the giant barrel of a machine gun. The feel of the bullet casing in my hand came back to me and I instantly understood Kaji's distress.

"Come on," I said more confidently than I felt. "This happened a long time ago. It's not happening now. Let's get this over with."

I felt Kaji nod and move forward. Despite my brave words, I couldn't help but duck instinctively under the gun's barrel as we passed it. The thick plastic wall came to an abrupt end, but it didn't meet up with the metal wall of the corridor. Having nowhere else to go, Kaji and I squeezed through the gap to continue onward. Here there was a faint light coming from the left. It illuminated very little of the hallway where we were, but it was enough to make out the obstacle we had been maneuvering around.

There were two machine guns positioned to defend this place – the room at the end of the hall where I had been instructed the main server was located. They were set up like turrets to be manned from behind a plexiglass wall, which I now assumed must be a bulletproof shield of some sort. There were still several magazines of bullets loaded into the machine guns and stacked behind them ready for use, but the corpses draped across the guns showed how the battle had been lost.

On the far side of the hallway – the side we had not ventured near, as we had determined early on was the most damaged – I could see the shield had been melted away somehow. The metal behind it looked as if it, too, had been subjected to an intense heat.

I forced myself to turn away from the horrific scene and focus on the task at hand. Kaji was already ahead of me in the dimly lit room. I followed him quickly.

The room was similar in shape and size to the cryogenic bay, but was not kept cold, and lining the walls was not frost or ice, but wires and pipes of all descriptions. The whole place was in disarray, much like Binaris' room in the outpost had been. In the center of the room was a shocking sight.

There was a metal pillar in the direct centre, bowl-shaped at the top as if meant to hold some form of liquid, though it was empty now. To either side of the raised bowl were, for lack of a better term, two corpses. The one furthest from the door was desiccated, but still recognizable as what it had been before – a Croatin. He had been rather large and the parts of him that had been bionic were still intact.

Opposite him stood a figure much like Binaris, only male in shape, and with its head sliced cleanly in two so the severed wires were clearly displayed. The male Binaris had a cord trailing from his lower half to an oversized plug over on the far wall.

Nothing else in this room appeared to be damaged, with the exception of the door, which no longer seemed to exist. Was the male Binaris the main server, then?

"Kaji," I addressed him, "we have to bring Binaris here. We should be able to get her set up and she might be able to activate this place for us."

"I'll go get her. You stay here."

Kaji left and as I was alone in the room looking around at the ancient scene, recognition came crashing down.

"Reset the program." The robotic voice spoke metallically.

"There is not enough time," a guttural Croatin voice responded anxiously. "The Vile Emperor is almost here. If we do not get them out, they will die."

I saw them through an air duct vent. A Croatin and an android like Binaris facing each other over a basin of water...a pool of water that reflected an aerial image of me on the hospital rooftop about to die.

My mind edited in what must have happened next.

The door crashed in, lava spewing into the room. Shots and screaming and the sounds of tearing metal could be heard in the corridor beyond.

"Agreed," the android said emotionlessly, 'Terminating the program."

The Vile Emperor himself entered the room. Kai-een, the blond teenage Goth was beside him, his blades drawn. No hesitation. No mercy. Kai-een killed the Croatin and removed the robot's head in one swipe.

As the scene came to an end in my mind, and I came slowly back to the present, I realized I was panting uncontrollably, my hand on the edge of the basin the only thing keeping me upright. The Tuesdays had been a program and that program had somehow miraculously come to completion before this atrocity occurred. I shuddered at how close we had unknowingly come to death.

"Yukari?" Kaji's voice snapped me fully back to the present.

"I'm fine." I composed myself as quickly as I could. "Bring Binaris over here."

The Roughlanders carried Binaris over to the spot I indicated near the plug on the wall. With effort I pulled the plug out of the deceased android and brought it over to Binaris. I looked for a similar place to hook her up and sure enough the models were functionally identical. My hand stopped, hovering for a moment over the plug on Binaris. Just above the socket it read: *Made in Japan.*

"Here goes," I whispered, and plugged Binaris into the system. Her eyes lit up immediately. "Binaris?" I addressed her, but there was no response. "Binaris? Pass code: Sapphiros."

She didn't answer, but if her glowing eyes were any indication she was online with the system. "Kaji, I'm going to go back to the other computer. If she says anything, can you come and get me?"

Kaji agreed, and without further explanation I headed back to the hallway of death. Unfortunately, or fortunately depending on your perspective, plugging Binaris in had the added effect of turning on some of the lights in this area. I could now clearly see all of the carnage and destruction, but somehow it seemed less scary in the light, and at least, being able to see it, I could safely navigate my way back through it.

The cryogenic bay's computer awaited me, and when I got there I noticed Yue was in the room now as well, inspecting the frozen man I had discovered earlier. I ignored her, took my seat at the monitor, and got down to work.

System operating at 58%...62%...66%

I let out a relieved breath; the system was repairing itself. I navigated through the menus back to cryogenics.

Initializing cryogenic release. Estimated time: 00.04 32

Four and a half minutes? I jumped up off my stool. "Yue! We need to leave this room," I announced and hurried to the open door.

At the threshold I looked back for her. She appeared to be mesmerized by the people frozen in the tubes. It was only now that I realized there was certainly more than one of them cryogenically frozen here. How many people had I just released from presumably eight hundred years of stasis?

"Yue, come on," I called again and this time she looked over at me with an unimpressed expression.

I heard the motion before it happened. The doors behind me made a telltale whooshing sound – they were closing. I had two choices: stay in there with Yue or go back out to safety.

Some preservation instinct kicked in before I had the chance to make a conscious choice and without realizing I had stepped back, the door closed on my face. "Yue!" I screamed in distress and rammed my fist on the closed door, "Yue!"

"What happened?" Masaru asked from behind me.

I spun around to face him. Hotaru was there as well, a little bit behind him. "Yue is in there, and the cryogenic program is running. She could be in danger."

That was enough for Masaru. He stepped up to the right hand panel and raised his hand to it before looking back at me expectantly. Picking up on his cue, I took the left hand panel and together we repeated the command for the doors to open.

Nothing happened; the program had caused a lockdown. I leaned against the wall, feeling worried and defeated.

"She'll be all right," Masaru said comfortingly.

If anything, Hotaru looked more scared than I was, but she thankfully kept her worries to herself as the three of us waited anxiously for the doors to open once more. Eventually they did, but the scene they revealed was not one any of us could have expected.

Yue's back was to us, so we couldn't see her expression, but she appeared no more injured than she had been from the fire blast earlier. She was backing up in a defensive stance toward the door where the three of us stood. Beyond her was the real shock. There were not just one or two newly awoken relics from a time long past, but five, and they could not have looked more different from us or from each other.

Directly in front of Yue stood a tall man in a broad suit of white armour with no helmet, his face visible. He had darkly tanned skin, with dark brown hair, and his features looked stern, but in a fatherly way. He carried a massive weapon in one hand – I believe it would be called a mace, but it was larger than any I had seen depicted before – and he had a sword handle visible over his shoulder.

Closest to him – and looking just as threatening if not more so – was a woman. She, too, was covered in armour, with a metal coif around her smooth, proud features. She also had a large mace, but hers was wooden, and in her other hand she held a massive shield, beautifully decorated with a coat of arms.

To the woman's right stood another armoured female, though this one looked pleasant and was trying to smile at the rest of us in greeting. She had no weapons drawn, though I could see her sword sheathed at her waist. Her red hair was straight on either side of her face, but despite her armour she didn't look like much of a fighter.

On the far left, standing slightly apart from the group, was the man I had seen in that first tube. He was fully clothed now in rather normal-looking pants and a ragged shirt, though the scaled arm was not covered by a sleeve and was more intimidating now that the claws had come to life. He looked relaxed, however, and had leaned himself up against the tube where he had been frozen only moments before.

The fifth being was by far the strangest, though she seemed the least dangerous at first glance. She stood behind the others and was much smaller, but I could make her out between the two armoured women. She appeared to be covered in a short fur and her features were bat-like, with large open ears that rose above her head and large wings that drifted out behind her like a cloak. She was surreal, but undoubtedly beautiful.

Surprisingly, Masaru was the first one to break the tableau. "Who are you?" he asked rather bluntly, no doubt caught off guard by the mysterious appearance of these strangers.

"I am Sir Sabien," the tall man with the mace responded in a deep, authoritative voice. "I am the Knight Commander of Sapphiros. These are the Knights of Sapphiros. Lady Adel," he said, indicating the woman beside him, "her squire, Aysel," the red-haired woman, "Ris," he gestured to include the bat-woman, "and Jeth."

"Hey, how're ya doin'?" the man with the scaled arm, presumably Jeth, said in a rough, mellow-toned voice.

The armoured woman was still glaring icily and Yue hadn't yet backed out of her defensive crouch. I figured I had better diffuse this situation if I could. I stepped forward, presenting myself to them with a formal Japanese bow. "I am Yukari Namikoya…" I hesitated only an instant before adding, "Chosen of Sapphiros."

At this, the Lady Adel's eyes widened in surprise before narrowing into slits. It seemed not only was I not what she expected to find, but I also displeased her in some way. The others' expressions remained much the same.

"This is Yue Noh," I said, indicating Yue, beside me, "and–"

"Hotaru Hatsumuya," Hotaru jumped in, offering her own bow just as I had done. "I'm very pleased to meet you."

"You four are the Chosen of Sapphiros we've been waiting for?" Lady Adel asked, her voice slightly accented with a proud and regal bearing. "But you are still only children!"

"I'm not one of the Chosen," Masaru said quickly. "I'll go get Kaji. He'd be the one ye're wanting."

"We weren't exactly expecting this either," I addressed Lady Adel. "We recently arrived on this world without a clue as to how or why we were here, only to learn of Sapphiros and this place by Binaris at the Roughlander outpost. We were left a message from Yuko Seig to come here and so we have."

"Roughlander outpost?" Sabien questioned. "Did you not arrive here at the Temple?"

"We were dropped in the middle of the desert with nothing," Yue informed him tartly. "We were lucky to be brought to the outpost."

"Then you have united the Roughlanders and reminded them of the pact with Yuko Seig?" Sabien asked.

"No," I responded unfalteringly. "We could not be certain the outposts had not been compromised by the Vile Emperor's forces, even if they all stood after eight hundred years. I didn't think it was wise to alert the Vile Emperor to where we were, though it seems he already knew we had arrived."

Even the armoured Sabien looked a little faint at my news. "Eight hundred years?" he asked incredulously. "Have we been asleep for that long?"

I nodded, realizing perhaps I should not have sprung that information on them without warning, but I had received it in much the same way. "It apparently took us that long to arrive here."

"So you say you arrived in a desert and were brought to the nearest outpost. Do you have a map?" Sabien asked, regaining his composure.

Kaji, who had returned with Masaru at some point during the discussion, came forward to hand Sabien our Roughlander map. "We landed here," he said as he pointed to the rough center of the Sand Lake, "and we were taken to this outpost here," he pointed again, "which was destroyed by Deathsquads. We were told they were likely hunting us, but we did not stay to find out."

"You have managed to evade the Deathsquads and make it this far?" Sabien asked, sounding concerned. "Do they know you are here?"

"No," Kaji responded. "They may be able to guess where we would be headed, but they did not see us and they were not able to follow us."

"Is it possible for the Splitter to have malfunctioned?"

"Anything is possible, Adel," Sabien responded. "Jeth, go to the control room and make sure everything is in order. I think we should let the Chosen speak with Yuko Seig."

"I thought Yuko Seig was dead?" I asked.

"In a manner of speaking," Sabien agreed, "but her spirit remains here and she can still be reached. Save your questions for her. After you have spoken with her, we can see about your training."

Unsure what to make of these Knights, we followed Sabien and at the large central door, left Masaru behind to introduce the female Knights to Dahlia and the Roughlanders. The door was now open; Jeth had gone on ahead to the 'control room' as per Sabien's request.

A steep ramp led upwards to a round platform surrounded by a metal railing. The walls outside the platform were covered in computer monitors, and Jeth sat on a familiar Earth-style swivel chair, tapping away at the keys.

"Jeth, is everything operable?"

"Yeah, man," Jeth responded, "but we don't quite have full power, so I don't know how long it'll last."

Sabien turned to us. "Chosen. You will be able to speak with Yuko Seig, but you may have to be brief." A door suddenly opened in the metal wall to our right, revealing another room attached to this one. "Arrange yourselves around the pillar in the centre of the room and place your hands upon it, but do not touch anything else, and once the process has begun, do not move until it is over. Do you understand?"

We nodded, eyeing the strange room. It was completely circular, like this one, but smaller. There was perhaps room for the four of us, but no more. The pillar in the centre appeared to be made of crystal and was the approximate height of a speaking podium. Along the ceiling of the room and lining the walls were spring-shaped metal coils pointing inwards. We all dubiously filed into the room and did as we were told. Sabien and the others had been expecting us at the instruction of Yuko Seig. We did not know them, but it seemed we had no choice but to trust them if we wanted to learn what we had come here to learn.

I stood across from Kaji, with Yue and Hotaru to either side of me, and the crystal plinth between the four of us. We each placed a hand on the pillar before us as instructed. The door shut, cutting off our view of the Knights. I waited anxiously for something to happen, and then instantly regretted when it did.

A whirring sound picked up and the metal coils lining to the room began to rotate slowly. They were elongating and coming toward us in the center. We all looked around at them worriedly. I cursed myself for not bothering to ask how this process worked and what it was going to do.

As the coils got closer and closer, Hotaru lifted her free hand to reach out to one. She drew her hand back quickly with a gasp, "They're really sharp all the way along, like razor blades."

The news was not comforting, but if Sabien and the others intended to kill us, we had already walked right into their trap. We watched with dread as the coils drew ever closer and winced as they got close enough to reach skin and they kept on coming.

Inexplicably, we found ourselves standing on Shinjuku High's school rooftop. It was a sunny day with a few clouds in the blue sky and a light cool breeze wafting against our faces. The four of us stood facing each other each with a hand raised between us. Confused, we lowered our hands and looked around.

It felt very real, but I also knew it couldn't be.

"Welcome Chosen," Yuko Seig's voice spoke and I whirled around to face her. She looked just as she had been depicted in Binaris' files, from her white, blue-tinged hair to her outfit decorated with a star motif, and her red eyes glowing faintly in the light. She stood on the empty rooftop as if she belonged there, though surely she would have appeared surreal in Tokyo.

"I am sorry I could not greet you in person," Yuko Seig apologized. "This setting was chosen from your memories as it is one you are all familiar and comfortable with. You may ask what you wish of me. I'm sure you have many questions."

We had come so far to reach this place and been through so much, but I found all of a sudden I had no idea what to ask. All my focus had been expended on trying to reach this place and I found myself without purpose.

"Everyone's been telling us since we arrived here that we're the Chosen of Sapphiros, but what does that mean?" Hotaru was the first one to voice a question.

"Sapphiros chose you to represent him on this world and to restore balance to it. You four were marked at birth to be his Chosen ones."

"But the mark did not appear until we arrived in the desert," I noted.

"It has always been there, but had no need to manifest itself until now," Yuko Seig responded serenely.

"How did we get here and why did it take so long?" I demanded, irritated by her calm demeanor when it was our lives she had altered irrevocably. "What was the point in bringing us here if we were going to be too late?"

"When the Vile Emperor threatened your lives in the park, I knew you either had to return and face him or be destroyed. You are this world's last hope. The Splitter is the method used to travel between our two worlds. Two Splitters are needed to bridge the gap between worlds, so when I felt the Vile Emperor was on Earth, I fought for control of the Splitters in order to bring you through to escape him.

"You were supposed to have arrived immediately, but the Vile Emperor did his best to prevent that. As time went on and the war continued, I did not know how long it would take or if you would ever make it through. I am glad you did."

"But we're not," Hotaru said plaintively. "It's great that you saved us from the Vile Emperor, but how're we supposed to get home?"

"I am afraid the only way to get back to Earth is to have control of two of the Splitters. There are only three I know of. Jedeite destroyed his out of rage, and I don't think Damos ever had one, as he has no Chosen. That leaves ours, Machalite's, if you can find it, and Rubia's, which is controlled and closely guarded by the Vile Emperor."

We all took a moment to absorb this new information. No way home? Eight hundred years had passed on this planet while we had travelled here and there was no way of knowing how much time had passed back on Earth. Even if we did manage to gain control of the Vile Emperor's Splitter and learn to work it, we might be eight more centuries returning. The world we knew might well not exist anymore.

"But we weren't the only people to come here from Earth, right?" Hotaru asked suddenly, far off-topic in my opinion. "There are Japanese military uniforms at the Temple, and Japanese writing. I even found some yen."

"Yes, that's right," Yuko Seig confirmed with a slight smile. "We had a number of Japanese people from Earth come and live with us at the Temple, including your parents. You four were actually born on this world."

"We were?" Hotaru asked, incredulous by this revelation. "But how did we grow up on Earth, then?"

"I should probably tell it to you from the beginning so you can understand how this all came to be," Yuko Seig admitted finally. "When the Splitters were first activated, the Vile Emperor and I travelled to Earth and established trade with your government."

"Wait a minute," Yue spoke for the first time, "you took the *Vile Emperor* to Earth?"

Yuko Seig's cheeks reddened slightly, as her composure broke for the first time to show embarrassment of all things. "He wasn't called by that name then."

"What was he called?" Kaji interjected.

"His name is Verasheen." When Yuko Seig spoke the name it was like a caress. I shuddered despite myself, wondering how this surreally beautiful woman could have had feelings for that armoured monstrosity in any form. "And though I didn't know his intentions then or what he would eventually become," Yuko Seig continued, her voice filled with regret and longing for a simpler time, "I am sorry I brought him to Earth.

"For a time our two Splitters remained open and travel was possible between the two worlds. Some humans from Earth decided to colonize and they came to live in the Temple. They were all military personnel and your parents were among them. When you were born, Sapphiros blessed you with the gift of his Choosing.

"When the war started, your parents didn't want you to fulfill your destiny. They didn't want you to grow up as Chosen on a world where you would have to fight to survive. I didn't want them to take you, but your parents insisted on returning to Earth.

"So you grew up there, never knowing what you were supposed to be."

"Are you blaming our parents for this?" Hotaru demanded heatedly. "It sounds like they gave us a chance to live! The Vile Emperor would have killed us by now on this world."

Hotaru was right, of course, but I didn't think Yuko Seig, misguided as she was, would see it the same way.

"Your parents are to blame for your ignorance of your responsibilities and your powers. Had you grown up here with me, you would be ready now to face the Vile Emperor and to win this war."

Hotaru was crying out of frustration and I couldn't blame her. Personally, though, I didn't have it in me to hate this ghost of a woman. She certainly deserved a large portion of blame for the state of things and the fact that we were trapped into this fate, but it was all just too much for me to take in at the moment. All I could think was the world our parents had shown us – Earth – had been a fleeting paradise, and this dried out desert planet was our reality now, as it was apparently always meant to be, if one believed all this woman had told us.

I had to accept the facts. I had felt how real and brutal and vivid this world was, and I now knew I was likely never going to leave it.

Chapter 5 – Remember Fear

We came out of the visit with Yuko Seig just as abruptly as we had entered it. The menacing metal coils lining the walls retracted and the door opened with a whoosh to the side.

Unbeknownst to us, hours had passed during our conversation with Yuko Seig, but we were safe now within the Temple, able to rest and recuperate from the ordeals we had faced to reach this place. The surreal visit with Yuko Seig stuck with me and its very orchestration was all the proof necessary for me to believe these Knights were quite capable of operating the Temple's systems, so I didn't need to bother to continue trying to figure them out.

"As Chosen, you all have access to near-limitless power given to you by Sapphiros," Sabien informed us once we had gathered at his request in the central command room.

We stood together with Sabien and the bat-woman, Ris, on the railed platform in the center of the space. At Sabien's instruction, Jeth operated the controls and the platform we were standing on began to descend. A large, metal-walled room about the size and shape of Shinjuku High's gymnasium was revealed as we descended to the lower level of the Temple. It was well lit by the fluorescent-style lighting that was commonplace in the temple.

"This is the training facility," Sabien indicated. "Yuko Seig left instructions that I was to show you what I could of your powers and help you to develop them. I am certain you will soon outstrip me with your abilities, but there is no reason I can't start you on the right path."

"Powers?" Hotaru asked, her tone confused. "What sort of powers, Sir Sabien?"

"Every person's powers manifest differently, and with Chosen this is especially so," Sabien lectured, "but generally speaking there are three ways a gem god's power can manifest: elementally, physically, or magically."

"But if they are powers, doesn't that mean they are all magic?" Hotaru questioned.

"Not exactly," Sabien answered. "Allow Ris and I to demonstrate for you."

Sabien drew his sword from his back and held it in his left hand with an easy confidence. "Physical powers can boost a person's or an object's – in this case a weapon's – natural abilities." As he spoke steam began to rise in the air around the blade.

"My power is mainly elemental in form. Watch," he instructed, and when he was certain he had our full attention, Sabien disappeared.

His form seemed to melt right in front of us to splash to the floor in a puddle. The oversized puddle drifted left, and then right, before rapidly coming toward us. I moved out of the way, alarmed and unsure of what to make of this man and his magic.

"That would be an elemental power," Sabien's voice came from behind us.

I whirled around and sure enough he had reformed; there was not even a trace of water remaining on the floor. I think we were all in shock because for once even Hotaru said nothing.

Next, Sabien indicated we should watch Ris for an example of a magic form of power. I did as instructed, not knowing what to expect from the bat creature, but a steaming sword and a man that could turn himself into a puddle seemed pretty much like magic to me. I wasn't sure I yet understood the difference Sabien was trying to illustrate.

Ris lifted off into the air and held her hands aloft in front of her slender form. She hovered in the air, flapping her wings gently to stay aloft, and she closed her eyes in obvious concentration. Between her outstretched hands a blue pulsing light formed. I recognized the colour immediately – it was the same as the blue light we had encountered in the park the night we had fled the Vile Emperor.

The mysterious light pulsed and grew until she held a small ball of it, and the pulse became an electrical current, licking at the palms of her hands. Ris opened her eyes and grinned wickedly at Sabien before releasing the ball she held. The crackling energy surged through the air toward Sabien. To my surprise he met the blast head on with his sword held before him. The sword seemed to absorb the energy and Sabien wisely dropped the blade before the electricity could reach him.

"That would be magic," Sabien informed us, shooting a dangerous look at Ris, who settled herself serenely back upon solid ground.

"Why are you showing us this?" I asked when it seemed like he was finished with his demonstration.

"I do not know what form your powers will take," Sabien responded, "but depending on what you can do or wish to try and learn, you will be training with different Knights. We each have our specializations and I'm sure we can help you develop quickly, whatever path your powers choose.

"Now, close your eyes. I'm going to teach you something." Kaji, Yue and Hotaru closed their eyes, so I did as well, and Sabien continued with his lecture. "In the beginning, your powers will be triggered and fuelled by strong emotions. Anger, fear, determination, and love, among others, but as you become more attuned to them that will no longer be the case, and you will find strong emotions will inhibit you.

"You must learn to master your emotions and use them to become stronger. I want you all to remember fear," Sabien said, his deep voice commanding, "Remember feeling afraid, remember terror and being unable to act because of it. Then, defend yourself.

"Can you picture it?" Sabien asked, "Can you visualize your fear and make it real?"

My mind summoned up the most dreadful image without hesitation. I recoiled mentally from the vision of the undead torso scrabbling toward me in the dark, cavernous tunnel. I couldn't move; I couldn't act or even draw the bow in my hands to defend myself. It was coming for me. I opened my eyes and gasped with relief to see I wasn't still in that tunnel. I filled my lungs with air gratefully; I had made it out of there alive – we all had.

"Good," Sabien stated, having seen our various reactions to his little exercise. "You may open your eyes. Hotaru," he addressed her first, turning to face her. "Remember your fear and defend yourself."

Sabien drew his mace and Hotaru nodded, taking a defensive stance. I stared at the two of them, my jaw dropping. Was he going to attack her? Did Hotaru think she stood a chance against this trained Knight Commander, unarmed and unarmoured?

Sabien brought the mace back behind his head and moved in deliberately with a full-motioned swing. Hotaru, despite herself, took a step back, but then raised her arms in front of her body as if they would be enough to save her from the mace's blow.

Hotaru closed her eyes tight and waited for the blow to strike. The mace struck solidly on the air before Hotaru's outstretched hands. What? There was a glint of that same colour of blue light, then the mace's motion stopped and bounced back.

I heard clapping from beyond where we all stood and I looked up in surprise. Ris was happily smiling and clapping her delicate hands together. Hotaru opened her eyes and looked over at Ris with a satisfied expression.

"I did it, didn't I?" Hotaru asked. "It's just like the blue light in the park. I just asked Sapphiros to protect me."

This statement took me aback. Had we all made this deal with Yuko Seig and requested the help of Sapphiros, then? Is that why all four of us had been brought here and 'chosen'?

Sabien nodded, seeming satisfied by Hotaru's success, but not surprised by it. "Kaji," he turned to face Kaji next. "Remember fear."

Kaji nodded, looking determined, and Sabien repeated the process of raising his mace for an attack. I found myself holding my breath, anticipating the blow, but the mace didn't connect this time either. Kaji kept his eyes open and focused on Sabien's attack. At the last possible second, he did as Hotaru had done and raised an arm. I noticed immediately it was the one he had injured trying to unlock the door to this place – the one that had been frozen solid.

The mace slowed to a stop just before connecting with Kaji's arm. The mace and half of Sabien's armoured arm were covered in a thick layer of ice.

I stared at this phenomenon in shock. It was one thing to see these strange Knights from another planet perform startling feats of magic, but it was quite another to witness ice pouring from the hands of someone you had known your entire life. Kaji seemed pleased, however. He was even grinning at Sabien, who smiled back at him encouragingly. "Creative."

"Yue." Sabien turned to her next after having hit his arm off the wall to remove the ice. "Remember your fear."

Yue, always so contrary from the rest of us, did not seem in the least bit intimidated by Sabien's training methods. She stood relaxed and she met Sabien stare for stare over his massive weapon. He repeated his earlier motions and raised the mace. Yue's calm demeanor did not falter. Sabien brought the mace down for the swing and Yue simply waited for it to fell her.

Once Sabien had committed to the swing, Yue pounced, like a cat. She leapt forward into the attack and grabbed hold of the mace at the shaft, as if she intended to divert the force of the blow or to disarm him. I marvelled at her bravery and her easy confidence for less than a second, and then I marvelled at something even more amazing.

The mace was gone.

There was no trace of it having ever existed. Yue took a step back and I was pleased to see even she looked surprised by this.

Sabien also looked taken aback. "Where is my mace?"

Yue shrugged, looking confused. "I just willed it away. I didn't want it to hit me."

Sabien's eyebrows raised, but he didn't offer any sort of explanation for this strange occurrence. "Ah. Well, good job, then," he congratulated her. "Yukari? Are you ready?"

I met his eyes and clearly saw that he intended to face me next. He did not believe for a second I could not do what my friends had already done. I wished I had his confidence.

Sabien reached for his sword on the ground and took up position with it. I swallowed apprehensively. There was something about the sharp blade of the sword that just seemed so much more deadly than the mace had – never mind that they were both equally fearsome weapons.

I tried to take in a deep breath and failed. I saw Sabien raise his sword for the strike and I shut my eyes tight to concentrate. Just like he had instructed, I made myself picture what scared me, and I saw in my mind's eye the torso, clawing its way along the dark tunnel floor under its own power. I felt the bow in my hand and this time I drew back an arrow, focusing everything on striking one vital spot to slow the ravenous creature down.

Surely by now, Sabien must have struck me down or stopped. I opened my eyes slowly to see a glowing blue light focused to a point between my hands and aimed at Sabien's chest. He was holding the sword before him, point down and he looked pleased.

Ris started clapping again and I was so startled I lost my concentration and the light arrow winked out of existence. I stared from my empty hands to Sabien in shock.

"It will get easier with time and practice," Sabien stated. "I will speak to the other Knights, and as soon as you have rested we will continue your training."

Hotaru was assigned to work with Aysel and Ris, learning to deflect different types of attacks and also to fight with the sword she had picked up at the Roughlander outpost. Yue practiced her hand-to-hand skills against armoured Lady Adel, and Kaji worked with Jeth doing who knew what.

I, alone, continued to study with Sabien, and occasionally Ris would provide a moving target for my arrows, which I learned to produce quickly and accurately. I found I could shoot them regularly, as if loosing an arrow from a bow, or if I focused enough on my target I could let the arrow seek it out on its own. Using this method the arrow struck true every time, even if it had to turn and weave in the air to do so.

We trained in the Temple of Sapphire for nearly three weeks. It was hard work, but it felt wonderful to feel relatively safe and fed and not have to flee for our lives. I thanked providence every day the Deathsquads did not know where we had gone or how we had escaped them.

"Remember fear, Yukari," Sabien said to me again one morning. We had met in the training room below the Temple and it was just the two of us seated face to face across a bowl of water.

I nodded. I remembered fear well. The deadly torso from the valley, of all the sights I had seen since arriving on this awful world, was still my inspiration for creating my arrows.

"Do you know why I turn into water?" Sabien asked me.

"No," I responded truthfully. It still perturbed me – even after I had developed powers of my own – that Sabien could liquefy his body at will.

"Water cannot be injured. Water cannot be stopped," he stated. "It flows where it will and there is not much on this world that can harm it."

"That's true," I stated, thinking about it. "Water, like basic matter, cannot be created nor destroyed, but merely changes from one form to another."

"I think you've got the idea," Sabien informed me, standing and gesturing for me to do the same. "Defend yourself," he stated simply, drawing his sword once more.

Not this again. I felt my fear rising and then I realized what he had said. A sword could not hurt water. I didn't know if I, like Sabien, could become water, but he seemed to think I could. I forced myself to breathe deeply in and out, and willed myself to allow the sword to pass right through me. *Water cannot be harmed*, I told myself, repeating it internally like a chant followed by, *I cannot be harmed*.

The sword strike came and slashed across my middle, but I did not feel the pain. The blade had passed right through me, but I did not bleed. I felt a little light-headed, like I wasn't fully present in the world, then the feeling passed and I felt solid again.

I felt my middle, but there was no wound and no exposed flesh – even my clothes were undamaged. I looked to Sabien for an explanation, my eyes wide with disbelief. I had felt the sword pass through me, I was sure of it.

"What did I do?" I demanded of Sabien.

"It was like slashing at air," Sabien responded and held the blade aloft so I could see it. The metal was covered in drops of water, not blood. "You became mist for just an instant. Remember this lesson, Yukari. You may need it again someday."

"I will, Sir Sabien," I answered, still overwhelmed. "Thank you."

"Thank Sapphiros," he responded. "I am here only to show you the way," and he left me there alone, contemplating the bowl of water at my feet.

"You have all worked very hard these last few weeks, and although training never stops, I believe you have all proven yourselves capable of using the power you have been given," Sabien announced to the four of us out in front of the Temple in the courtyard.

The Roughlanders and Knights gave a cheer, and I felt very self-conscious looking out at them all as Sabien praised us.

"In light of your achievements, I have arranged a chance for you to put your abilities to the test," he continued. "Myself and the three other Knights will face you in combat. Ris can heal injuries as long as they are not fatal, so I expect none of you will take it easy on us."

I was surprised by this announcement, but perhaps not as much as I would have expected. I had experienced firsthand the realism of Sabien's training and I knew he meant it – we were to defend ourselves and the Knights would not hold back on his command.

"What about Aysel?" Hotaru asked suddenly.

"Aysel is a squire," Lady Adel responded derisively. "She will do what she can to tend to the injured until Ris can get to them."

"We begin at the bounce of the sun," Sabien announced and I eyed the sky apprehensively. We didn't have much time.

The four of us gathered together where we stood and the Knights left us to it. The Roughlanders could be heard chattering excitedly about the show they were about to witness, but I tuned them out and faced the others.

"We'll have to work together if we are to have any chance of beating them," Kaji said and I nodded at the truth of his statement.

"Unfortunately, they know a lot about what we're capable of, but we don't really know much about what they can do," I pointed out. "We're at a severe disadvantage here."

"All we can do is try our best Yukari," Hotaru stated. "Just like training."

"Somehow I think this is going to be more serious than just training, Hotaru," I informed her. "I think it best if we each tackle those we know best, divide them up."

The others agreed and we relocated to the far side of the courtyard to wait for the match to begin. The Knights had already done likewise across the courtyard. The Roughlanders and Aysel had gathered to watch, and only Aysel and perhaps Masaru looked anxious among them.

The sun dipped below the buildings to touch the horizon and immediately started its return journey through the sky, as was considered normal for this world.

"Begin!" Sabien called and immediately began his change to water.

I focused on him as his form melted away, narrowing my eyes, and as the puddle that was Sabien flowed into the cracks between the cobblestones he began to glow with a cyan light. I had him in my sights. I knew as long as he was water I could not harm him, but at least I would know where he was and would have at least a second's warning should he reform for an attack.

Ris took to the air and to my left Hotaru surged forward, running full tilt toward the remainder of the Knights. Lady Adel stepped forward, mace and shield held ready to meet Hotaru's attack, while Jeth simply looked bored and remained where he stood.

Kaji appeared to be biding his time to my left and Yue further right of me had not moved to engage the Knights yet either. I spared them no more than a glance before turning my attention to Ris in the air, tracking her motion with my eyes while trying to keep at least a part of my awareness on the motion of the glowing puddle that was Sabien.

Sabien circled wide across the courtyard, coming toward us. I had some time before he reached us, so I focused my thoughts and formed an arrow between my hands to let loose on Ris, who was still above and slightly behind the other two Knights. Ris dodged my attack easily, as she was used to avoiding my arrows by now.

Sabien's puddle swerved suddenly and headed straight for Yue.

"Yue!" I called out. "Sabien glows!"

My meaning sank in immediately and Yue caught sight of the cyan puddle stalking her. She made as if to run from it and abruptly she disappeared.

"Yue?" I scanned the courtyard and surrounding area quickly. Hotaru was closing in on Lady Adel and Kaji was circling away from Sabien, who was still in water form where Yue had been moments earlier.

The sudden motion caught my eye and I saw Yue reappear far to my right, clear of the battle, before she disappeared again. She was too fast for my eyes to follow, but it seemed she was running. Another power, perhaps? Sabien had mentioned that physical powers could enhance a person's natural abilities and Yue had always been fast.

Unable to keep up with Yue any longer, my attention was drawn to Hotaru. Instead of facing Lady Adel as I had anticipated, she leapt into the air, as if to leap over the female Knight entirely. Hotaru thrust her hands sharply to her sides and, for a wonder, powerful jets of water shot out from her palms to connect with the cobblestones beneath her and propel her even further upwards. I saw her intentions as soon as I saw how far her momentum was going to carry her. Hotaru hadn't been intending to engage Lady Adel at all — she was after Ris.

Lady Adel's affronted expression showed clearly what she thought of Hotaru's slight to her worth as an adversary. Lady Adel spun around, her heavy mace following her motion to connect solidly with Hotaru's exposed back. Hotaru cried out suddenly, her back arching unnaturally with the force of the blow and the flow of water from her hands ceased instantly with the loss of her focus. She crumpled to the ground immediately, and before she had so much as settled there, Aysel was at her side.

In my distraction at Hotaru's plight, I almost didn't notice Sabien's puddle form nearing the place where I stood. I was sure there was nothing I could do to him and plenty he could do to me, so I ran.

Ris was still circling overhead, watching everything with her wide eyes. She looked torn between continuing in the fight and dropping out to treat Hotaru's injuries. Making her decision, she focused on Kaji, who had yet to take on any of the Knights, and she began to form a blue ball of energy between her hands.

We had already lost Hotaru and we needed Ris off the field to tend to her. I couldn't let Kaji also be injured, so I focused my will on Ris. I knew Sabien was after me; I didn't need my targeting to tell me that anymore. Working as fast as I was able, I used the training I had been given to summon three arrows, loosing them one after the other on Ris.

Ris, of course, saw them coming, and dissipating her energy attack, she weaved to avoid the arrows. I had her in my sights, though, and the arrows dodged and weaved with her, separating to strike her from three sides. The arrows sunk into her middle and the sudden pain of the impact caused her to plummet from the sky.

I winced, watching her fall. I felt awful for having actually struck Ris, who, though silent, had been a kind presence these past few weeks in the temple. I knew this was a training exercise, and it was best to treat the other team as if they were our enemies, but it didn't feel right, somehow.

In my preoccupation with Ris, I didn't notice until it was too late that Sabien had finally managed to catch up with me and was now in the ground at my feet. All of a sudden I felt terribly weak. I dropped to my knees, unable to stand, and it was a struggle to even take in enough air to keep breathing. What was happening to me? Was this Sabien's doing?

Time slowed as I fought internally for the strength to overcome this sudden disability. Ris' wings shot out fully to either side in a desperate attempt to slow her rapid descent. She caught the air close to the ground and she might have made it if it wasn't for Yue who appeared out of nowhere to leap onto her back. The two of them crashed to the ground and within seconds – even in my dazed perception – Yue had Ris' wings and arms locked within her own.

"Yield!" I heard Yue demand and Ris nodded, panting, but with a smile on her face.

I could hear the pounding of my heart slow until the beats came softer and softer and further apart. Blackness threatened around the edges of my vision. I had enough consciousness left to be grateful Ris was not too badly hurt, and so I watched as Yue let her up and Ris headed over to where Aysel was still guarding Hotaru.

I took my last breath with effort as Yue disappeared and reappeared once more, using the force of her unreasonable speed to ram into Lady Adel from the side. Not anticipating this maneuver,

Lady Adel toppled into Jeth, who had been fighting Kaji close by, and they went down in a heap.

Across the courtyard and far away from the action, I crumpled with them and the world went black, Sabien's magic or my own feebleness having done me in.

When I came to, Ris was hovering over me anxiously. I could feel the warm cobblestones against my back. "I'm fine, Ris," I croaked out, but I didn't feel fine. I felt as if I had had the flu for a week and there was no strength left in me.

Ris gave me a disapproving frown, but left me to my own devices. I sat up very slowly to see what was going on. Sabien had removed me from the fight; that much was clear. He was still out there, remarkably still glowing, though I hadn't been concentrating on him for some time now.

Kaji was the only one of the four of us left standing. At first I thought Yue was performing another one of her disappearing tricks, but I must have missed something because Yue was being tended by Ris less than ten feet away. Lady Adel also was out of the fight, though she did not appear to be injured in the slightest. She was standing with Aysel and watching Jeth and Kaji still in the center of the courtyard.

There didn't appear to be any fighting happening, however. Jeth and Kaji, both in martial arts style fighting stances, seemed to be talking to one another. After a moment, they both stood, their poses relaxing.

"I yield!" Kaji called out. "Even if I could hurt Jeth, which I'm not sure I could, Sabien would have me."

Sabien reformed at these words. "A wise choice. Well done, Chosen," he directed his words at all of us, "I'm impressed at your progress."

The Roughlanders cheered once more; whether they agreed with Sabien or had just enjoyed the show I could not tell, but it was over and I fervently hoped I would never have to face these Knights in combat again. Not only because of their skill or power, but because I truly felt now that I had begun to get to know them that it was infinitely better we were on the same side.

I laid back once more, relieved there would be no more fighting today, and enjoyed the feel of the sun on my face.

"We may have a wee problem," Dahlia announced, interrupting my very brief moment of peace. "I found this little guy comin' out of the Sand Lake."

I sat up a little too quickly and my head swam. When my vision focused once more, I was able to see what Dahlia was talking about. At her feet was the little coffee-robot we had left behind at the Roughlander outpost where we had met Binaris. The little robot looked happy to see us, if a walking espresso machine could express emotion.

"If it could follow us all the way here from the outpost, then it may be someone could have followed it, or tracked us in some way," Dahlia informed us.

"Dahlia, have you seen any Deathsquads approaching?" I asked.

"Not as of yet," she replied.

"I think it may be time we moved on from here," I suggested a little regretfully. Our time at the temple had been the most peace we were likely to encounter on this world. "Sir Sabien, would you and the Knights be able to organize the supplies together?"

"I'll head back to the rooftop to keep an eye out, then," Dahlia proposed.

"I'd like to have a look as well," Kaji seconded.

Hotaru and Yue were both up and about now that Ris was through with them, though they both looked to be taking it easy after their beatings. "The four of us won't be much use with hauling and lifting right now," I noted. "Maybe we should all go with Dahlia and we can discuss where we should go from here."

Kaji and Dahlia agreed, so we left the Roughlanders and the Knights in the charge of Masaru and Sabien, and we climbed back up to the roof of the abandoned buildings where Lilyth had dropped us off upon our arrival here.

Kaji pulled out his Roughlander map and showed it to Dahlia as he asked, "Would you be able to mark the outposts on here?"

Dahlia hesitated a moment. "Not all of them are recorded or known. There are quite a few we like to keep hidden from the Vile Emperor. I know where they all are, because I'm a Corporal, but if I mark them down for ye, and that map gets in the wrong hands..."

"I will guard this map with my life," Kaji swore with the utmost sincerity.

Dahlia nodded. "Well, ye are the Chosen of Sapphiros. I know whose side ye're on. I'll tell ye where they are."

"Thank you, Dahlia," Kaji replied respectfully and the two of them got to work plotting the twenty-something Roughlander outposts, and even a city or two, on the map.

While they did so, I was deep in thought. It had not escaped my attention there was only one real fertile area depicted on the map we had been given. There were Roughlander outposts here and there across the four great Sand Lakes, and some near mountains or on other rough rocky terrain. There were yellow squares on the map depicting cities, of which I counted only four.

One, to the northeast, was labeled 'The Ruby City'. I decided right then and there I would not willingly choose to go there. The one below it on the eastern side of the map was labeled 'Espearia'. I didn't know its allegiances, but it was a little too close to the Vile Emperor's seat of power for my liking. The one closest to our current location was to the west and labeled 'Sresh'. Dahlia had just informed Kaji that Roughlanders mainly occupied the city, but the city was well known by the Vile Emperor and was likely watched, if not controlled, by him because of its prominence.

There was also a city in the fertile area. That whole section of the map was labelled, 'Taiyou'.

"Taiyou is where we get most of our supplies," Dahlia was telling Kaji. "Not directly, o' course, as it is rather far, but through trade. In one way or another, all Roughlanders work for Taiyou, and are paid in water and supplies."

"Is there a central outpost there, then?" Kaji asked. "An outpost that is in charge of the others, or has more say in the affairs of the Roughlanders?"

"Well, not exactly," Dahlia replied. "Each outpost looks after its own. That's not to say that we wouldn't help each other out or keep in contact with one another, but we're pretty well separated out here.

"There is a sanctioned outpost in Taiyou itself, though," Dahlia continued. "That's where the supplies come from."

"In a desert world, those who control the water have a lot of power," I noted, indicating the lake and river that surrounded Taiyou on the map. "Why hasn't the Vile Emperor overrun Taiyou yet? Wouldn't he want to control the water supply?"

"Oh, I'm sure he does," Dahlia agreed, "but Taiyou's protected somehow. The Vile Emperor has been trying to take Taiyou for over eight hundred years, but every time he has been held back."

Kaji was nodding, "I asked Binaris about it before I disconnected her. Apparently for the last hundred years or so Taiyou has had a ceasefire with the Vile Emperor."

"If they are so protected, why would they need a ceasefire?" I asked.

"Binaris didn't know," Kaji replied. "I tried to ask. She said the Vile Emperor had been repelled four times and afterwards an agreement was made, so there has been peace ever since. From what I can see, Taiyou is the safest place this world has to offer."

"Then that's where we should go," I said and not because Kaji had said it was safe, either. If this Taiyou place had managed to stave off the advance of the Vile Emperor for eight hundred years, then they must have been doing something right, and we could do well to learn the secret of their success. "If Taiyou still stands against the Vile Emperor, then it would be a strong ally to have."

"What I want to know is how they've done it – kept him at bay," Kaji stated. "If his army has been enough to overrun the rest of the planet, it doesn't make much sense that he wouldn't be able to crush them as well."

"If we go there, maybe we can find out," Hotaru suggested.

"We can't go alone," I remarked. "If we are still being followed, the small group of us will not be enough to survive out there against the Deathsquads. Besides, any outpost we stop at for supplies will be in danger for having sheltered us. We should warn the Roughlanders what's coming. We should stop at each outpost and gather together those that are willing to follow us."

"And draw more attention to ourselves?" Yue spoke for the first time. "Gather an army together so the Vile Emperor thinks we're becoming a threat and sends his Deathsquads to eliminate us?"

"Yue, he already thinks we're a threat," I informed her, "and the Deathsquads are hunting us at his command."

"We don't know that for sure," Yue countered. "Destroying the outpost we were at could have been a coincidence. He could be destroying all of the outposts in turn, attacking the Roughlanders, not us."

"He could be," Kaji agreed, "but Yukari is still right that we should warn them. It's their decision whether or not they want to fight with us."

"I don't like it," Yue declared.

"Well, do you have a better plan?" I asked her bluntly.

"As a matter of fact, I do," she stated. "We split up. We'd be in smaller groups and less noticeable that way. Half of us visit these outposts," she picked off a few outposts in a rough line to Taiyou, "and the other half of us go to the rest of them and warn them the Vile Emperor may be coming for them. Then we sneak into Taiyou and have a look around, figure out whose side they are on before we make any demands of them."

I pursed my lips into a thin line of disapproval. "Splitting up is suicide," I remarked. "Even with the Knights and these new abilities of ours, we're no match for a Deathsquad even half the size of the one we encountered in the Sand Lake."

Yue sulked, but Kaji deliberated over what both of us had suggested. "Well, we are at least agreed our best bet lies in Taiyou." He looked between the both of us and took in Hotaru's nod before continuing, "I agree with Yukari that I don't think it is wise to split us up just yet."

"Me too," Hotaru piped in. "I wouldn't want to have to worry about everyone and not know what was happening."

"So it's decided, then," Kaji stated. "We'll head to Taiyou, stopping at each outpost on the way and informing them about what's going on. They can send runners to the outposts that aren't on our direct path and spread the word that way, which will be much more secure than that general announcement Binaris tried to send when we first arrived.

"We can ask the outposts what they know of Taiyou and decide more specifically what to do about the place when we know a bit more and are closer to it. Sound fair?"

Hotaru and I agreed. Kaji was speaking sense. Yue still didn't seem pleased with the plan, but she was clearly outnumbered, so she had no choice but to go along with what we had decided.

Meanwhile, Dahlia had been looking out over the horizon with her strange hammer-telescope device. "I don't mean to disturb ye, but there's something coming this way fast, and I don't think it's a Sand Crawler."

Kaji headed over to her and held out his hand for the hammer. "May I?"

She handed him the device while continuing to peer over the edge. Hotaru and I wandered over to see what they were both looking at.

"I think it's a man," Kaji said with a note of wonder in his voice. "He'd have to be moving as fast as Yue does."

Far in the distance I could make out a dark speck and a whirl of sand surrounding it. The man, if that's what it was, was coming toward us very quickly. At his current speed he would be here in moments. Kaji and Dahlia continued to trade off looking through the hammer-scope as the unbelievably fast runner got closer, until Dahlia's face fell in horrified recognition. "Fuun," she breathed. "It's Fuun."

My mind made the connection to where I had heard that name before. "The Chosen of Machalite?"

"The very same," Dahlia confirmed. "He's probably already seen us. There's no use running now, he's too fast, but keep yer wits about ye and don't make him want to kill ye, or ye'll be dead."

I swallowed apprehensively. The last thing I wanted was to meet another Chosen, knowing what little I did about the powers of the lava-spewing Vile Emperor.

"Yue," I called back, "can you get Sir Sabien up here, and any of the Knights that might know how to deal with this Fuun person? Tell them the Chosen of Machalite will be here any second."

Kaji, Dahlia, Hotaru, and I waited with a mounting sense of unease for the legendary Fuun to arrive. I didn't feel up for a confrontation, and I wasn't convinced that even at full strength we would be enough to defend ourselves from this being who apparently, according to Binaris, had massacred armies *before* he proclaimed himself the Chosen of the gem god representing order through chaos.

Too soon he was upon us and Yue had not yet returned with Sabien.

"So it is true, then," Fuun spoke with more feeling in his voice than I would expect from a mass murderer and the feeling I was hearing was most definitely contempt. "The Chosen of Sapphiros have arrived at last."

Fuun was tall and imposing, and the narrowness of the battlements we stood upon did not help make me feel at ease at his nearness. He was dressed in black, with an impossibly long katana sheathed at his waist, reaching almost to the floor. He wore a tattered cape made from strips of material hanging off of his shoulders and there were pieces of metal armour on him, a bracer or a shoulder piece here and there. His entire left arm was sheathed in metal – or made from it – and it ended in a wicked claw, encrusted with dried blood.

I drew back instinctively – I didn't want to have to face this new menace, now or ever. We had unwittingly made enemies of the Vile Emperor, wasn't that enough for anyone to deal with?

Fuun smirked malevolently. "Don't tell me you're shy."

"What business does the Chosen of Machalite have here?" Kaji demanded brazenly.

"Whatever business I please," Fuun responded, his smirk widening into a full grin. "Who's going to stop me from going where I like, you?" He shifted his gaze over to me. "Or your girlfriend?"

I felt something inside me snap. Fuun, overgrown bully he was, was just like all the other boys back in Shinjuku High, no matter how much power he had attained in this world. Were we not Chosen like him? Did we not have access to the same level of power as he did? He had no right to push us around and I had the sudden insight that was the reason he had come – to intimidate us into fearing him. It wasn't going to happen.

"My name is Yukari Namikoya," I addressed him with authority in my voice, "Chosen of Sapphiros. If you have some purpose to discuss with us, do so, otherwise we have things we must attend to."

"Tell me," Fuun began conversationally, "is there a reason I should not kill you where you stand?"

I gritted my teeth – this was far from over. "I assume, since you follow Machalite, that you have no love for the Vile Emperor?"

"I have been a thorn in his side for more than eight hundred years," Fuun stated with pride. "Neither of us have managed to kill the other yet, but we each grow stronger, and one day when he emerges from the Ruby City, I will be waiting for him."

"Then killing us now would be a mistake," I stated with conviction.

He was so fast I didn't have the time to react. Before I even had the chance to draw another breath his hand – thankfully not the metal one – was around my neck, tight enough to restrict air, but not enough to strangle me, yet. Fuun deliberately took one step, then another, toward the edge of the building's roof, pushing me before him, until I was leaning over the edge.

"I don't make mistakes," Fuun growled dangerously.

I drew rapid shallow breaths and tried to remain calm. If Fuun had wanted to kill me, I would be dead already. I silently thanked Dahlia for that piece of advice concerning this madman.

"Wrong choice of words," I conceded, relieved to find that he wasn't fully cutting off my air supply and that I could still speak to defend myself. "I simply meant no matter what gem god we represent, we are on the same side."

"What use would you be to me?" Funn demanded "I could kill you now easily and it would change nothing."

"We are nothing – yet," I countered, "we are learning quickly and may one day stand a chance against the Vile Emperor. If you kill us now, not only would it not be a challenge to you, and therefore to no purpose, but it would also be destroying potential allies."

I couldn't believe he was still listening to me. I didn't even know what I was saying anymore and I realized I would say almost anything to live through this encounter. I didn't want to die today, or any day, even if my life had suddenly become a thing out of nightmares.

"And who would rule," Fuun demanded, "if you or I defeat the Vile Emperor? Would you seek to take his place? Or your Knight Commander there?"

I managed to shift my gaze to beyond Fuun without moving my neck, which was still in his deadly grasp. Sabien, Ris, and Yue had arrived, and they were all staring at the scene before them in shock. Sabien looked murderous, but he dared not interfere while I was held so precariously over the edge.

"No," I whispered, tired now of the strain. "If we can see the planet free of its tyrant, I would not seek to replace him. When the Vile Emperor is defeated, balance will be restored and our job will be finished."

He abruptly let me go. I thought for a moment I had been flung off the rooftop, but as I stumbled to a halt, I realized my feet were still on solid ground. I rubbed at my neck gratefully and took a few deep breaths.

"I want to see what you are capable of, Chosen of Sapphiros," Fuun stated. "Allies..." he considered the word, "it might be interesting."

"Regardless," I told him, "we mean no harm to you and yours."

Anger flashed in the madman's eyes for a moment. "Only me," he said, and then his calmer demeanor returned. "If I am to be your ally, what is your plan, Yukari Namikoya?"

"Our plan hasn't been fully decided yet, Fuun." I addressed him as an equal; I had committed myself now, and there was no turning back. "If you wish to be of use, though, there may be Deathsquad soldiers approaching this place. If you are as powerful as your reputation claims, it should be no trouble for you to detain them."

"And afterwards?" Fuun asked, smiling now. "Where should I meet you?"

"I am certain, with your abilities, having found us here, you should be able to find us again," I stated calmly, hoping against hope we would never see this man again, until maybe when it came time to face the Vile Emperor, and only then if we could trust he would not betray us.

"Very well," he agreed, sounding amused, "we shall meet again. I look forward to testing your skills in battle."

As abruptly as he had arrived, he leapt off the rooftop and disappeared, leaving us stunned by his presence. I almost collapsed with relief, but I had the presence of mind to turn to the others. "We need to get out of here, quickly."

There was no argument at this pronouncement. We rejoined the Roughlanders and Knights in the courtyard below as quickly as we were able. Someone, it seemed, had managed to find a Japanese-designed truck somewhere and a large quantity of the supplies had been loaded into it.

"A truck!?" Hotaru exclaimed. "There *were* Japanese people here!"

"Yeah, there were," Jeth replied from the driver's seat of the truck. "They were good people. Weird, but good. We had a whole military unit living with us here."

"Does that truck still run?" I had to ask – it had been eight hundred years, after all.

"Yeah man, it works, check it out." Jeth revved the engine of the truck and steam shot out of the front hood.

"That doesn't look healthy," Hotaru noted. "Aren't they not supposed to do that?"

"Turn it off, Jeth," I directed him wearily.

I approached the truck as the Roughlanders scurried around me, getting the last of the supplies together for our departure. Going around to the cab, I faced Jeth through the open window. "Do you know much about cars?"

"About what?" Jeth asked, clearly confused.

I took in a deep breath and let it out to keep my calm. At least there wasn't much out in the desert Jeth could hit if he didn't know how to drive. I didn't know too much about cars either and I doubted Kaji, Yue, or Hotaru would know much, but being from the planet that had manufactured this truck, I figured one of us would have the best chance of getting it to run smoothly.

I reached in past Jeth and pulled the lever to open the hood, ignoring Jeth's exclamation of surprise as I worked my way around to the front of the truck to have a look at its eight-hundred-year-old engine.

It was in remarkably good shape for its age – which was a relief – but I could spot right away it was completely out of engine coolant. Coolant would be crucial to running in this desert's heat.

"Do you have coolant stored anywhere?" I called back to Jeth.

"No, probably not," Jeth replied. "We didn't really need it, not with the snow everywhere."

I considered his words for a second and I remembered the picture Binaris had showed us of the Temple of Sapphiros. It had been covered in snow, but that must have been eight hundred years ago. It would take some getting used to remember the knowledge these Knights possessed was so far out of date.

"Right, well, we're going to need some now if you want that thing to run in this heat," I informed him. "I assume, at least, that you have gas to make the truck run?"

"Yeah, there's gas, barrels of it in the back," Jeth answered. "Don't know where you're going to get that coolant stuff, though."

It came to me all of a sudden. It was a marvel that after everything that had happened to me today that my mind was still working. I knew how to make engine coolant, or at least something that would pass for it; it had been on the science test I had lived through several times during the Tuesday in the Splitter's program.

Either way, I knew the answer – I had memorized it along with the others.

I gave orders to Jeth to bring me what I needed. We would be on the road – so to speak – in no time at all. Hopefully our newfound potential ally, Fuun, would keep the Deathsquads at bay long enough for us to make it to the next outpost. Either way, it was going to be a long and hard road from here.

Chapter 6 – Long Roads

"Pact with Yuko Seig, or no pact with Yuko Seig, the Vile Emperor is coming and we're going to need all the help we can get to stand against him." I spoke with conviction, repeating the words I had used at the last three outposts where we had stopped. "Separated like this, he can pick off each outpost one by one, like he already did with the one at the center of the Sand Lake. We'll have a better chance if we are together."

"You speak sense," agreed Lady Sirrah, the leader of this particular outpost, a tough woman with her long, dark braid reaching most of the way down her back. "The Roughlanders had long given up hope this day would come, but we can't deny the opportunity to fight back against the Vile Emperor now that it is here. Though it means leaving our home, my people are with you."

I was a little taken aback by Lady Sirrah's easy acceptance of what we were asking her to do. The other outposts had not been so easy to convince and we hadn't gotten as much support as we had been hoping for. Perhaps word was finally beginning to reach ahead of us, giving the Roughlanders some warning of our coming and our request.

We were seated around a circular table on the top floor of Lady Sirrah's outpost. At the table were the four of us Chosen, Sabien, Dahlia, Masaru, Lady Sirrah, and the two other outpost leaders we had managed to gather en route to this place.

"So what is your plan, then?" Lady Sirrah asked. "Where do we go from here?"

Kaji and I had spent most of our journey deliberating just that with occasional input from Yue or Hotaru, so we were somewhat prepared to answer that question.

"The majority of the Roughlanders will be coming with myself and Hotaru. If you could advise us as to the quickest route to Taiyou, we hope to stop at this outpost," I said, indicating the nearest outpost to where we were on the map we had laid out in front of us. It was just beyond a ridge and on the edge of a long sinuous stretch of Sand Lake. "Then we will continue on to this outpost," I said as I indicated another, much closer to Taiyou, "before making our way to the sanctioned outpost in Taiyou, where I hope we might be able to secure an alliance with the city."

The other half of the plan, which I did not explain to Sirrah, involved Kaji, Yue, and half of the Knights splitting off to tackle another three outposts – including one said to be ruled by Croatins – on a longer route around to the far eastern border of Taiyou. From there, they would enter Taiyou with any allies they had gained to meet us in the city and be our reinforcements if it turned out Taiyou was not the safe haven we had been told it was.

Lady Sirrah frowned. "It's a long way around to that outpost, unfortunately. We don't have much contact with them because of it. There is a path between here and there – it's a tunnel through the cliff. Some of the Croatins use it for trade and to bring supplies through from Taiyou, but they don't generally allow us down there."

"Well, they're going to have to make an exception," I stated. "It would be better by far to move everyone discreetly than to travel the whole distance overland."

"I'll see to it then," Sirrah agreed. "Give us some time to get everyone ready to move."

It was decided, then. Kaji and I finalized our plans of which of our original party would be going where. I wasn't fond of the plan to split up, but I saw the benefits of being able to reach more places, while still having some of us get to Taiyou quickly and hopefully safely, as well.

We both agreed it was best that he and I head the two teams, and to separate Yue and Hotaru between us to keep an eye on them. Yue was likely to get in trouble by herself because she was headstrong and independent, and Hotaru had the tendency to act or speak before she thought about the consequences. Also, I knew Hotaru would feel more comfortable having me around and Yue wouldn't mind either way. Kaji was prudent and capable, so I wasn't worried about his ability to take care of himself, and I knew he would also do his best to look after Yue.

As for the Knights, I was taking Sabien with me to Taiyou. His position, authority, and poise would help me to gain an audience with the ruling body of the city and perhaps convince them to listen to me. I didn't relish the prospect of so great a task, but this was the hand that had been dealt to me. Jeth was to continue to drive the truck of supplies, which would go with Kaji, as he had the longer route to travel and potentially more danger to face out there on the open wastelands. Ris, we had learned on our journey from the Temple of Sapphire, had an ability that allowed her to cloak an area and make a small group invisible. It was taxing to her, but she would be a good resource to Kaji's group, should they encounter any trouble and need to hide or flee. This left Hotaru and I with Lady Adel, and in addition Aysel, who was Lady Adel's squire and so went where she did.

As for the Roughlanders, Kaji suggested Hotaru and I take charge of the transport of Binaris, as we should reach the safety of the sanctioned outpost sooner and have somewhere to potentially store her. Corporal Dahlia and her remaining crew would go with Kaji to represent her outpost, and to support Kaji's claims as to the state of affairs among the Roughlanders. She would confirm Kaji and Yue's status as the Chosen of Sapphiros and the new leaders of the Roughlanders as a whole.

Masaru, as Dahlia's second, would come with Hotaru and I for the same reason, acting in his Corporal's stead. In the two days we waited for Lady Sirrah's people to ready themselves to move out, we said our goodbyes to Kaji, Yue, and the others, and let them get somewhat of a head start, as they had further to go.

It was an uncertain farewell, as neither group could really know what might await the other. Since our arrival on this world, the four of us – the only four in our particular predicament – had not been separated. Now our experiences and dangers would differ, and I fervently hoped our newfound abilities would be enough to keep us safe individually until we could be reunited again.

Trying to direct ourselves forward, Hotaru and I set out at the head of an unbelievably large group of migrating Roughlanders. After conferring with the outpost leaders, I was able to put together a rough number and learned we had approximately nine thousand people with us. Not all of them were with us to fight; there were a few that were either too young or too old, but their people were relocating, so they were too. The sheer number of people that had put themselves essentially in my charge overwhelmed me, so I was glad I had Sabien and the Roughlander outpost leaders – who were used to their positions of authority – with me to look after these people.

The mouth of the tunnel was much larger than the one we had encountered at the entrance of Lilyth's valley, but I could not help the sense of unease I felt at descending underground and out of the sunlight. This time we, as a group, were more prepared for our tunnel journey, however, as there were lamp-like devices here and there held by various Roughlanders. This tunnel was also not as small or as dark as the other had been. After we had traveled some distance, it became evident there seemed to be a glowing substance oozing here and there from the cavern walls. It added an eerie yellow light to the tunnel, but ensured no one would be walking blind down here.

According to Lady Sirrah, the tunnel would take an entire day to cross on foot, or so she had been told. We decided roughly halfway to take a short midday rest before continuing. I was curious about the foreign substance oozing from the walls, so I decided to take a look at it to determine if it was worth harvesting for a natural light source.

Not wanting to touch an unidentified substance with my skin – Sonoma-sensei had taught me better than that – I drew an arrow from the quiver on my back and used the flat arrowhead to scoop up a sample. The yellow liquid was viscous and by placing my hand in the air above it I could tell it gave off some warmth. I didn't really have any manner of testing it, but immediately I was overcome with the feeling that I should know what this was.

Scanning around the tunnel while thinking furiously, my eyes lit upon the dormant form of Binaris, surrounded by those Roughlanders that had continued their task of transporting her. I remembered abruptly one of them mentioning Binaris had been partially operational since the time she spent active at the Temple of Sapphire, so I scooted over to where she was.

"Would she have enough power to answer a question for me?"

"Oh, yeah, she should," one of the Roughlanders answered. "We've left her off to conserve her power since we left the Temple, but she was working fine once we got her unplugged."

They unwrapped Binaris from her tarp for me and activated her on-switch. Her eyes lit up their customary light blue and she fixed her robot gaze on me immediately. "Yukari, Chosen of Sapphiros."

"Yes, Binaris," I confirmed my identity. "Are your systems fully operational?"

"Operating at twenty-two percent capacity on reserve power," Binaris reported.

I winced, but twenty-two percent was better than nothing and I only had one quick question for her. "Binaris, are you able to identify substances?" I held up the arrow with my sample.

She tilted her head downward and the blue light from her eyes glinted off the yellow glow on the arrow, turning the resulting light green for a brief moment.

"Scan completed," she reported. "Substance consists of sixty-five percent plutonium, thirty-two percent uranium, and the remaining three percent is unknown."

Plutonium and uranium? I felt the floor drop out from beneath me – both of those substances were known to be highly radioactive. I dropped the arrow in my hands and backed away from it instinctively. "Turn her back off," I instructed the Roughlanders, "and whatever you do, don't touch that arrow, or any of the yellow substance on the walls, understand?"

They nodded their agreement, a little surprised at my sudden vehemence, and I stood quickly, looking about for Sabien. I found him a little ways ahead, speaking with Lady Adel and Hotaru. I made my way over to them, still feeling a little unsteady with shock.

"We have a problem," I announced.

"Yes, we do," Sabien confirmed. "The path ahead is blocked. It appears there was a cave-in here at some time."

Blocked? I started to breathe a little heavier – we were trapped in here? How long did it take radiation poisoning to take effect? How long until people started falling sick, or worse, dying?

"Sir Sabien, I've discovered something," I told him. "The yellow glow here and there on the walls is extremely dangerous. It is radioactive and exposure to it is eventually fatal. I'm not sure how long we have, or if it would be better to try and go on or turn back."

"Other than the rocks in our way, I believe we are much closer to the exit going forward than we would be turning around," Sabien responded, taking my news calmly. I could tell the word radioactive was lost on him and Lady Adel both. "Not to mention, it would be difficult to redirect all of these people from back here."

Hotaru, unlike the Knights, had understood me. "Radioactive?!" she exclaimed. "We have to get out of here!" Hotaru's instant panic got through to the Knights as my pronouncement had not.

"Is it as dangerous as you say?" Lady Adel asked, her expression concerned now.

"Yes," I answered decisively. "Proximity to it causes a poisoning effect. The symptoms may not be evident at first, but soon enough the children and elderly will fall sick and weaken quickly, and the rest of us will not be long after. The only way to deal with radiation is to stay away from it."

Sabien nodded. "Very well. I will see how far this blockade goes. If it is clearable, we shall forge ahead and get out of here as quickly as possible."

Hotaru and I went forward with Sabien to see the cave-in. Lady Adel stayed behind to relay our predicament to Aysel and Masaru, and to warn the Roughlanders to stay as far as they could from the poisonous glow. The blockade created by the cave-in looked pretty densely filled in by pieces of rock, both large and small, and to my dismay, more of the uranium and plutonium compound leaked between the piled rocks.

Sabien eyed the obstacle with a determined expression, and before Hotaru or I could anticipate what he intended, the Knight splashed to the ground in his puddle form and whooshed forward to seep between the rocks.

"Sir Sabien!" I called out to him, knowing it was futile. He had made his decision and he was going to go through with the consequences.

Lady Adel rejoined us and we could hear the sounds of the Roughlanders getting ready to move again, either forward or backwards, whatever we eventually decided. Adel said nothing, but she eyed the yellow-coated rocks with distaste, and the three of us waited anxiously for Sabien to return.

It was not too long before he did; his puddle form glowed slightly, a sickly yellowish film coating the surface of the water. He reformed and staggered with the sheer effort of standing. Hotaru made as if to run to him, but before I could stop her Sabien put up his hand to warn her not to come near.

"I'm all right." Sabien said, his voice sounding tired, but still strong. "It does not continue very far. We should be able to make it through."

"But, Sir Sabien, the radiation," I pointed out, "even if we cleared the way, getting the Roughlanders through there would poison them all."

"Hotaru may be able to help with that," Sabien suggested, looking to her..

My friend nodded, her face filled with determination, and I wondered at what Sabien meant.

"Adel," Sabien addressed her, "I am going to need your assistance and that of your mace."

Adel nodded and stepped forward, removing her mace from her back and holding it at the ready. Sabien spoke to Adel privately for a moment before addressing Hotaru once more. "If you are ready, Hotaru, I know you can protect everyone. Trust in your power."

"I will, Sir Sabien," Hotaru responded and raised her hands in front of her, creating the tiny blue disc of a shield, the first power she had learned to manifest.

I wasn't certain what Sabien thought Hotaru was going to be able to do with her shield, but Hotaru retained her determined expression as she closed her eyes to better concentrate on what she was doing. Her shield grew, the blue field expanding outward from her hands to hug the tunnel wall. At its full expanse the cyan shimmer of the shield was barely visible, except where it touched the walls.

"Will that keep out radiation, Hotaru?" I asked, but she didn't answer me, her expression indicating an intense level of concentration.

Beyond the barrier Hotaru was maintaining, Sabien had become water once more and Adel seemed to be using some sort of power to spin her mace at an impossible speed, holding it before her like some sort of drill. My amazement grew as I realized exactly what Sabien had been intending her to do – drill through the irradiated rock. In addition to this, I quickly came to understand what task Sabien had given himself in all of this. He recklessly placed himself between Adel's whirring mace and the rock, using the force of the water to drill more quickly and effectively through the fallen stones.

The hole they rapidly created was large enough for one person, maybe two, to pass through at a time, and thanks to Sabien's water form it was relatively clean of the radioactive glow. I shuddered at the thought of what this was doing to Sabien's body and I hoped he would be strong enough to survive it.

"Hotaru," I addressed her, "can you move with that?"

"I don't know," she responded after a moment's thought, "I've never tried."

"Try it now," I instructed.

Hotaru, arms and shield outstretched before her, took one step forward and then another. The shield moved with her, but I could hear it scraping against the tunnel's walls and I could see the effort it was costing Hotaru to push against the rock.

"You can do it, Hotaru," I encouraged her. "Hug the rock as closely as you can to keep us safe, but it'll get easier soon. The tunnel gets smaller ahead."

Hotaru nodded and we began to move forward, one painstaking step at a time. I kept up a steady string of encouragement and I gestured behind me for the nearest person to come forward. Aysel and Masaru both came over to me.

"Have everyone follow us through," I instructed them. "We're getting out of here, now."

Hotaru was drooping with exhaustion when the shield finally flickered out of existence and we emerged out the other side of the previously blocked area. Up ahead, Sabien was reformed but unconscious on the ground, with a wilted Lady Adel worriedly looking over him.

Aysel hurried to them and I followed more slowly after her while supporting Hotaru.

"We'll have to make a litter," I informed them. "We can probably use Binaris' tarp. Lady Adel, I know you must be feeling pretty awful, but can you walk?"

Adel looked a little green, but she nodded and climbed to her feet, so I took her at her word. Aysel supported her, and Masaru and the Roughlanders with Binaris saw to the litter to carry Sabien; as quickly as we could be we were on our way. Thankfully, it wasn't long before we were out of the tunnel entirely and we got our first sight of the sprawling community around the large outpost below.

I had over nine thousand Roughlanders with me and it was still the largest, most bustling outpost I had yet seen. Due to the trials we had faced in the tunnel to gett here and the current state of my two Knights, I was very glad to see it.

Hotaru and I left Adel and Aysel to look after Sabien and the Roughlanders we had brought with us, while we searched out the person in charge of this outpost. Masaru came with us as our Roughlander representative, and after asking around, we were led to a comfortable meeting room about the same size as the other ones we had seen at the various outposts we had visited, but much more ornately decorated.

The table was an elongated rectangle and the wooden chairs surrounding it were richly padded. Prepared dishes were arrayed in the center of the table, as well as pitchers of chilled beverages. The walls were a strangely distracting pitted texture, all in the colour of bronze, which when combined with the bold red velvet curtains made the room seem overly opulent, at least compared to anything else we had come across on this world.

The three of us took seats as instructed and I felt distinctly out of place in our shabby – not to mention filthy – Roughlander clothing.

"Do you know who's in charge here?" I asked our escort, a young man I would place at about twelve years of age – officially the youngest Roughlander, if that was what he was, I had yet seen.

"What makes you think it's not me?" he asked belligerently, and I gave him a look that told him what I thought of that statement. "Yeah, yeah, I'll go get him," the kid – I mentally reduced his age to ten, whether or not that was the case – agreed reluctantly and left us to our own devices in the room.

Hotaru was already reaching for the food. I supposed we were expected to partake, since it had been placed out and we had been brought there to wait, so I also poured myself a glass of water and offered to do the same for Masaru.

"Welcome, welcome!" The fattest man I had ever seen, either here or back in Tokyo, waddled his way into the room, shifting his bulk from side to side to make it through the door. I could not help but gape at him. This man lived in a harsh desert – no matter how large and well-off his outpost appeared to be – surely supplies were still sparse? Or perhaps they weren't, this close to Taiyou. "What can I do for you two ladies?"

"American?" Hotaru whispered incredulously to my right and I gave her a quelling look.

I stood to give some height to my position. This man needed to take me seriously and I could tell immediately my age, my gender, and my shabby appearance were not going to help my case.

"I am Yukari Namikoya, Chosen of Sapphiros," I introduced myself. "We have travelled from the outpost south of here and some of our party has taken sick on the way."

"There are quite a few of you, aren't there?" the man said, shifting his massive bulk into the oversized chair at the opposite end of the table from us. "It's quite a surprise to see you all here, but if you are looking for shelter of course you are welcome to stay. But you will have to make yourselves useful. We have some of the finest medics as well, so we can see to your sick…it's not contagious, is it?"

"No it's not," I assured him, "but we will not be staying–"

"Why ever not?" he asked in surprise, his chins wobbling with the effort of speaking. "Where would you go? I assumed you've fled your outpost because of some nasty sand crawler or something? I've heard they can get quite big out there and take down whole buildings. We don't have those kinds of troubles here, you'd be quite safe."

I took a deep breath to calm myself; this rather large man was getting on my nerves. It was clear he did not often leave his outpost and had little knowledge of what the real world was like to live in.

"We've come a long way to warn you that the Vile Emperor is threatening the outposts and to ask if any from this outpost would like to join with us to stand against him," I said in a rush to get it out before he interrupted with something else.

"Do you know of the pact the Roughlanders made with Yuko Seig?" Hotaru chimed in.

"Yuko Seig?" the fat man questioned, "Oh, you're that chosen one or whatever you called it. Of course I've heard that old fable, who hasn't? 'The Chosen will return and lead us to freedom against the Vile One' or some such." He laughed, his whole form rumbling with the motion of it.

He sobered after a moment. "So you're saying that you are here straight out of legend to lead the Roughlanders against the Vile Emperor? If it's an army you're looking for, you can ask, of course. I won't stop you, but I don't think anyone's going to want to follow you."

My eyes narrowed in displeasure. "What would make you think that?" I demanded sharply.

The fat man leaned forward in his chair, his expression abruptly becoming serious. "This outpost is a safe place. We shelter anyone who requires it." He leaned back in his chair again as if his shift in personality had never even happened. "Why, we even have some people from the Ruby City sheltering here. Most of them are retired Deathsquad, but they do their part, same as everyone else."

My spine straightened abruptly at these words – Deathsquad, here? I had been right; there were some outposts that were compromised by the Vile Emperor's forces. I had been so stupid, stating my intentions flat out to this man as I had done at the previous outposts.

"In that case, I suppose we have no further business here. I regret we could not come to an understanding," I stated diplomatically, internally itching to get out of this place and get back en route to Taiyou as soon as possible. At least we hadn't told this man where we were headed so that he couldn't report it to his Ruby City contacts.

"I hope you will keep our presence here a secret," Hotaru told him and I groaned inwardly. There was little else Hotaru could have said to make him want to share his knowledge of us more.

"A secret?" he repeated. "But that won't do at all! How am I supposed to let the Roughlanders know about your request if I don't tell them you were here at all?"

"We have reconsidered due to the information you have given to us," I informed him. "We'll be leaving immediately, so there will be no need to inform anyone we have been here. Come on, Hotaru."

"Well, it was nice meeting you," the fat man said pleasantly, but I could hear the obvious false note in his tone, now that I knew what to listen for. "Remember my offer of shelter. It wouldn't do for all of your people to die out there in the Sand Lake."

My eyes flashed as my patience for this man suddenly ran out. "And I hope when I pass through here again I find that your people have been spared."

And with that said, I walked out of the room and the outpost's main building without a backwards glance. Hotaru and Masaru caught up to me before I reached the bottom floor, as I was walking with purpose but not hurrying.

"If I could have everyone's attention," a familiar voice rang out loudly all over the outpost on what I could only assume was some sort of speaker system, "I've had some interesting visitors today! The Chosen of Sapphiros has come to ask you all to fight with her against the Vile Emperor. If any of you are interested, I dare say you will find her in the storehouse next to the main outpost. Now, if you'll all excuse me, my bath is waiting for me. Have a nice day, everyone!"

Hotaru's shocked expression matched my own, and without any words being spoken, we both started running back to the aforementioned storehouse where we had left the Knights and Aysel. It was now imperative that we leave this place, sooner rather than later, and in case said Rubian citizens or Deathsquad soldiers or whatever they were answered the fat man's summons, I didn't want to leave the unconscious Sabien and the weakened Lady Adel undefended.

The gall of that vile, vile man – I shook my head in disgust as I ran out of the fat man's outpost and into the storehouse, Masaru and Hotaru at my heels.

"Lady Adel," I addressed her immediately upon entering the building, "has there been any change with Sir Sabien?" She shook her head to indicate he was still unconscious. "We need to leave now. How fast can we get everyone together?"

"It might prove difficult," Adel informed me. "It seems the Roughlanders have dispersed somewhat among their own kind. We'll see what we can do."

Nodding to Adel, I searched the bustling storehouse crowd – as many of the Roughlanders that could fit seemed to have stayed together, at least – for Lady Sirrah, or the other two outpost leaders.

I was speaking to Lady Sirrah concerning the need to move out immediately, when I noticed something strange out of the corner of my eye. Six obvious newcomers had surrounded Adel and seemed to be having a conversation with her. Their clothes were still vaguely Roughlander in style, but markedly different from the styles of the people we had brought with us, so they stood out right away.

The leader among them – or at least the one who was doing most of the talking to Adel – was rough around the edges, but good looking, with light brown hair and a rogue-ish expression. As I watched with curiosity that turned to mild amusement, the man got down on one knee in front of Adel and the five other men with him followed suit.

"We want to join you," their leader pronounced, attempting a tone of complete sincerity, but falling just shy of the mark. I didn't gather this was a man who swore oaths often.

"You want to join me?" Adel responded with scorn, taking the fact that this man had thought she was in charge here in stride. "Why should I ever trust you?"

"I know you would have little reason to, especially after that fat man's announcement," the man conceded, "but I'm willing to swear to you."

The man lifted his left hand followed by his right, which held a small knife. He balanced the knife against his pinky finger and met Adel stare for stare. After a moment, the five other men behind him did the same. Adel did not seem impressed by this gesture. She raised an eyebrow as if to say, 'Well, what does that prove?'

Without flinching, all six men sliced off their own pinky fingers. I flinched myself, watching them, but I couldn't look away.

"Do you accept our loyalty?" the lead man asked Adel, not looking at his severed finger lying in a small pool of blood on the floor before him.

"I accept," I said, walking over to where they knelt, even before I realized I had spoken.

As one, the six turned to face me and I noticed these were tough men. They all bore the marks of old injuries and their leader in particular had only one eye. The other was covered with a weathered leather patch that seemed to be as much a part of his face as his scraggly facial hair.

"I'm Yukari Namikoya, Chosen of Sapphiros," I introduced myself before gesturing to Adel. "This is Lady Adel, my Knight." I just barely caught Adel rolling her eyes at the whole scene.

"I like a woman in charge. My name is Razor," the leader said with a charming smile, almost offering his bloody hand before he realized that wouldn't be the best idea, "and these are my boys."

"You should get bandaged up," I commented. "We're moving out immediately."

So, as much as the fat man's outpost had been a failed journey, we had gained six very interesting new members to our procession – and what a procession it was. Razor proved himself useful nearly as soon as we had reached the desert, our slightly reduced column of Roughlanders in tow. Some, I supposed, had decided to stay at that awful place, but I couldn't blame them if safety in numbers was what they were looking for.

Far off in the Sand Lake, a massive tail broke the surface of the sand before disappearing once more below. If we had been on Earth and this had been water, I would have sworn up and down the fabled Loch Ness monster was real and I had seen it.

"What was that?" I asked no one in particular.

"Sand crawler," Razor responded, and I started a little; I hadn't realized he had been so close. Until I was sure of him, I would have to keep a closer eye on my own safety in his presence. "They get real big out here. The best way to keep one of them from killing you is to move in a big group and act like you're bigger than it is. Stragglers or individuals will get eaten immediately and draw it right to the rest of us." His voice was gruff, like the rest of him, but he curiously did not have the accent I had come to associate with Roughlanders.

"What's bigger than a sand crawler?" I asked him curiously.

He smiled lopsidedly. "Nothin'."

I gave him a look that clearly told him I didn't care for his humour. "Would a larger sand crawler keep another sand crawler away?"

"Oh probably," Razor responded, his tone still nonchalant, "as long as it wasn't injured."

"Well, we'll have to move like a very large and very healthy sand crawler, then."

I left Razor to his own devices as I moved forward to speak to Adel, Masaru, and the outpost leaders to tell them what I wanted them to do. Before long, we had arranged ourselves to my specifications. We moved sinuously and in a long column, alternating periods of rest with periods of walking. The end result was that to anything out in the sand we would appear to move in a wave like a giant snake might.

Masaru, Hotaru, the Knights, and I headed the column as the snake's head, and the other outpost leaders had taken up in different groups to ensure the smooth operation of our new method of transport. On our group's first rest period, I looked back to discover which group Razor and his men had taken up with and how they were getting along.

Masaru and Hotaru beside me seemed to follow my gaze, wondering what I was looking for. I located Razor six groups back – his group was walking now – when suddenly Masaru whipped past me, running full tilt through the sand.

"Masaru!" I called after him, angry that he had broken the formation we had worked so hard to set into motion.

Masaru ignored me and everyone else, running full tilt back to Razor's group. At the sound of my voice, Razor's head snapped up and his eyes lit onto Masaru barreling toward him.

The wave of people walking to imitate a sand crawler blocked my sight of what happened next, but as they moved aside once more I caught the signs of a scuffle in the sand in Razor's group.

Then I saw it; not far from the moving column there was motion out in the sand. My eyes snapped to the source of the motion and I saw a strange and terrifying creature. It swam in the sand as if in water, and as it rose up briefly I caught sight of its head, which was shaped almost like a hammerhead shark with baleful eyes on either side. The beast was grey in colour, except for the underside, which was the same colour as the sand through which it moved. It had fins for arms, but powerfully clawed back legs. At one glance I was able to tell it was large enough to swallow a person whole, and that person was sure to be either Masaru or Razor, as they were separated from the pack.

Instinct kicking in, I reached for the bow at my back. I didn't bother to string an arrow – truth be told I didn't even think of it. I remembered fear and power was within my grasp.

However, just before I formed an arrow with my mind, something changed about the scene before me. Someone – it was too quick for me to see who it was – shot out of the scuffle, skidding over the sand directly toward the sand shark, who abruptly shifted direction to head for the new tasty morsel presented to it. Without conscious thought, I formed an arrow and loosed it at the lone Roughlander out on the sand. It was not a simple arrow made of light this time, but one with a long white rope trailing after it impossibly far over the sand to wrap around the stunned Roughlander. Surprised, but still full of adrenaline enough not to question what I had done, I dropped the bow, as I grabbed hold of the rope and tugged with all the strength I could muster.

The Roughlander skidded out from the jaws of certain death and slid across the sand to land close enough that he could scrabble the rest of the way back to the group before the creature could discern what had happened to his meal.

I let myself breathe again as soon as he was safe and I looked dubiously at the bow at my feet. Whatever I had done, I was glad I had done it, but it was strange indeed to see the white trail of rope lay across the sand from here to the man I had saved.

Meanwhile, the scuffle had ended, and after a moment Masaru came walking back, weaving his way through the Roughlander groups this time and not striding openly across the sand.

"I assume you had a hand in that?" I accused, my voice cold.

Masaru didn't respond or even look at me. He had a bruise on his face near the jaw and was limping slightly. His expression was as dark as a thundercloud and his eyes darker.

"You don't need to tell me what happened and I don't need to know why," I said to him in the same tone, "but I want your promise this is not going to happen again, Masaru. Razor and his men swore to follow me, which means they are a part of this."

"It won't happen again," Masaru spoke at last, his words grudging and he left me behind, walking faster so he could head the column and not have to talk to anyone.

Thankfully, the rest of the journey passed without much incident. Eventually, Hotaru also tried to talk to Masaru, but where before they had been conversing amiably about cell phones and other pieces of Japanese culture that Masaru did not understand, now he would not even look at her.

By resting and walking by turns, we made our way across the Sand Lake until we could make out a large outpost ahead. We were asked to stop when we encountered a group of about twenty or so Roughlanders wearing partial armour, armed with various weapons, and riding mounts like the ones we had abandoned long ago in the mountains. Their leader, a man who looked the least like a Roughlander out of all of them – he was wearing full armour and his head was helmeted – called forward for no more than five of us to approach to speak with him.

I realized what we must look like – an army approaching for an attack – even though we were largely Roughlanders like them and not Deathsquads.

"Hotaru, Lady Adel, Masaru and Lady Sirrah," I named four people to accompany me. "Aysel, can you look after Sir Sabien?"

Aysel nodded from near Sabien's tarp-litter and the others came forward. Masaru looked surprised I had included him. I didn't know if that was because he didn't think his position warranted it or if it was because of his behavior during this stretch of the journey, but he was someone I had begun to rely on and, truth be told, I didn't know any of these people half as well, except for Hotaru, of course. Considering Masaru gave me an idea of how best to approach this scenario.

"Masaru," I said as I walked over to where he stood, separate from the others.

"Aye?" he asked cautiously.

"We might have more success if you explain the circumstances to them," I told him.

"Why me?" he questioned, seeming shocked out of his earlier despondency.

"I'd rather not have Hotaru and I announce ourselves until we are sure of this outpost's allegiance," I explained. "You're a Roughlander with a valid reason for having left your outpost. See if you can't get us in to speak to the leader here."

Masaru agreed, though reluctantly, and when we reached shouting distance to the other Roughlander group, their leader dismounted and strode forward, and Masaru joined him just out of earshot.

Hotaru, Adel, Sirrah, and I waited and watched as Masaru said his piece to the armoured man, who seemed unmoved by whatever Masaru was saying to him. Hotaru fidgeted beside me with the delay until she just couldn't take it anymore.

"It's not working," Hotaru complained. "He's not listening to Masaru."

Hotaru was right; it seemed whatever Masaru was saying, he was having no effect on the armoured man.

"Alright," I conceded, "I'll go speak to him."

I took a few steps forward, but stopped abruptly when the Roughlanders across from us raised their weapons meaningfully in our direction. I wondered briefly what sort of a threat they thought I was – I hadn't touched the bow on my back and I was otherwise unarmed. I looked back over my shoulder and I realized Hotaru, and worse than that, the impressive Lady Adel, had started to come forward with me.

As I stood there deliberating, Hotaru raised her hands as if in surrender and walked forward until she had passed me, headed for Masaru. The men kept their weapons levelled at her but they did not fire, and Hotaru made it to Masaru's side safely. Wishing I had been the one to make it over there, I listened closely to see if I could hear what Hotaru was saying and discover if she was hurting our chances at all.

"What reason do we have to trust your word?" the armoured man asked in response to whatever Hotaru had stated to him upon her arrival.

"Well, eight hundred years ago, Yuko Seig made a pact with the Roughlanders," Hotaru began, giving the man a history lesson in order to explain in the most roundabout way why we had come.

"Yes, I know that piece of history, but what does it have to do with the present?" he responded tonelessly.

This was getting ridiculous; I didn't know what angle Masaru had tried, besides the one I had suggested to him, but I knew Hotaru wasn't going to get anywhere quickly with this one. It was not as if we were in a dire hurry or anything, but I wanted to either get into that outpost to state our case or move onto Taiyou – either would have been better than wasting time out here in the harsh desert sun.

"I'm a Chosen of Sapphiros," Hotaru stated.

"Again I say, what reason do we have to trust you?" the man repeated, not moved by Hotaru's pronouncement.

"We can prove we are who we say we are," I said loudly, so the armoured man could hear me, as I took a single step closer. I was still wary of the weapons pointed at me, but I felt this had gone on long enough and I should have perhaps taken charge of this from the beginning. "Understand that as you have no reason to trust us, neither do we have reason to trust you."

The man in charge gestured to the men behind him to lower their weapons and then gestured me forward. Adel and Sirrah followed me of their own accord as I walked forward to join Hotaru and Masaru.

"My name is Yukari Namikoya," I informed him "Hotaru," I gestured to indicate who I was speaking about, "and I are both Chosen of Sapphiros. We have come with important news and a request for the leader of this outpost. Should it be impossible to speak with him or her, we ask only that you allow us to pass safely through your territory, so we may continue on to the sanctioned outpost in Taiyou. Now," I said, with as much authority in my voice that I could muster, "you know what we want of you. What is it you require of us?"

The man nodded before pointing at Masaru, "We will hold onto him to ensure you speak only the truth. Should you cause any trouble or be caught in a falsehood, he will be killed."

I nodded reluctantly in agreement; I didn't intend to speak falsely to this outpost leader or any other, and as long as everything went okay, Masaru would be spared.

Masaru looked from me to the armoured man with a shocked expression as if he wanted to flee. Before he could think to do so, the weapons of the men before us lifted once more, centering on him this time, and some of the men moved forward to surround him. His betrayed expression made me feel a flash of guilt, and I couldn't meet his eyes as the mounted Roughlanders surrounded him completely, putting blades to his throat. I rationalized with myself that we had to see this through and for now that meant doing as these Roughlanders asked us to, but the guilt did not fade.

The small group of us accompanied the mounted Roughlander crew toward the outpost, leaving our Roughlanders behind to wait and rest in a large cluster. No one spoke until we reached the door of the outpost building.

"He stays here," the leader of the crew announced.

Hotaru set her mouth into a stubborn line. "We'll get you out of here safely, Masaru."

Masaru, still wary of the pointed blades under his chin, did not so much as nod, and he didn't chance speaking. Avoiding his gaze, I entered the building and braced myself for whatever was necessary to see us out of here safely.

We were led to a round room on the top floor. I was getting rather used to the layouts of these outpost buildings, which were all roughly the same, but varied in size and height. This one I placed at being medium-sized. The room at the top, however, was not a meeting room like it had been at Lady Sirrah's outpost or a lavish apartment like it had been at the fat man's outpost. Instead, it was a very stark room with a small round table in the centre, with electrical devices here and there on the walls. Though more orderly, this room reminded me sharply of Binaris' room or the main server back at the Temple of Sapphire.

The leader of the Roughlander crew was the only one to accompany us inside; the others had stayed behind with Masaru. Upon reaching our destination, our guide removed his helmet to reveal a metallic face beneath. I started in surprise, staring, perhaps rudely, at the android's face. The mental image of the male Binaris filled my mind, but I abruptly realized this man, or robot, whatever he was, had spoken normally and not with the computerized-sounding voice I would have expected from one of his kind. Perhaps – my mind supplied a possible explanation – they had improved the technology somewhat in the past eight hundred years.

"I am called X-en," the android introduced himself at last. "You may speak to my master now, if you wish."

I looked about the room, confused. "Where is he?"

"I am here, Yukari," a deep voice rumbled from several points around the room. I assumed immediately that whoever X-en's master was, he did not intend to reveal himself to us.

"Well you seem to know who we are, but we do not know who you are," I stated the obvious.

"And you still have not provided proof you are who you claim to be," the voice countered.

I deliberately unlaced the collar of my Roughlander clothes to pull the fabric back enough to reveal the blue mark upon my chest. I turned myself so X-en could see the mark for what it was.

"This mark is not fake. We are the Chosen of Sapphiros," I announced to the room. "We have come to ask for your aid against the Vile Emperor and his forces."

"Ah…" the voice said, as if what I presented to him was something he had long awaited. "Chosen Yukari, Hotaru, I am glad you have come at last."

"So you remember the pact with Yuko Seig, then?" Hotaru asked hopefully.

"I know of the pact the priestess of Sapphiros made with the Roughlanders, but that is not why I am glad of your coming. I have waited here these long years to ally myself with you. The Vile Emperor has ruled for too long."

"If we are allies, then why do you not show yourself?" I asked, still unconvinced by the strangeness of this encounter.

"I fear my appearance may frighten you," the voice said regretfully, "but if we are to be allies, I suppose you are correct."

The voice went silent then and we all looked around the room expectantly.

"My master is coming," X-en informed us as the door opened, whooshing to either side like the automated doors of the Temple of Sapphiros had done.

The monster that stooped to enter doors not nearly large enough to accommodate him was like nothing I had ever seen before. His legs and arms were like tree trunks and his body was even thicker. His form was vaguely birdlike, with glossy, black-feathered wings protruding from his back and reinforcing the likeness. I would have most closely compared him with a giant vulture, but there was some humanity in the way he moved and his abashed expression. He was hunched over and his limbs were gnarled with obvious signs of age. His eyes gleamed blackly as he waited for us to recoil from his presence.

I fought the urge to do so with everything in me. This vulture creature had already proclaimed himself to be my ally and I did not want to throw away the chance I had to leave here with more than I had hoped for.

Beside me, Adel gasped a little in recognition and I looked to her sharply, startled that she out of all of us was the one to react to this creature's appearance.

"Lady Adel of the Kusabana house," the vulture creature spoke with the same deep voice, only more intimidating now he was so near. "Why have you come here? Do you seek death?"

"I am not the person I once was, Lord Hex," Adel stated, determination evident in her tone.

"Do you no longer give your allegiance to the Ruby City and the Lady Lilyth, then?" Hex demanded, a trace of danger in his tone that clearly warned Adel of what he would do should her answer not satisfy him.

"Lady Adel is a Knight of Sapphiros now, Lord Hex," I addressed him, using the name Adel had used for him. "She is our ally and I trust her with my life."

I did trust Adel, I realized abruptly. I did not know much, if anything, about the past of the Knights, but they had already proven they would each give their lives to protect us, the Chosen, even if it was only at the request of Yuko Seig, a woman long dead.

"I trust her also," Hotaru seconded.

"Very well," Hex desisted this line of questioning and approached where Hotaru and I stood.

I tried not to flinch or step back, but he was large enough that he could have picked up both Hotaru and I easily from where he stopped. Instead, he reached out with both of his gnarled clawed hands and held them out to us. Reluctantly, I put my dwarfed hand in his. With a sudden motion, he broke the skin of my palm and Hotaru's with his claws, then brought our palms to his mouth to lick the trickle of blood he had released.

He stepped back, letting us both go. "We are allies now," he stated. "I will give you the help you require against the Vile One."

Taken aback, Hotaru and I were at a loss for words.

"You should probably know I am not the only one who has been waiting these past eight hundred years for you. It will not be easy to search them out, but there are other allies…"

Chapter 7 – No One Here But Us, the Trees, and the People

Nothing is ever simple. It wasn't that I thought it would be, but our trip to Taiyou was turning out to be more complicated than I would have thought possible. The difficulties we were facing made me worry about how Kaji and Yue might be faring, and when we might see them again.

"Come on, I don't bite," Razor said, offering me a hand in climbing the ridge up out of the Sand Lake and onto the solid ground of the rocky outcropping before us.

My feelings toward Razor were still mixed, but in an effort to get to know him, and because he had offered, I had gone ahead with him to scout the way. My uncertainty towards him was reinforced by the fact that Masaru clearly distrusted Razor and had looked very displeased when he had learned of my intentions to venture anywhere alone with him. Personally, I was confident enough in the prospect of being able to defend myself from Razor should he prove to be a danger to me, but his declaration of loyalty back at the fat man's outpost had impressed me, and deep down I did not feel as if I had anything to fear.

I stared out at the vista before me. To Razor, or anyone else who might stand here, there was nothing out there to see except for the dun-coloured rocks of the wasteland and the piercing pale blue of the constantly sunny sky. I, however, had been working at something that allowed me to see further than I had ever been capable of before.

The idea had come to me as a method of being able to hit a target very far away. I had found that if I concentrated on a point in the distance, I could focus on it like I did with any target. Suddenly, it would seem much nearer and I would be able to see it more clearly than before. I tried my new trick now and I caught movement as I scanned the horizon.

Centering in on the source, I saw them as if they were much nearer to me than was the actual case – a Deathsquad encampment. Hex had warned us it would be between us and the entrance to Taiyou. I couldn't make out the numbers or the details, but it was enough that I could tell they were there.

I felt my mouth settle into a grim line. "All right, Razor, I've seen what I came to. We can head back."

Razor was looking off in the direction I had been staring at with a slightly puzzled expression. "All right," he finally agreed, "you're the boss," and proceeded to hop back down the cliff edge we had so laboriously climbed up.

I turned about to begin the climb down, only to notice Razor was holding out his arms for me to jump down into them. Ignoring him, I scooted to the edge and began to let myself down one foothold at a time.

"You know you're going to have to learn to trust me eventually," he commented blithely.

I reached solid ground and turned to face him, dusting myself off. "And you're going to have to accept there are some things I can do for myself."

He smiled lopsidedly. "All right, fair enough."

I returned the smile tentatively; Razor was hard not to like.

Together, we headed back to where the others had made a temporary camp so we could rest before continuing our journey. We were at the edge of the Sand Lake, where the sand was shallower, so we were less likely to encounter sand sharks and other dangerous denizens of the Sand Lakes.

There were much fewer of us now, so our previous method of travel was no longer effective or necessary. We had left Binaris and our Roughlander forces behind at Hex's outpost, and only twenty of us had continued on to Taiyou. Until we secured an alliance, or at least knew the state of affairs in Taiyou, I thought it best not to march an army to their borders to demand entry like we had effectively done to Hex.

"There are Deathsquads between us and Taiyou," I stated once I was in earshot.

"How many?" Sabien asked, having now recovered somewhat from his radiation poisoning.

I shook my head. "They weren't in rank and file, so it was hard to make out. It's a permanent encampment, though. It seems like they are stationed there." Razor was giving me a speculative look, which I ignored. "We're going to have to find a way to get through."

"It's a Rubian encampment," Razor elaborated, startling us all. "They have been stationed there since the ceasefire was established, as far as I know. It's as close as they can get to Taiyou, so they stay there to remind the city of their presence. They're not supposed to stop anyone from crossing the border, but they'll rough you up if they get the chance."

"Have you ever been to Taiyou, Razor?" Hotaru asked the question I was busy pondering.

"No, not personally," Razor responded, "but I've heard things from the Roughlanders who run the supply caravans. Unfortunately nothing current, though."

"Do you know who rules the city?" I asked.

"Uh," he hesitated, "it's a king, I know that much. Narlhoop? Or something like that...wait, I remember, it's Narlhep. King Narlhep."

"Do you know anything else about the place?" I pressed. "Their laws or customs? How they feel about the Vile Emperor?"

"Well, they've got a Deathsquad camped on their doorstep and a ceasefire to try and ensure he doesn't attack them again, I figure they don't care much for the man," Razor surmised. "But I do know one of the Talons, Fuzen, is the official ambassador of the Ruby

City. He's the only one of them who's allowed access to the place, and it was him who negotiated the terms of the ceasefire.

"Also," he added, "they don't like other races in Taiyou. They're prejudiced. We're lucky we don't have any Croatins with us or they probably wouldn't let us in."

"Well that's more than we knew before," I noted, "but we still don't know how to get past the Deathsquad. We have to remember they are probably looking for Hotaru and I, and I don't doubt they know what to look for."

"I have an idea in regards to that too," Razor offered.

We heard him out and debated amongst ourselves according to the information Razor supplied about the Deathsquads. Adel, though not very forthcoming, was also a good source of information regarding the history and the tactics the Deathsquads had used in her day.

"I was a general. I trained Deathsquad soldiers," Adel revealed when questioned as to how she knew so much about the Deathsquads. "I am a Knight of Sapphiros now, but I was born in the Ruby City."

If any of the others were surprised by her admission, they kept it to themselves.

Razor's plan was fairly simple, but it involved disguises. With Aysel's help, he spent a good while trying to muck up my face and dull the colour of my hair with sand and water in the hopes they could make me appear to be a young man. Aysel's worried frown was not encouraging, but when Masaru walked by and couldn't suppress a chuckle, I was immediately fed up with the whole process.

"This isn't going to work, Razor," I stated, unimpressed. "Just find me a scrap of cloth to use as a scarf over my hair. That and the dirt should convince anyone I am a penniless refugee."

"What's a penny?" Masaru asked.

I was startled by the question, but it served to remind me just how far away from home I was. "Money…you know, currency?"

"Oh, ye mean like a krevel?"

"Possibly," I hesitated, but then I remembered I had a coin on me – it was the one Hotaru had found in the Temple of Sapphire. I pulled it out and showed it to him. "This is ten yen."

"That's ten of 'em?" Masaru asked incredulously and dug around in his pocket to produce a couple of cube-shaped bits of bronze. "This is two krevels, see? One, two," he said, counting them out for my benefit.

The krevels immediately reminded me of something, and I wondered for a moment where I had seen them before. Then the memory of the fat man's outpost struck me and I could see the pitted bronze of his walls hadn't been some strange sort of building material – they had been krevels.

"Masaru, how much is a krevel worth, exactly?" I asked, a little reluctant about hearing the answer.

"Well, it'll likely take us a few more of these to pay our way across the ferry into Taiyou," he answered and I shuddered to think how much money the fat man was putting on display to impress upon everyone his own self-worth. If I had only known what they were then, I might have been able to guess that man was in someone's pay and therefore not to be trusted.

"I didn't know it was going to cost us," I commented at a loss – until this moment, I hadn't even known there was a currency system on this planet. "I don't have any…krevels. You can have this," I said, offering him the ten yen coin, "though I don't know how much good it'll do you, beyond a souvenir."

Masaru took the ten yen coin from me and he seemed pretty pleased about it, so I tried to let go of my concerns over the fact that the Roughlanders were pooling together their limited money to pay for our trip across.

Thankfully, Hotaru's dark hair and average appearance had the benefit of not causing her to stand out as much as I did, so she was able to pull off disguising herself as a young member of Razor's gang.

We also changed our story a little, so I was just a frightened Roughlander seeking refuge in Taiyou, like the others we had brought with us. The Knights were too strange to fully disguise and they refused to remove their armour to do so, but they assured us they would be able to make their own way across should they encounter any trouble. In a worst-case scenario, they could return to Hex's outpost and await us there with the rest of our forces. I was still worried about Sabien in his weakened state should it come down to a conflict between our Knights and the Deathsquad soldiers, but I didn't want to doubt his abilities aloud in case I offended him.

Without further ado, we were off. The Deathsquad encampment, and therefore Taiyou, was still a ways off, but that only served to give me time to worry about what we would be facing. When we arrived we found a small crowd of refugees, presumably seeking entrance to Taiyou like us. By joining them, we easily tripled the quantity of people trying to reach the ferry to cross the lake of Taiyou. There was a bridge as well, but once we were off into the water we would be home free, whereas on the bridge the Deathsquads could have a better chance of following us or hemming us in if they discovered who we were.

The sight of so much water brought awe to the Roughlander faces around me, even Masaru. I tried to copy his expression, though to me this body of water was small compared to any I had seen. What gave me pause were the several thousand Deathsquad soldiers roaming the encampment bordering Taiyou as if they belonged there. My skin itched with uneasiness at being so close to them and knowing none of these soldiers would hesitate in seeing me dead – or worse, brought bound and gagged to their master.

At first I tried to control my fear, but then I realized as the Roughlander refugee I was supposed to be, my terror would be expected and could only help my disguise, so I let it take over and I felt my body tremble.

Most of us had paired up and grouped off to reinforce our stories that we were refugees and family units from the destroyed Sand Lake outpost. Masaru was my partner, and as he noticed my trembling he put an arm around me to lead me forward. I huddled in close to him, playing the part now as I was expected, so I did not have to see the horrid Deathsquad soldiers. I let him guide me toward the ferry docks, effectively hiding my identifiable face from view.

A group of four Deathsquad soldiers were stationed before the ferry, interrogating passengers before they could reach the relative safety of the loading dock, which was manned by what appeared to be Knights of Taiyou. Their armour was white with a white dove motif and the style abruptly reminded me of Sabien, who had disappeared as water before we got into view of the Deathsquad encampment and informing us he would see us in Taiyou.

The Deathsquad interrogators were roughing up the people that tried to get by them, but so far they had not prevented anyone from crossing their path or killed anyone, though one or two people would have some serious bruises. Some of the Roughlanders we had brought went on ahead of us, including Sirrah. Thankfully, their group made it through without much incident.

Razor's people and Hotaru were next. I could see the Deathsquad soldier interrogating Razor give him some trouble, though over the general din of the area I couldn't make out what was being said. Razor stood, his back straight, and gave back at least as good as he got verbally. Then the Deathsquad raised his hand in warning; still, Razor did not back down. I wondered if the man was crazy and trying to draw attention to us, but from back here there was nothing I could do about it if he was.

The Deathsquad soldier backhanded Razor with his gauntleted hand and I winced in sympathy. Razor's attitude changed immediately, and he kept his eyes on the ground and his shoulders hunched, as if he feared a worse beating. The soldier, seeing that Razor was cowed, let him and the others through, and I let out a sigh of relief. Thanks to Razor's little show, the Deathsquad soldiers had not even spared a glance for Hotaru in her flimsy disguise.

Masaru and I took our turn after that. I kept my face huddled to his chest as we approached the armoured bullies.

"Are you gonna give us any trouble?" the Deathsquad soldier demanded of Masaru. His helmet muffled his voice and I couldn't make out his accent, if he had one.

"No trouble here, sir," Masaru answered straightforwardly.

"What about your little lady here?" the Deathsquad soldier beside him commented a little slyly. "You wouldn't mind if she stayed here a little while first before you continue on, would you, boy?"

I didn't see or hear Masaru's reaction as I was too lost in my own. My fear was turning rapidly into rage; overgrown bullies, they were all the same.

"I said no," Masaru said, drawing me closer to him and away from the reach of the Deathsquad soldier that was trying to get his hands on me.

"We'll just see about that," the first Deathsquad soldier said and I looked up just in time to see him lifting his hand to strike Masaru down. I could feel Masaru getting ready to push me aside to defend himself. I knew if he started a fight here it would escalate. Emotions were too tense here on the docks and the Deathsquad soldiers were waiting for an excuse to flex their muscles.

"No!" I yelled suddenly in my most frightened voice. "No, don't hurt him, please!"

It was enough to give all of the men pause, if not to completely dissolve the tension around me.

Then abruptly the first Deathsquad soldier began to laugh. "This one'll be no sport," he commented. "Looks like he needs his little lady to protect him."

The other soldiers around him chuckled at this before returning to their duty and in the moment I was able to tug Masaru, who was red in the face and trying to control himself from lashing out, past the soldiers and onto the docks, where we at least were safely within the jurisdiction of the Taiyoun soldiers.

I let go of Masaru once we had blended into the crowd, so he wouldn't feel tempted to lash out at me for making a fool of him. I didn't regret my actions as they had kept the two of us safe, but I was disgusted at the necessity of having to pretend to be less than I was. I had never given into bullying before; I had always acted with pride and confidence, and not doing so left a sour taste in my mouth.

Through the crowd on the docks, I could see how the others were faring. I watched with a growing sense of unease as a very short cloaked figure – maybe four feet tall – made its way toward the Deathsquad soldiers stationed before the ferry platform. I gasped suddenly as I realized why the sight of that cloaked figure gave me such a feeling of distress – it was a Croatin. I recognized the way it moved from my association with the similarly-sized Croatin, Ticket. Razor had said Croatins and other non-humans – like Ris, I supposed – were not allowed within the borders of Taiyou. I didn't know why this Croatin was trying to sneak into Taiyou, but as one of the Deathsquad soldiers turned to face his next victim and his eyes lighted onto the small, cloaked form, my heart instantly went out to the mysterious non-human stranger.

Aysel, her bulky armour and weapons disguised only by an oversized cloak made from the tarp we had used to carry Binaris across the desert, was next to attempt the crossing, which caused me some anxiety for the more timid squire's welfare. I was especially worried should something happen with the Croatin's attempt to cross and if security measures were increased as a result.

I could see from her expression and where her gaze was trained that Aysel had also noted the presence of the Croatin and its plight. Without the hesitation or caution I would have expected from Aysel, she furled her cloak aside and drew her sword, advancing suddenly on the Deathsquad soldiers before the Croatin's true nature was revealed to them and the Taiyoun soldiers beyond.

"Move aside, I wish to pass," Aysel announced in an impressive impersonation of Adel at her most arrogant.

"Who do you think you are?" one of the Deathsquad soldiers demanded, while the rest of them took up positions with their weapons, ready to defend or attack as necessary.

"Lady Adel of the Kusabana house," Aysel stated proudly – so much for not calling attention to ourselves. She levelled her sword at the one who had questioned her. "Do you deny my right to go where I wish?"

The Deathsquad soldiers seemed to hesitate somewhat at the name and Aysel's absurd demand, but then the one who had spoken – perhaps the highest ranking of this particular group – spoke in an effort to take control of the situation. "I'm afraid I'm going to have to, Lady."

The Croatin stuck in the middle of this tense situation looked about himself in panic for a safe direction in which to flee. Catching the Croatin's eye in the shadow of his cloak, I waved at him to come to me. As the Deathsquad soldiers moved to surround Aysel, the Croatin took advantage of their distraction to duck between them and scurry to my side, careful not to walk too much like the frog-person he was, lest the Taiyoun soldiers catch sight of him.

Meanwhile, Ayselwas somehow taking on all four Deathsquad soldiers at once and was very clearly holding her own against them. I hadn't expected it to come down to a fight and I wondered very strongly what Aysel thought she was doing. I mean, yes she had created an effective distraction – the Deathsquad soldiers would likely remember little else from today besides her audacity – but she was also placing herself in great danger. There were thousands of Deathsquad soldiers here, all these four needed to do was to call for reinforcements – not even Adel could fight them all.

"Hey, thanks," the Croatin said, in a voice much like Ticket's, upon reaching my side, "my name's Stephen. What's yours?"

"Yukari," I replied and looked down at Stephen with an exasperated expression. "Tell me something, Stephen, why is a Croatin trying to get into Taiyou?" I whispered to him so only he might hear me over the din of the crowd and the noise of the fight.

"You're lucky my friend is distracting them or you would have been caught already."

Stephen worriedly looked from me to Aysel. "I didn't mean to get anyone in trouble," he said apologetically. "My family has tried for generations to make it into Taiyou. We're from here originally, though we live in Espearia now. Every generation we send someone to try and make it home and now it's my turn. None of them have ever come back. I'm hoping they made it in, but I'm not sure."

Stephen, though earnest, was a pitiable creature.

"Well, provided we get through this, if you stick with us and don't cause trouble, we'll see if we can't get you into Taiyou," I told him, against my better judgment.

"Wow, thanks," Stephen responded and took up position at my side to watch the conclusion of the battle between Aysel and the Deathsquad soldiers.

Three of the original four Deathsquad soldiers were now wounded – only one seriously – but now several others had approached to join the fray and Aysel found herself completely surrounded. The Taiyoun soldiers at the edge of the docks stood impassively; though these were their borders, they clearly had orders not to interfere with what occurred just outside of Taiyou.

Aysel spun about to face the newcomers and I held my breath in anticipation for her; even though she had done well so far, surely she couldn't take on three more in addition to the ones she was already fighting. One of the newcomers drew his sword from behind his back and leveled it directly at Aysel. The ruby eyes of his helmet glowed a deep red for a moment before the same light began emanating from the hilt of his sword.

My eyes widened in surprise – the Deathsquad soldiers had a power of some kind? The red light grew in intensity before all of a sudden pulsing to the tip of the sword blade and releasing in the form of a red beam, reminiscent of the powers the Talons had displayed back in the park in Shinjuku. The beam was only a short blast, not continuous, but it shot in a direct line for Aysel. She straightened, but didn't act to move out of the way.

I watched in horror as the blast hit Aysel full in the armoured chest and she exploded.

"Aysel?" I whispered, too shocked yet to feel the loss, but where I expected to see some sign of carnage and a spray of blood, there were only clumps of snow. The Deathsquad soldiers looked as surprised as I was, though I couldn't see their expressions. They converged on the small piles of frozen water and a few of them kicked the snow experimentally with their armoured boots.

As they mulled this over, another cloaked figure in the crowd caught my eye. The figure reached the ferry docks and tried to blend into the crowd. Not paying attention to whether my new Croatin recruit was following me or not, I took off for where I saw the cloaked figure disappear.

The crowd started to move and load themselves onto the ferryboat as I searched about, finally seeing the person again on the far side of the ferry where they had gathered with Masaru, Hotaru, Razor, and the others. As the hood of the cloak came down I was relieved to see it was Aysel.

"Aysel!" I let out, hurrying over.

"Actually, I'm over here," Aysel's voice said from behind me and I whirled about.

Aysel stood behind me, looking a little sheepish, with the cloak made from Binaris' tarp over Adel's armour and with Adel's coif in her hand. I turned back from Aysel to the person I had thought was Aysel and saw I was looking at an exact double. Hotaru and the others amazed expressions matched my own.

"You did a wonderful job, sister," Aysel said.

"You as well," the look-a-like wearing Aysel's armour responded in Adel's proud accented voice.

I, along with the others, gaped at the two of them – sisters? Adel and Aysel were identical twins. I realized now I had never seen Lady Adel out of her full suit of armour or without her coif. If I had, the truth of the matter would have been revealed long ago. Though vastly different in personality and demeanor, there was no telling them apart physically.

"Well, whoever you are," Stephen interjected from beside me, "I want to thank you for distracting those soldiers."

"You can thank me by staying hidden," Adel responded. "From what I understand, it wouldn't do for you to be discovered within the borders of Taiyou."

Stephen nodded solemnly in acceptance as the ferryboat took off from the dock. We had yet another refugee with us to keep hidden, but we were officially, for good or for ill, entering the city of Taiyou.

I could see the city across the open expanse of the lake, especially with my trick of looking more closely at things far away. The city was built largely of a grey stone, but here and there I could see wooden support beams – they must have trees there, I thought. The buildings were generally anywhere from one to three stories tall, and while they didn't seem to have any towers like the Roughlanders outposts, I could see fanciful-looking spires in the distance, so maybe it was just the area near the lake that was less developed.

While huddled together on the crowded ferryboat, we waited and had guarded conversation until the boat reached the other side and we unloaded ourselves in Taiyou proper. There was a massive gate guarded by more Taiyoun soldiers blocking the mouth of the bridge into the city and the edge of the docks.

"Roughlanders, to me!" one of the guards called out, gesturing to our party amongst others. "Your weapons will have to be confiscated, but we will lead you to the Roughlander Sanctioned Outpost. Are there any outpost leaders among you?"

Lady Sirrah stepped forward to speak to the guard as we all waited. Shortly after, she came over to speak with Hotaru and I.

"I didn't think it wise to reveal your identities to the city guard," Sirrah informed us, "but apparently as an outpost leader I am able to carry my weapons into the city. can designate three others as my guards and they can do the same. Should I name you, so you can keep your bow and sword?"

I considered her request as I looked around at the people we had brought with us. Adel and Aysel would never give up their weapons under any circumstances – for all I knew they were probably family heirlooms or something – and regardless they would be far more effective armed than myself or Hotaru would be. As for a third person, I instantly thought of Masaru. He was acting as an outpost leader in Corporal Dahlia's stead, even though his outpost was destroyed. It wouldn't do to undermine the authority of his position by stripping his weapons away like the others, and I remembered his reaction at having lost one of his knives earlier.

I looked regretfully at my bow; I didn't like the thought of giving it up, but I at least knew I could defend myself without it and I didn't need a bow to shoot arrows. I assumed Hotaru had some skills that didn't rely on her physical blade, since she was also trained by Sabien and the other Knights.

"No, Sirrah, thank you for asking," I answered her at last. "Can you name the Lady Adel, Aysel, and Masaru as your guards so they can stay armed?"

"Certainly, Yukari," Sirrah replied and headed back over to do so.

Hotaru was giving me a displeased stare, but I ignored her; she wasn't the only one who would have to give up her weapons. On my way over to the gate where the weapons were to be left behind, I informed Adel and Aysel of the arrangement I had made with Sirrah. Adel seemed pleased with my decision. I would have informed Masaru also but I could see Sirrah was already talkin to him, so I approached the guard by the gate with my bow and quiver held in my hands.

"Excuse me," I addressed him, "do you confiscate them for good or is it possible to pick them up on the way out of Taiyou?"

The guard looked surprised by the question. "You're not intending to stay in Taiyou?"

I abruptly remembered I was supposed to be a refugee and that someone seeking sanctuary in Taiyou was not likely to leave it once they had found it. "Well, I just got here. I have no idea what I'll find beyond those gates," I answered, sticking to the truth as much as I could. "If Taiyou's not what I'm looking for, then I might try somewhere else."

The man smiled pleasantly and I was thankful he hadn't turned suspicious after my slight blunder. "I'm sure you'll find Taiyou to your liking. Roughlanders that come here seem very happy, but if you want I can take your name down, so once you are settled in you can see about getting your possessions back. We only take them at the gate as a security measure."

I nodded, understanding the city's sensible precaution. "My name is Yukari. I'm with Lady Sirrah's group."

The guards accepted the bow and quiver from me and did likewise with everyone else's weapons, excluding those named as Sirrah's personal guards. They searched some of the Roughlanders, namely Razor and his gang, but curiously Stephen managed to slip under their radar as he proffered no weapons and perhaps they thought he was a child due to his lack of height.

The city guards of Taiyou who escorted us from the gate to the Roughlander Sanctioned Outpost were courteous, if not forthcoming. The outpost itself looked like others of its kind, except in miniature and made from grey stone. It was a total of three floors in height and was surrounded by a wooden fence, of all things. It had been a while since I had seen wood in such a quantity and the sight of the fence abruptly struck me as a waste of a good resource – I had been among the Roughlanders too long.

The wooden fence had an entrance gate manned by yet another city guard. I looked around before we were admitted into the compound and I realized I had not yet seen a single citizen of the city that wasn't in a guard uniform. There were buildings in the area and we still were not far from the main gate of the city, but they appeared to be mainly storehouses, not homes or businesses, which also struck me as odd. I didn't have much time to ponder this, however, as in short order our group was ushered into the compound, then the wooden gate was shut and barred behind us.

The Roughlanders of the Sanctioned Outpost were friendly and easygoing. They didn't have the natural caution and suspicion of outsiders I had gotten used to seeing, and even though we had been shut up in here with them, they welcomed us with open arms.

"Who is the leader of this outpost?" I asked a Roughlander who introduced himself to me.

"Tathos?" the burly man responded amiably. "Oh, she's the best leader this outpost has ever had. You'll like her, she's real smart."

"Thank you. Do you know where I might find her?"

"Oh, I'm sure she's about somewhere, you'll find her soon enough," he continued, his tone pleasant and disarming. "It's not like you're going anywhere, right?"

"Right," I responded dubiously, but I didn't want to press, so I left the man alone. "Thanks again."

"No problem, anytime."

The group of us that had arrived together soon disbanded and we were mingling with the Roughlanders of this strange outpost. By far the oddest thing about the place I discovered while wandering about the compound was that instead of sand there was grass beneath my feet on spongy ground, and there were trees and flowers aplenty filling in the backyard of the small outpost building. Most astounding was the fountain located in the center of the compound. It was round and ornate, and it gave off familiar splashing noises that indicated a plentiful source of water. I had seen the lake on the way in, but in my time on this world I had grown used to the absence of water, so seeing it again was a wonderful thing.

I approached the side of the fountain and watched the water for a moment with a slight smile on my face. "May I?" I asked a nearby Roughlander, uncertain of the custom here and if the fountain was just decorative or a general water source.

"Of course!" the Roughlander woman answered cheerily. "The water's for everyone."

The woman filled a bucket with water and went on her way. I lingered over the fountain for a moment longer and washed my face free of the dirt Razor and Aysel had decorated me with, and I took off the ridiculous headscarf. My hair was so disgusting and frizzy I couldn't even run my fingers through it – I would have loved a full bath, but I didn't think that was a luxury even the Roughlanders here could afford. My canteen was still relatively full from the lake of Taiyou, so I drank from that and didn't bother filling it, as I continued my tour of the grounds and my search for Tathos.

The compound was not large and there were fewer Roughlanders here than I would have expected, since Taiyou was spread about to be such a sanctuary, but I supposed the Rubian encampment must discourage most of the would-be settlers from making the journey here.

Hotaru had joined me by the time I was successfully directed to Tathos, and together we came across the outpost leader sleeping peacefully under a tree. Her hair was, if anything, a rarer colour than mine, being that it was lavender and fell well past her shoulders. She appeared young for her position and perhaps it was just that she was sleeping, but she also had an air of innocence about her.

She wore clean clothes of dark brown leather in the Roughlander style, with gratuitous belts and buckles. Her back was against the tree and her legs outstretched in front of her. On her lap there was a ferret, the first animal I had seen on this world that was recognizable to me.

Unlike Tathos, the ferret was awake and staring at Hotaru and I balefully. It reared up on its back legs and let out a warning hiss. The sound startled Tathos awake and she stretched her arms wide with a yawn before opening her eyes. As she did so, the ferret disappeared in a wisp of greenish smoke.

I started in surprise – had I imagined the creature? I looked to Hotaru for confirmation and sure enough her expression was as confused as my own. There were other people in the area, walking by, sitting, and socializing, but none of them seemed to have noticed this odd phenomenon.

"Hello," Tathos greeted us pleasantly as if she didn't have a care in the world. I supposed living there, perhaps she didn't.

"Tathos, is it?" I inquired.

"Yes, that's me," she replied simply, regarding me with an expression of happy expectation.

"My name is Yukari Namikoya and this is Hotaru Hatsumuya," I introduced us. "Is there somewhere here we may speak with you privately?"

"Of course," Tathos agreed with a friendly smile, but made no move to stand. "You may speak freely. There's no one here but us, the trees, and the people."

"Right…" I commented, narrowing my eyes.

I wasn't sure if this Tathos person was trying to be funny or serious. It was certainly possible in an open community like this they would have a no-secrets policy or something similar. Tathos waited expectantly for us to begin, her eyes wide open and seemingly guileless.

"We are the Chosen of Sapphiros," Hotaru said quietly so as not to draw everyone's attention.

"Really?" Tathos asked with enthusiasm. "Nice to meet you. I'm Tathos."

I quirked a brow in confusion – hadn't we already introduced ourselves? In fact, I distinctly remember addressing her by her name as we approached.

"Yes, Tathos…" I shook my head to clear it in order to focus on the task at hand. "We were told you are the leader of this outpost."

"Yes, I am," she confirmed, "and you are very welcome to make yourselves at home. We have everything we could want here. Have you seen the catalogs?"

I was momentarily distracted by this line of questioning. "No we haven't, but–"

"Oh, well, you should go and look at them right away. They're wonderful." She stood up, still smiling. "I can show you."

"That's not why we came, Tathos."

She pouted for a moment, as if what I had said upset her, before her face settled back into that same vacantly happy expression. I was beginning to get the impression that perhaps Tathos wasn't as intelligent as the Roughlander I had asked about her had led me to believe.

Tathos' eyes lit upon my face again as if seeing me for the first time. "Hello, I'm Tathos," she stated, her vacant smile now giving me pause. Something certainly was amiss here and I was starting to come to the conclusion that it was Tathos' mind.

"Nice to meet you, Tathos," Hotaru responded politely with a sympathetic smile in her direction.

The conversation, such as it was, continued for a little while in much the same fashion as Hotaru tried her best to string together what Tathos had to say, which wasn't much. I gave up on the endeavor much more quickly, having ascertained that Tathos – whatever was actually wrong with her – was not the competent outpost leader I had expected to find.

Unfortunately, that meant this outpost and the role it played was clearly not what the Roughlanders thought it was. Dahlia, and later Razor, had given me the impression that it was from there the Sanctioned Output that Taiyou interacted with the Roughlanders, and the trade of supplies, and potentially information as well, originated. Apparently, that wasn't the case.

I wandered back toward the entrance of the compound and knocked on the gate. A slit in the door opened and I could see a pair of eyes on the other side for a moment before they moved out of view.

"Excuse me," I addressed the guard stationed outside. "I was hoping to take a walk, or maybe visit the marketplace?"

"There's no need to do that," the guard answered. "If there's anything you need, I'm sure you can find it in the catalogs and it will be delivered to you."

Uh huh, it was just as I thought. The Taiyoun guards were polite, but this was a prison. The Roughlanders weren't allowed in the city at all, and now we were trapped in here with them. I looked around at the wooden fence and then at the people it kept within, wondering briefly if none of them had ever tried to escape. Surely I wasn't the first person to be alarmed at the idea of being kept like a caged animal.

By the look of the Roughlanders, they were all happy. There were a fair amount of people present, but the outpost wasn't crowded. The grass and trees were a wonderful sight to behold, and I was sure that went doubly for the Roughlanders who had grown up in the barren wastelands that existed outside of Taiyou. There was wood in abundance, and that meant furniture more comfortable than the metal chairs we had seen elsewhere. I could even see a few people whittling or working on some other hobby. Then, of course, there was the fountain, a constant source of nearby water. Perhaps it wasn't so strange the Roughlanders were simply glad to be here where it was safe and life was easy.

It all made sense, logically, but it still did not sit right with me. The Roughlanders I had seen and known since coming to this world were a hardy people, who prided themselves on their ability to survive in harsh conditions and thrive despite them. It didn't seem likely every Roughlander that came here would appreciate the trap they found themselves in, comfortable or not. Freedom was a word I was sure the Roughlanders believed very strongly in, or they would have given into the Vile Emperor's dominion long ago.

I found Adel without much trouble and Masaru was nearby, so I gathered them both to me.

"Have either of you noticed the strangeness of this place?" I asked without preamble, speaking quietly so as not to alarm anyone.

"The people here are a bunch of idiots," Adel stated bluntly. "I can't get a useful answer out of the lot of them."

"That's exactly what I mean," I stated. "I'm not sure what's causing it, but the people here seem too complacent. They are kept here by no more than a wooden fence and one guard." I looked to Masaru. "How many Roughlanders do you know would put up with being kept like this?"

"Not many," he answered. "It's nice and all, but this place makes my skin crawl." Masaru looked around at the people and trees uneasily. "And there's too much green."

"All right, well, we need to figure out what's going on here. There's something we're not getting," I informed them. "I want you both to ask around. Talk to people, find out what they know, how long they've been here, and how they feel about the place. If you come across any of the others we came in with, get them to do the same. We'll meet up here," I said, looking up at the sun to see where it stood in the sky to find it was shortly before a bounce, "just after the bounce."

I introduced myself to as many people as I came across. All were friendly, maybe too much so, and all praised Tathos as being the greatest mind the outpost had to offer. I had to force myself to smile so much at their inanities my face began to hurt.

"And you've never been out into the city?" I asked the same Roughlander I had originally talked to about Tathos.

"Nope," he replied, "don't need to. Everything I could want is in the catalogs."

I got similar answers out of most of the people I talked to; they were beginning to sound like a broken record. What I did establish, however, was the longer someone had been here the less coherent they sounded. Ones that claimed to have been here for a few weeks, say, or less than a year, seemed only apathetic or maybe content with their lot, whereas those who claimed to have lived here for a sizeable length of time – or in some cases couldn't remember how long they'd lived here – were in awe of these catalogs, Tathos, and had trouble remembering the simple things, like occasionally their own names. All this research served to make me more worried there was something seriously wrong in the outpost, and my belief that we should not stay there more than we had to grew ever stronger.

To further my research, and because I had by now heard so much about them, I had to investigate these catalogs everyone kept mentioning. My search led me to the middle floor of the three-storey outpost building, where I found Razor flipping through a magazine with a fruity-looking red drink in his hand, complete with a cherry and a little umbrella decoration.

A pretty young Roughlander girl with a flop of brown hair and a particularly vapid expression was explaining the use of the catalogs to Razor. I could see behind them on the far wall there was a pile of similar-looking magazines, and next to that was a serving table filled with plates of food and goblets of water.

"And you just pick which ones you want and then you get them…only bigger…" This girl was about the worst I had seen yet, other than maybe Tathos herself. She was in complete awe and wonder over the catalog ordering system, which I had gathered was run by the city to keep the Roughlanders supplied with food and anything else they wanted.

170

We had to get out of here; this place wasn't what I had been hoping for and dallying here in this penned-in enclosure was not going to help us get any closer to an alliance with Taiyou, or even in gathering Roughlanders to our cause.

I noticed Aysel in a corner of the room with a plate of food in front of her as she nibbled on a bit of cheese. I headed over to her to tell her about the meeting place and time, in case she hadn't been informed yet, but before I got to her Adel stormed into the room.

"Aysel, there you are!" Adel exclaimed, going over to her sister. "I've been looking all over for you. I thought I told you to stay with me?"

"I just wanted something to eat," Aysel responded, "and there are these catalogs here where you can order anything you want."

My hackles rose as Aysel spoke. She wasn't nearly as vacant as some of the Roughlanders I had talked to, but her words had a striking similarity to the disease that infected this whole place.

"We have to get out of here," I said, getting closer to Adel, "before this place starts to get to us too. Razor," I called over to him, "I need to speak with you."

"What is it Yukari?" Razor asked, getting up and coming over to our side of the room.

"Do you and your men have access to anything explosive?" I asked him, as strange of a request as it may sound.

He smiled lopsidedly. "Yeah, sure. What do you need?"

"I need the group of you to take up positions at separate points along the fence and bring the fence down at my signal. We're getting out of here."

"Okay," Razor responded, taking a sip of his drink, "but why would you want to leave?" He added after a moment, the awareness in his eyes seeming to fade, "They've got everything here."

I stared from Razor to his drink and back at him again, then something clicked. "The food…" I breathed aloud in realization, but the thought continued unbidden.

The food or the water; either one could be poisoned with something to keep the Roughlanders complacent and under control. My unease at this place solidified immediately into a dark shadow of suspicion about the nature of the city of Taiyou.

Adel was looking at her sister worriedly. "Come on, Aysel," she said, taking her by her armoured arm and tugging her to her feet.

"Okay," Aysel responded, agreeably. "Can I have some more cheese, though? It's quite good, you should try some."

"No," Adel responded, "and you will not have any more either. We're leaving – now."

Aysel protested, but Adel was the stronger of the two and forced her sisterout the door. As the two of them left and I made to follow, Masaru walked into the common room with a goblet of water held in his hands. I watched in horror as he lifted the cup to his lips for a drink.

"Masaru, no!" I called out, alarmed his free will would start to fade like Aysel's and Razor's already had. Without conscious thought, I dove forward and knocked the cup out of his hands. It clattered to the ground, spilling its contents all over the floor.

"Why'd you do that for?" he demanded, his eyes wide in startlement.

"Whatever you do, don't eat or drink anything here," I ordered him. "I'll find us a way out of here, even if I have to do it myself."

I stalked out of the outpost to find Hotaru and meet the others as we had planned. A quick look to the sky informed me it was about the time I had indicated to everyone. I found Hotaru looking concerned and Adel – still with a death grip on Aysel – explaining the situation to her sister.

"I have a plan to get us out of here," I informed them as I reached their side. "I don't know how many of us have already been affected, but for any who have, there will be no convincing them to come with us."

"Aysel is coming," Lady Adel stated forcefully.

"Yes," I agreed, "but we can't force everyone. It would be too difficult to control them all if they are like her." Aysel was already struggling and tugging to be free of her sister's grasp, in an effort to return to the outpost.

"I just want to look at the catalogs before we go," Aysel said, her tone almost a whine. "Can't I?"

"We'll wait here a few moments and see who else comes. They know about the meeting, right?" I looked to the sky to check the sun; it was past the time I had set.

According to Adel and Hotaru, they had spoken to nearly everyone from our group, though Sabien had apparently never joined us, either at the entrance to Taiyou or here in the outpost. I was concerned by his absence, but I had too much trouble of my own to worry about what might have delayed his rendezvous with us.

Several tense minutes passed and Aysel's distress increased, but no other person of our group joined us, not even Masaru or Razor.

"We have to go," I repeated. "We'll come back for them when we figure this out. Hotaru, I need a distraction."

Hotaru nodded with determination, but I could see the obvious worry on her face. She knew leaving was the right answer, but none of us felt at ease about abandoning those we had brought with us.

Not long after I had asked Hotaru for a distraction, the strangest thing occurred, which I supposed qualified it for a suitable distraction – it began to snow. White flakes drifted slowly down from a cloudless sky; there were only a few at first, but within minutes there was quite a thick flow of them. In no time at all, the sight of the abnormal occurrence mesmerized the near mindless Roughlanders.

I silently thanked Hotaru for her ingenuity as I took a deep breath and drew my power together into an arrow between my hands. I closed my eyes to better focus, as this was going to take everything I had to accomplish. I visualized four support beams of the fence I had noted on my earlier walk around the compound and then, working quickly, I summoned four arrows and charged them with as much power as I could invest in them before I let them loose. There was not a shred of doubt in my mind that I wouldn't strike exactly where I intended, and I opened my eyes to the sound of four explosions going off at once in four different directions.

The wooden fence fell.

We were the only ones who ran, but the rest of the Roughlanders suddenly milling about in the confusion were enough to distract the solitary guard and anyone else who may have been watching. The four of us ducked into the nearest alley and reached for the door of the first storehouse we came across – thankfully, it was unlocked.

The storehouse was also thankfully unoccupied. The ground level was filled with crates, with the exception of the wall that had one window. Going up the stairs, we discovered a single room with a small bed and a few belongings that looked abandoned.

I pulled out a pencil and some folded up paper from my belt pouch, and with Hotaru's help I plotted what we had been able to see of the area around the outpost, so we would have a map of sorts to be able to find our way back here in case we got lost.

All the commotion, or perhaps the struggling, seemed to have tired Aysel out. She didn't look well and soon she was sagging weakly in Adel's grip.

Having completed what I could of the map, I watched Aysel with a concerned expression. "She should probably lie down," I recommended. "She may be going through some kind of withdrawal from whatever they put in the food or water."

Speaking the words aloud gave me an idea, and I stood abruptly.

"I have to go back," I stated. "Stay here. I promise I won't allow myself to be affected, but I have to get a sample of the poison – or whatever it is – if we're to have any hope of discovering how to fix this, or even just to have it as proof of what is happening to the Roughlanders in there."

"Go and come back quickly," Hotaru agreed. "We should be okay here for a little while to let Aysel rest."

Asking Adel's permission, I took Aysel's water skin with me to collect my water sample, and I let myself back out onto the street. There was no one in sight, but I looked around and waited to be sure. I had never done what I intended to before, but after seeing Sabien travel around in his water form I thought it might be possible for me to do the same as mist.

I centred myself as Sabien had taught me, and I felt myself lighten and become less substantial. Then I let go of the control I had over my form and I hoped for the best.

The wind picked me up immediately. I could still see everything around me, but I couldn't feel my own form. I drifted on the wind, feeling slightly dizzy and light-headed, but thankfully the wind took me in the vague direction of the outpost, which wasn't far. I tried not to dwell on the strangeness of my own circumstance, but instead I focused my will on learning to control this new aspect of my power, directing myself along the wind currents to where I needed to go.

It wasn't as easy as moving with the wind, but I managed to angle myself to drift to the place I knew would have both food and water – the common room on the second floor of the outpost building.

Oddly, Masaru was the only one there when I willed myself to come together and reform in front of him. I was more than slightly relieved when I reformed easily and, other than a surreal sense of dislocation, I didn't feel any parts of me were amiss.

"Yukari?" Masaru was dumbfounded by my sudden appearance, or maybe it was just the contamination talking.

With a deep sense of regret at abandoning Masaru to this fate, I tried to make myself ignore his presence and do what I came here to do. I reached for the hunk of cheese off of the plate Aysel had been working on, thinking it was best to get it from the same source that had infected her.

"I thought ye said…not to eat anything?" Masaru said from behind me and I whirled about to face him.

He looked troubled, like he was working very hard to remember what I had said to him. He shook his head in an attempt to clear it.

"You remember?" I asked him, feeling a sudden glimmer of hope – maybe he hadn't been as badly infected as I had feared.

"Remember what?" he asked, the blankness in his eyes returning.

I sighed in regret, and with a pained feeling in my chest, I turned my back on him again to pour two goblets of contaminated water into Aysel's water skin.

"You said…no drinking, either…"

I whirled around once more, and I saw in his expression that he was clearly doing everything in his power to overcome whatever was affecting him, and struggling to let his own will resurface.

"Masaru?" I said his name, trying to will him to succeed. If I could get him to snap out of this, maybe it wasn't too late to try and take him with me back to the others.

I took a few steps towards him, putting the cheese in my belt pouch and pulling out the map Hotaru and I had pieced together. It wasn't a good map by any means, but it had the storehouse we were hiding in clearly marked on it, and the route we had taken to get there.

"Masaru, look at me," I commanded him, locking my eyes with his. "Gather as many of us as you can and meet me here." I pushed the map into his hand and closed his fist around it. "I'll wait there for you."

I was loathe to leave him here like this, knowing as soon as I drifted back out that window he would probably succumb to the will of the place and be lost again. He was on the verge of coming out of it; I could tell I almost had him. I wracked my brain for something I could do that might be enough to startle him out of it completely.

Without a conscious decision having been made, I did the most shocking thing I could think of – I leaned in and kissed him.

I had been aiming for shock value, but I got a little more than that. His lips were warm and pleasantly soft, and the kiss lingered a little longer than it probably should have. I had never kissed anyone before, and though I had done it out of necessity; I felt something more pass between us in that moment.

As the kiss broke, I saw past Masaru and into the doorway of the common room. Razor was standing there, drink still in hand, a look of surprise and hurt on his face.

I felt my face flush, and I wanted nothing more than to be away from there, where no one could see me. I got my wish; my power manifested itself on my behalf and in less than a breath I was drifting away on the wind out the open window, leaving Razor and Masaru behind – a crumpled, hand-drawn map still held tightly in Masaru's hand.

Chapter 8 – Boiling Point

Aysel's condition worsened and there was no sign of Masaru, Sabien, or anyone else. I had hoped perhaps that her system just needed to crash from withdrawal before she began to recover, but as time wore on, she showed no signs of improving.

As it turned out, the area of town we found ourselves in was not as unpopulated as we had originally thought. We watched through the upstairs window as citizens of Taiyou went about their daily business, and we worried at any time the owner of this particular storehouse, or some employee, might come in and find us.

I hadn't been able to ascertain anything as of yet about the samples of food and water I had taken from the outpost and we were running out of uncontaminated food. The storehouse we had holed up in was full of food, but being so close to the outpost we couldn't be certain if it was free of contaminants. As for water, Hotaru could apparently create or summon it using her power, which was a welcome gift.

When we started seeing city guards making rounds in the area – presumably to gather any escaped Roughlanders, though we couldn't be sure – Adel, Hotaru, and I had to make the hard decision to move on and leave the chance of the others joining us behind.

There were various pieces of discarded clothing in the room we had hidden in and we shared them between ourselves. Hotaru and I pulled off our gratuitous belts and stored them in sacks, which we could carry, and pulled presumably Taiyoun-style shirts over our Roughlander ones. Adel and Aysel did not look like Roughlanders in any case, so aside from a cloak for Aysel, they went without disguise.

"We have no choice," I stated. "We'll have to see if we can meet up with Kaji and Yue."

We had walked what felt like the length of the city before we stopped at a bench in a quiet area to rest a little. Taiyou was beautiful and well populated; we had done our best to stick to streets less filled with people, but even still we noted the city was in good repair and the citizens cared for it. It was clean, there were areas filled with trees and grass, and the people were happy – and not in a vacant, infected by the Sanctioned Outpost's water supply kind of way.

"Ris is with them. She should be able to fix Aysel," Hotaru stated optimistically.

"Or Jeth," Adel added. "He knows a thing or two about poisons."

I looked over at Aysel, whose head was in her sister's lap as she slept, which she had been doing more and more of, coming in and out of consciousness and never being more alert than a dazed state. I hoped it wasn't a poison, for on an alien world there was no way of knowing the antidote, but if Jeth or Ris had even a chance of fixing it, then we had to try and reach them.

We walked until we were drooping with exhaustion, but had come far enough away from the city that we hoped we wouldn't encounter anyone. The countryside we found ourselves in was covered in healthy green grass and sparsely treed. We had been following a cobblestone road headed northward, but now we headed over to a copse of trees to make camp.

As Adel put her sister down, I inspected Aysel immediately. She had a fever and she was conscious, but unresponsive. She was also sweating profusely, even though Taiyou was so much cooler than the desert we had gotten used to. I gave her some water from my canteen and it dribbled over her lips. I pried open her right eyelid with my fingertips and noted her pupils were wide. She also didn't seem to register the motion of my hand as I waved it in her line of sight.

"Do you know what you are doing?" Adel asked, concerned.

"I don't know enough about what is wrong with her," I admitted reluctantly, "but I promise you, Adel, I will do my best to bring her through this. Hotaru, can I have some more water so I can try and bring her temperature down?"

Adel did one better than that; she repeated her strange trick of creating a double of herself made of snow, which served to leave behind clumps of the frozen water once she destroyed it.

I shook my head at the strangeness, but did not question the providence of having such gifted individuals around to make such things possible. After soaking a cloth in the melting snow and applying it to Aysel's forehead, I got her to suck on a piece of ice while I sent Hotaru and Adel to look for firewood. Adel was reluctant to leave her sister's side, but she could clearly see Aysel was not going anywhere, so she complied.

They were gone for some time, which gave me a chance to think without Hotaru's constant chatter or Adel's hovering to distract me. Something about Aysel's glazed eyes gave me pause. I thought back to the people at the Roughlander sanctioned outpost; it had been in their tones and their stares where I had first realized something was wrong.

Now Aysel was suffering from some sort of withdrawal from the substance. I had some of the tainted water and cheese with me, but I was reluctant to give it to her in case she was able to pull out of this on her own, and this was just the process her body had to undergo before she could burn off whatever was affecting her.

I lifted Aysel's eyelid again to get a better look at it and see what had originally caught my attention. I studied her pupil for a moment before I became aware that there was a faint tinge of green on the eye itself. I suppose I had rationalized it away until now by assuming it was a reflection of all the green in the landscape around us.

I focused on the anomaly and my eyes adjusted like they did when I was trying to shoot an arrow at something impossibly far away. Suddenly, I could see into Aysel's eye as if I had a magnifying glass, or better yet, a microscope.

Green – tiny, crystalline-shaped molecules danced along the surface of Aysel's eye and were busy replicating themselves to make a film over her vision. Occasionally one would degrade and dissipate, but the others replicated fast enough to take their place and then some.

I blinked and came out of it to find myself an inch or so away from Aysel's face, startled by this new application of my growing powers. Now I knew what they looked like, the particles of this particular substance, and how they spread so quickly, having a near immediate effect on the host's body.

I dug through the mostly empty pack of supplies and drew out an empty glass jar that used to contain an unsavoury pickled vegetable we had already consumed as our rations dwindled. I rinsed out the jar with the help of Adel's snow, and when it was as sanitized as I could make it I poured a sample of the contaminated water from the Sanctioned Outpost.

Lifting it to the light of the ever-present sun, I repeated the process of focusing my vision. I wanted to see the particles before they had a chance to infect someone. Sure enough, they were present, but not replicating nearly as quickly, nor moving as fast.

I pulled the cheese out of my belt pouch to try the same thing, but it was a wasted effort; the cheese was too dense for me to see more than its pitted surface. If it was also contaminated, there was no way to tell.

I tried adding uncontaminated water to the sample and was pleased to find I could dilute the substance so the green in it was less potent. Perhaps weaning Aysel off of the substance slowly might help to rid her body of its dependence. She had certainly wanted more of the food and water back at the outpost, which indicated it may be some sort of addiction. Thinking I would get the best of both worlds and try to cool her off at the same time, I added snow to the jar and checked it one last time to see how that affected it.

The movement and division of the particles slowed down immediately, until they looked like they were struggling against being frozen themselves. Cold helped! The realization struck me immediately – I could slow the rate of infection if I could get Aysel's temperature down.

Hotaru and Adel returned then, with firewood in their arms.

"Adel, we have to bring Aysel's temperature down," I informed her. "It seems cold slows the progress of what's happening to her."

Adel and Hotaru set to cooling Aysel down with the piles of snow, while I built up a fire some distance from Aysel for the rest of us. According to Adel, once the cold snow had taken effect, Aysel settled into a more relaxed looking state, and eventually a deep sleep. I assured her that was probably a good sign, though I wasn't certain that was true.

As we sat around the fire, roasting a small animal Adel and Hotaru had managed to catch, a question occurred to me. "Adel, Hotaru," I broke the silence suddenly, "while we were at the Sanctioned Outpost, did either of you eat or drink anything?"

Hotaru shook her head no, but Adel's answer was the opposite. "I had some water almost immediately after our arrival. Someone handed both Aysel and I a glass, and after all the time we have spent traipsing through the desert, I thought it pointless to refuse."

I quirked a brow at her. "But you seem to be fine, whereas Aysel…" I mulled over the thought for a moment, but no way I spun it made any sense. "If you both drank from the same source, you should both be infected, unless you are immune in some way. Would you mind if I checked something, Adel?"

"If it will help Aysel, you may check whatever you wish," Adel responded.

I looked into Adel's eyes as I had done with Aysel, and for good measure, I checked Hotaru's too. Hotaru had green eyes naturally, but I could see no little particles moving on or in them. Adel, on the other hand, had some of the miniature green crystals, but they were being destroyed slightly faster than they were replicating.

Blinking to come back to regular vision, I looked at Adel questioningly. "What would be different between you and your twin sister that would allow you to fight this off, but her to suffer from it?"

"I am a Knight and was given power. Aysel was not," Adel answered promptly, but with a twinge of bitterness in her tone. "She was not found worthy of the gift, and so she is still in training."

Adel's explanation made sense; Adel's powers could be what allowed her to combat the substance in her body. I had no explanation for the effects of magic, but when everything else about

Adel and Aysel was the same down to their DNA and the manner in which they were infected, something had to explain the phenomenon I was witnessing. Hotaru and I had powers too, but I wasn't willing to test the substance on either of us.

Having reasoned through this as much as I could, I decided to finish off my tests as the other two settled down to sleep. Adel said she would relieve me after she had rested, and I nodded my acceptance of her plan of us taking watch so no one came upon us unawares.

I had one more test I could perform, considering the rudimentary tools I was operating with – what I wouldn't have given to be back in the Shinjuku High science lab with proper equipment! I took my sample jar, and with the use of a forked stick I suspended it over the flames of our campfire.

I left it there, focused in, and watched to see what heat would do. The particles replicated rapidly, picking up speed the hotter they got. It wasn't long before all I could see was a roiling green. I blinked and stared at the jar in horror. The water inside of it – if it could be called that anymore – had hit its boiling point and was visibly green now, even to a casual observer.

The human body – no matter now cold we made Aysel – still had a minimum internal temperature. These things would continue to replicate and spread; even freezing them wouldn't destroy them, it could only slow or maybe stop their progress.

I looked over to where Aysel lay motionless. There was blood leaking slowly from her nose and even from here I could see her skin was clammy and colourless. Her condition was still worsening and I was certain that if we didn't find her help soon, it was only a matter of time before this disease, or whatever it was, killed her.

Maybe if Aysel had been a Knight, this wouldn't have happened, but she didn't have any power of Sapphiros, and neither did Masaru, Razor, or any of the others we had left behind.

The most horrific epiphany struck me at that very moment. I had left Masaru with instructions to stop eating or drinking, and to leave the Sanctioned Outpost to follow me. If he had, by now he would be like Aysel, the disease spreading rapidly in his body, and with no one to slow its progress or treat him for it. I had ordered Masaru to his death and condemned anyone he might have tried to take with him.

I had an awful vision of Masaru, pale and sweaty like Aysel, stumbling along in the city of Taiyou with the crumpled map I had left him in his hand and blood leaking slowly from his nose. His eyes were green and unseeing as he took his last breath, falling limply to the cobblestones.

It was very hard to live with myself after that.

We tried feeding Aysel the diluted contaminated water and keeping her temperature down, but she did not seem to improve at all as Adel carried her and we walked still northward until the next bounce.

Tormented by my realization and the nightmares that had plagued me when I had taken my turn to rest, I was not much company, but we were so very lucky Yue – flash-stepping ahead of the rest of her group – found us and led Kaji and the others to us.

I was somewhat relieved to see Sabien was with them, but silent Ris immediately took charge with the help of a pair of strange-looking cloaked Croatin healers Kaji and Yue had apparently picked up at the Croatin outpost they had visited. There wasn't time for reunion stories, and at the time I wasn't interested, but I was sure there was much to tell.

I somewhat mechanically filled Ris in on what I had been able to discover about the disease and how Aysel had become infected. The fact that the others we had brought with us would now be in the same boat I left unsaid, as I couldn't face speaking it aloud.

With my duty done, I let Ris and the other two strangers work, and I watched them from a little ways away. Amidst all the confusion and concern over Aysel and over the group of us being reunited, no one noticed we had been spotted until it was too late.

A group of knights, armoured differently from the ones I had seen in the city, came over to investigate what the commotion was about. They wore white armour like the Taiyoun knights had, but these seemed more regal. They were decorated with a lion motif and carried shields carved with a lion head design.

There were only two among their group of about twenty or so that were unhelmeted. One, I presumed, was their leader, and the other looked to be an advisor of some sort, or perhaps a priest. The former appeared young for his position – he was maybe a year or two older than the four of us from Shinjuku – but he carried himself with poise and authority. His hair was a startling white, but it helped him to appear just as regal as the lion head on the pommel of his sword hilt and the platoon of knights in tight formation behind him. The latter wore black robes in stark contrast to the white of the other men's armour, and his head was completely bald. In fact, by paying more attention to him I noticed he had not a single visible hair on him, not even eyebrows or eyelashes.

"I am Sir Rama," their leader spoke and I was surprised to realize he was addressing himself to me, but then I understood I was simply the closest one to him. "Is there anything amiss here?"

I saw no reason not to be honest. We were far enough away from the Sanctioned Outpost that no one would link us to it and with the entire group of us together I did not think twenty knights could force us to go anywhere we did not wish to – not that I was looking for a confrontation.

"One of us has fallen ill," I explained. "I am a medic of sorts, but as of yet nothing I have tried has been much use."

"We have some of the best medics in Taiyou back at the keep," Rama replied. "Do you know if the illness is catching?"

"She's not contagious. The disease is transmitted through liquid," I responded.

"Would you mind if I had a look at her?" One of the knights stepped forward, removing his helmet as he did so. I could see he had a leather pack strapped to his chest with a lion head badge on it. "I'm a medic."

A second, or even third, opinion could not hurt, and I was somewhat curious to see if the Taiyoun medics knew of what ailed the Sanctioned Outpost. If they did, perhaps they might have a way to cure it.

Rama, the bald man, and the medic came away from the other knights and accompanied me to where Ris was looking very frustrated and upset. Aysel's condition had not changed and she was still unconscious. As the newcomers approached, the Croatins wisely backed up and hid their frog-like faces in the cowls of their black cloaks.

I waved Ris back; I wasn't sure how these Taiyouns were going to react to her kind, since apparently they didn't like Croatins, but Rama and the other two didn't even give her a backwards glance.

The medic took off his leather pouch and began removing things from it. I leaned forward curiously to watch and no one protested – but I supposed, after all, this was my patient. He pulled out a few strange looking instruments, some of which I could identify their use, and others I could not.

The first was a tube device with a little glass lens at the end that magnified light; he used this to quickly check Aysel's eyes. After doing so, he gave a startled expression before gesturing for me to look as well. I had already seen what there was to see in Aysel's eyes, but I humoured the medic since I had no way to explain how I had examined her so thoroughly without the tools to do so.

It was almost a relief to watch the man go through the motions I had not seen since that day Hotaru and I had spent camped out in the hospital, which I had to remind myself hadn't exactly happened. With the strange devices he had, he seemed to check Aysel's temperature, test a sample of her saliva, and monitor her breathing, heartbeat, and blood pressure. After all this, he pulled out little sanitized wipes to clean all of his tools and the gloves he had put on, before taking them off again. I found myself staring longingly at the sanitary wipes and the gloves, not to mention the little vials and tongs I could see poking out of his medicine kit.

"You don't have access to proper tools, do you?" Rama asked from beside me. In my preoccupation with the medic I had entirely forgotten his presence.

I shook my head. "I had to leave them behind," I answered, mostly truthfully – he didn't need to know I was referring to another planet's science lab.

"If you will not bring your friend to the keep," Rama continued, "we can at least leave you this," he said, indicating the medical kit. "And if there is anything else we can do to help, you need only ask."

I looked down at the medical kit again and my heart soared – Rama and the medic likely had no trouble reading my expression. The feeling lasted only a moment before I remembered the dire state we were in and how I still had no idea how to save Aysel, let alone Masaru and the others.

"Have you encountered this before?" I asked the medic, indicating Aysel.

"There's something familiar about it, but I'll have to monitor her a bit more before I can be sure," the medic responded.

"We shall stay here for a bit, then," Rama agreed. "I see someone I should like to speak with also."

Rama and his bald-headed companion left Aysel's side, heading over to speak to Kaji, of all people. Ris returned to Aysel's side to watch the medic work and I was left with my newly acquired medic kit in my hands, minus the few things the Taiyoun medic had said he might need to treat Aysel.

I saw Jeth over by a large tree in the distance and I remembered what Adel had said about him being the person to talk to about poisons. With a shrug, I headed over to him – anything was worth a try, though Jeth didn't strike me as being particularly knowledgeable about anything.

"Adel told me you might be the person to ask about the contaminated water."

"Yeah," Jeth answered with a pained expression, "she talked to me. I'm working on it."

I sat down cross-legged before him and fully opened my medic kit to see what it contained while I waited to see if there was anything Jeth could tell me. The first thing I recognized I was very pleased to see. There was a collapsible Bunsen burner and a handful of empty vials. There were also some vials that were full; one contained a flesh-coloured paste, another a purple syrupy liquid, and one held a vibrant pink powder. I had no clue as to the purpose of any of them. There was also the sturdy pair of gloves, a packet of sanitary wipes, a nice set of surgical scissors, a suture kit, and tongs of a few different sizes, not to mention the expected bandages, gauze, and et cetera.

By the time Jeth spoke, I had my Bunsen burner set up and was setting out samples of the infected water in various vials to test everything I could think of against the little green crystalline particles.

"You said they were crystals, right?"

I looked up at Jeth sharply, surprised he was still there and wondering just how much Adel had explained to him. Then I realized I had been muttering under my breath in my preoccupation.

"Yes, little green ones. They replicate faster when heated, slower when cooled," I explained my findings. "I'm not sure how concentrated they are elsewhere in her body, but they seem to be attacking her eyes."

"Have you tried a saline substance?" Jeth asked and I met his stare blankly. "You know, like salt."

"I know what it is, but what gives you that idea?" I asked.

"Just might break 'em down, that's all," Jeth answered somewhat cryptically.

Unless one of these unidentified vials contained salt, I didn't have access to any…except maybe my own sweat. Not the most sanitary test, but I could still see if it worked before I ignored Jeth's advice completely. I cleaned my hands before I started rubbing them together. The heat of the day, combined with the heat coming off the Bunsen burner, was enough to get a small sample of sweat. I dripped it into the last vial, then added some of the diseased water and zoomed in to watch the reaction.

It worked; I couldn't believe my eyes, but I watched as the salt from my hands broke down the crystal particles. With the Bunsen burner's heat on, the particles were replicating at about the same rate, so neither side was winning, but it was definitely more headway than I had made yet.

I tested the other substances from my medical kit with mixed results, none of which were at all promising; one even sped the contamination process up.

"Jeth, I need more salt," I told him. "It seems to be working."

Jeth smiled at me. "There you go, girl, I knew you'd figure it out."

I gave him an odd expression, but I couldn't help being pleased the solution was now possibly within my grasp. "Jeth, please, get everyone to run around or something. I need sweat if I can't have salt." A realization struck me then – we had not had any salt in our diet since our arrival on this planet, was salt rare on this world? "Jeth, make sure to get Kaji, Yue, and Hotaru's sweat in particular. They're more likely to have what I need."

"Ew," Jeth commented, "whatever you say, Yukari."

I shut off the Bunsen burner and then I was off, running toward Rama.

"You can help me," I announced as I reached his side. He had been preparing to leave, but stopped as I reached him. "I need salt, as much of it as you can provide."

He smiled at my odd request, but did not question it. "You shall have it."

We worked out the logistics of where he could drop off my request before Rama and his knights were on their way.

No one got much rest during our stay in the field as I had them running about and training to work up as much sweat as possible, which I then collected in the shoulder piece of Sabien's armour, the largest container I could find.

"You need salt water?" Kaji asked me once everyone had gotten started with their exercise.

"Yes," I answered him, "it seems to be the only thing that works, but I think maybe those of us from Earth are more likely to have a higher salt content."

"Would this help, do you think?" Kaji asked and suddenly a double of him appeared at his side.

I stared at it in mild shock; it looked exactly like Kaji, except it was less animated and had no pupils in its eyes.

"Is it like Adel's? Does it turn into snow?"

"I didn't know Adel could make clones of herself," Kaji remarked. "But no, it does better than that…if it's actually my water making them."

I was confused by what Kaji was trying to show me, but I did as he asked and placed Sabien's armour piece below his still motionless clone. Then Kaji punched his double as hard as he could in the face.

The double splashed into water like Sabien could, but it didn't reform or move; it just filled the container before it. I was thoroughly disturbed, but if it had the salt content I needed, I wasn't going to turn down what Kaji and his creepy clones had to offer.

"I'll boil it down and see what I get. I may need you to do that again a few more times if it works," I told Kaji. "It doesn't hurt, does it?"

"No, not at all," Kaji replied, smiling with a hint of pride. "I'll go back to exercising in case it wasn't what you needed."

Building another fire, I distilled, and hopefully cleansed, the gathered salt-water to use it to treat Aysel. The clones, though not high in salt content, were salt-water, and we did discover that it was a much faster way to collect more water, as disturbing as it was to watch Kaji destroy copies of himself.

We kept Aysel cool, feeding her the salt water at intervals, and every time we did I checked her eyes with my uncanny ability. No one seemed to question that I knew exactly what I was doing, since I so effectively took charge of Aysel's healing. Even Ris, whose healing magic was having no effect, left me to my own devices.

The only other test I ran was trying extremely diluted salt water dropped into Aysel's eye. I didn't want to run the risk of blinding her, so I made sure to drop the solution as close to the edge of her eye as possible, but I needed to see how effective the salt was when applied directly. I watched as the particles exploded in Aysel's eye and were replaced much more slowly than before. As dangerous as this method was, I decided to keep it in mind in case it became necessary.

After the next bounce, Rama returned with the promised salt and in addition, a most welcome crate of medical supplies, including a couple of Flaqqers. When we all finally settled down to rest, Kaji and the others told us about their adventures at the Croatin base and on the route into Taiyou. In return, Hotaru and I filled them in on the state of things at the Roughlander outpost and the existence of Lord Hex.

Kaji and Yue had apparently managed to convince – and I heard tell it was no simple matter – the First Spawn of the Croatins to commit his entire forces to fight against the Vile Emperor. Apparently a few Croatins chose to become Roughlanders or live elsewhere, but most of them stayed in their ancestral home, which was the base Kaji and Yue had visited.

We were introduced to Pine and Dudgi, the two Croatins Yue and Kaji had brought with them into Taiyou. The rest of the army was waiting behind at the base, much like ours was at Hex's outpost. Pine and Dudgi were like no Croatins I had yet encountered, and Yue informed us they were of the Second Spawn.

They were both brightly coloured – Pine neon green and Dudgi yellow – and they both had purple markings over their skin. They reminded me instantly of poisonous tree frogs and my suspicions were confirmed when Yue informed us it was deadly to touch them.

After the Croatin base, Kaji and Yue had moved on to an outpost located to the east of the border of Taiyou and had found it in ruins, with only a few survivors remaining. According to Yue, she had learned a power that allowed her to read the memories of a person, and she had learned a massive ribbon of destructive power had fired from somewhere within Taiyou, destroying the outpost along with everyone inside.

"And that's where I met Sir Rama for the first time," Kaji informed us. "He doesn't like Croatins much, but a survivor had crossed into his lands to request aid, so he brought his troops over to provide it."

Continuing on northwards, the group of them met up with Sabien, who had crossed the lake of Taiyou in his water form, and from there they had crossed the border to make their way down to meet us.

"Did Dahlia make it to you in time?" Kaji asked as we were taking our turn telling what had happened to us on the way here.

"Dahlia?" I questioned. "No, we haven't seen her…I didn't even realize… why isn't she with you?"

Kaji abruptly looked worried. "We learned from the Croatins that there were Deathsquads in your path and Dahlia took some of her Roughlanders back across the Sand Lake to warn you. She figured with you walking and her crew mounted, she should be able to warn you in time. I didn't want her to go…I knew it wasn't safe, but she insisted."

"Maybe she's back at the Sanctioned Outpost. She could have arrived after we left," Hotaru suggested.

It was possible Dahlia could have been behind us, or maybe even ahead – we had stopped at Hex's outpost for a few bounces. Had she followed us, she might have been at Hex's outpost with the rest of the people we had left there, or she might have been at the Sanctioned Outpost. I didn't want to consider what else might have happened to Dahlia, especially with the danger I had left Masaru in.

Aysel did seem to be improving, but it was a slow process. On the way back towards Taiyou she came around enough to be able to drink some water on her own, though she coughed and sputtered at the salty taste. She was still dazed, and her eyes mostly unseeing, but all of us were glad at her progress.

We decided not to all enter the city in a large cluster, so we did not draw as much attention to our group's odd appearance. Hotaru, Kaji and I, along with the invisible – thanks to Ris' abilities – Ris and the Croatins, were one group, while Adel stayed with her sister and the others to show them the way to the Sanctioned Outpost.

Hotaru and I led our group back to that storehouse where I had directed Masaru. I had to know if he had followed and what had happened to him, and it seemed Hotaru felt the same way.

Upon our arrival we found the storehouse door was locked. Hotaru, having learned a thing or two from Sabien herself, melted into a puddle and slithered beneath the door to open it for us from the inside.

My heart thudded in my chest, dreading and hoping simultaneously at what I might find. I stepped past Hotaru into the main room and my heart leapt up into my throat as I saw what awaited me.

There was a body on the floor before me, partially hidden by the staircase. It was a Roughlander by his clothes, but it wasn't Masaru. I didn't know this man personally, but it was one of the men from Sirrah's outpost we had brought with us. His corpse was clammy-looking and colourless, and there was a pool of sticky blood on the floor where he lay, which had come out of his nose and mouth.

I averted my gaze and ran up the stairs past him – my nightmares were coming true.

The room at the top of the stairs looked lived in, which was not the way we had left them. The sheets were rumpled, the pillows from the bed had been tossed about to make sleeping areas on the floor, and there were also the remains of a meal in the center of the room. My eyes, however, were riveted to the sight of the black-bladed knife Masaru had picked up in the Temple of Sapphire to replace the one he had lost. It was jutting out of the wall and holding up a crumpled piece of paper, which had been smoothed out.

There was no mistaking who had left this message; the back of the page even had my badly drawn map on it. With a sinking feeling, I pried the knife out of the wall, holding the note in my other hand.

Yukari,

I had to focus a little to make the characters legible. With my glasses it would have been effortless, but my new power was just as good. The letter wasn't written in Japanese and it took me a moment to figure it out. The characters were reminiscent of English, which I knew, so though it took me a little longer, I puzzled out the letter Masaru had left for me in a shaky hand.

I did as you asked me to. The six of us have been waiting here for the past few days, but one by one we've all grown weaker. The man who owns this storehouse, Marc, has been a friend and allowed us to stay here, giving us food and water, but there is only so much he can do without the city guard becoming aware we've escaped from the outpost.

Hennin died today. None of us are doing very well, but we know now we have to move on and hope we can still meet up with you. I believe you would have headed north, so that's where I'm going.

And Yukari…my memories from the outpost are a little fuzzy, but there's something I'd like to talk to you about.

Masaru.

I was crying by the time I deciphered the rest of the message and I could feel the roughness of the knife hilt I was gripping a little too tightly.

"Yukari?"

I looked up with a hopeful expression, but it was only Kaji, coming upstairs to look for me. He noticed the tears on my face and the knife in my hands, and his expression softened into one of concern.

"I have to go," I whispered. "Go back with the others and take the supplies to the Sanctioned Outpost. I'll meet you there."

"You don't need any help?" Kaji asked.

I shook my head. "No. I'll find him."

With the knife and letter in my hand, I abruptly turned myself to mist and floated out the open window, leaving Kaji to stare after me.

Unfortunately, the wind was moving southward, back toward the Sanctioned Outpost, so I wasn't able to go much faster as mist than I could while walking. I floated a little ways before my patience ran out, so I lowered myself to the ground in an alleyway and reformed.

I put the knife and letter in my medic kit and headed generally northward, sticking to the uninhabited route we had followed on our way out of the city. I figured Masaru would have been just as cautious as we were, if not more so, in his Roughlancer clothes.

It was pure happenstance that I noticed a smear of blood and a handprint on the corner of a building as I entered yet another alleyway; there were drops of blood on the ground below it as well. Though I fervently hoped the blood did not belong to Masaru, my mind kept returning to my vision of him stumbling through the city of Taiyou with blood leaking from his nose, and the memory of poor dead Hennin back at the storehouse and the pool of blood beneath him.

I peered in through the window of the warehouse I found myself at and checked the door. It was locked, but there seemed to be no sign of the Roughlanders I was searching for, other than the mysterious bloody print on the corner.

I scanned the view ahead for more blood. Sure enough, I could see a few drops on the cobblestones ahead. I couldn't be sure they belonged to the people I sought, but what other explanation could there be?

I ran forward, and upon reaching the next few drops of blood, I repeated the process again of scanning ahead for more signs to see if they had been this way. I found a bloody scrap of cloth leading me still northward. I grew more panicked with each find until they abruptly stopped. I was still in a warehouse district of Taiyou and I hadn't seen any people in some time. The door of the building I found myself near was slightly ajar. I forced myself to breathe and turned with the strongest feeling of dread to enter the warehouse to see what awaited me.

I pushed the door open tentatively. It was relatively dark inside, and the crates in this warehouse were stacked in some places almost up to the roof. The windows inside were high up near the ceiling and dirty enough that the light was filtered.

I found my first Roughlander barely ten steps into the building. He was flopped over a crate and his face lay in a pool of his own blood. He was near death and I didn't know his name any more than I had known Hennin's when I found him. I gently lowered him to lie on the ground, and checked his pulse and eyes quickly. His heartbeat was sluggish, but present, and his eyes were far more glazed than Aysel's had ever been.

I drew the water skin from my belt, dribbled some salt water into the man's mouth, and then I dropped some into each of his eyes. I had no time to be more thorough than that, though. There were others there I needed to find and I hoped against all odds they would be in a better state than this man.

Leaving the man there to rest and for the salt water to begin to take effect, I headed deeper into the maze of crates, moving quickly, heedless of how the dark impeded my vision.

I almost tripped over the next Roughlander. A quick examination told me he was already dead, as were his two companions seated around the remains of a small fire. The scene before me was horrific, but there was still no sign of Masaru.

Did he leave after his friends had died? Was he strong enough to move on from there and keep searching for me?

I worriedly looked about the warehouse and I caught sight of yet another pool of blood. A beam of light from one of the windows illuminated where blood had dripped down the side of a tall stack of crates to pool on the floor below. I followed the trail upwards with my eyes until I saw a limp hand hanging over the edge of the highest crate.

Without a thought I turned to mist and floated up through the air toward him. He lay below a window, his body draped over two crates. There was just enough room for me to reform beside him, so I did, reaching for my water skin of salt water before I was fully solid.

"Masaru?" I whispered to him, panic rising, "I'm here – I came…"

I checked his pulse; he was still alive, but his heartbeat was faint – he didn't have long. I turned his head so I could give him a dose of the salt water and I immediately noticed his breathing wasn't any stronger than a shallow gurgle. His airways were clogged with blood. I tried to ignore the puddle he had been lying in, so like the others I had found who were already dead, and not thinking to reach for my gloves, I used my hands to clear some of the blood away to allow him to breathe.

While monitoring Masaru's pulse with one hand, I reached into my medic kit with the other and pulled out a square of gauze. I soaked the gauze in the salty liquid and put it in his mouth. I knew he wouldn't be strong enough to drink – he was so much worse than Aysel had been.

I couldn't move him like this; I was fairly certain he was weak enough that if I tried he would die. In any case, I wasn't strong enough to carry him easily or get him down from there. Soaking another piece of gauze, I dropped a few drops into each of his eyes, as I had done for the man below. I was just about to go back to re-soak the first piece of gauze when I heard footsteps in the warehouse and I froze.

Whoever it was – by the sound, it was only a single person – they had come in through the door I had inadvertently left open behind me. The person did not call out, nor did they slow their steady pace. I peered through the darkness and focused my vision to try and see back the way I had come.

From this vantage point, and with what little light there was in the warehouse coming from behind me, I was able to make out a figure of a man in a long coat as he came across the three dead Roughlanders I had left behind.

In the man's hand he held the neck of the first Roughlander I had found – the one I had tried to treat. He was dead now, his neck clearly broken, no doubt by the one who held him.

I gasped in recognition at the same second the man looked up and our eyes met – it was Fuzen, Talon of the Vile Emperor.

I remembered him well from that night at the park and the subsequent Tuesdays that had followed. On the Tuesdays that had not really happened, he had been the doctor assigned to Shuzhue's grandmother. The coat he wore now was similar in cut to the doctor one he had been wearing then, but this one was dark brown. He still had the sinister eye patch over his right eye and his hair was long, straight, and black. If he spoke, no doubt I would hear the mocking European accent I remembered from the hospital.

There was no time; I was certain this man was here to kill me and had undoubtedly hunted me down for that purpose. I couldn't even spare a glance for Masaru. It was my fault he was there like this, and if I died then I would never be able to make it up to him.

I had to try; I couldn't just let Fuzen stop me. I wouldn't go down without a fight, especially not if it meant abandoning Masaru again.

I raised my hands and summoned four arrows as Fuzen drew his sword, a Japanese-style katana. Practically no time had passed, but I could count the rapid beats of my heart in the space between the seconds. After selecting my targets, I loosed all four arrows at once.

One smashed through the window directly behind me, two others hit windows to either side, and only one went straight for

Fuzen. He parried it easily with his sword, as if it was nothing but a passing insect to him, but I had made the arrow I sent after Fuzen special. The deflected arrow continued into the stack of crates behind the Talon where it exploded forcefully, showering the warehouse with debris. At that exact moment, Fuzen leapt.

I watched him fly straight for me as my arrow had come for him. He leapt impossibly far and impossibly fast with his sword held before him, prepared to strike.

At that moment, with death coming for me, I was not afraid.

I had found something more important than fearing for my life. I knew with absolute certainty that I had to save Masaru and somehow it had to be within my power to do it. My grip tightened on Masaru's limp form and I willed the two of us away from here. I felt my body begin to lighten, but my grip on Masaru remained.

When the sword sliced through the space we occupied it struck nothing but air and water – the look of shock on Fuzen's face was something I would never forget.

Letting the wind take us, I soared out through the hole I had made in the window and I drifted up, high above Taiyou on the air. Fuzen could leap, yes, but I did not think even he could follow me up there.

Chapter 9 – I Dub Thee

I let the wind carry me southward and I didn't reform until I was back in the common room of the Roughlander Sanctioned Outpost. The table where the water and food had been left out for everyone to partake of the contaminant had been cleared. I reformed the two of us upon it, so I would not have to move him.

I choked back sobs as I climbed down from the table and with shaking hands I forced myself to examine him. Thankfully, travelling as mist had not made Masaru any worse for wear, but he was still dangerously weak. I felt a comforting hand rest on my shoulder and I tore myself away from the sight of Masaru to look up at Sabien.

"Is he going to be okay?" he asked, his voice deep and caring.

I struggled to regain control of myself. "I…I think so." I met Sabien's kind blue eyes and focused on them to steady myself. "He has a chance, now that he's got someone to treat him."

"I saw what you did for Aysel. He could do much worse than have you care for him," Sabien encouraged me. "His spirit is strong. He'll make it through this."

I nodded to his words, but I wasn't as convinced. It was going to be a long, hard fight for Masaru to come out of this, and with Fuzen searching the city for us – which he no doubt was now that I had escaped him – I didn't know if Masaru would have the time he needed to recover.

Sabien gave my shoulder a squeeze. "The others of your group are not back yet. Do you know why that might be?"

"I left them at the storehouse not far from here," I told him and Sabien frowned, but said nothing.

Aysel was brought upstairs and laid on a table across the room from Masaru, so I could more easily look after both of them. I repeated the salt water treatments for them and noted that Aysel was actually improving, which was heartening. With the uncontaminated water I had from my canteen, I cleaned the blood off of them the best I could. I made myself a schedule for Masaru's treatments based on what had worked for Aysel and what I thought he could handle, and by the time I had finished there was a commotion in the yard below.

I dared not leave Masaru and Aysel alone. It didn't seem likely Fuzen had found us so quickly – or that he would make much of a commotion about it if he had – but I had to know what was coming, so I leaned out the window I had been using as my way in and out of the building.

Just inside the gate in the courtyard below, I could see Ris, the Second Spawn Croatins, and my crates of medical supplies from Rama had arrived, but oddly Kaji and Hotaru were not with them. The commotion I had heard was the mindless Roughlanders' reaction to the sudden appearance of a bat creature and two strange Croatins.

I looked around the room with an anxious expression as Adel came in to check on Aysel.

"She's doing much better," I informed her. "I need her to drink some more salt water any time she wakes, even if just a little, and Masaru could probably use as much as he'll take every fifteen minutes or so. Do you think you could keep an eye on them for me while I instruct everyone else on what needs to be done?"

Adel nodded solemnly, taking the canteen of salt water from me.

I hurried downstairs past several infected Roughlanders and outside to where the Knights had gathered around the crates, keeping curious Roughlanders away from the 'new delivery'. I hoped they, and the city guard for that matter, thought the crates had been ordered from the catalogs.

I divided what uncontaminated water I could find – mostly from the canteens the Knights had carried into the outpost – into water skins I requisitioned from the curious Roughlanders around me. The infection made them agreeable if nothing else, so it was a simple matter to get them to drink the salt water I offered them.

"Here you go, Razor," I offered him a drink. "Try some."

Razor amiably switched the glass in his hand for the proffered salt water, though he didn't know what I was handing him. He took a long drink and then made a face at the salty taste. "What is this stuff?"

"It's an acquired taste," I suggested. "Maybe you should share it with your friends." I gestured to the Roughlanders behind him and soon enough everyone wanted to try some of the new drink I had supplied.

Ris, Jeth, and Sabien helped me to see that the salt water was spread about, though until Hotaru returned, we would quickly run out of clean water to use. My concern at this point was checking the fountain to see what its level of contamination was and if it could be salvaged in any way. If I poured salt directly into the fountain, then maybe I could make sure everyone got the required dose and eliminate the infection once and for all.

Hefting a bag of salt onto my hip, I set off purposefully for the center of the compound.

The fountain gurgled innocently while Tathos sat on the edge of the pool, running her fingers absently through the water with a contented expression. As soon as I got within ten paces of the fountain, the mysterious ferret appeared in a wisp of green smoke. It met me stare for stare and when I went to take another step forward it hissed menacingly. Tathos seemed blissfully unaware of the vicious animal at her side, but I noticed Yue, sitting by a tree beyond the fountain, had locked eyes onto the creature.

I considered the ferret for a moment; it was evident to me that it could be no natural animal. For one thing, it was too expressive; the look from its eyes was too calculated, belying an almost human intelligence. Not to mention its method of simply appearing and disappearing where and when it wanted to. The greenish colour of the smoke was also telling; I had seen more than my share of green over the past few days and the shade was exactly the same as the virus in the water I had been studying.

The ferret was involved in this, though I couldn't say exactly how; instinct told me that at the molecular level the water in the fountain the ferret was guarding was as green as the grass surrounding it.

Faster than my eyes were able to follow, Yue was up from her place by the tree and leaping at the creature. She landed in the fountain, splashing herself and Tathos – who giggled at the sudden deluge – and reaching for the ferret with both arms. The ferret puffed into insubstantial green smoke with uncanny reaction time before Yue could even touch it.

I took my chance while the ferret was 'gone' to rush forward with my bag of salt.

"No, wait!" Yue said suddenly. "There's more to this."

I stopped less than five paces from the fountain. "There's a lot to this, Yue," I agreed, unable to keep the trace of bitterness from my tone, "but that water is killing people and taking their minds away. Salt works against it."

"What about the people who have been here for much longer?" Yue indicated Tathos beside her. "They might not survive without it now."

Seemingly on impulse, Yue grabbed the sides of Tathos' face. "What happened here, Tathos?" The question wasn't meant to be answered aloud, I understood that immediately. Yue held Tathos' face between her hands and shut her eyes, touching their foreheads together. "Tell me."

A moment later, she made a frustrated sound. "Ugh! I can't get past the fog of this place!" She scooped the slight Tathos into her arms and made as if to leap.

Just before she took off, the ferret reappeared in her line of sight. The mystical animal regarded Yue curiously, without the animosity it had shown me thus far.

Yue paused, staring down at the creature. "Will you let me see?"

After a moment of what looked like consideration on the ferret's part, it leaned toward Yue, as if offering her something. Yue put Tathos back down gently on the edge of the fountain before reaching her hand out to tentatively touch the ferret. Tathos displayed no sign of even noticing she had been moved. I wasn't sure what to make of this odd tableau, but I waited for it to play out, unsure whether or not I should interfere.

I felt more than saw Sabien, Jeth, and Ris come up behind me, drawn over by the scene at the fountain. The tableau lasted only a moment in any case, as Yue's eyes shut and the ferret disappeared with its usual flare.

"Yue?"

Her eyes opened wide, showing her pupils were covered in a visible green haze.

"I am King Taiyou." When Yue spoke it was with a deep male voice, completely unlike anything I could imagine coming out of her. I narrowed my eyes, feeling anger bubbling to the surface. I didn't know for what reason this ferret-king had possessed Yue, but if he meant her harm, or intended to keep her, I was more than prepared to throw my bag of salt into his face – if that would even work against him.

"Please," the King's voice continued in a monotone that sounded less a request and more a command, "stay your hand."

"Why should I?" I demanded of him, anger over the effects of this disease overrunning any sense of caution I had.

"I love her."

Yue? But no, it wasn't Yue he was speaking of. King Taiyou, through Yue's eyes, was looking at Tathos with reverence.

"Tathos?"

"Yes," King Taiyou answered in his inflectionless tone. "She was to be my wife, no matter how bitterly my brother hated we had found each other. She was a Roughlander, and I, the heir of the Taiyoun dynasty. My family knew of my love for her and in the end it was only my brother Narlhep who opposed our marriage. Narlhep took it upon himself to see I would never wed the one I loved. He was jealous of my position and my happiness. He wanted everything I had for himself, so he turned to Oujou magic and it consumed him."

I listened to King Taiyou's story with only half of my attention; the other half was busy trying to understand how it related to the current issue and keeping a careful eye on Yue's body, in case it showed any signs of strain from the ferret's occupation.

"On the day I came to propose to my queen, my brother followed me here in secret," King Taiyou continued. "He had prepared a curse he believed would rid him of the one person who had always stood in his way."

Yue's eyes lovingly drifted back down to Tathos, and it was hard not to believe in King Taiyou's sincerity. "She was so happy when I asked her. I wanted her to stay happy forever, but my brother had other plans.

"He stepped out of hiding and unleashed his magic on me. He killed me, but Tathos tried to save me. She shot him in the heart, but it was too late. The Oujou curse still linked the two of us together, and if an Oujou curse is to be ended it must be done in the proper way, or it will have disastrous consequences.

"The curse rebounded upon its maker, shattering him into a green mist. It was raining that day, and the rain caused the mist to settle on this land and into the water of this fountain. Tathos cried and cried and cried, but I was no more than mist myself then and she was alone, destined to live out her life in sadness.

"I have done what I can to save her from that destiny," King Taiyou concluded. "She lives on now, but she is happy and I am always here with her."

"But her mind...?" I whispered, horrified someone had put Tathos in her current state on purpose. "Would it not be better for her to grieve than to lose herself?"

"It is my will that keeps her alive," King Taiyou stated. "I took away the memories of her sadness and I will let nothing upset her ever again."

I could tell by the finality of that statement there would be no reasoning with the spirit of the dead king. For however long he had been there guarding and controlling Tathos' mind, he believed he was doing what was right and necessary, and was unlikely to change his view now.

"What about everyone else?" I demanded. "Surely you see you can't keep them all like this?"

"Without my influence, they would die," King Taiyou stated with certainty. "They have been affected by the curse, and like Tathos, it is only my will now that keeps them alive."

I swallowed hard, thinking about the state in which I had found Masaru and the other Roughlanders who had escaped. Aysel's near immediate symptoms of withdrawal made perfect sense now that I understood that leaving here was a death sentence for those affected.

"How can the curse be broken?" Sabien asked from behind me and I belatedly remembered his presence.

"An Oujou curse can only be ended by the blood of the one responsible for it. Since my brother is dead, one descended from his line would be needed."

"Narlhep is dead?" I questioned. "But Razor said the name of the current King was Narlhep."

"It may be possible the current king is a descendent of the murderer's line," Sabien suggested. "If all we have learned is accurate, that would have made Narlhep next in the line of succession. If his brother died, Narlhep's line may have taken the throne."

Meanwhile, Yue, standing on the edge of the fountain this entire time, was swaying somewhat and blinking to clear her vision. Without warning, her eyes rolled up into her head and she toppled. Before she could fall and injure herself, Jeth was there. "I gotcha, kiddo, you did good."

While I had perhaps more information as to the origins and nature of the problem, I still did not have a solution, nor more peace of mind. Masaru and Aysel were still in somewhat dire straits and the rest of the Roughlanders, though not in any immediate danger of dying, had still lost their minds and their identities to this awful place. A disease or a poison was something I could at least understand, but a magical curse was entirely new territory for me. I didn't like the implication that it was something by its nature I could not understand.

I contemplated Tathos – essentially patient zero – for a moment. Her condition and her circumstance unsettled me on a deeper level; I could not help but feel pity for her, even though she sat with the expression of the utmost contentment upon her face. The realization that someone else had arrived at the outpost startled me out of my contemplation. I spun about to find Hotaru and Kaji had returned.

There was also a new person with them I didn't recognize. He was dressed in what I had come to recognize as Taiyoun clothing – in this case a long tunic over comfortable looking linen pants – and was carrying a wooden chest in his arms, straining only a little under the weight of it. He appeared friendly enough, but it was strange to see a visibly Taiyoun citizen entering this den of Roughlanders.

Leaving Tathos to her own devices, I hurried over to see what had taken Hotaru and Kaji so long to return, and Sabien and Ris came with me.

"We got the cure!" Hotaru announced happily.

"You what?" I demanded, incredulous.

"Apparently Roughlanders who want out of the Sanctioned Outpost are allowed to leave if they join the City Guard," Kaji explained. "After they leave here they are taken to the infirmary where they are treated against the disease Aysel contracted." I didn't bother to correct him about the nature of the problem being a curse, not a disease. "Marc took us to the nearby barracks and we took a chest of the stuff."

"You mean you stole a chest of the stuff," the Taiyoun man corrected Kaji, his voice faintly accented in the Roughlander style, and I realized this must be Marc. The name abruptly struck a chord and I remembered Masaru had mentioned someone named Marc in his letter.

"You're the owner of the storehouse, right?" I asked Marc, who nodded. "I'm sorry if we've caused you any inconvenience...and I want to thank you for letting Masaru and the others stay with you for a time."

"You must be the blue-haired girl my daughter saw," Marc greeted me warmly. "I won't say it was no trouble at all, but I'm glad I could help. I was a Roughlander myself once and Masaru's a good fellow. Is he doing any better, do you know? I didn't realize it was the sickness affecting him, or I would've tried to get him the cure sooner. By the time I realized what was wrong with him, he and the others had left...with the exception of the one they left behind..." Marc added the last bit with regret in his tone. "I've made arrangements to have the body buried as if he was a relative of mine. I hope that's all right."

I nodded to indicate it was all right with me, but at the same time I was fighting my emotions over the reminder of what my orders had done to Masaru and the Roughlanders who had gone with him at my request. "He's..." I tried to reassure Marc that Masaru was going to be okay, but I couldn't get the words out when I wasn't sure they were true.

"Oh," Marc said, immediately abashed. "I'm sorry. Don't cry, please. He's still alive, though, isn't he? We're not too late with the cure?"

I nodded again, this time through my tears, "He's alive…"

I led Marc and the others upstairs to see Masaru, which also let me relieve Adel and check on my patients. I found Razor at the table with a glass of salt water in his hands and a resigned expression. "Why is it when something is supposed to be good for you, it tastes awful?"

"Razor!" I exclaimed, rushing forward to hug him gratefully, surprised and pleased by how like himself he sounded again. "You're okay?"

"Whoa, careful there," he said. "I'm still a little confused and I've got a killer headache." Letting go of his drink, Razor hugged me back. "Hey, are you okay?"

I hadn't realized it, but I was crying again, and relief over Razor's return to sanity wasn't exactly the reason. I pulled away from Razor and wiped the tears from my face. I really needed to pull myself together; there was a lot of work to be done. "I'm fine," I lied. "I'm just glad you're back."

I looked around the room. Aysel was awake and taking salt water from Adel, and I was relieved to see she was aware enough to make a face at the taste. Masaru, on the other hand, was most definitely still unconscious, though he was hard to make out through the crowd of well-wishers around his bedside.

"Don't crowd him, please," I requested as politely as possible. I knew they were only there to offer support for his recovery, but there was nothing worse than a crowded sickroom and Masaru was having enough trouble breathing already.

Hotaru was visibly upset at seeing Masaru so weak. "But we got the cure, so he'll be okay now, right?"

"What exactly is this 'cure' and how does it work?" I asked, looking to Kaji more than Hotaru for the answer.

Somewhat surprisingly, it was Marc who spoke. "I don't know what it's made of." He opened the chest as he spoke and handed me a vial of the stuff. It was a smoky grey colour I had never encountered before and it shimmered slightly in the light. "They gave it to me when I got out of this place. Of course, I wasn't as sick as Masaru at the time, but they gave it to me all the same. Seems they dose everyone who comes out of here.

"Stuff doesn't taste too bad, but it doesn't settle either. The body rejects it, I think," he explained. "It bubbles in your stomach and it's all you can do not to vomit, but they make you hold it in. After a few doses, you don't feel like you want to come back here anymore and you can remember who you are again."

"How many doses?" I asked, eyeing the viscous liquid in the glass tube with curiosity.

"Three, I think, but I don't remember too clearly. It was over a couple of days and it was a long time ago for me."

"Then we should have enough to dose almost the whole outpost," Kaji noted, counting the vials in the chest.

"You are not using that on Aysel unless you can prove to me it works safely," Adel stated forcefully. "Yukari's method is working and Aysel is recovering. Until you can say the same of your miracle cure, she'll have none of it."

"And neither will Masaru," I stated. "I don't think his body would be able to handle it like this, if it's as violent a process as you say."

"I'll try it," Razor offered, not moving from his seat at the table. "I'll try anything that'll save me from having to drink this crap."

"You're sure, Razor?" I asked him. "We don't know exactly what this will do to you."

"Bring it on," he stated boldly. "I'll be fine."

I opened the vial in my hand and stared at the stuff inside. Even peering into it with my special vision, it was hard to make out the nature of it. It seemed the shimmery part of it was solid, but the rest of it was the consistency of syrup. If Razor was going to try it, I had to know first if it was safe at all, so I dipped my pinky finger into the stuff and reluctantly touched it to my tongue.

It didn't taste bad – it tasted kind of like sand. It also had a coppery finish to it and a hint of salt. Blood? I questioned, eyeing the substance warily. King Taiyou had said the blood of Narlhep's line would be needed to end the Oujou curse. Was it perhaps possible the Taiyouns knew this fact and had used royal blood to manufacture a cure?

"I don't think it'll kill you," I said aloud to Razor, handing him the vial. "If you're willing to try it, go ahead."

He gave me a wink with his one eye and bravely downed the vial in one gulp. "Doesn't taste so bad–" he began before his body convulsed with violent shudders.

Sabien stepped up to hold him and Ris stoically held his mouth shut with a long, slender finger, until Razor sagged limply between them and the tremors stopped. I winced in sympathy, but it seemed Razor, though still looking a little green – figuratively speaking – was still awake and alert. Sabien and Ris helped him back into his chair.

"How are you feeling?" I asked him tentatively.

"Like I've been trampled by a mount," he answered a little waspishly, "but I can tell you if anyone offers me food or water or one of them goddamn catalogs right now, I'll punch them in the face."

I smiled a little despite myself; Razor was going to be fine.

"Anyone who's coming out of it because of the salt, ask them if they want to try the cure," I suggested. "And make sure no one goes near that fountain. Hotaru can make us all the clean water we need."

"Aysel will wait until you've had your third dose," Adel said to Razor, "if you make it that far."

Razor glared at Adel, who met him stare for stare. Satisfied he was recovering nicely and Adel would ensure Aysel's full recovery, I returned my attention to Masaru, who most certainly needed me more than anyone else did at the moment.

Hotaru settled herself into a chair by Masaru's side as I worked to get him to take in more of the salt water. He was nowhere near to coming around and his heartbeat was still faint. It was a struggle to put on a brave face for Hotaru, who would certainly worry much more if she knew I doubted Masaru's chances.

With Hotaru there, I didn't feel it was right for me to linger over Masaru's side. I tried to make myself useful, but with most people drinking the salt water on their own and the testing of the cure underway with those who showed interest, there wasn't much for me to do. I found myself downstairs on the main level contemplating Sabien as he stood talking to Jeth.

"Sir Sabien," I asked when he was finished and Jeth had wandered off to wherever Jeth went, "I know you've mentioned to us before you were dying when you became a Knight, but can you tell me what happened?"

I was referencing a passing comment Sabien had made to us during our stay at the Temple of Sapphire. At the time the comment had held no real meaning for me, but now in light of Masaru's circumstance, I was suddenly curious.

"Of course, Yukari," Sabien agreed amiably without a hint he knew why I might be asking.

"I had been struck through the heart with a blade," he said it easily, as if it really had been over eight hundred years ago in his memory. "Yuko Seig rescued me by my Knighting. She granted me the power of Sapphiros and as soon as she had done so, I turned immediately to water. It took me almost a full month to reform the first time, but when I finally did, there was no mark – it was like I had never been injured."

"So it's possible that making Masaru a Knight might save him?" I asked.

"What happens when a person is Knighted is different for everyone, but it's very possible, yes," he answered. "Remember, though, I was knighted by Yuko Seig, who was only a priestess of Sapphiros. As I understand it, a Knight made by a Chosen is a different matter altogether."

"Different, how?"

"You four have a much stronger connection to Sapphiros. Your power is without limit. I would assume a Knight made by one of you would be stronger than any of us save Ris, who was Knighted by Sapphiros himself while he was in mortal form."

"Sapphiros was mortal?" I questioned, trying to keep up.

"Yes. Sapphiros, alone, of the gem gods, wanted to experience a mortal existence. He died shortly after you all were born, after he had designated you as his Chosen, of course. I didn't know him personally. Only Ris, of the Knights still living, did."

I nodded, trying to absorb all of this information for pondering over later.

"So if I wanted to make him a Knight, then, how does it work?" I asked Sabien, returning the conversation to my original intention.

"If you are certain of your choice, I can show you how it is to be done, but the rest of it is between you and Sapphiros," he answered. "But Yukari, before you decide I feel I should tell you I have seen a darkness in Masaru's heart. In all other respects I agree he has the qualities needed to be a Knight of Sapphiros, but that darkness worries me."

"I know," I responded, thinking back to the time I had seen Masaru in his rage over seeing Razor had joined us, "but I have seen him control it and I know if anyone deserves to be one of you, it's him."

Sabien nodded with a sudden smile. "In that case I would be glad to have Masaru join our ranks. It would be wonderful to have another Knight to train."

Sabien made me recite the passage he dictated until I could do it word-perfect without his prompting, before the two of us headed upstairs to the common room. Upon seeing Masaru again, I had no doubt what I was trying to do was the right answer. He looked much the same, and even if he could heal naturally I knew deep down he would never get the chance to do so. Every time we had found a place we thought we were safe enough to rest and let our guard down, we had been found by some danger or some agent of the Vile Emperor. Fuzen was after us now and our trail could easily lead him to Marc's storehouse. From there it wasn't much of a logical leap to where we had come from and had returned to. If I wanted to save Masaru and repair the damage I had done it had to be now, and there was no better way than to share the power I had been given.

"Hotaru, can I have a moment alone with him, please?" I asked a little awkwardly, approaching Masaru's bedside where Hotaru still sat, her head down.

When she looked up, she had tears in her eyes and tear stains down her cheeks. "I'm not leaving him like this."

Her refusal abruptly angered me, but at the same time I felt sympathy for Hotaru. She didn't know how important my request was, or that I was so close to being able to bring Masaru back to health if it could be done. I sighed and opened my mouth with reluctance to try and explain myself to Hotaru – always a frustrating experience – when Sabien stopped me.

"It doesn't matter, Yukari. She can stay. Just concentrate like I told you."

I did as I was told, closing my eyes and trying to ignore Hotaru's presence. It was surprisingly easy; I had gotten used to

Sabien's meditation methods, and had grown adept at focusing my will and my power to whatever task was set before me.

"*Sapphiros*," I began as Sabien had instructed me:
My friend and father
My patron and my benefactor
I lift up Masaru towards you
I seek to give my gift of your blessing
To this man
To assist in keeping balance
Hear me, Sapphiros."

Sabien's beliefs in Sapphiros were not my own – his life had been saved by Sapphiros' power and mine had been thrown into turmoil – but I spoke the words he taught me with as much conviction as I could muster, because I fervently desired for this process to work and I was very much aware of Masaru's life hanging in the balance. In addition to the words, I was told I needed to visualize something dear to me in an offer to Sapphiros, so in my mind's eye I was standing on the highest diving board at Shinjuku High's swimming pool. It was my favourite place in the world – well, in my world – high up above the water below and free of any restraints.

That was how I had thought to picture it, anyway, but in my vision it was different – Masaru was with me.

I held Masaru's unconscious form aloft, like I was offering him to the heavens. Light beamed in through the expansive windows and reflected off the smooth surface of the water below.

As if the light had been some sort of signal, I dove with Masaru still in my arms. As we fell through the air, coming closer and closer to the water's surface, Masaru's eyes opened slowly and he took in the view around him with wonder.

I prepared myself for contact with the water below – I would keep Masaru safe and see us through the water's surface – but we never made contact. I felt myself lifted up just enough to barely skim the surface of the pool. My reflection showed glowing blue feathered wings flowing from my back and propelling the two of us safely above the water below.

The vision faded and I opened my eyes to Sabien's softly spoken instruction, "Dub him your Knight."

I took two uncertain steps toward Masaru, who was still lying as he had been on the table-turned-bed. I wanted to offer him something, some token that was both gift and apology for what I had done to him, and the presumption I had made in making him my Knight. For however it was a gift, I also knew it would likely prove to be a responsibility – one I had not asked him if he even wanted.

"I have nothing else to offer you," I whispered, conscious of Hotaru practically at my side and the rest of the audience in the room, including Sabien and Adel.

Throwing caution to the winds, I leaned down and kissed my new Knight softly on the lips, heedless of the opinions of those around me and thankful Masaru was still unconscious. As I stepped back, I watched Masaru's eyes flutter open. I felt my face heat, but Hotaru stepped in between the two of us before Masaru could see my reaction.

"I dub thee, Friend of Sapphiros," Hotaru announced, using her power to summon a sword made of ice and tapping the confused Masaru once on each shoulder before stepping back.

My embarrassed expression abruptly changed to one of confusion as I stared at Hotaru. It came back to me suddenly that I had heard another voice repeating the words Sabien had taught me as I was saying them. I had been too lost in the concentration necessary for the ritual, so I hadn't realized what that had meant – she had Knighted him too.

A bitterness welled up in me as I watched Hotaru hug Masaru, grateful he was awake and looking much like his old self again. A part of me wanted so badly to join them in the celebration and hug Masaru myself, crying with happiness that I had saved him, but with Hotaru there I couldn't. I took a deep breath to steady myself, and with all the control I could muster, I walked away from the happy scene.

"Is that *Fuzen*?"

Kaji was peering out a window-sized opening in the outpost wall near the top of the stairs headed to the second floor. I ran to his side, my fear spiking at the name, and adjusted my vision to see further than Kaji could have managed.

"I don't see anyone," I told Kaji, speaking softly, so I would not betray how I felt.

"He's gone now, but there was a flash of power on the top of that roof there," Kaji pointed to a rooftop in the distance.

"Power?" I questioned.

"Yes," he replied. "I can see it now. You know, our powers and magic in general. It…glows."

I understood immediately what he meant; he had developed some sort of vision power like I had, only his was much different in application. I was immediately ashamed I had not told the others sooner, but there had been so much on my mind since we had returned to the Sanctioned Outpost. "Kaji, I had a run-in with Fuzen earlier."

"What?"

"He found me in the city where I found Masaru," I told him, still speaking cautiously, lest the tears start again. "He was there to kill me and he tried, but I turned the two of us to mist and floated out a window."

Kaji smiled suddenly, likely imagining the scene as more of a successful escape than a desperate attempt to flee. "I bet that made him mad."

I nodded. "But that's just the problem. Kaji, what if he tracks us and comes here?"

"If he comes I guarantee he'll get more than he bargained for," Kaji replied resolutely. "All four of us are here and all of the Knights. I heard he's the only one of the Talons who's allowed into Taiyou. The others are kept out somehow – even the Vile Emperor."

"I hope you're right about our odds, Kaji," I told him. "I better let Sabien know what to expect, so at the very least we can be ready for him."

If Sabien was overly alarmed at my news he didn't show it. In fact, he seemed just as proud of my escape as Kaji had been. However, Sabien did take my warning with the gravity it deserved, and he had Adel and Jeth set up defenses at both entrances to the outpost building.

Secure in the knowledge the Knights were well prepared to deal with whatever came our way and that someone would wake me if I was needed, I climbed up to the top floor of the outpost, to where there were a multitude of cots set up for sleeping. The long day – however many bounces it had actually been since I had last slept – and the various events that had taken place, including the flight from Fuzen and the Knighting, had completely exhausted me. Thankfully, I fell into a peaceful and dreamless sleep.

When I woke, the sun was high in the sky as usual, but it was a new day. Sabien gathered the four of us together to tell us what he knew of the Oujou and their curses. "The Oujou, in my day, were a tribe of sorceresses and shapeshifters from the swamps of Taiyou. When I first heard the name I recognized it, but it took me a little while to link it with what I remembered.

"The Oujou came to the Temple of Sapphire once. They only sent one of their tribe and unfortunately for us, we underestimated the threat, which no doubt was their intention. The Oujou walked right up to the temple in the dead of winter wearing nothing more than was necessary for modesty's sake and barely that.

"She demanded entry into the temple and she was apparently looking for the Chosen. When we denied her, she attacked us. She reached a Knight named Lorne first. He screamed at her very touch and fell writhing to the ground.

"The Knights all fought valiantly, and in the end she was driven back and forced to retreat. She never came back, but those men and women she touched didn't live through the week. It was the most horrific thing and there was nothing we could do to stop it, or even to alleviate their pain. Their skin just melted off until only their bones remained."

"That is horrific," Marc agreed, entering the outpost past Jeth's guarded door and coming up behind Sabien. "Do you always tell such disturbing stories?"

"Only when they are true," Sabien replied seriously. "I hope you four think on this if you intend on concerning yourselves with the Oujou."

"Well, I'm sorry to interrupt," Marc said, putting down a crate he had carried in. "I just thought I would stop by and see how everyone was making out. I also brought over some Taiyoun-style clothing in case some of you wanted to get out and see the city. I wouldn't want you to be stopped by the guard because you looked like Roughlanders."

"That's going to have to stop soon," I noted, "especially now that most of the Roughlanders are getting their minds back. They're not going to be content just to stay here as prisoners."

"I suppose you'd have to take that up with the Regent," Marc said with a shrug.

"The Regent?" Kaji asked. "Who's in power now and how would we go about meeting with that person?"

Marc looked a little taken aback by the seriousness of Kaji's request. "Lord Viron is Regent until Prince Narlhep comes of age in a few months and takes the throne," he answered. "You want a meeting with Lord Viron?"

"Yes, we would," Kaji confirmed.

"Pardon my saying so, but why would the Regent want to talk to you?" Marc questioned. "Not just anybody can walk into the palace and demand to speak with whomever they like, especially not now."

"Because they are the Chosen of Sapphiros," Sabien explained. "They've come a long way for an alliance with Taiyou."

Marc looked at the four of us again as if seeing us for the first time. "The pact with Yuko Seig wasn't a myth, then, was it?"

"No, it wasn't," Sabien confirmed.

"Would you know how we'd be able to get a meeting with Lord Viron?" Kaji asked again, now that Marc knew who he was dealing with.

He hesitated a moment. "I have some connections with the city guard still, from when I was one of them. I'll pass the word along and see what I can do, but I'll have to tell them who you are. It's likely the only way Viron would agree to a meeting."

"We've got nothing to hide," I stated with a look to Kaji, who smiled slightly.

"Okay…well, I'll do that then," Marc finished, seeming a little overwhelmed. "Enjoy the clothes. If you need anything else, I'm just down the street." He turned to leave, but then stopped and faced us all once again. "Listen…I'm a Roughlander – at least I used to be. I'll help you in any way I can, because I've come to like all of you and Masaru as well, but please don't ask me to fight. I have a daughter and she's all I care about in this world. I don't want to leave her without a father."

"You have our word," Kaji promised easily.

"And if you ever need somewhere safe to go, you can come here," Hotaru added.

Marc smiled at Hotaru's words and the feeling behind them, but he clearly had no intention of accepting the offer. "I'd rather not have to come back to this place," he admitted. "I hated it here – that's why I joined the guard."

We all had to laugh at that. Like most Roughlanders, Marc had a certain charm about him and a relaxed way of looking at the world. I abruptly recalled Masaru's first words upon waking up after he was Knighted and suddenly aware of himself and his surroundings again: "Ugh, not this awful place again!" I smiled, remembering it, though at the time I hadn't wanted to listen. Masaru was back, the Roughlanders we had brought with us were recovering well, and the four of us were united again, so I had reasons to be joyful.

I had yet to speak to Masaru and to apologize for my actions, but now at least I would get the chance. As for Taiyou, we had made progress today; things were changing there because of us. We were beginning to have an effect on the world around us, and hopefully that would soon include an alliance with the only known nation to repel the Vile Emperor for the past eight hundred years.

It was a lot to hope for, but it was no worse than the hand we had been dealt upon our arrival here. In some ways it was better – at least we had that small hope now.

Chapter 10 – Field Trip A.K.A the Dog Part of the Story

Sabien took the task of training Masaru with the utmost seriousness. From bounce to bounce, he pushed Masaru to the limit in order to prove he was a capable fighter both with and without his newly developing powers.

"What do you fear, Masaru?" Sabien asked, as the two of them faced off on the ground floor of the outpost building, weapons held at the ready.

Sabien had his signature sword, but Masaru was fighting with two glowing blue curved knives made from pure energy, much like my arrows were. As strange as it was to see Masaru wield power like we now did, it also seemed right somehow. The blades came easily to his hands when he summoned them, which was impressive considering how much effort it had taken me to draw those first few arrows.

"Well right now I fear you with that big sword," Masaru quipped, trying to sound more energetic than he obviously felt. "Mostly because I know ye intend to use it."

Sabien didn't prove him wrong, but I hardly thought Masaru was being honest or forthcoming about whatever it was he feared. There was no way Sabien was going to let up on him until he did – and maybe not even then.

I had mostly avoided Masaru over the past couple of days. He was almost always training with Sabien, being healed by Ris, or surrounded by others who were curious or congratulatory about his change in status, and I felt awkward around him due to all that hung between us.

I spent most of my time thinking over everything that had happened and what it all meant. It was certainly time for me to catch up to current events. I had done my best to work out how long we had been here, and over the last month and a half or so, it had been one danger to the next without much chance to absorb it all.

I had come to the conclusion I had to be honest with myself; my feelings toward Masaru weren't as confused as I wanted to pretend they were. In that moment when I had realized how important his life was to me, there was no shying away from the truth anymore – I was in love with him. The problem was, I had no idea what to do about it.

Earlier, as the sun rose from its bounce, I had read and re-read Masaru's letter to me. I was now certain I would be able to read the alien script perfectly, should I come across it again. He had concluded the weighty note by saying we needed to talk, and there was no doubt about that, but I was uncertain how much I should tell him. Of course, I now knew how I felt about him, but there was no guarantee he would return my affection or welcome it. I had never once felt this way towards anyone, nor had I believed I would ever fall for someone – especially not this drastically or quickly.

Regardless, I knew I couldn't avoid him forever, so I resolved to face my fears and approach him, see what it was he wanted to talk to me about, and answer him as truthfully as I could. Giving him that much was the least I could do for him. Truth be told, I wanted to see him again, and not just to watch Sabien train him into the ground.

Masaru was panting with the effort of keeping Sabien's blade at bay with his knives. Masaru was holding his own, but it was obvious, even to me who had little knowledge of combat, save archery, that Sabien was the better fighter.

"Remember your fear, Masaru," Sabien instructed and pressed his advantage, driving Masaru back a few steps.

Masaru, quick-witted and sure-footed, dropped suddenly and rolled through the bigger man's legs, emerging on the other side of Sabien and hoping to catch him off guard. They had been training for days now, and it was obvious Masaru was slowing down and Sabien was quickly learning his student's strengths and tactics.

Sabien spun in time to catch Masaru's outstretched knife with his sword, but then Masaru did something I gather Sabien wasn't expecting. He threw the knife he had purposefully kept back with his other hand.

The knife, once loosened from Masaru's hold, didn't disappear as one might expect, but surged forward to strike Sabien around the middle, bending to wrap around its target like a band of energy more than a blade. Sabien was pushed back by the force of the throw and struck the wall behind him, the band of energy remarkably pinning him there.

Masaru wasted no time and leapt forward to place his first knife to Sabien's throat, to make clear who the victor of this match was. As he landed, I began walking forward, thinking I would use this pause between matches to try and get a moment to speak with him. It seemed like I would get no better opportunity, as Sabien wasn't likely to let up and give Masaru any free time.

Masaru caught the motion out of the corner of his eye and turned his head to look in my direction. Sabien – whose arms had been left free – used this moment of distraction to act, driving his sword blade through Masaru's shoulder and out the other side.

I gaped in horror at having to watch it, but being unable to act.

"Remember distraction, Masaru," Sabien said coldly, his gaze locked on his target. "Ris, heal him."

Ris flew over as commanded and immediately covered Masaru in her blue healing field as soon as Sabien had removed his sword in a smooth motion. Sabien walked away to pick up his towel and wipe his face. I took a deep breath to steady myself and walked purposefully in his direction.

"Sabien," I addressed him coldly and without his title, as I was unable to fully reign in my anger after what I had just witnessed. "I know Masaru's training is important, but may I request a few moments to speak to him?"

"You have fifteen minutes from the time he is healed," Sabien responded in a tone even colder than my own. For some reason, he also seemed angry.

I nodded in agreement to his terms and he walked away. With another deep breath, I headed over to where Masaru was being healed by Ris, and I sat myself cross-legged before him on the floor.

All too soon Ris was done and Masaru opened his eyes, absently rubbing his wrist, which he also seemed to have twisted, but Ris hadn't healed. We were face to face and I had asked for this opportunity, so I had to take it.

His expression was puzzled as I met his eyes, outwardly calm, but with my heart fluttering. I reached into my medic kit and pulled out Masaru's knife that he had left behind for me to find at Marc's storehouse, holding it out flat before me in offering.

"You said you wanted to talk to me?" I asked, still meeting his eyes and exercising control over my voice to keep it steady.

"Aye," Masaru responded, studying my face.

"Was it about anything in particular?" I pressed, trying to have him initiate the conversation I wasn't certain I was ready to have.

"Aye…" he began, even more hesitant than before. "It's just that…I was wondering…well, why exactly did ye kiss me?"

The first thought to float through my head was a question: *the first or the second time?* But I didn't dare speak it aloud.

I felt my face heat suddenly at being put on the spot, my control over my expression and voice wavering with embarrassment. "I…well…I wanted to save you." I blushed furiously at even coming so close to the truth of the matter. "I needed to snap you out of it – the water…"

"Oh," he commented, perhaps a little surprised and maybe even disappointed by my answer, though I hardly knew what it was he had been expecting. "Is that all, then?"

This was it; this was my chance to tell him if I was going to, but I couldn't bring myself to say the words. "No…it's," I struggled with what to say to him. There was just so much that needed to be said and I didn't know where to start. I was also very much aware of the fact that Sabien's clock was ticking and he would be back any minute. "I'm sorry that you are going through this – with Sabien, I mean," I said, changing the subject to something that was on my mind, but was a little easier to talk about. "I never got the chance to ask you if you wanted to be a Knight."

"Did ye want me to be your Knight?" he asked with that hint of uncertainty still evident in his tone.

"Yes," I said, nodding in agreement. "I did it to save your life, but as I told Sabien, you deserve it – more than anyone." I tried to explain my actions in regards to the Knighting, wanting to make sure he understood why I had done it without asking him first. "I also wanted you to be able to defend yourself. I don't want anything like what happened to you to happen again."

Masaru nodded slowly, absorbing all this. "Then I would be honoured to be your Knight, Yukari – and thank ye."

I smiled slightly, feeling a little relieved that at least I hadn't forced him into his new position and that he accepted it, but my smile fell when I saw Sabien was returning for more of the brutal beatings he called 'training'. I wondered briefly why he was being so hard on Masaru, when he had taken it somewhat easily, at least in comparison, with the four of us. It was possible he also realized Masaru would not have the time to learn any slower, since Fuzen was in the city and could be upon us at any time.

"I'll try and stall him," I offered suddenly, standing. "Give you a little more time to rest."

Masaru smiled ruefully, "Good luck."

I headed purposefully to intercept Sabien before Masaru's time was officially up.

"Sir Sabien, can I ask you something?"

Sabien raised his eyebrow, implying he suspected I might have an ulterior motive, but he gestured for me to continue.

"I know we might soon gain an audience with the regent of Taiyou, but in the meantime is there something we should be doing?" I asked, searching for the words to describe how I felt. "I know it's not safe in the city for us because of Fuzen, but we don't really know enough about Taiyou – what they want, or how they feel about the Vile Emperor. I mean, they have a ceasefire and a Rubian encampment on their borders, but Fuzen is also allowed to walk freely in the city. We don't know why any of that is or what it might mean to Lord Viron. We could be walking into a trap if Taiyou has stronger ties with the Ruby City than we think they do."

"You could be right," Sabien agreed, "there is much we don't know. But I think I know what might help with that. Jeth," he called over to the door where Jeth had been stationed for the past while, awaiting Fuzen's possible appearance. "I want you to tell Yukari about the time you defeated the Duke of Espearia."

For a moment, I thought Sabien was passing me off to Jeth so he could go back to torturing Masaru, but to my surprise, Sabien headed over with me to where Jeth stood guard.

"Yeah, sure thing, but it's really not that great of a story, not compared to some of the other ones I could tell."

"Just humour me, Jeth," Sabien instructed.

"All right, all right," Jeth gave in. "Once upon a time, long long ago, there was a man who called himself the Duke of Espearia, who, it was said, could not be defeated. There were three reasons for this. One was no one could find him, two was no one could get to where he was, and three was that he was invulnerable.

"I had heard about this Duke, like everyone had, and one day my curiosity got the better of me, so I decided to take it upon myself to see if the rumours were true. But first, I had to find him.

"So I dressed myself up as a woman." My eyes widened at this pronouncement. I couldn't picture Jeth ever having done such a thing, and I started to wonder if there was any truth to this tale he was spinning, and also what the point of this telling was.

"I was too recognizable as myself, you see, and I've always thought people are more likely to talk to a pretty woman than to me," Jeth clarified. "So I walked around town and into all the places where people go and I talked to them. I talked to them about regular, everyday stuff, like the weather, the local area, and sometimes I would bring up stories of the Duke of Espearia.

"By the time I was getting bored of talking to people, I had pieced together enough clues and I figured it out. The Duke of Espearia was hiding in the only place that didn't have a way in or out and was big enough to contain his ego – a nearby mountain.

"So I became a dog." Jeth stopped his tale suddenly and turned to Sabien. "Wait – is this the part where I turn into a dog?"

"Yes, Jeth," Sabien confirmed tiredly, as though he had heard this story more than a few times, "this is the dog part of the story."

"Yeah, okay," Jeth agreed and I rolled my eyes, gesturing for him to continue. As much as I had no idea where this was going, at least I was succeeding in my task to allow Masaru a longer break. He had looked so strained and battered; it was the least I could do to put up with talking to Jeth for a little while.

"So I became a dog and I scouted out the area around the base of the mountain. Dogs have a really good sense of smell, so all I had to do was pick up the scent of a man coming in or out of the mountain and I would have found the Duke. Unfortunately, it took longer than I thought, but I didn't give up. By the end of the week, I knew every inch of that mountain and the area around it too. I even thought I knew which scent belonged to the Duke, since it went straight to the mountain and disappeared, but I couldn't figure out how he'd gotten inside.

"One day, I ran into a man in the forest and he patted me on the head. I was bored out of my mind by this point, so I followed the man because I needed something to do. It wasn't until we got back to the mountain that I realized this man was the Duke of Espearia. He stood in front of the mountain and asked it to open – and it did.

"Being the good little dog I was, I followed him inside. I lived with the Duke for months, watching his every move, studying his habits. He was like a hermit. He hardly left his mountain – I think he was worried about ruining his reputation. It turned out he was just a fat and plain little man. And as for whether he was actually invulnerable, I couldn't tell.

"One night, the Duke was eating supper and I had reached the limit of my patience, so I got up. I was gonna tell him what I thought of him and end this, and I was going to get out of the mountain. I opened my mouth to get his attention – 'Boo,' I said.

"And just like that, he died," Jeth concluded.

"He died? But how, what killed him?" I found myself asking, annoyed by the conclusion of the lengthy tale.

"Choked on a bone," Jeth stated with the utmost seriousness.

"But then you didn't defeat the Duke of Espearia. He did it to himself – it was an accident," I protested.

"You know, I never thought of it that way," Jeth admitted.

"Either way," Sabien interrupted, "the reason I wanted you to hear this story is because getting to know Lord Viron before you meet him and gaining an understanding the affairs of Taiyou is similar to the problems Jeth faced trying to learn about the Duke of Espearia."

"So what you're saying is we should go out about the city and see what we can learn?" I asked.

"It might be a good idea."

I shook my head a little in wonder; it was strange Sabien hadn't just come out and said that in the first place in response to my question. Perhaps he had wanted me to learn it for myself, or perhaps, in a way, he was trying to humour me by letting Masaru rest without seeming to soften towards him. Sabien was perhaps more cunning than I gave him credit for.

"Thank you, Sir Sabien." I told him. "We'll do that."

I found Kaji first and explained to him what Sabien had said, and what I thought we should do. I didn't feel as if we four should separate completely – that would be foolish with Fuzen in the city looking for us – and Kaji agreed teams of two would have a better chance to watch each other's backs.

"Would you mind if we switched partners?" I asked Kaji, not wanting to get into the reasons why I didn't want to spend the day with Hotaru right now.

"I was going to ask you the same thing," Kaji admitted. "You go ahead with Yue, I'll take Hotaru."

I nodded in agreement. "I'll bring the clothes Marc brought us to the courtyard. We can change out in the trees."

The Taiyoun robes were very comfortable, being made out of a light, airy material reminiscent of silk, and they were surprisingly similar to Japanese-style kimonos. I changed into mine gratefully, resolving that if I was ever going to change back into my Roughlander clothes, I would be washing them first. My hair, though knotted, was surprisingly not as filthy as I had supposed. I rationalized it had something to do with turning myself to mist and back again having a cleansing effect.

When the four of us met in the center of the courtyard again, I was surprised to see we looked moderately presentable and normal for what I had seen of the Taiyoun citizens. Yue was the only one who hadn't needed Marc's clothing donation; she had taken it upon herself to order what looked very much like white Shinto-style priestess robes from the catalog ordering system.

"I figured it would look suspicious if the Roughlanders suddenly stopped ordering things from the catalogs," Yue said defensively, but the robes looked very good on her and were a small piece of home, so no one was going to begrudge her.

Kaji and Hotaru left via the gate, assuming since the guard knew them from when they came in with Marc that they would be allowed out again. I remained with Yue, intending to have to mist us both out into the city, like I had transported myself and Masaru before.

"Hop on," Yue instructed, indicating her back.

"What?" I asked, surprised.

"Just trust me."

With a shrug, I did as Yue asked and climbed onto her back; I was going to need physical contact to try and turn us both to mist anyway. But as soon as I was settled, Yue was off faster than the speed of light. I was exaggerating, of course, but it was ridiculously fast.

The scenery of Taiyou whizzed by on either side like a wind filled with colour. It took me a little while to adjust my eyesight to be able to make out anything at all, and I found myself wondering when we had actually gone over or around – or through – the fence, which had been rebuilt by the mindless Roughlanders at the Sanctioned Outpost while we were gone.

When Yue stopped moments later, we were somewhere I didn't recognize in the middle of the city. It took another shaky minute for the world to stop spinning, and I found I was gripping Yue's shoulders tightly.

"So where do you want to go?" Yue asked brightly, pleased with her insane method of travel.

I looked around for a minute, a little at a loss. Through some buildings in the distance, I could see the palace spires. I struck me then – there was a monarchy here, of course there would be a palace.

"We should probably start in the area near the palace," I told Yue. "The people there would likely know more about Lord Viron and the prince."

"You're the boss," Yue agreed and without warning we were off again. This time I managed to adjust to our speed more quickly and I was actually able to make out that Yue was indeed running. She was just moving so quickly that the people we passed didn't even register we were there at all.

She let me down in an alley between buildings, just out of sight, so our appearance wouldn't be remarked upon. The people here had the look of wealthy government officials going about their daily business. There were also a number of city guards, and near the entrance to the palace drawbridge there were some more Taiyoun knights in their white armour, like we had seen by the ferry on our way into the city.

The palace itself caught and held my attention for a moment. I was overawed – it looked like nothing other than a fantasy palace straight out of a Disney movie. It had a drawbridge and a moat, along with spires and towers that jutted elegantly in a symmetrical fashion – and because this was Taiyou, it also had vines and plants climbing out of the palace grounds.

Tearing myself away from the view so as not to continue gawking like a Roughlander might, I forced myself to examine the people once again. I hardly thought we were going to get any information out of the palace guards or the businessmen, but across the street from us I could see a beautiful little café patio with a small group of girls, giggling and chatting amongst themselves. I pointed them out to Yue as possible sources of information and people who were less likely to be suspicious of us for asking what every citizen of Taiyou should already know.

"Leave it to me," Yue said confidently and the two of us casually walked by the café to eavesdrop.

"What does Prince Narlhep see in her, anyway?"

"You mean aside from the fact that Kosetsu's drop dead gorgeous and Viron parades her about the palace in front of him so he gets to see her everyday?"

"Well, yeah, I guess so, but if he doesn't want them to marry like he says, then the Regent should let the Prince out every once and a while and give the rest of us a chance."

"Hello ladies," Yue said, sidling up to the fenced-in patio and throwing herself right into their conversation. "I couldn't help but overhear that you were talking about Prince Narlhep. It's totally a shame the Regent keeps such a tight hold on him, otherwise we might see more of him."

"Yeah," one with long, blonde-haired one spoke – it was somewhat difficult to tell them all apart – as she lowered her voice to a conspiratorial whisper, "ever since the assassination attempt,

Prince Narlhep's been kept in the palace for his own safety. He's not allowed to do anything anymore."

"But he's the Prince!" Yue protested, really getting into her role of teenage gossip.

"I know!" one of the other ones agreed with her. "You'd think that'd count for something, but Lord Viron's in charge until Prince Narlhep turns sixteen in a couple of months. I suppose then he can do whatever he wants. Who'd argue with the King?"

"What happens to Lord Viron when the Prince becomes King?" I asked, hoping that I managed to sound only mildly curious since I knew I could never manage to imitate the mindless chatter these girls were used to.

"I don't know," the blonde admitted and looked at the others, who seemed to blankly return her stares.

One of them with a short bob of dark hair looked thoughtful, however, and I focused on her as the likely one to have a response.

"Well, Lord Viron's always said he didn't want the responsibility of kingship. My dad said he doesn't even like being Regent," she said at last. "I suppose he'll go back to his lands in the north, unless of course his daughter marries the prince and becomes queen. Then he'd stick around, wouldn't he?"

"Hopefully, she'll go back north with him and then when Narlhep is king he can have his pick of who to marry instead of just choosing Kosetsu," the one who had first bemoaned the Prince's ineligibility said. I gathered this Kosetsu was Lord Viron's daughter, who was potentially the queen-to-be.

"Well, we've got a good chance of that!" the blonde one exclaimed. "The prince isn't allowed to marry until he turns sixteen, anyway. I read it on one of those dusty old scrolls at the museum when my tutor dragged me there. It was the only interesting thing I came across."

"Where's the museum?" I jumped at my sudden insight; there could be no better place than a museum to learn the history of Taiyou and perhaps understand what had happened here in the last eight hundred years, especially concerning the Vile Emperor.

The gaggle of girls all looked at me strangely, but Yue was quick to cover for me. "We've just come into the city…so we're still learning our way around."

"Oh, which province are you from?" the somewhat more intelligent girl with the short bob asked curiously.

Yue looked blank, so I stepped in with the only province I could say I had actually been to, "Sir Rama's lands."

"Oh," the blonde one said, returning to her favourite subject – gossip. "Sir Rama, now there's a catch. I hear he may be taking his father's place on the council."

Having most likely exhausted our newfound source of information and not wishing to have to answer questions about Rama or his lands – of which we knew little about – we decided to get directions to the museum and make a hasty retreat. The girls – I can't for the life of me remember their names – were kind enough to give us a parting gift of some pastries they had ordered and were sharing amongst themselves. We took them gratefully and walked, instead of running at the speed of Yue, to the museum, which as it turned out was not far away.

The pastries – the girls called them crumblecakes – were the most wonderful and decadent thing I had ever eaten. We had had fruit since our arrival on this world, but until my first bite of crumblecake I had not noticed or felt the absence of sugar. The crumblecakes were a remarkable combination of crumbly, warm, sugared pastry with a tart berry filling, and Yue and I both scarfed them down as if we had never had anything sweet before in our lives.

The museum was a rather large and imposing building not far at all from the palace. As we approached we noted there was a lineup of girls our age waiting to get inside, so we joined the line to wait for our turn to enter.

"Stay with your partners and don't touch anything!" an elderly woman's voice called out suddenly from near the front of the line.

"Yes, Madam," the girls around us chorused.

It seemed as if Yue and I had stumbled upon some sort of girl's school field trip. It was too late to back out now, so we entered the museum with the rest of the students, realizing as awkward as it would be if we were discovered, this would help our cover story. It also meant we wouldn't have to pay any krevels – which we didn't have – to enter.

It was darker within the museum than without, and we were able to squeak by the near-sighted and elderly teacher in the crowded entranceway. The first room of the museum was the one the blonde girl had mentioned; it was covered wall to wall with scrolls, both ancient and modern, and had displays of ancient artifacts on pedestals in the centre.

I was inordinately pleased with our find, but Yue looked unimpressed, though she had little choice but to follow me around as I perused the scrolls. The teacher was keeping a close eye on the students and we didn't want to risk drawing attention to ourselves, lest she discover we weren't actually a part of her class.

The scrolls were mostly written in the lines and squiggles I had come to call Taiyoun, whether that form of writing was restricted only to this country or not. Thanks to Masaru's letter, I could now read it fairly well, and it wasn't long before I got the gist of how the scrolls were laid out.

It seemed there were different eras in Taiyou's history. Long ago, the land had been divided into a multitude of warring tribes. Occasionally one tribe would ally themselves with another and a simple treaty document would be signed, and as I gathered, often broken, as the alliances would shift and the wars would resume.

In the center of the room, there were a series of very important documents written on ancient artifacts that were themselves from a time where the tribes formed together to unite under the single banner of Taiyou. which marked when the formal kingdom was first established. There was one particular document outlining the rules and traditions of the kingship they established. It was ornately carved into the inside of a rather large turtle shell, and my eyes were drawn to a faintly glowing blue signature among the many carved into the bottom of the document. The name was illegible, but beneath it I could read: *Mediator, and Chosen of Sapphiros.*

Reading the shell top to bottom was a task that strained my knowledge of Taiyoun script, but in doing so I learned some rather important things about the laws that governed the monarchy of Taiyou, especially with regards to ascension to the throne.

As a group, the students plus Yue and I moved on to see the rest of the museum. The room that most caught my attention was a rather long hallway depicting famous moments in history in elaborate paintings along the walls. Below each painting was a descriptor telling about what the paintings represented. The best part about it was the paintings were in chronological order, which was a big help in piecing together the information presented.

There was a curious picture early on in the hallway that depicted a flaming comet in the sky, hurtling toward the planet, and a lone figure in spiked armour silhouetted against a vivid orange and purple sunset, waiting for the comet to strike him down. The caption read: *The Lady Lilyth, a comet, was said to have crash landed. This artist's rendition depicts the Vile Emperor awaiting Lady Lilyth's coming. Though a vivid reconstruction, this image is generally believed to be inaccurate, as it has been ascertained that the Vile Emperor arrived separately on this world at a later point in time.*

According to a nearby painting showing a starscape on a night sky, this world used to have both day and night in equal measure, which changed at some time after the arrival of the Vile Emperor and the Lady Lilyth, though unfortunately no dates were given. Disappointed with the vagueness of that history lesson, I moved on to the others, and by that point, Yue had already moved on ahead to look at whatever she found interesting.

Moving ahead, I decided that more recent events might be of more use to me in the current circumstance. I stopped when I reached the end of the line. A young man, perhaps twelve years of age, was depicted in a silver suit of armour and seated on the leftmost of three thrones, holding a sword too big for him in his hands. *Prince Narlhep the Fourth,* the caption beneath read, *Current heir to the throne of Taiyou.*

The one back from that was a picture of an oversized man in a dark suit of armour, with spiked black hair and a serious expression. The backdrop of the painting was a study with a roaring fireplace. *Lord Viron, Regent of Taiyou until such time as Narlhep the Fourth is crowned.*

There was no new information there, other than a visual representation of who it was we were supposed to meet. It helped to know in advance how imposing a man this Viron was. We would have to ensure we were well prepared to speak with him if we had any hope of convincing him of our legitimacy.

King Narlhep the Third, was a spindly man with a roguish grin and a sinister gleam to his eye, *slain by his only living son, he was reputed to have an obsession with Oujou magics.* Well, there were a couple of facts I hadn't known. I glanced back over at the current prince's depiction once more – he had killed his own father?

Out of simple curiosity, I examined the pictures of King Narlhep the Second and the First, and of course of old King Taiyou, who was now presumably a ferret trapped in the Roughlander Sanctioned Outpost. A pattern very quickly formed, in that each

Narlhep king was responsible for the death of the one prior. I hadn't seen any mention in the scrolls of this being a necessity of kingship, but among the Narlhep line it seemed it was a tradition, which had begun with the death of the last King Taiyou.

I continued my walk back along the wall of paintings to see if I could find anything about the mysterious Oujou tribe or their strange magics, when I noticed that other than me, most of the female students were hanging about talking and were not really interested in the paintings at all. I was abruptly reminded of similar field trips I had been on back in Tokyo. Lost in a wave of nostalgia, I happened upon one girl who had a notebook in hand. She was busy scribbling and taking notes in front of a picture of a boat on water, with a full moon suspended in a night sky.

She had long, straight, brown hair, slight features, and was a little shorter than the other girls around her. I instantly felt a kinship for this girl who seemed so serious about her studies; it seemed she had no partner with her and no friends to chat with. I also wondered briefly what she found so interesting about the picture she was studying. Then, bolstered by my new confidence gained through trying to blend into Taiyou, I decided if I wanted to know, I might as well ask her.

"Oh," she seemed startled that I was addressing her. "It's not for school…" her already shy and quiet voice trailed off, examining me. "You're not in our class, are you?"

"Uh, no," I admitted. "I've just come into the city from Sir Rama's lands. My name is Yukari."

"I'm Mifa," she introduced herself, smiling slightly. "Well, it'd probably seem pretty boring to you, but I'm studying the moon. We used to have one, over eight hundred years ago, back when there were oceans too." Mifa indicated the picture in front of us and she lowered her voice conspiratorially. "I know the moon is still there, in the sky, I've seen it sometimes."

I nodded in agreement. "Yes, it would still be there, but just not visible because the sun never sets."

Mifa looked startled that I agreed so readily with her theories; I gathered she was generally looked at askance for being interested in things other people overlooked.

"Mifa, I have a project of my own I'm working on," I ventured, wondering if perhaps this inquisitive girl might be the fountain of information I was looking for. "Do you know anything about the Oujou?"

This also seemed to be a controversial topic, but Mifa seemed to trust me enough from our few minutes of acquaintance. Apparently the Oujou were a hidden topic of interest of hers as well – as I gathered many things were – and Mifa had a theory that the Oujou were still around, teaching their magics in hiding somewhere. She even had suggestions of where I might begin to search for them, if I was so inclined. Mifa and I continued our conversation until we were through the next room and the class was about ready to leave.

This last room was largely filled with historical weapons and artifacts, and there I found Yue staring up at a sword made of green jade, completely encased in glass. The students began filing out as I rejoined her.

"I have to take this with me," she whispered urgently as I reached her side.

"What? Why?"

Yue swallowed visibly. "Jedeite told me to." She wasn't pulling my leg; I could tell by her expression she was serious.

I considered this a moment as I waited for the last of the students to follow the teacher out. "Well, if I'm going to help you steal something from the museum," I whispered, against my better judgment, "there's something I want too."

"This isn't for me!" Yue protested.

"Neither is mine, technically, but we might need it if things don't go as planned with Viron. You help me and I'll get us both out of here undetected."

"Fine, but how do I," she said, gesturing at the sword, "you know, get it out?"

"Can't you just make it disappear like you do other things?" I asked, referring to the power she had developed in training. I had seen her disappear and reappear Adel's mace and Jeth's pants on separate occasions.

"If it's Jedeite's sword, it's magic. I can't affect magic things or living things…just stuff," Yue admitted. "Wait! The glass – I can dissipate that!"

Yue used her power to make the glass case disappear. I tried to control my panic, but as Yue's hand closed on the hilt of the Jade sword, I put my hand on her shoulder and turned Yue, myself, and that sword to mist. And if the mist was tinged slightly green from the magic of the sword, there was no one there to notice us.

We drifted slowly back to the room with the scrolls to give everyone else time to leave the museum without us. I struggled with my morals the entire way, but I knew this might be my best chance at getting hold of what I needed, and if I didn't do it now I would never work up the courage to try again.

I reformed us in front of the turtle shell scroll, after ascertaining we were alone in the room. I silently thanked the fact that this wasn't Tokyo, where the technology level would have dictated hidden cameras and digital alarms.

"Yue, the turtle shell," I indicated.

The shell was on a pedestal, but not enclosed in glass like the sword had been. Yue reached in, touched her finger to the shell, and it disappeared to wherever it was she stored the things she made disappear. As soon as it was done, I turned us both back into mist and we were soon drifting back out into the sunshine, our crimes against Taiyou completed.

We made our way back to the Roughlander Sanctioned Outpost by the same method we had used to leave it. Before Kaji and Hotaru had returned, Yue had the sword of Jedeite wrapped up with strips of cloth and bound to her back in such a way that it seemed more of an elongated pack than a sword. I could tell from Kaji's expression he could see the power emanating from Yue's back, but if he mentioned it to her, I never heard anything about it.

"So did either of you have any luck?" I asked Kaji.

"We went to the marketplace–" he began.

"Someone gave me this cool bracelet!" Hotaru announced, thrusting her arm into my view. "It's got some Japanese on it, see?"

Sure enough, the bracelet had a single Japanese character on it, which stood for *Wooden Log*. The rest of the bracelet was covered in Taiyoun script.

"Can I see that, Hotaru?" I asked, intrigued by the little bit of Taiyoun I could make out before she moved her arm away.

"Sure," Hotaru replied, handing me the bracelet.

The wearer of this bracelet is invited to the gathering at the Wooden Log *at the change of the sun with five of their closest friends.*

I repeated the message aloud to the others. "The Wooden Log must be a place, then."

"Oh, yeah," Hotaru agreed, "that must be why the guy tried to give me directions."

"Who was this person, Hotaru?"

"Just someone I talked to in the marketplace," she answered. "He was about our age."

"So, do you think we should go?" Yue asked.

I was uncertain and my expression showed it, but Kaji was the one to answer. "Definitely. We wanted to be taken for Taiyouns and it looks like it worked. A party would be a good chance to socialize and get a feel for Taiyou."

"I guess you're right, but let's get our story straight before we go," I suggested.

"It says I can bring five people with me, right?" Hotaru asked. "So maybe we should bring Masaru and maybe Aysel with us."

"Bring Aysel where?" Adel called from her post at the back door entrance of the outpost building.

"To a party," Hotaru replied. "I was invited and I thought maybe I could take some of the Knights along."

I could see Adel's expression hardening from here. "Aysel is a squire. Why would you think to take her and not me?"

"Well, Masaru and Aysel are both younger..." Hotaru tried to wriggle her way out of Adel's wrath.

"Aysel and I are twins!" Adel exclaimed and Kaji, Yue, and I used this opportunity to make ourselves scarce.

It wasn't for Hotaru's sake, but more for my own and for Masaru's, that I ended up requesting Sabien's permission for Masaru to accompany us to the party as a bodyguard in case something unexpected happened during our excursion. He agreed it would allow Masaru a chance to adjust to his new position, but I felt the benefit was more that Masaru would be given some time off from training.

The group of us, Masaru included, napped until we were to leave. The constant sun was so disorienting, so I never felt I knew when a full day had passed. We had agreed we would set off separately and regroup at the marketplace to follow Hotaru's directions.

Kaji left through the main gate, as he was now known to the guard there as a friend of Marc's, and Yue used her speed to hop over the fence easily. There was no reason why Hotaru, also known to John, the usual gate guard, couldn't have gone with Kaji, but she insisted on accompanying Masaru and I.

"Hold my hands," I instructed them, and the three of us formed a circle.

I reached out with my mind until I could feel my hold over both of them, then I turned myself to mist, pulling them along with me. We drifted over the fence as a slightly larger cloud of mist and I took us as far as Marc's storehouse, where we reformed in the empty street. Hotaru would have to lead us to the marketplace and then to the Wooden Log from there, as I didn't know the way.

Hotaru took off across the street in her excitement. I moved to follow at a more reasonable pace, but I hadn't gone more than a few steps before I felt a tugging and I realized I hadn't yet let go of Masaru's hand. I did so hastily and hid a blush by scurrying after Hotaru, leaving Masaru no choice but to hurry to keep up with us.

The Wooden Log was indeed a place, recognizable by its sign, which consisted of that same Japanese character. It was an out of the way building that looked more like a shed or storage unit than anything else. Hotaru rapped on the wooden door expectantly.

A slit of wood opened at eye level and someone peered out of it at us. "Invitation?"

Hotaru held up her wrist with the bracelet on it and after a moment the door opened to reveal a bored-looking, dark-haired girl, carrying a long wooden staff with a bladed tip. She wore bits of metal-plated leather armour strapped to her here and there over her Taiyoun clothing.

"If you've brought any weapons, you better get rid of them," the girl commented, inspecting us.

None of the four of us had brought any, not having or needing them, but Masaru was a different matter. He still had his two knives, which Yue helpfully caused to disappear for him with a touch and a whispered, "I'll give 'em back later."

Upon entering the Wooden Log, we had no choice but to go down a set of narrow stairs, leading to an open door at the bottom. We could hear music and voices from the room below before we entered it, and it seemed the small building held a much larger underground bunker beneath it. The room was long but not wide, and there was already quite a crowd of people socializing at tables or dancing in front of a band of musicians set up at the far end.

With the exception of perhaps Masaru – who looked and sounded like a Roughlander, no matter that we had forced him to leave his extraneous belts behind – we blended in nicely with the general populace of the party. The Taiyoun robes Marc had given us matched what most of the people were wearing and it seemed this party was solely for people of our own age group.

We mingled a little and lost track of each other quickly. Hotaru was whisked away by the boy in the marketplace who had invited her there and remarkably I ran into someone I knew – Mifa.

"Mifa?" I questioned, and she looked up from where she had been sitting by herself with her nose in a small notebook.

"Oh, Yukari!" She seemed just as startled to see me. "Some party, huh?"

"I didn't figure this was the sort of place I would find you," I remarked honestly.

"Well, it isn't," she admitted. "I only came because my sister asked me to. She got one of those bracelets." Mifa pointed her sister out in the crowd and I recognized her as the girl with the short dark bob I had met earlier in the day at the café. She had been the smart one of the bunch who had given Yue and I the most insight into the current politics of Taiyou.

"My friend Hotaru got one too," I explained. "I'd introduce you to her, but I don't see her at the moment."

"You're not from the Raman province, are you?" Mifa asked suddenly.

I couldn't evade the direct question and I didn't want to lie to the one potential friend I had found in Taiyou. Not only that, but Mifa had been honest and forthcoming with me when I had asked her many controversial questions.

"No, I'm not," I admitted, "but I can't tell you just yet where I am from. Not here, anyway," I said, indicating the party.

Her eyes widened as I spoke, showing that she hadn't expected anything quite so secretive as the reason for my little white lie about being from the Raman province. I smiled awkwardly in an attempt to reassure her, but she just kept staring at me like I had grown a second head.

"Who's your friend?" Kaji asked as he joined us.

"Kaji, this is Mifa," I introduced the two of them, welcoming the interruption. "Will you two excuse me for a moment?"

I had noticed Masaru across the room, leaning up against an unoccupied wall not far from the door. He stood alone, an untouched drink in hand, watching the people around him as if he was very much an outsider. My heart went out to him; I, more than anyone, knew what it was like not to belong. Leaving Mifa to Kaji, I crossed the room to him.

"Yukari," Masaru met my eyes with surprise.

We stood staring at each other for just a beat too long.

"Don't worry about me," Masaru said suddenly. "Ye should be, ye know," he said, gesturing beyond me to the socializing crowd.

"I didn't invite you here just as a bodyguard," I said, indicating the position he had taken up so close to the door where he could watch everyone's comings and goings.

Masaru didn't seem to have an answer for that. He avoided my gaze for a moment, staring uselessly at the drink in his hands.

"Would ye like to dance, then?" he mumbled, looking up suddenly, and it struck me that his eyes were now blue and not brown as I remembered them being.

The song was coming to an end before I realized I had not spoken or answered him. I felt my face flush abruptly in embarrassment, but I noticed Masaru's awkward expression nearly mirrored my own.

"I have crossed the Sand Lakes," Masaru spoke at last, breaking the silence, "fought sand sharks and faced down sand crawlers…but you…you make it difficult for me to speak."

I felt my heart thud in my chest at his words, but I didn't know how to answer them or even what they meant. Unfortunately, being so close to the door, neither of us had the chance to say or do anything else, as with some fanfare and the cessation of the band's music, a crowd of people entered the party.

In the center of the group was a beautiful young lady in a long blue coat, with gold embroidered edging setting off the light gold of her long hair that cascaded down her back. She was elegant, and held herself with an easy confidence and a friendly expression. The group surrounding her, I understood immediately by the armour some of them wore, were her guards.

Masaru, by some instinct, or perhaps by Sabien's instruction or training, placed himself unobtrusively between me and the armoured guards.

"If you're going to insist on keeping your weapons," the girl spoke, her voice chiming like a bell but filled with the tones of someone used to being obeyed, "you can stay right here and not even think about using them."

Leaving the guards where they were, she stepped out from their protection to join the party, but stopped when she saw Masaru to look him up and down appraisingly. "Are you enjoying my party?" she asked him bluntly, and now I knew at least who had thrown this event, if not who she was.

"Aye, it's lovely," Masaru answered politely, his accent ringing clearly in the now quieted room.

The young lady's eyes opened wide in surprise and she took an unconscious step back from Masaru, looking about for someplace else to be. I was taken aback by her sudden change in behaviour and I felt my temper flare at the slight to Masaru and his Roughlander heritage.

"You must be the Lady Kosetsu," Kaji introduced himself to the party's hostess. I assumed he had learned her identity from socializing with the other guests, and the sudden revelation of her name stopped me from saying something I would regret later.

Kaji led Lord Viron's daughter to a nearby table where he had been seated with Mifa, her sister, and some other girls, most of whom I had met earlier at the café. Wanting to hear what was said, for the sake of the information we had come here to gather, I deliberately took hold of Masaru's hand to pull him with me to the table. I didn't want him to take Kosetsu's prejudice to heart and feel as if he wasn't wanted here. I wanted him there, even if no one else did.

We sat down in chairs next to one another and this time neither of us let go of the other's hand. I was extremely conscious of Masaru's hand on mine, but I tried as best I could to follow the conversation, as Kaji skillfully guided Kosetsu and the others to topics that interested him and might gain us some insight into Viron, Narlhep, and current affairs at the palace.

Most of what I heard only solidified the information Yue and I had gained from the gaggle of girls at the café earlier in the day, and the experience only served to impress upon me that Kaji was far better suited to manipulating social situations than I could ever dream of being.

Eventually, Kaji asked Kosetsu to dance in a bold move, and Yue, who had apparently been on the dance floor the whole time, sidled over to steal Masaru, as she also wanted a dancing partner for the next song. Embarrassed by our somewhat lengthy contact, I said nothing as Yue whisked Masaru away, and I was left at the table with Mifa, who was busy chatting with her sister.

My moment to myself did not last as Hotaru slid into the chair Masaru had just vacated. She was holding the invitation bracelet in her hand now, instead of wearing it on her wrist.

"I think you should give this to Masaru." Hotaru began inexplicably, pressing the object in question into my hands. "I'm really very happy for you two," she continued. "I sort of liked him myself, but I can see the way you both look at each other, and I wanted to tell you I'm not going to get in your way."

I held the bracelet between my hands tightly to control my emotion. I was startled by Hotaru's insight, embarrassed my feelings for Masaru were so obvious, and touched by Hotaru's sincerity all at once – the combination was overwhelming.

"Thank you, Hotaru," I whispered.

"You're welcome," she answered with a bright smile. "I was getting tired of wearing that bracelet, anyways. It seems that it's a Taiyoun custom that means as long as I wear it I'm claimed by the person who gave it to me." Hotaru gave a shifty expression around the room, searching for the boy who had invited her and sighing with relief when she didn't see him. "So I think you should give it to Masaru, and then no one in Taiyou will try and take him from you," she finished.

I had to laugh a little at her suggestion, but I could tell she was serious, so I gave her the benefit of the doubt and fastened the bracelet to my own wrist. "I'll think about it, Hotaru."

The music stopped abruptly; on the dance floor, Kosetsu was backing away from Yue, whom she had apparently been dancing with briefly. I looked up at the sudden change in the room's atmosphere to see Kosetsu's horrified expression. "No!" she exclaimed, aghast, staring between Yue and Kaji, before turning and fleeing the room, the guards forming up around her.

Before I realized it, I was on my feet and running over to Yue.
"What happened?"

"I couldn't lie to her," Yue said, abashed. "I told her who we are."

The party wound down rather abruptly after that, and we, along with everyone else, made our exit. I was outside first among the five of us and I looked back to see what was taking the others so long, only to see Masaru coming up the stairs with his arm around Hotaru's shoulders.

I didn't know what to think after Hotaru's words to me downstairs. I felt the weight of the bracelet on my wrist as the heaviest thing about me, as without my conscious direction my body floated into mist, and I found myself hovering insubstantially above the yard of the Wooden Log. Sabien had said in our training that our emotions were tied into our powers and they could prove a liability if we couldn't learn to control them, so I floated there, unable to reform until I sorted out my feelings.

To my left, I could see Kaji had an angry expression on his face. I watched as he vented his anger by punching the side of the building, leaving a fist-shaped dent in the wood. Kaji was strong, now. I didn't know if that was a reflection of his powers, or just the physical training he had undergone with Jeth, but we were all changing so rapidly from who we had been back in Japan.

Masaru and Hotaru noticed Kaji's little outburst but Yue was nowhere to be seen – she had probably started back on her own already.

"Go on Hotaru," Masaru advised. "I'll talk to him."

With a nod Hotaru looked around – presumably for me – but seeing no one, she began the long trek back to the Sanctioned Outpost on her own. Satisfied Yue was fast enough that no one would bother her and that Masaru had Kaji's back, I drifted after Hotaru, deep in thought.

I had no real claim to Masaru, whatever Hotaru believed, and while I was glad Hotaru felt our friendship important enough to give me her blessing in regards to him, I had no real reason to believe Masaru felt the same way towards me as I did about him. If he chose Hotaru, or anyone else for that matter, I would have no choice but to accept his feelings, though I doubted mine would change in any case.

Having come to this conclusion, I was a little saddened, but subdued enough to drift down and reform next to Hotaru. Together as friends, we returned to the outpost to end a long and eventful day.

Chapter 11 – The Oujou Curse

When I next woke, Masaru and Sabien were at it again. I couldn't bring myself to watch after what had happened last time, but I caught the tail end of it as I was coming down the stairs.

Masaru took a hit and fell hard. He wiped the blood from a split lip with the back of his hand while getting up and without wasting a moment he charged full tilt at Sabien. At the last possible second, Masaru ducked in to slide between the larger man's legs. Sabien somehow managed to anticipate the move, or just make use of Masaru leaving himself open, and he dealt a blow to Masaru's exposed back between the shoulder blades, driving him forward.

Masaru, surprisingly still kicking, rolled over and thrust his black-bladed combat knife between two overlapping plates of

Sabien's armour. A thin stream of blood trickled from the cut in Sabien's leg.

"Resourceful, Masaru, but that won't always be enough," Sabien commented, taking a step forward and freeing himself from the blade.

"Aye, but what about the mortar?" Masaru asked, holding up something in his hand.

From where I was at the mouth of the staircase on the opposite side of the room, it was difficult to make out what he held. Using my vision to focus in, I determined it was some sort of device attached by a thin wire to a cloth packet on the ground beneath Sabien's feet.

"That packet of explosives would destroy the both of us," Sabien noted calmly, eyeing Masaru.

"Aye, but it would mean I'd win, wouldn't it?" Masaru asked, equally as calm.

Sabien smiled suddenly, an expression I had not seen on his face for days. "That it would, Masaru. Thankfully, you don't have to die today."

"Oh, well that's a relief," Masaru replied, climbing to his feet and winding up the wire to his mortar. "Shall we go again, then?"

"No, I think you've proven your point," Sabien told him. "Remember your fear, Masaru. Death is a worthy adversary, but sometimes also a necessary one."

Sabien left the room then, leaving Masaru standing there and looking bewildered. "That was it? I just had to threaten to kill him?"

"No man," Jeth answered Masaru's rhetorical question from his usual spot at the outpost's front door, "you overcame your fear of death. Remember fear, man."

Seeing the training was done, I intercepted Masaru before he got to the stairs.

"Give me your shirt," I requested, without explanation.

Masaru, generally an obedient soul, did as I asked and removed his shirt, handing it to me without verbalizing the questions that must have been on his mind. I took it from him and spared only a glance for his bare chest – I couldn't not look when the opportunity presented itself – before heading out past him into the yard. There I found Hotaru filling a bucket for me as I had asked her to with her remarkable ability to manifest clean water at will. I took my bucket and the bar of soap I had maneuvered Tathos into finding for me and

Ruins of Sapphire

I retreated into the furthest corner of the outpost's fenced-in yard. I was still wearing my Taiyoun robes from Marc, but I did my best to cleanse every inch of me I could reach. That accomplished, I scrubbed Masaru's formerly white shirt and my filthy Roughlander clothes until they were cleaner than I was sure they'd ever been.

Laying the clothes out on a tree branch to dry. I laboriously worked out each and every knot in my hair and thought through exactly what I wanted to say to Lord Viron in order to secure an alliance with Taiyou.

Marc had stopped by earlier to let us know that Viron had passed the message back through Marc's contacts that he had agreed to an audience with us. Marc had informed us of all he knew about Viron – which wasn't much – but he did warn us it was Viron's custom to have a person at every meeting who could detect lies and falsehoods through some magical means or arcane training. Apparently this person was known as a Visionary and, though they were not common, they had long been used in an official capacity in Taiyou, so it was important we came as prepared as possible to this meeting and not be caught in any sort of falsehood.

When my clothes were dry I changed into them, carefully arranging each extraneous belt just so, tightening them with purpose and loosening the neck of my shirt to ensure the exposure of my mark of Sapphiros. Though I was a Chosen of Sapphiros and not a Roughlander, I very much intended to represent the Roughlanders at this meeting with the Regent of Taiyou, and it wouldn't hurt to be a visible reminder of their right to exist within this city. I was determined if nothing else, and I wanted attitudes changed toward the Roughlanders in Taiyou – they had been kept under lock and key for too long.

When I rejoined the others by the fountain as we had arranged, I noted the four of us had each decided to dress a little differently, which was fitting considering the balanced nature of the gem god we were supposed to represent. Kaji had elected to remain in his Taiyoun-style robes, depicting that he was willing to fit the expectations of the culture he was dealing with. Hotaru wore the same, but she had altered hers slightly by tearing the sleeves off, shortening the robe length, and draping over a few of her Roughlander belts. I assumed she was going for an eclectic 'best of both worlds' sort of image, or perhaps she was just seeking more freedom of movement for running or sword-fighting. Yue, in her

Shinto robes, was a little piece of Japan in a strange world and I, of course, had opted to look the part of a Roughlander.

"I have a request to make," I announced.

Kaji, Hotaru, and Yue looked to me expectantly, but I was distracted by motion from the back door of the outpost building. Adel had stood aside to let Sabien pass and following behind him was Masaru, Ris, Jeth, and even Aysel. I watched as Sabien and the others encircled us and the fountain, taking up positions facing outwards.

"I heard there was going to be a meeting," Razor said from between Ris and Jeth.

"It was supposed to be a private meeting," I retorted, looking about at the Knights' backs in confusion.

"There's no better place for a private meeting," Tathos joined in, coming out of the trees with some of the other mindless Roughlanders with her. "There's no one here but us, the trees, and the people."

"They've got a point," Kaji noted, unbelievably taking Tathos' inane statement into consideration, "what we decide to say and do affects everyone."

I nodded in agreement. "One moment, then, please."

I had noted Masaru was still without his shirt, and it wasn't fair for me to hold onto it and make him go without it. Picking it up from the edge of the fountain where I had placed it only a moment ago, I crossed the distance between us and tapped him on the shoulder.

He turned just his head around in surprise and I held up the shirt for him. Masaru gaped at it for a moment before taking it from me, his expression awed. "It's so white," he whispered. "I don't think I've ever seen anything so white before. Are ye sure this is the same shirt?"

I shook my head with a smile and left him to marvel over my handiwork, as I returned to the task at hand.

"I was wondering if I could be the one to present our requests to Viron," I began as diplomatically as possible. "I'm not saying I should be the only one to speak to him, but I'd like a chance to try and present our case first before all four of us start tugging in different directions. I've managed to piece together quite a bit about Viron and the affairs in Taiyou at present, so I think I might have a good chance of convincing him to take us seriously and listen to what we have to offer."

"But we're all agreed there should be no more hiding, right?" Kaji asked.

"Viron knows we are coming. We have an official invitation to visit with him at the palace. I say we should walk straight out that gate and up to the palace doors. I, for one, have had enough of pretending to be less than I am."

"Walk tall," Kaji agreed with a smile. "We don't need to scare anybody off with our powers, but if Fuzen is allowed to walk freely in the city there's no reason why we shouldn't be."

"Also, it's about time that Taiyou realizes they can't hold the Roughlanders in here anymore against their will," I stated.

"Should we bring the Knights with us?" Hotaru asked. "What if Fuzen attacks the Sanctioned Outpost while we're away?"

"You'll take an honour guard," Adel spoke from the outer circle. "It is the right of your position as Chosen."

"Some of us will have to stay behind to ensure the outpost is also protected," Sabien stated. "Adel, you will command the honour guard. Ris, Masaru, and Aysel will accompany you. Jeth and I should be enough to defend this place."

The Knights all nodded their agreement to the Knight Commander's orders, and just like that everything was decided; there was no more reason to delay our meeting with Lord Viron. There was a Knight assigned to each Chosen: Masaru to me, Ris to Yue, Adel to Kaji, and Aysel to Hotaru. Forming up ranks, we walked with purpose and confidence to the outer gate of the compound.

Kaji knocked on the gate and waited for it to open. John's eyes could be seen through the slit. When John saw it was Kaji looking to leave, he opened the gate without question, because he was under the mistaken impression Kaji was a relation of the storehouse keeper and former city guard, Marc. As soon as the gate door was open and he took in the rest of us – including the armed and armoured Knights – his welcoming expression changed to one of concern.

"What's going on here?" John demanded.

"We," Kaji indicated the four of us, "the Chosen of Sapphiros, have a meeting with the Regent, Lord Viron, today."

John took a cautious step backwards. "You know I can't just let you all walk out of here."

"I understand your position, John, but we're leaving and we're going to come right back in the same way," Kaji stated bluntly. "I would strongly suggest you let us pass. We're here to make an alliance with Taiyou and we have no wish to harm any of its citizens."

John swallowed visibly, but wisely stepped aside. It was unfortunate if he got in trouble for neglecting his duty, but there was no legitimate way he could have stopped any one of us from doing as we pleased, and certainly there was no detaining four Knights and four Chosen.

The eight of us continued on in our formation with pride and determination, making a straight line through the city toward the palace. The citizens of Taiyou stared at our strange procession, which included not only two ladies in foreign-looking armour, but also two Roughlanders – I included myself in that number – and a Kumori, as it turned out Ris's race was called. Apparently the rumour of who we were and where we were headed spread quickly, and I began to hear 'Chosen of Sapphiros' as a whisper through the crowd. Despite their stares and whispers, I also noted they gave us a wide berth and there was fear on more than one expression. Apparently 'Chosen' was a title they had come across before and didn't view positively.

When we arrived before the palace drawbridge, Fuzen was there waiting for us in front of several palace guards; they were called legionnaires, according to Marc. I met Fuzen stare for stare. He hadn't gotten the best of me on our first meeting and he wasn't going to that time, either.

"Well, the Chosen of Sapphiros," Fuzen commented in his thick European accent. "Have you finally decided to crawl out from the rock you've been hiding under? Go home, Chosen, there is nothing in Taiyou for you."

"We have as much right to be here as you do," I stated calmly, but with authority. "Step aside."

"Ah, but I am an Ambassador from the Ruby City," Fuzen gloated, looking over us all with contempt, "and you are nothing to Taiyou."

He focused his gaze on Hotaru who, along with Aysel was furthest to the right. "You wasted your time coming here. The best you can hope for is failure." He looked past Hotaru to Aysel and continued much in the same tone, "This is the best you could do for a Knight? She barely has any power at all."

Fuzen's eyes lighted on Adel as he took a few steps toward us all. "Ah, Miss Kusabana, I would have thought the reason for defecting would have been to join the winning side, but no matter…

"Kaji," Fuzen turned abruptly and addressed Kaji knowingly, as if they had met before, "still too afraid to face me alone?"

Kaji's fists shook at his side, but he did not rise to Fuzen's taunts. It was obvious what the Talon was trying to do. He was either afraid to face us, or he couldn't risk his political position by attacking us openly within Taiyou without consent from the ruling body. Either way, he had no power here, and as I saw him turn to face me next, I fought to remember as long as we had no buttons to push, we were in control.

"I see you managed to save one," Fuzen commented to me, as if he was speaking about the weather rather than Masaru's life. I kept my expression still as he continued, "What about the others you left behind to die?"

I didn't react; I knew every Roughlander I had left behind in that warehouse had been dead when I left it – one of them by Fuzen's hand – but I felt Masaru, standing behind me, stiffen.

"She didn't tell you, then," Fuzen commented with a sly smile. "I bet they were friends of yours."

Masaru wisely said nothing, so Fuzen moved on to Ris and Yue. Outwardly I kept my calm, but inwardly I cringed. I would have to clarify things with Masaru when next I got the opportunity; I couldn't let him go on thinking I hadn't done everything in my power to save those people I had damned by ordering him to leave the outpost.

I was lost in my own concerns, so I didn't hear what insults or tauntings Fuzen had come up with for the blameless Ris or the usually silent Yue. Having put up with his hurtful words long enough, I leaned over to address Adel in a whisper, "Wait here and keep him occupied if you can. If things go well, we'll rejoin you here as soon as we can, and if they do not, we'll try and send you word to return to the outpost, so we don't give him the chance to stop us."

Adel nodded her understanding, and gesturing to Kaji, Hotaru and Yue, I stepped forward. Within moments we were being escorted inside by the legionnaires and Fuzen was powerless to stop us.

The palace of Taiyou was like nothing I had ever seen before, though we didn't get much of a chance to admire it as we were ushered through it by the palace guards. The walls and floors were largely constructed of white marble inlaid with green, with tapestries interspersed here and there to break up all that white. The dove theme from the armour of the legionnaires was carried through the décor and indoor plants were also plentiful, though it was unclear how they got enough light to survive as there were no windows in the inner halls. Roman-style pillars upheld majestic ceilings, particularly in an area leading to a large set of double doors encased in silver. I could only assume by the ornate carving of an imposing visage with emerald green eyes that this was either the throne room or some other equally important chamber.

We didn't stop at the double doors, however, but turned left and continued on down the hall. The legionnaires stopped outside a wooden door, leaving us with a bald man with no facial hair or eyebrows; Marc had informed us that this hairlessness was the mark of a Visionary. His features were completely different, but his peculiar lack of hair reminded of the bald man who had accompanied Rama and I realized now he must have also been one of these Visionaries.

The Visionary bowed to us before opening the door to allow us entry. I was expecting him to enter the room with us as we had been told he would, but the hairless man stayed where he was, though he left the door open behind us.

The room appeared to be a study of sorts; in fact, it looked much like the setting of the painting of Lord Viron from the museum. The walls were lined with bookshelves and there was a fireplace set into the right wall, though due to the general hot weather it was not lit. I wondered if it ever got any use or if it was just a show of luxury. In the center of the room was a heavy wooden table, and Lord Viron stood before a floor to ceiling window with his back to us.

In a comfortable chair before the fireplace there was one other person in the room. Kosetsu – Lord Viron's daughter – sat covered from head to toe in a black robe and looking somewhat ill at ease, her eyes darting from her father's back to the four of us, before returning to stare at the floor.

The four of us arrayed ourselves so we could all be seen and heard easily. Yue was to my left, Kaji to my right, and Hotaru was on the far side of Kaji. The four of us and Kosetsu waited awkwardly for the imposing form of Viron to turn around and take notice of us.

"Why now?" he spoke at last, his deep voice rumbling through the room. "The Chosen of Sapphiros," he commented as if to himself, though he still had not turned to face or acknowledge us. "Why now show your hand?"

At these words, he turned slowly to look at the four of us. Viron was tall and he was certainly imposing. He wore a long, black cloak over a rust-coloured embroidered jacket in what I associated with a medieval style, and below that he wore black pants over heavy boots which set him firmly on the floor. His thick black hair was dressed to one side over thick black brows, pulled down in a severe expression. His dark colouring looked nothing like the light gold of his daughter beside him, for whom he spared not a glance.

As I studied him something flickered and for a moment I saw him in very different attire. His cloak covered not an elegantly embroidered Lord's outfit, but a suit of heavy, dark, rust-coloured armour, complete with metal boots and gauntlets, and a black-bladed sword in his hands, the point held down before him. I blinked and the vision faded, but it left me feeling uncertain of what I was seeing. The shape of the cloak over his clothes indicated he was larger than he should be and Viron was already a large enough man.

I shook my head and focused myself on what I had come here to say. The others were waiting for me, as I had asked for the right to speak first. "We realize the timing of our visit may seem strange," I began in response to his question, "but we arrived on this world eight hundred years too late, and we have come to Taiyou as quickly as we have been able."

Viron said nothing, but he turned his attention to me, as I was the one who had answered him. I found his penetrating gaze most uncomfortable, but I had come here with a purpose and I wasn't going to let this man or his position intimidate me. My vision flickered again to reveal the suit of armour and the sword under Viron's cloak, and a strange wavering shimmer around him.

"We've travelled a long way to reach Taiyou to seek an alliance. We understand there is currently a ceasefire between Taiyou and the Vile Emperor, but we wish to offer our aid to Taiyou should it ever be needed." There was no reaction from the stoic Viron; he was still watching me intently. "We have reason to believe the Vile Emperor is unlikely to remain satisfied with the ceasefire, and if the treaty is broken and he attacks Taiyou, we would like to be here to help you defend it."

Viron said nothing when I had finished, he only shifted his gaze to Hotaru next. Hotaru smiled awkwardly under his intense scrutiny but said nothing, and after a long and awkward silence Viron shifted to Kaji.

"I am in agreement with Yukari," Kaji stated. "The Vile Emperor has tried more than once to take Taiyou in the past and failed, but for the past hundred years while Taiyou has considered itself safe, the Vile Emperor's forces have only been growing stronger outside of its borders. We sincerely hope the day will not come when our assistance will be necessary, but in case it does, we would be valuable allies to have."

Viron turned his attention to Yue next. I spared a glance to my left and noticed Yue's fists were clenched tightly at her side and her mouth was pursed in a thin line, like she was trying to prevent herself from speaking out against something she disagreed with.

Yue and Viron stared each other down for another uncomfortable moment before Viron finally broke the silence with his deep rumble. "Do you also have nothing to say, then?"

"I have plenty to say," Yue stated suddenly, the floodgates of her anger opening wide. "What was the weapon fired from Taiyou on the Croatin outpost to the east and for what reason were over six hundred Croatins slaughtered?"

Viron gave away nothing by his expression. "I have heard you speak," he intoned, his deep rumble a monotone. "Now hear me speak. What action Taiyou takes within or without its borders is the concern of Taiyou and none other. Do you come here to judge or do you have some other purpose?"

Without waiting for a response, he continued on to address Kaji next, "Taiyou has stood against the Vile Emperor since he first rose against us and we will continue to do so. What advantage could you offer Taiyou that it does not already possess?"

Then he spoke to Hotaru, "You have declined to state your reason for coming. Why are you here? Do you attempt to hide your true purpose?"

Lastly he faced me once more. "You seek to offer aid, yet you have not made any demands. What do you ask for in return for your assistance?"

As his gaze remained with me I gathered it was my turn to speak again. "Sanctuary," I responded. "We ask that you allow us and our allies who help you access and sanctuary within the borders of Taiyou."

"I'm not trying to hide anything," Hotaru spoke when Viron looked to her for her response to his question. "I, too, agree with Yukari. We're here to help."

"The Vile Emperor is the Chosen of Rubia and he has four Talons amongst his innumerable forces," Kaji explained. "It is evident that Taiyou must have some means of protecting itself other than just soldiers or it would have fallen long ago, but nothing lasts forever. One day that method of protection might not be enough, or the Vile Emperor might find a way around it, and that's where we can be of use to you."

I worried about what Yue might say, having been left to stew while the rest of us answered the questions we had been asked. She was usually so quiet, but could be fierce when riled, especially in defense of another, and it seemed the fate of the Croatin outpost she had visited was a cause she had decided to champion. "I asked why an attack was made on the Croatins, who are our allies." Yue fought to control her temper. "I will not help the ones responsible for the slaughter of innocents. I know the weapon was fired from somewhere in Taiyou. I watched it happen and I can show you the memory of it as evidence."

"I have heard you speak. Now hear me speak," Viron intoned once more when Yue was finished and I began to understand this must be a formal ritual of some sort.

"That will not be necessary," Viron told Yue. "The weapon was indeed fired from Taiyou. The Croatins were marching for our borders. They sent an armed force six hundred strong toward our eastern border and action was taken to stop them."

This time Viron skipped both Kaji and Hotaru – there being no questions he needed to answer and presumably none he wanted to ask – and returned his attention to me. "You are the Chosen of Sapphiros. This is not your home, why offer to defend it?"

"I have seen your lands. I have walked through the city and across the countryside. Taiyou is beautiful," I told Viron in all honesty. "The land is green and the people are happy. This is not the case everywhere else on this world. Taiyou, with its water and its fertile soil, is the last bastion of hope for the rest of the world. If the world is to survive, it must be kept safe. If the Vile Emperor gains control of Taiyou and its resources, then he controls everything."

Viron seemed to consider my response for a moment. "I have heard you speak and you have heard me speak. Now, I decide."

Throughout all this, Kosetsu in her chair to the side had not so much as moved or spoken. I looked to her now to ascertain her response to all this, only to notice an intense look of concentration on her face and a sheen of sweat across her brow. The shimmer I had noted around Viron throughout the ritualistic question and answer period was around her too. As I examined the shimmer I was able to follow it from her to her father, and I realized when I focused on the abnormality I could see the suit of armour hidden beneath clearly. It seemed as if Kosetsu was using some sort of magic to alter her father's appearance and hide his defenses, but maintaining the illusion was a strain on her.

"You have been honest with me, so I will be forthcoming with you," Viron said suddenly, then glanced over his shoulder at his daughter. "You are dismissed."

With a barely perceptible nod, Kosetsu slumped in her chair and the wavering shimmer I had been so distracted by disappeared, leaving Lord Viron decked out in his real attire, the suit of armour and the black-bladed sword. Hotaru was the only one to be visibly startled by this revelation.

"I will take you to meet Prince Narlhep, so you can relay your offer to him," Lord Viron informed us. "He is the Crown Prince and will take the throne on his sixteenth birthday. As your proposal deals with the future of Taiyou, it is he you will have to convince."

"Will you help us convince the Prince?" Hotaru asked.

"I will neither help nor hinder you in regards to him," Viron stated bluntly. "Come."

Viron himself led us back down the hall toward the large silver double doors, which opened at his command, not seeming to have hinges or anyone on either side to push or pull them. Within was indeed a throne room, like I had surmised.

The room was large and only the centre was lit by a glow emanating from the ceiling. There were no windows and I got the impression we were in the very centre of the palace. The floors were black-and-white checkered marble with a single strip of red carpet leading to a dais with three thrones. Behind them an inexplicable garden of trees began, fanning outwards to encompass the room.

The centre throne was the largest, but a boy in armour – looking older than his picture in the museum, but not by too much – Prince Narlhep the Fourth, sat on the left hand throne, slumped over with his head in one hand, absently twirling a sword with the other.

According to the facts we had received, he was our age, but he didn't quite look it. He was slight of build, with brown lanky hair that hung in his eyes and a weak chin. When he finally looked up to acknowledge the newcomers into his throne room, I noted his eyes were the same dull brown as his hair. His metal and white dove-themed armour was splendid, but it seemed to overshadow him and make him seem unsuited to his kingly birthright.

Regardless of his appearance, whether anyone liked it or not, this boy would be king on his sixteenth birthday. I stood dumbfounded for a moment; this boy-king would be what stood between the Vile Emperor and control of Taiyou. Granted, Narlhep the Fourth would likely have advisors – Viron among them – and I couldn't legitimately judge the prince based on his age considering we – also fifteen – were apparently the Chosen of Sapphiros. Had we arrived when we were expected on this world, that title may have held considerably more political influence than it did today, although it had gotten us in to see this king-to-be.

"Prince Narlhep," Viron announced to the bored looking monarch, "the Chosen of Sapphiros are here to speak with you."

Narlhep studied us a moment. "The Chosen of…" His eyes widened perceptively, and the spinning of the sword in his hand stopped abruptly. "Why would you bring them in here?!"

"They have gone through the ritual and passed my tests," Viron informed the prince emotionlessly. "They have no intent to harm you."

"Oh, well in that case…" The prince straightened himself up in his throne and held the sword point down between his legs in an attempt at a more regal position. "What can I do for you?"

I had to stop myself from rolling my eyes at this display and remember not to judge or offend the future king of Taiyou. I opened as diplomatically as possible, "We have come to offer our allegiance to Taiyou in the event the Vile Emperor seeks to break the ceasefire and threaten your borders once again."

"The Vile Emperor?" The prince snorted. "He's left us alone for a hundred years, why would he attack us now? It's not like we've done anything to him."

I gritted my teeth at this as I tried to prepare a suitably calm response, but thankfully Kaji stepped in. "It's not what Taiyou has done to the Vile Emperor, but what he can hope to gain by conquering this land. Taiyou has quite a monopoly over the natural resources of this world, correct? He's tried before to take the land, and as patient as the Vile Emperor must be with having been alive so long, he will try again."

"And he'll fail," Narlhep stated with confidence. "He's failed every time he's tried."

"Can you be certain of this?" Kaji asked bluntly.

"Taiyou is protected," Narlhep answered, somewhat cryptically.

"By the weapon?" Yue spoke up suddenly. "The weapon that was fired on the Croatin outpost?"

"I didn't order it fired on the outpost, they were marching for our borders!" Narlhep looked uncomfortable at his outburst and glanced around the room. "No…it's not the weapon," he responded, then met her eyes, "but how do you know about that?"

"I lived through it," Yue told him bitterly. "I watched it happen through the memories of the only survivor. He's dead now, too."

"If it's not the weapon," Kaji interjected, "then how is Taiyou protected? I have seen soldiers, but not nearly enough to defend the whole of Taiyou."

"I'm not going to tell you that," Narlhep protested. "You're just like Fuzen. All you're after is Taiyou's secrets, so you'll have access to our weapons and our defenses. Well, I won't tell him and I won't tell you either. I'm not that stupid."

I was beginning to doubt that, but I was glad this fool of a monarch hadn't yet sold out Taiyou to the Vile Emperor's Talon.

"We're not here for your secrets," Hotaru joined the conversation. "We want Taiyou to be safe. We're here to help you."

"Yeah, I got that part," Narlhep said, "but Taiyou doesn't need help and we don't need interference. As soon as I'm King, I'm going to get rid of Fuzen too."

"You can't get rid of him now?" Hotaru asked.

"He was my father's friend and was granted rights to the city," Narlhep admitted in a frustrated tone. "I can't overrule any of my father's decrees until I'm King, so Fuzen's allowed in Taiyou until then."

"What about the Rubian encampment on your southern border?" I asked, curious now.

"Oh, them? They're outside of our borders and they haven't caused any trouble, so we let them be. Besides if we attacked them, the Vile Emperor would take that as breaking the ceasefire and likely retaliate–" He cut off abruptly and looked at me sharply, "Is that what you're trying to do? Get me to break the ceasefire so you can 'save Taiyou' and take it over from the inside?"

"No, of course not," I responded, slightly offended. "I was just mentioning them because I wasn't sure if you were aware they are terrorizing refugees trying to enter Taiyou, and likely harassing the supply caravans that go to the Roughlanders out in the wastes as well."

"So you'll fire that weapon against six hundred Croatins scouting near your borders, but you leave a Deathsquad camped on your doorstep?" Yue asked incredulously.

Narlhep ignored her question as he studied me intently. "Are you one of those Roughlanders? You don't have that disease, do you?"

"It's not a disease, it's a curse," Yue informed him.

"One we've found a way of stopping," I added.

"But not curing," Yue emphasized and quoted what we had learned from King Taiyou, "'an Oujou curse can only be broken by the blood of the one responsible for it'."

"And who's that?" Narlhep asked.

"You," Yue declared.

"Me? But the Roughlanders have been sick for generations and I've never even met one of them. Except maybe you," Narlhep said as he gestured at me.

I rolled my eyes at Yue's dramatics. "She means your bloodline," I explained. "Your ancestor King Narlhep the First killed his brother, King Taiyou, using Oujou magic. It rebounded on him and infected the water supply at the Roughlander Sanctioned Outpost, and has been trapping people's minds there ever since. If an infected person tries to leave the outpost they sicken and die, but if they remain at the outpost their minds fade away, while their bodies live."

"Is this true?" Narlhep asked, looking to his Regent, Viron, for the answer as he wasn't yet sure to trust any of us.

"I do not know," Viron answered. "Your father, in his wisdom, sought to imprison all of the Roughlanders so their disease would not spread. I told you it was a mistake to re-open the Sanctioned Outpost and allow them to continue to enter Taiyou."

"I always thought they got the sickness from the waste," Narlhep admitted, "but if it's an Oujou curse as you say, we can confirm that."

"I can show you the evidence," Yue offered, holding out her hand to Narlhep.

"She has the ability to give people memories of what she has seen," Kaji explained.

"No thanks," Narlhep declined. "I'll just ask the Oujou."

All of us, except Viron, were taken aback by this statement, but immediately after he had spoken a woman appeared behind the throne in a wisp of green smoke, just like the ferret King Taiyou was so fond of doing.

She was just the same as how Sabien had described the Oujou sorceress he had met over eight hundred years ago. The woman was tall, with skin so pale it was on the verge of being translucent, and her clothing – if the spider-like webbing of interlocking black metal pieces could be called that – barely covered any part of her except what was absolutely necessary for decency's sake. Her hair was jet black to complement her outfit and her fingers ended in delicately pointed claws of the same black metal.

"Our prince has called, so here we are," the Oujou spoke, her sultry voice lilting. "We come when called, be it near or far."

"Is there an Oujou curse on the Roughlander Sanctioned Outpost?" Narlhep asked directly.

"A curse upon the damned may yet prove a blessing," the Oujou answered in a roundabout fashion, smiling slyly.

"I'll take that as a yes," Narlhep decided, eyeing the Oujou distastefully. He turned to us once more. "That explains quite a bit. How did you say the curse can be ended again?"

"'The blood of the one responsible,'" Yue repeated. "I'm not sure if that means you'd have to bleed into the fountain or by how much."

"Is it true?" Narlhep addressed the Oujou, still curved sinuously behind him on the throne. "Would my blood free the Roughlanders from the curse?"

"If the curse you seek to break," the Oujou addressed us rather than Narlhep, "then the prince you will have to take."

"Well, I won't die for it," Narlhep stated, "but if something can be done for the Roughlanders to stop the illness or curse that's been affecting them this whole time, I'd be willing to try. Especially if it was something my father, or his father, was responsible for."

Yue nodded. "Then will you come with us to the Sanctioned Outpost?"

"I do not think that is advised," Viron interjected. "The Roughlander Sanctioned Outpost is a dangerous place and you are not supposed to leave the palace by order of the council."

"I'm going, Viron," Prince Narlhep declared. "You can send as large of an entourage as you want, but fixing the Roughlander illness once and for all is important, and only I can do it. You can't keep me cooped up here forever."

"What about the alliance?" I asked, trying to return to the main point of discussion. "It is wonderful you are willing to help with the Roughlanders, but in regards to the future, would you be willing to accept our help if the time comes when it is needed?"

"Viron," Narlhep addressed his Regent, "get your entourage together while I finish discussing matters with the Chosen of Sapphiros. I don't believe I have anything to fear from them or you wouldn't have let them in here, and I also have the Oujou to protect me."

Viron nodded, without any hint of the displeasure he likely felt at being commanded to do something he disagreed with. "Guard the Prince," he commanded the Oujou, before shutting the massive silver doors behind him and leaving us in the throne room with Narlhep and the sorceress.

"Unfortunately, I can't agree to an alliance right now," Narlhep said, his tone sounding a little more relaxed and sincere. "As much as I would like to, I can't overrule my father's decrees until I'm King, and allying with you would be a slight to Fuzen and the Ruby City. I can't risk ending the ceasefire. I don't want to begin my reign by being the King who provoked the Vile Emperor.

"I can offer you continued access to the city, the same as Fuzen has, but no more than that."

Meanwhile, Kaji was eyeing the door and looking a little concerned. "Prince Narlhep, are you aware we are sealed in here by magic? The door has no handles either, does it just open on its own?"

"Well, Viron can open it and so can I," Narlhep answered, "or failing that, the Oujou can."

Taking Kaji's worried expression into consideration; Narlhep got off his throne and walked to the door. He stood there a moment expectantly, but then he turned around with a confused expression. "Oujou, why won't the door open?"

The Oujou declined to respond, but gave a wicked smile instead.

"Open the door," the prince commanded, "immediately."

Her smile got wider, but again she said nothing.

"You are supposed to obey my commands," Narlhep informed her in a frustrated tone. "I told you to open the door."

"As the prince commands, the Oujou obeys, but the prince is not yet a king and it is not quite the same."

"What are you saying?" Narlhep demanded, his face white and his expression shocked; I gathered the Oujou had never disobeyed him before.

"Bound we may be, but to the crown, not the boy," the Oujou answered again in her roundabout way of speaking. "The Oujou obey, serve, and punish with the utmost of joy."

"But there is no king, I'm the prince!" Narlhep exclaimed. "You're supposed to obey me."

"Prince Narlhep," I interrupted to get his attention, "is Viron able to command the Oujou?"

"Of course he is, he's the Regent…" Narlhep trailed off as the realization hit him. "Viron locked us in here? Why would he do that?"

"Obviously he didn't want you to leave the palace to help the Roughlanders," Yue stated.

"No, it's more than that," I realized suddenly, beginning to piece it all together. "The assassination attempt – was the perpetrator ever caught?"

"Well, sort of," Narlhep responded. "I mean I know who it was. It was the Oujou."

All of us were taken aback by this statement and we eyed the Oujou warily. The Oujou seemed the most unconcerned of us all; she merely leaned on the throne once more, as if to watch us dance to her tune.

"The Oujou?" Hotaru questioned. "She tried to kill you, but you consider yourself safe around her, and you let her guard you and stuff?"

"Well, yeah. Once I found out, I ordered her not to try it again and–" He cut off abruptly and backed away a little further from the throne where she was lounging.

The Oujou was the key to all of this, that was clear, but Viron – supposedly the only other person with the power to command the sorceress – evidently had a hand in it as well. The only possible motive I could see for Viron having commanded the Oujou to assassinate Prince Narlhep was to either take the throne himself for real, and not just as Regent – a position that would end in a few months when Narlhep turned sixteen – or to scare the prince into hiding here in the palace, allowing Viron control over Taiyou in the meantime. Neither outcome was good and now there we were, trapped in the throne room with the outcast prince and his would-be assassin, while Lord Viron, the Regent of Taiyou, was out there doing whatever he wanted with no one to oppose him.

I studied the Oujou. I focused in on her – really focused – and I noticed she didn't seem to be as solid of a presence as I had first thought. Intrigued by the constant motion of the particles that formed her image, I used my ability to peer very closely and zoomed in to see what she was made of.

I raised a hand to my mouth in horror to keep from crying out; the Oujou was not one solid being. She was made up of a multitude of green, crystal-shaped particles, identical to the ones that infected the fountain's water at the Roughlander Sanctioned Outpost and had so greatly affected everyone who had ingested them.

The Oujou could kill with a touch, Sabien's warning tale came back to me. *Those she touched died a week later, their flesh melting off of their bones.*

It made sense now how it was possible. If the Oujou was able to control her particles, and no doubt by the forming of her own image and her method of appearing she was, then she could use them to infect others with whatever curse she wished.

I abruptly remembered the effect salt had on the crystals, but all I had on me was one wasterskin with maybe the faintest trace of salt left inside. I doubted that would be enough to slow her down, let alone to stop her from killing the four of us or Narlhep.

"Whatever you do," I warned the others, "don't let her touch you."

The Oujou repeated her wicked smile, this time in my direction.

It struck me then; this sorceress was the same one Sabien and the Knights at the Temple of Sapphire had met eight hundred years ago, and she was likely the only one of her kind there was. She addressed herself in the third person plural because she was many in and of herself. If each of those particles and the way they spread, infected, and took over indicated sentience, then the Oujou really were many; they were infinitely small and just as deadly for it.

"Who ordered you to assassinate me?" Narlhep asked the Oujou from near the doors. "Or did you think of it on your own?"

"The Oujou are bound to the crown, as we said," the Oujou answered with a tilt of her head, "ordered, then, we are not blamed when our prince is dead."

Yue flashed-stepped to the door and tried with all her might to push or pry it open, but to no avail. I loosened my waterskin from my belt and held it in my hand, as it was the only weapon I thought might be of some use against the incorporeal form of the sorceress. Kaji kept himself close to Narlhep, in case he should have to be defended.

The only person unaccounted for, I realized suddenly, was Hotaru. I scanned the room, but tried not to let on to the Oujou what I was doing, in case I alerted her to the fact that one of us was missing. My eyes lighted on Hotaru as she reformed from a puddle of water in the trees beyond the triple thrones and behind the Oujou.

Hotaru manifested two swords, one short and one long, and I worried for a moment she intended to attempt to strike the Oujou from behind, instigating a battle I wasn't sure we could win, but as it turned out that wasn't her intention. The sword in Hotaru's right hand was the one made of ice I had seen before, which shimmered with a white frosted blade, but the one in her left – the shorter one – was different. It was made from water miraculously held into the shape of a sword, with an extremely fine, bladed edge. Lifting the water-sword into the air above her head, Hotaru struck at the floor and to my surprise, her sword cut right through the marble, leaving a visible slash at her feet.

Hotaru's repeated slashing was not silent by any means, but remarkably the sorceress did not seem to care that she was attempting to escape through the floor. The Oujou either didn't understand what Hotaru's aims were, or didn't think it was possible Hotaru would succeed. Or maybe – just maybe – her orders did not include us, as Viron could not have foreseen our intentions, our powers, or the fact we would help Narlhep oppose him.

The Oujou regarded us with a bored expression and I decided it would be far better to keep her occupied than to provoke her. "Narlhep, if we're right about Viron, of which I have little doubt," I informed him, backing up until I was a little closer to him and Kaji, "you can be King now. You don't have to wait to turn sixteen."

"The only way I can be crowned early is in a time of war," Narlhep responded, "and I already told you I won't restart the war with the Ruby City."

"Foreign or domestic," I stated and Narlhep regarded me blankly. "The war doesn't have to be external. If it can be proven to your council that Viron is an enemy to the crown, then the fact he is a traitor would be enough to declare a civil war on his lands and his person, and you could be crowned King immediately with all that entails," I said, indicating the Oujou with the slightest gesture of my eyes.

"Even if you're right, I'd still need the official document stating that law, and if you haven't noticed we're stuck in here and Viron is out there," Narlhep pointed out. "If this was his plan all along, I'm sure he's already thought of that and removed any chance I'd have of outsmarting him."

"Well he might be going to the museum to do just that," I allowed, "but thankfully Yue and I already stole that particular document and we have it in a safe place for you."

Narlhep regarded me wide-eyed for a moment before regaining his composure. "But that still leaves us trapped in here, with her."

I glanced up suddenly and noted Hotaru waving her arms silently in our direction.

"No, it doesn't," I stated, "let's go."

At my words, Yue flashed-stepped once more and picked Narlhep up bodily, swinging him over her shoulder in a smooth motion. The Oujou simultaneously snapped to attention, and I watched in horror as she exploded into green mist and rapidly expanded outwards.

Yue disappeared, running faster than my eyes could comprehend, and thinking fast, I grabbed Kaji's hand and turned us both into mist. In the distance, Hotaru jumped down the hole she had made in the marble floor to avoid the countless green particles of the Oujou that were rapidly fanning out from the dais at the centre of the throne room.

I prayed my mist would keep Kaji and I safe from the particles of the Oujou, and even though water had been susceptible to the curse at the Roughlander Sanctioned Outpost, the attack of the Oujou didn't seem to have any effect on me as I drifted through the expanding green mist and propelled the two of us through Hotaru's hole.

The room below seemed to be a small common room for palace guards, but it was thankfully empty. Kaji and I drifted through it after Hotaru, but Yue and Narlhep had travelled so quickly they were nowhere to be seen.

The three of us made for an open window where Hotaru turned herself into water once more to slide down the side of the building into the moat and presumably to the other side, while Kaji and I drifted out into the city. All I could do was hope Yue and Narlhep made it out of the palace with no trouble and assume everyone would meet back up at the Sanctioned Outpost. That was the default plan in case our meeting with Viron, and subsequently Narlhep, had gone somewhat awry.

Once safely far enough out into the city that the guards or Fuzen were unlikely to find us, I reformed Kaji and myself in an alleyway.

"How are we going to tell the Knights to go back to the outpost?" Kaji asked.

"I'll handle that," I responded, raising my arms to try something I had been working on.

I formed an arrow and attempted to attach a message to it with my mind. The glowing blue energy arrow appeared between my hands, but the shaft appeared more in the shape of a wound-up scroll. I smiled at my success and then focused on Adel as my target before letting my arrow fly. I knew where she was even if I could not see her, and I knew without a doubt my arrow would fly true and land at her feet.

We're done here – go home.

Chapter 12 – Temple of Jade

Adel and Fuzen faced each other, neither one prepared to back down," Masaru related to the crowd of gathered Roughlanders and Knights. "So then Aysel told Fuzen, bold as you please, 'You know my sister can kill you with a thought'." Masaru's imitation of Aysel's faintly British accent was passable, but it had his audience lost in various degrees of hilarity.

"And that's when Yukari's arrow whizzed between the two of them to land at Adel's feet. Fuzen looked like he was going to wet himself," Masaru described with a laugh, "and Adel took it in stride, like she could command arrows from the sky to strike him down any time she pleased."

I couldn't help but smile at Masaru's retelling of what had happened outside the palace and how we had collectively managed to get the best of Fuzen once again. I stood in the doorway of the outpost building, torn between joining the Roughlanders and their easy camaraderie, and watching the long awaited possible resolution of the Oujou curse on the Roughlander Sanctioned Outpost.

Out in the yard, Yue and Prince Narlhep stood before the fountain, speaking with the ferret-king through Sabien, whom I gathered had volunteered himself for that purpose.

"So my bleeding in the fountain willingly will break the curse?" the prince asked.

"Yes," King Taiyou responded, his deep voice not sounding as strange when coming from Sabien's vocal chords. "All those affected would be released and I could return their minds, but I am afraid their bodies would revert to the age they should be. Some, like my Tathos, have been here since the beginning. The curse is what keeps them alive now. If you break it, they will die."

I abruptly remembered the riddle the Oujou had given us, *A curse upon the damned may yet prove a blessing,* and her meaning was suddenly clear. The Roughlanders who had come here unknowingly or been the victim of unfortunate circumstances had drunk of the cursed water and become destined to die from it. The other alternative was living forever, but without access to their minds or memories – what sort of life could that be?

"After all I have done to protect her, I cannot let you kill her," the king stated, but with a deep sadness in his voice. "I never wished for any of this and I've tried to keep those who come to this place away from the fountain, but once they are cursed as well, all I can do for them is keep their minds locked away so they can be happy, like my Tathos."

"But you said yourself she isn't happy," Yue interjected. "The last thing she did was cry for days and she only seems happy now because she can't remember otherwise. Wouldn't it be a mercy?"

"I know it is unfair and selfish of me to allow the curse to continue," he admitted, his voice lonely and tired, "but what of the others? Their lives would also be forfeited."

"What sort of lives are they?" I asked, entering the conversation as I strode forward closer to the fountain. "They retain no memories of each day, so today is much like the day they arrived for them. If they hadn't ever come here or if they had left, their lives would be over now, regardless. It's not fair to keep them imprisoned like this and I'm fairly sure if you could ask them, being Roughlanders, they would want to be free."

"I would willingly give my blood to see this curse ended," Narlhep ventured. "I don't want anyone else to get infected because of what my ancestor did, and just sealing this place up isn't enough,

I know. Please, King Taiyou," Narlhep asked, sounding sincere, "let me make amends for what my line has done."

Tears filled Sabien's eyes – I assumed they were King Taiyou's – and after a moment he nodded. "It is time the curse was ended. I will hold on as long as I can to see that the ones who lose their lives do not feel any fear or pain and then I, too, will fade. At least then Tathos and I can be together, as we couldn't be in life."

A puff of green smoke wafted from Sabien's eyes and mouth, and the Knight Commander wilted but kept his hold on consciousness. The green smoke reformed on the fountain's edge into the familiar ferret form of King Taiyou's spirit, and Tathos could be seen approaching the fountain a moment later, as if summoned.

Tathos reached the fountain and sat on its edge, the ferret climbing into her lap and snuggling her affectionately, before looking around at the rest of us with its knowing eyes. Narlhep nodded to the ferret-king and made his way to the fountain, drawing his sword and removing his gauntlet.

"My blood is freely given," he announced. "Let the curse upon this place and these people be ended and their freedom returned."

Wincing, Narlhep drew the sword across his own hand and made a fist to squeeze the drops of his blood into the fountain as penance for his great-grandfather murdering his royal brother with the use of Oujou magic. The blood dripped into the fountain, but did not stain the water. Instead, a green mist slowly began to rise from the surface.

All around the yard there were infected Roughlanders and as the green mist began to rise, they all stopped whatever it was they were doing and stood, looking upwards to the sky. Like the ferret-king had come out of Sabien, the green particles of the Oujou – which were, in essence, her magic and her being – rose out from the eyes and mouths of the Roughlanders, freeing them from the curse that had held them prisoners in the Sanctioned Outpost.

The mist rose and joined together to form a green fog over the outpost yard, filtering the sun until it was no more than a green haze. Narlhep looked up at it worriedly, but the rest of us, including our Roughlanders and Knights who had come outside to watch, were looking at Tathos, who was smiling through her tears as she reached up for the hand of the ghostly form of an impressive-looking man. As her hand made contact with King Taiyou's, she became just as insubstantial as he was, and the two of them drifted up to join the green cloud above, which dissipated as quickly as it had appeared, fading on the wind and in the sun's light.

Out of the Roughlanders who were freed by Narlhep's actions, some were never found or accounted for. Others left behind only a pile of dust and the rest were revealed to be of varying ages, depending on how long they had been imprisoned here. The ones who survived were some of the oldest Roughlanders anyone had ever seen, and as they grew acclimatized to their new situations, they were extremely grateful to be able to live their lives again, though bitter at the years they had lost.

Together the Roughlanders, old and young, gathered the piles of ash and dust for a proper burial within the trees of the outpost yard, where they vowed they would plant a garden to commemorate all who had lived and died here under the influence of the curse.

"Prince Narlhep," I addressed him as I bandaged his hand and we watched the Roughlanders go about their work, "do you have any idea what Viron might try to do next?"

His brow furrowed. "Well, that would depend on what his goal was all along and why he wanted me out of the way."

"I know Viron has spread about that he doesn't want to be King and that he would be content when his term as Regent ended," I remarked, "but wouldn't that be the perfect cover? When you conveniently died, by assassination or otherwise, as Regent he would 'reluctantly' step in and the council would hand him the crown with thanks. I heard you and Viron's daughter are close?"

"Yeah," Narlhep swallowed visibly, with embarrassment perhaps. "We're betrothed, but Viron didn't want us to get married."

I considered this with what I had learned from the gossiping girls the other day. "That could also have been a part of his cover," I ventured. "If he didn't want you married, he could have sent his daughter back to his own lands, but he kept her in the palace, didn't he? He might have wanted you to become attached to her so that if you didn't die, he would still have a connection to the throne."

"I love Kosetsu," Narlhep stated, startling me with his conviction. "That has nothing to do with Viron manipulating me. I understand there's a lot I wasn't told about and I was a fool for letting him and the council lock me in the palace, but my feelings for Kosetsu are real. She's not a part of this."

"Who fired the weapon? Was it the Oujou?" Yue asked, approaching us with purpose. I could see from her expression she would have asked this question much sooner, but she had been kept occupied by the Oujou curse and then presiding over the burial of the less fortunate Roughlanders in the Japanese fashion, as her mother, a Shinto priestess, had taught her.

"What?" Narlhep asked, taken aback.

"You said you ordered it," Yue accused, "so that means you didn't fire it yourself – who did?"

He looked extremely uncomfortable. "Well, only those trained in Oujou magic can fire the weapon, but it wasn't the Oujou. We don't let her have access to that kind of power."

"So if it wasn't her, who was it?" Yue pressed. "That Croatin outpost was destroyed and I want to know who's responsible."

Narlhep's look changed to one of confusion. "I ordered the weapon fired on a Croatin patrol and I'm sorry for that. I didn't think about the lives that would be lost, but Yue, I promise you, I didn't order anyone to fire on their outpost."

"Well, somebody did," Yue declared. "They are all dead. I can show you the memory to prove it."

"Does that mean there were two shots fired, then?" I asked. "One on the patrol and another on the outpost?"

"Must have been…" Narlhep answered, "but that would mean that Viron–"

"Viron fired the weapon, then?" Yue interrupted him.

"No," Narlhep responded with a sigh, "not Viron…Kosetsu. She's a sorceress, but she wouldn't have fired it twice on her own. Viron must have changed my orders or made her do it."

"Can the weapon fire within Taiyou?" I asked. "If Viron knows he can't get a hold of the tortoise shell document and the Oujou told him you escaped with us, could he fire the weapon at us if he knew where we were?"

Narlhep looked immediately worried. "He could – well, he could make Kosetsu do it. Do you think that now that I've escaped, he'd want to finish the job he started by ordering the Oujou to assassinate me?"

"It would make sense." I gave Narlhep a dubious expression. "He knows we were staying here and that you were supposed to come with us to break the curse. Even if he doesn't intend to fire on us, I don't like the thought of a weapon powerful enough to destroy an outpost in Viron's hands."

"We'll have to stop him," Yue declared. "See if we can get to the weapon before he can convince Kosetsu to fire it for him."

"Yue has a point," Kaji said, joining the conversation. "If what you're saying is true, then we can't stay here or he could shoot us down whenever he'd like."

"I suppose I have no choice but to tell you where the weapon is," Narlhep stated. "I'm not supposed to tell anyone, but if you're going to help me get it back and save Taiyou, then I trust you won't try to take it for yourselves." We nodded our agreement and Narlhep continued, "In the rough center of the lands of Taiyou there is a singular mountain made of jade, though it looks like regular rock from the outside. It's a school for sorceresses," he said, as I noted with some satisfaction Mifa had been right in her theories on where to find the Oujou's secret school, "and it's where the weapon is housed.

"The only problem is if we try to go there," Narlhep finished, "Viron is going to know we're coming and he'll be able to tell exactly where we are within Taiyou."

"How is that exactly?" Kaji asked.

Narlhep grimaced. "The ruler of Taiyou is connected to the land. They can feel the land and the people on it. It's how our defenses work. The King – or in this case, the Regent – can direct the army or the weapon to where the threats are."

"He can feel everyone all at once?" I asked. "Wouldn't that be a little confusing?"

"It doesn't work that way," Narlhep struggled to explain without giving away too many of Taiyou's secrets, but then gave up resisting. "I hope I'm doing the right thing by telling you all of this, but I have to trust you. Taiyou is divided by lines of power known as Leyins. The Leyins criss-cross all of Taiyou, linking together at the jade mountain in the center – it was once the Temple of Jedeite, though the people of Taiyou don't follow the gem gods anymore. When someone becomes King or Regent they are connected to the Leyins somehow – I haven't been told what the process is yet – and they can feel it any time someone crosses a Leyin. They know instantly who they are, where they've come from, where they're going, and their intentions toward the land, too, or so I've been told."

"But we could avoid these Leyins, right?" I asked.

"We'd have to cross several of them to reach the mountain. It's in the middle of Taiyou and the Leyins get more frequent the closer you get."

"The Leyins are the weapon, aren't they?" Yue asked. "I crossed one on our way here and it felt the same, like a ribbon of power. I almost lost control of it and Jeth had to pull me out."

"You can feel the Leyins?" Narlhep asked, taken aback. "That shouldn't be possible…but I guess you are a Chosen. They're not exactly the weapon," he tried to explain. "I mean they are…but they're just power. They cover all of Taiyou, including the borders. As far as I understand it, the weapon just draws on the power of the Leyins."

"So unless we can somehow avoid the Leyins, Viron will know we are coming and what we intend," Sabien summarized. "In which case, there is no reason to hide and we can ride out in force before Viron takes it upon himself to destroy this outpost."

"There is no way to avoid them," Narlhep said, "but I can show you where they are."

I handed Narlhep a sheet of paper and the length of pencil I had carried with me since the Temple of Sapphire and he drew, as best he could from memory, a map of Taiyou with the locations of the Leyins marked on it.

"If we go this way," I indicated on the map, "we can give Viron the impression we're headed for the Raman keep. Would Lord Rama support you if we showed him proof of Viron's treachery?"

"Lord Rama took himself away from the council after my father died. He might not want to come back to the city, but he hates Viron and he was like a father to me growing up. I know I can count on his support, even if I don't have the rest of the council's."

"Perfect," I said. "I know Sir Rama, Lord Rama's son. I can send him a message to meet us here," I said, pointing to the map, "on the border of the Raman province and away from any Leyins. If he'll support you, then we'll have a witness to your claims of Viron being a traitor and soldiers in case we need them to secure the mountain."

"But if Viron feels us go over the Leyin with troops, he might just fire on us all," Narlhep pointed out.

"Firing on the Chosen of Sapphiros who could be said to be kidnapping the Prince is one thing," Kaji pointed out, "but Viron would have to be pretty stupid to fire on Lord Rama's troops while they march with the rightful heir to the throne, which could only be taken as proof he's a traitor. We'll be much safer with witnesses."

I had the Prince compose a message to Rama and assured him it could not be intercepted, unless someone was there to pick it up off the ground in front of Rama's feet. I did my best to visually imprint Narlhep's seal onto the bottom of the note and with intense concentration I even managed to include a small map of the Raman province, so Rama would know where to meet us. I was quite pleased with my efforts and I didn't even think to question that my arrow might not be able to shoot so far as to reach its target, a whole Taiyoun province away.

Sabien and Masaru informed the Roughlanders we were all leaving and why. There wasn't a single Roughlander who didn't want to come with us, even though it would mean they might have to fight to support Prince Narlhep. They were fully aware of who had finally released them from the curse and evidently he had won their allegiance by doing so.

Everyone picked up what belongings they had or might need, including weapons and supplies ordered at one time from the catalogues supplied by Taiyou. Without delay, the four of us, the Roughlanders, the Knights, and the three Croatins – including the two Second Spawn Yue and Kaji had picked up and Stephen, the Seventh Spawn from Espearia – stood ready to depart, with the pallet from Rama filled with supplies and salt and carried by four Roughlanders.

Ris cloaked the group of us with invisibility, so we could leave the city without alarming the citizens of Taiyou. Kaji and Sabien stayed ahead of Ris, so they could be seen as they knocked on the outpost gate.

John slid the eye slit open cautiously, "Kaji, are you looking to leave again?"

"Yes I am, John."

John looked past Kaji and Sabien, and seeing no one else, he let out an audible sigh of relief and opened the door. "Just the two of you, then?"

Kaji walked past John, but Sabien stood with his back against the open gate door to keep it propped open. The rest of us took this as our cue to exit through the gate as silently as possible.

"John, a piece of advice," Kaji addressed the gate guard, stalling for time as the rest of us shuffled past. "Today might not be a good day to be guarding the outpost. Just in case something was to happen, I think you might be better off being elsewhere."

Just then, Stephen the Croatin sneezed and John's eyes darted about, looking for the source of the noise, but of course he couldn't see past Ris' magic.

"I only have your best interest in mind, John," Kaji informed him.

John's eyes continued to dance nervously, but he forced himself to look Kaji in the eyes. "I know that, Chosen," he said with as much sincerity as he could muster under the circumstances, "and thank you."

Kaji nodded and John didn't stick around to find out what in the world Kaji was up to – he ran.

Masaru closed the outpost door behind us and we were off once again through the streets of Taiyou, this time with no one the wiser and with the Prince of Taiyou sandwiched between myself and Yue to keep him safe, should Fuzen, or anyone else, detect our presence.

Once out of view of the city, Ris let the invisibility field drop and we marched through the countryside of Taiyou toward the Raman province. It was nearly a full day to the first Leyin. I remembered the journey well from when we had come through here with Aysel, when I was just learning about the effects of the curse and trying so desperately to combat it.

It was almost a certainty Viron could and would reach the mountain of the sorceresses before us, if that was where he was headed, but we had little choice but to press onwards and hope we could outmaneuver him, or at least wrest control of the weapon from him upon arrival.

As we neared the Leyin, Sabien suggested we rest before we make the crossing. "We'll want to confuse Viron as to our speed of travel if we can't confuse him about anything else," he recommended. "If we rest now, we can press for speed after the Leyin and reach this Lord Rama all the sooner. Until we cross that line, we're essentially invisible to Viron. I'd like to rest while he doesn't know exactly which way we've gone."

Sabien allotted himself and the other Knights as guards around the group and told us to get some rest. Hotaru offered to stay near the Prince, in case she needed to shield him from harm, so with a nod to Narlhep, I left him with her and went to look for where Masaru had been stationed. There hadn't yet been time for me to speak with him and there were some things I needed to say to clear the air between us. I found him on the southern edge of the camp, seated on a rock and looking out at the trees. He was far enough away from the group that whatever I said to him wouldn't be overheard, which suited me just fine.

"Is this spot taken?" I indicated the ground next to the rock he was perched on.

"No." Masaru didn't smile, or even turn his head, but kept his eyes on the tree line.

Settling down beside him, I sat with my legs crossed. "Is this a bad time?"

"Not exactly," he answered, still distant, "but I'm supposed to be keepin' a lookout for danger and I don't want Sabien to think I'm not doing what he told me to."

"Ah," I commented, at a loss, "well, I wanted to talk to you…because I know Fuzen said some things at the drawbridge…"

"Are they true?"

"No. I mean…well, yes, they were dead, but–' I took a deep breath to collect my thoughts. "When I got back to the city the first place I went was to the storehouse where I found your letter. I was extremely worried, you see, after seeing what that curse had done to Aysel. I left the others behind at that point and I followed your trail to the warehouse.

"The first one I found was still breathing." I forced myself to relive the horror of that day so I could do Masaru the justice of telling him how his friends had died. "I did what I could for him, Masaru, I really did. I left him where he lay because it would have done no good to move him, and I continued on looking for you and the others.

"The next three were already gone," I said it as simply as I could, with no description of the horror of what I had seen, but I could tell by Masaru's expression that he was picturing it anyway. He kept his eyes on the trees, but I could see how my words were hurting him.

"That's when I found you." I had to continue and get it all out now, or I likely would not work up the courage to try this again. "There was a trail of blood along the crates."

"Aye," Masaru replied, his voice controlled, "I had climbed up there to keep a lookout for ye."

His words cut sharper than a knife and my guilt over ordering Masaru to leave the outpost with the others was overwhelming. Fuzen had been right in saying it was my fault those men were dead.

"I tried to come sooner," I said, my voice breaking. "I got there as fast as I could with the salt water so I could treat all of you. You were in a bad state. I didn't think the salt was going to be enough and I couldn't move you without risking your life.

"And that's when Fuzen showed up," I continued my story. "He killed…" I was at a loss; I didn't even know the man's name.

"Jorne," Masaru supplied, "he had been guarding the door, so he would have been the closest."

I nodded, swallowing. "Fuzen killed Jorne. After that, you were the only one left. He attacked us and I had to get you out of there…" I hesitated on explaining what I had realized in that second – how important Masaru was to me and that I loved him. "So I broke the windows with my arrows and turned us both to mist. Fuzen couldn't follow us into the air…"

Masaru was nodding, his expression grim. He still had not so much as glanced in my direction.

"I'm so sorry, Masaru."

He looked down at me then, and I saw the sadness in his eyes. "I should be thanking ye for trying and for doing what ye did, or I wouldn't be here now."

I shook my head. "But it's my fault you were there in the first place. I told you to stop eating and drinking and to leave the outpost."

"Aye, and I listened to ye," Masaru replied. "We're all responsible for our own actions and you didn't kill anyone – Fuzen did. I don't blame ye, Yukari."

I was thankful for that small kindness, but I blamed myself and that was enough.

"I'll need some time, though, to sort through it all," Masaru said. "I miss them."

"Do you mind if I stay here?" I asked carefully. "I'm supposed to be resting, but I don't want to go back to the others just yet."

Masaru nodded his consent, looking out at the trees again, and I stretched myself out a little ways away from his rock to try and get some rest. I found myself watching his back for a time as he worked through the death of the people he had led away from the outpost and I gathered Masaru was likely feeling as much guilt as I was, in addition to the loss of his friends.

When I awoke Masaru was nowhere to be seen, but there was a pillow from the Sanctioned Outpost under my head and a light blanket draped over me.

"You're awake, good," Razor said from behind me as I sat up. "Here you go." He handed me an apple and a bun. "Sleep okay?"

I nodded, feeling subdued after my conversation with Masaru.

"That a girl. Sabien was looking for you," Razor informed me. "Something about Kaji saying you would be the best at finding people. It seems Yue is missing."

I stood abruptly, "Yue? How?"

Razor shrugged. "I have no idea, but she's the fast one, right? Maybe she decided to scout ahead and just didn't think to let anyone know."

"Thanks Razor," I said, indicating the breakfast he had given me. "I'm going to go see Sabien."

"No problem," Razor responded and I left him staring after me with an odd expression on his face.

I shot off a message arrow in Yue's direction at Sabien's request, which Ris followed west into the trees to find her. Thankfully, Yue hadn't gone far, and when she returned to camp we learned that Jeth had been with her.

"She just had a bad dream, is all," he informed us. "Nothing to get all worked up about. I saw her leaving all in a panic and followed her, but she'll be okay now."

I wasn't sure what Yue had been dreaming about, but it was true we had a lot to worry about and had seen some pretty awful things since coming here. I gathered that Yue, having seen the effects of this weapon in action through the memories she had absorbed, perhaps had a better idea of exactly what danger we faced from Lord Viron, should he order his daughter to fire on us.

I hoped that Yue – and indeed all four of us – would be able to handle what was coming and not break under the strain of what we had to face. For now, potential crisis averted, our eclectic group continued on its way, crossing the Leyin in the direction of Lord Rama's lands and picking up speed for the duration to hopefully cause Viron to misjudge our exact location.

Throughout our journey I was Narlhep's constant companion. Yue would sometimes walk with us when she was not conferring with the Second Spawn Croatins, Kaji mainly spoke with Sabien concerning tactics, and Hotaru helped the Roughlanders carry the pallet of supplies. Narlhep and I spoke of Taiyoun history and customs, both political and traditional, and I learned a great deal about Narlhep's life as heir to the throne.

"While my father was alive, I was shunted off to the Raman province to live with Lord Rama, so I couldn't be a threat to my father's power. Lord Rama's son, Leon, was like a brother to me, but since my father died and Lord Rama left the council I haven't seen either of them. It'll be good to see someone I know I can trust. Not that I'm saying you're not trustworthy," Narlhep corrected himself, "but we've only just met and I've known Leon Rama my entire life."

I smiled to show him no offence was taken. Everyone I had met on this world, including the Knights, whom I was beginning to rely on, and Masaru, whom I felt so strongly about, were all people I was still just getting to know. It wasn't the same as the bond I had with Hotaru, Yue, and Kaji, whom I had known since childhood, even if we didn't always get along.

Narlhep did not mention how his father had died and though the museum had informed me Prince Narlhep had committed regicide at age twelve, I still couldn't fathom it, especially after getting to know the prince as a person and not just a figure of history.

"I've known since I was a boy I was going to be King one day," Narlhep continued, "but it's not something I think I'll ever be good at. I just hope I can do a better job than my father did, you know?"

I nodded in understanding. I felt sympathy for him – I was quickly learning myself what it meant to be destined for a position you didn't feel qualified for – but after Narlhep's noble behaviour at the Roughlander Sanctioned Outpost, I felt he had the potential to be a great King once he grew into the role. Although, being from a distant world where democracy reigned, I did not feel I was perhaps the best person to judge such things.

Yue was able to call forth the tortoise shell from wherever it was she had stored it and Narlhep and I pored over it as we walked.

"You're right, you know," Narlhep told me after a time spent reading and re-reading a certain passage of the ancient document, "it says right here a civil war is enough to declare immediate kingship. I wonder why I never knew that."

"It's probably something your father and Viron didn't want you to be aware of, so you couldn't find a way to use it to become king sooner," I replied, going off of what I knew of the previous monarch's personality and inclinations.

Narlhep smiled lopsidedly. "I don't doubt you're right about that, too."

Before the next Leyin, we stopped at the place where we were supposed to meet Rama and were a little concerned to discover we had managed to arrive first, considering we had the longer distance to travel. We allowed the Knights some rest, as they had stood guard before the last Leyin, while Kaji, Hotaru, Yue, and I decided to take watch and wait to see if Rama would arrive.

Yue offered to scout, but to my surprise she didn't run around the group of us at top speed like I expected, but instead she sat down in the grass and lowered her head in a meditative position. Before her on the ground, a cyan blue bird made of energy, similar to my arrows, emerged from her hands and took off into the air, circling higher and higher before shooting east in a dive.

Narlhep and I waited impatiently on either side of Yue's slumped form for her to come out of her trance and tell us what was going on. Eventually, she obliged.

"We're surrounded," Yue said. "Tell Kaji and Hotaru to get back here. It's Sir Rama's troops and he'll be here shortly."

I sent message arrows to both Kaji and Hotaru to let them know and Yue flashed-stepped off at high speed to escort Rama himself back to us. Sir Rama's expression was stony when he reached the center of the camp surrounded by Yue, Hotaru, Kaji, and flanked by five of his own personal troops, who Narlhep told me were called the Lion Brigade, along with his Visionary, whom we had also met before.

"I'm relieved to see you well, your Highness," Rama said formally upon reaching Narlhep and I. "I received a most interesting communication in the form of an arrow."

Narlhep smiled, which eased the tension considerably amongst the group. "I was just as surprised as you when I learned how Yukari intended to send the message. Sir Rama, meet the Chosen of Sapphiros," Narlhep said as he gestured to the four of us.

"Actually, we've met," Rama said with a hint of a smile. "I found them trespassing in my father's lands. So am I to understand the message was indeed from you and you were not under any form of duress?"

"I can see how you might think that," Narlhep replied, letting out a laugh before his expression turned serious, "but unfortunately the message Yukari sent for me is real. Viron tried to have me assassinated, and when that failed he tried to imprison me in my own throne room. I have the Chosen to thank for getting out of there and giving me a chance to prove Viron a traitor to the crown."

"You have proof, then?"

"The Oujou admitted to the assassination attempt," Narlhep answered, "and Yue has a helpful gift of being able to transmit memories from one mind to another."

"Show me."

Touching Rama's face gently, Yue presumably gave him her memory of the throne room and all we had discovered therein. Most of it was conjecture, but hopefully it would be enough to condemn Viron for his actions. Yue had to repeat the process for the Visionary and when she was through with that, which took no more than a moment, the Visionary nodded to Rama – what Yue had shown him was the truth.

"My father has given me leave to speak for him in all things, and to act as his voice in regards to this event and in council until such time as he returns," Rama informed us and his prince in a formal tone. "I have the document written in his own hand stating as much.

"I have seen the evidence and confirmed it true," he continued. "Lord Viron is a traitor to the crown of Taiyou and the House of Rama lends its support to you, Prince Narlhep. The Lion Brigade is yours to command."

Rama knelt before his Prince and I could see tears in Narlhep's eyes. "Thank you, my friend." Narlhep helped Rama up and the two embraced.

We gave Rama and the prince some time to get reacquainted, and to let the Knights rest, before we gathered to discuss our strategy for the coming confrontation.

"Our first issue will be crossing the Leyins. There are only two more we will need to cross between here and there, but when we do, Viron will know our exact numbers and location," Narlhep restated for Rama's benefit.

"Well, my men and I patrol our borders all the time, so we have legitimate reason to be travelling in this area," Rama informed us.

"That will work for your men, but the rest of us are a different matter. Kaji," I addressed him, "can you see the Leyins?"

"Of course," Kaji answered to Narlhep and Rama's surprise.

"Did you get a good look at the last one we crossed?" I followed up. "How tall are they and how thick? Can we go over or under them?"

Kaji considered the question a moment. "Definitely not under, they seem to emanate from the ground. They're taller than a man, but not much more so. I'd say maybe seven to eight feet high?"

"They're not much more than a person thick," Yue added. "I got stuck in one, remember?"

"Well that's something at least. I can probably carry at least the group of us over it as mist," I explained. "I might have to make a couple of trips, but Viron wouldn't be able to sense us if we never touch a Leyin."

"What about the Roughlanders?" Hotaru asked. "Can they go with Sir Rama's soldiers?"

"Viron would be able to detect them and the presence of so many Roughlanders so far inland would point directly to us," Sabien noted.

"He's right," Masaru spoke up, "but we don't need to fly to be able to go over a wall. We've got a lot of carpenters with us. They rebuilt the fence at the Sanctioned Outpost in less than a day, I'm sure they can make a ladder or something."

"Wouldn't it have to be a bridge to go all the way over safely?" I asked. "There's nothing to lean a ladder on."

"Well I was thinking more like one of those platform things – like over water," Masaru added.

I stared at Masaru in confusion. It seemed like he was describing a diving board – which would work perfectly with something on the other side to cushion the fall – but I was wondering how in the world he even knew what a diving board was, let alone how he thought of one.

Masaru looked a little sheepish, "I saw one…when ye Knighted me. There was all that water…"

I blushed with the realization Masaru hadn't been as unconscious during the Knighting process as I had thought he'd been; it was very possible he also remembered me kissing him for the second time. I didn't think to question how it was possible he had seen something I had imagined; magic rituals were funny that way, I suppose.

"More to the point," I said, recovering somewhat, "that's a perfect idea, Masaru. Do you remember enough to explain to the Roughlanders what it looks like?" Masaru nodded. "Perfect. So all we'll need is something for them to land on on the other side. I suppose we can toss over the pallet first with the supplies and use the blankets and pillows to cushion the fall."

"All that's well and good, but what are we going to do about the Oujou?" Yue interjected. "Getting there won't do us any good if she's just going to curse us so we can't stop Viron. We already know she takes orders from him."

Yue had a point, but it was one I had already thought of.

"Well, we know what works against her – salt," I said. "So we need salt and lots of it."

"There was only so much left at the outpost from what Rama gave us," Kaji informed us. "We had to use most of it to treat the disease and the rest we had people drink as a preventative measure, so they wouldn't get infected again."

I nodded. "Sir Rama, would you happen to have any more salt?"

"I do, in fact," Rama replied, "but it's not a common request, so unfortunately it's only kept in one storehouse I know of." He pointed to the map of the Leyins we had spread out before us. "It's a ways from here and you'd have to cross at least three Leyins to get there. You could send for it, I suppose, with your message arrows, but it would still take some time to get here."

"I don't know how I would even send an arrow to a place I've never been to," I responded dubiously. "Without someone to lock onto, I wouldn't know where to shoot and I wouldn't want to hit anyone accidentally by trying."

"I'll get it!" Yue announced.

Rama gave Yue a surprised look. "Do you fly or something? Or perhaps can appear and disappear at will?"

"No," Yue responded with all seriousness, "I just run really fast."

Rama's brow furrowed. "Presuming my countrymen believed you had the right to requisition the salt, how would you carry enough back here? On your back?"

Yue shook her head. "Not exactly."

"Yue, you would be the perfect person to send," I told her. "You can jump the Leyins and store the salt. You should probably take one of Sir Rama's men with you, so you'll be believed." Rama nodded in agreement, though he still seemed bewildered. "We'll keep moving. Can you meet us, say…here?" I indicated a spot on the map close to our destination.

"Better than jumping the Leyins, Yue should cross as many as possible and keep Viron's attention for a little while, before jumping them on the way back to us. It might help us to confuse him," Sabien suggested.

In agreement, Yue commandeered Rama's captain and made him strip off his armour so he would be lighter for her to carry. Within moments, she was off into the Raman province to give Viron a merry chase and requisition the salt we would need to face the Oujou, should she try and stop us. Rama's men formed up around our group and together we proceeded to the next Leyin, where the Roughlanders, recently freed from the lengthy Oujou curse, were given a chance to put their skills learned at the Sanctioned Outpost to use.

"Everyone hold hands," I instructed the Knights, apart from Ris, who with her wings was able to fly herself over.

Taking a deep breath, I felt the connection between myself and the people to either side of me, and then reached outwards from there to feel them all. There were seven people besides myself, and repeating the process I had used that first time to rescue Masaru from the warehouse, I turned them all to mist with me and was relieved to discover it was possible to take so many. As a large cloud, we drifted up and over where Kaji had informed me the Leyin was and reformed a short distance away on the other side.

"That was awesome," Jeth remarked to the relieved laughter of Prince Narlhep.

Hotaru and Kaji, along with the other Knights – among whom I counted Aysel, even though she was only a squire – seemed to take my strange method of travel in stride.

In remarkable time, the aged Roughlanders managed to construct an elaborate wooden diving board to pass over the seven-foot tall, invisible – to everyone but Kaji, at least – magical barrier. The rest of us could have waited for the diving board to be completed, but we hadn't wanted to chance any of us accidentally touching the barrier, as we would have been more noticeable to Viron than a singular Roughlander would. We also needed people on the other side to construct the landing pad for the divers.

In due course we were over the Leyin en masse and the diving board was left standing to mark the Leyin border. It was a monument to the newfound freedom of the Roughlanders in Taiyou and this potentially historic day, when the Chosen of Sapphiros and the Roughlanders marched with the Taiyouns to denounce a traitor and restore the rightful King to the throne.

We repeated the procedure at the next Leyin and rested on the other side to await Yue's return, so we would be prepared to face Viron and the Oujou when the time came.

The mountain of Jade, formerly the Temple of Jedeite, was a striking oddity on the flat countryside of Taiyou that for some inexplicable reason was not visible until one was almost upon it. I suspected some illusionary magic was being used, like what Kosetsu had done to hide Viron's armour, but on a grander scale.

The mountain itself was not large, but it was perfectly straight and tapered, as if it had somehow been constructed by man and not nature. At the base of the mountain, there was a small village of wooden cabins and storage huts; on the southern side a staircase was carved into the rock, leading up to a large entranceway framed by two identical jade pillars. Upon closer inspection, the jade pillars were not straight, but carved replicas of the feminine form of the Oujou, complete with her spider-like webbed clothing and pointed claws. The implications of her form decorating the entrance were enough to make me shudder, but we had come here with a purpose and we meant to accomplish it, whether the Oujou interfered or not.

We met no resistance and found no other troops waiting for us anywhere near the mountain, though the Lion Brigade did scout for them. There was also no sign of Viron, but without going inside there was no way to tell if he had gotten here before us and was perhaps already at the weapon.

"Not all of us can or need to go in," Sabien advised. "Adel, I leave you in command. I will accompany the Chosen and the Prince."

"I'm going with you as well, your Highness," Rama informed Narlhep and gave orders to his own troops.

With that being decided, the four of us, Sabien, and Rama, accompanied Narlhep up the stairs to the entranceway. We were met in the open doorway by an ancient woman clad in a floor-length black robe, her silver hair done up in a tight bun, with black webbing to hold it in place.

"Ah, our prince has come at last to see us," the woman spoke in a thin, reedy voice, her exceptionally long fingernails clacking together ominously. "Has the time come already?"

Narlhep ignored the woman's question in favour of getting directly to the point. "I seek the traitor Lord Viron. Is he within the school?"

The woman seemed to consider this a moment. "I know not of treachery within Taiyou, but the Lord Regent is within. He has asked not to be disturbed."

"Disturb him," Narlhep instructed. "Viron will be tried for his treachery."

"Very well," the woman replied with a tired sigh, "come along."

The woman drifted along the floor through the entranceway and further into the mountain, as if she hovered more than an inch off the ground. I shuddered once more watching her – it was unnatural.

Narlhep followed the woman within, so we had little choice but to accompany him. I didn't like the feeling of entering a mountain I had seen only one entrance to. I understood this was some sort of school, so likely there would be a multitude of people within, but from the outside I had not seen even a singular window or airway. On the inside, the walls were lined with Jade and the colour and feel of the rock reminded me forcefully of the throne room in the palace, though I couldn't place why until I remembered the green eyes of the silver visage of the throne room door. Was it possible the throne room doors had also been made of Jade and encased in silver, like this mountain was encased in rock? Jade – Jedeite, sapphire – Sapphiros? It was becoming clear to me that precious stones had a bit more meaning in this world than they did on our own.

The center of the mountain was a hollow circle with a similar ambient light to that of the throne room in the palace, which came from no discernable source. The circular jade walls were broken up by wooden doors all the way around, and by looking up I could see a second floor balcony and even a third, with no evident way to reach either level. On the very top level, high above us, there was a jade statue of a menacing figure looking down upon us. The shape of it looked vaguely Croatin, though larger and more reptilian, but even from here the face was recognizable as the carving on the throne room doors. Was it a likeness of Jedeite, perhaps?

I was right about the multitude of people; there were women – presumably students – in the signature black, floor-length robes, scurrying from room to room, some with books or instruments in hand, others floating like the ancient woman was.

In the center of the mountain floor, the ancient woman stopped abruptly and spun about in place to face us. A loud grinding noise filled the hollow mountain, and when I turned to see where it was coming from I could do nothing but watch as the massive stone and jade doors grinded shut with deafening finality. We were sealed within the mountain with the traitor Lord Viron, a veritable army of trained sorceresses, and potentially also the deadly Oujou.

Chapter 13 – Punishment for the Forgotten

The students and trained sorceresses went about their tasks or attended their lessons, floating or walking by us with only mild curiosity, if they glanced our way at all, while we essentially cooled our heels, waiting in the main chamber of the mountain for Lord Viron to grace us with his presence.

The sorceresses' lack of concern over strangers in their midst did nothing to lessen my sense of unease. As large as the school was, we were still sealed inside a mountain made of solid Jade; another sealed temple to a gem god, only this time the temple was not our own and there was no computer system I could override to get the doors to open.

"So we just wait?" I asked, the entire situation causing my patience to wear thin.

"What other choice do we have?" Sabien responded stoically.

"While we are stuck in here, the people we left outside are still in danger from Viron," I noted. "He knows exactly where we are now."

"Ris and I are connected," Sabien told me. "If she was in danger, especially so close, I would know it instantly." By the tone of his words, I understood there was a deeper meaning. Ris and Sabien were together; I suppose that meant Krox and Dahlia weren't the only inter-species couple I knew.

If it was possible to court disaster just by speaking of its possibility, Sabien had done so. I watched the Knight Commander's expression change abruptly from calm to frantic. "She's in danger," he breathed, with a vulnerability I had never heard from him before.

Masaru – I had left him out there along with the others. I forced myself to breathe and control my rising panic. Sabien's premonition of Ris' well being was not enough to confirm that the weapon had been fired. It would be wonderful if we could somehow get out of this mountain and help those outside, if they really were in danger, but we had a task to accomplish in here and stopping Viron could be the answer to protecting everyone we had brought with us.

I felt for Sabien. If Ris was important enough to him that he could feel when she was in danger, then if a way out could be found for him, the rest of us would do what we could to handle Viron without him.

Obviously what Sabien sensed was enough to make him believe his place right now was outside with Ris and the others. As I scanned the room with my particularly sharp vision looking for a way out, Sabien splashed to a puddle on the floor and was zooming about, feeling for cracks that would let him escape to the world outside.

Yue flash-stepped over to try the doors themselves, but like the ones in the throne room they had no handles or hinges, so no amount of pushing or commanding them to open seemed to have any effect.

"They're magically sealed, Yue," Kaji informed her.

Narlhep looked concerned. "If they're like the throne room doors, maybe I can open them. I know she told us to wait, but that just means Viron has me exactly where he wants me – trapped again."

Narlhep headed back to the door to see if they would respond to his commands like, presumably, his throne room doors were supposed to, but I didn't hold out too much hope for his success. Narlhep was right, this felt like too much of a trap for my liking.

"I'll check the other levels," I announced and turned myself to mist to float upwards toward the tapered ceiling, scanning the walls as I went.

"I'll just wait here," Rama added unnecessarily.

Short of trying every door in the place to look for windows, which I sincerely doubted existed, I could find no cracks in the surface of the Jade that might indicate a weak point and no drafts of air, fresh or otherwise. It had been a windy day outside, but in here the air was still and slightly stale.

As I reached the ceiling, I noted the top did not taper to a point like one might expect, but instead ended in a flat surface of smooth jade. The topmost floor of the inside of the mountain was a balcony, upon which the massive statue of the Croatin-like form stood like a sentry in front of an ornately carved wooden door. I almost left to float back down to the ground level and inform everyone that my search had proved unsuccessful when I felt it; there was the faintest of drafts coming from beneath the wooden doorway.

The imposing form of the statue was not enough to deter me from reforming beside it, but it came close. I was beginning to suspect Jade and perhaps Sapphire, or the other precious stones— though we hadn't come across any yet – had some inherent magical properties. If I was right, it would explain the magic Kaji had detected on the doors of both this place and the throne room, and how they had operated presumably on their own, unless of course the doors were another manifestation of the Oujou's will, in which case we knew who was responsible.

The statue did nothing, but as I reformed and reached for the handle, the door opened with a whoosh to reveal the matronly sorceress, hovering her standard inch from the ground, and coming toward me quickly. The door seemed to have opened for her of its own accord. Despite myself, I took a step back out of her way, but by her expression she was just as surprised to encounter me as I was to see her.

"What are you doing up here?" she demanded sharply, fixing me with a baleful stare.

I didn't answer her, as there wasn't really a good explanation for my presence on this balcony. The sorceress didn't wait for my response, but instead drifted past me to the edge of the balcony to look down. Her brows furrowed in displeasure as she studied the scene below.

Tearing myself away from the door through which she had come, I looked past the woman to see what was going on. Far below on the ground level, there were two puddles of water visibly swooshing around looking for exits – Sabien and Hotaru, I presumed. Narlhep looked impatient, but stood with Rama to wait; Kaji and Yue were out of sight for the moment.

"This won't do," the woman muttered and winked out of existence before my very eyes. I blinked for a moment in surprise, but then realized she had somehow managed to cause herself to appear on the ground floor and was now speaking to Narlhep below.

I gave one last furtive look at the door behind me before deciding I could always come back if it were necessary. For now, it would be better to check if the sorceress had done what she had told us she would before doing anything to antagonize her. With a sigh, I turned myself back to mist and floated down to the others.

"My request is simple, open the doors," Narlhep demanded of the sorceress, obviously frustrated.

"I'm afraid that is impossible," the sorceress stated simply, as I landed behind her and reformed. "Once one of the royal line has entered the school, the door may not be opened again, except by the ruler of Taiyou. Only you can shut the door and only you can open it."

"How do I open it, then?" Narlhep asked, trying for patience.

"You do not know? It is not for I to teach you, but for your predecessor. In this case the Lord Regent has command over your teachings. Perhaps he intended to teach you when it was time for you to ascend to the throne and not before."

"Viron is a traitor, which forbids him from continuing in his position as Regent, and the form of his treachery is grounds for a civil war, meaning that I am to be declared King immediately," Narlhep proclaimed, his patience having run out entirely.

The sorceress' sudden shift in expression betrayed her surprise. "Have you proof of these accusations?"

"Yue, show her please," Narlhep requested and Yue stepped forward to give the memories to the sorceress. "These memories have been confirmed as truth by Sir Rama's visionary and Sir Rama is here acting on behalf of his father, a prominent member of council. I ask that you recognize my legitimacy and co-operate."

The sorceress nodded despite herself, a little stunned at the turn of events and likely still reeling from the odd experience of having memories given to her by Yue. I had never experienced the phenomenon myself, but I had seen the bewildered expressions of her victims many times and had gathered that it was a less than comfortable experience.

"Good. Firstly, tell me how to open the doors," Narlhep continued.

"I can't do that," the sorceress said, hesitating. "Only those of the royal line, or the current Regent, know how. We don't shut the doors – ever."

"Then where is Viron?" Narlhep demanded.

The sorceress took a deep breath and recovered some of her previous demeanor. "The Lord Regent has been advised of your request and has said that he will be down shortly."

"Did we not just prove to you that Viron is no longer the Regent?" Hotaru asked.

"Until the Prince is crowned, there must be a Regent in place. Unless the council rules otherwise, that Regent is Lord Viron," Rama explained to her.

"Indeed," the sorceress agreed, "and I ask that you retire to a chamber to await him, so my students will no longer be disrupted by your presence." She gestured to a door and it opened at her silent command.

"If he is actually coming, we will wait a short time longer," Narlhep conceded, "but in that room over there." He pointed to a room on the other side of the mountain – one that was not of the sorceress' choosing – in case she had any ulterior motives.

The room in question was one that two younger students had entered not long ago and therefore was more likely to be safe. The sorceress nodded her head with a tilt to the side and said, "Very well," before drifting over to the door Narlhep had indicated and allowing it to open wide before her.

The group of us followed behind her. Within the room there were the two students standing before a Kumori, like Ris in size and shape, but white with a few reddish-brown markings. The students faced each other with their hands outstretched and between them hovered a crackling ball of green-tinged energy. As we entered, our footsteps – especially Sabien, Narlhep, and Rama in their armoured boots – clattered loudly on the Jade floor, causing the girl on the right to break her concentration and glance just once over her shoulder.

That single moment of distraction was all it took. The crackling ball of energy lost its precarious balance and hurtled away from the first student to envelop the hands of the one who had showed it a moment of weakness. The unsuspecting student cried out in sudden intense agony as the energy wrapped around her hands, searing them thoroughly.

While the first student looked on in horror, the Kumori raised her hands in a deliberate motion and the vengeful magic energy winked out of existence, leaving the injured student crying fiercely, cradling her burned and ruined hands.

"Heal her and then go," the sorceress commanded. "This room is no longer available."

With a nod, the Kumori – in a way so reminiscent of Ris that I looked over my shoulder to see how Sabien was doing – raised her hands and created a small field of red light to encase the girl's hands in order to heal them.

As the Kumori and the students filed past, the sorceress directed a disapproving frown at us, as if to say the girl's injury was our fault. When the room had been cleared for us, the sorceress made as if to leave again and floated toward the open doorway, when she stopped abruptly and her feet landed on the jade floor. The suddenly grounded sorceress staggered back a few steps into the room and we were able to see what had caused her to falter. Filling the open door was the menacing form of the Oujou, holding an ornate gold crown carved with doves and adorned with small pieces of Jade.

"A King declared, but our Prince he remains. We gift the crown and our King is regained," the Oujou said, bowing her head in a slow and deliberate motion.

The others watched the Oujou warily, but my eyes were on Narlhep. On the one hand Narlhep wanted to take the crown now, so he would have the authority to break free of Viron's control and begin his kingship immediately, to try and make amends for all his father and Lord Viron had done to Taiyou. On the other hand, Narlhep was not stupid and, though tempted, he knew the Oujou meant him harm, so any crown given from her hands was bound to come with definite strings attached.

"Narlhep, don't," I cautioned. "It's not worth it."

"I know," Narlhep answered, the continuing struggle in his voice, "but…"

"We will find another way. The correct way," I told him. "You don't want to be a slave to the Oujou's will like your father and the Narlhep kings before him, destined to be killed by your own son as soon as he is of age."

Narlhep gasped; I hadn't known the truth of that fact I had picked up at the museum, but now I did. Each King in the Narlhep line had killed the prior ruler and I would bet any number of krevels those acts of regicide played into the Oujou's hand perfectly. The shock of my statement caused Narlhep's foot to drop and he hung his head in shame.

"Our Prince to decide if King he will be," the Oujou spoke again with only a hint of displeasure, tilting her head to look between Narlhep and myself. "The crown is his, by royal decree."

Narlhep snapped his head up to stare at her directly. "Yes, the crown is mine," he stated with conviction. "I will be King of Taiyou – but not by your hand. Your time is finished, Oujou."

The Oujou's patient and seductive expression abruptly turned malicious as she stared down the monarch who had defied her. The ornate crown between her hands wafted into nothing more than green smoke as she took a step toward the Prince, her clawed hands held menacingly before her.

"We are Oujou and forever we are. A princeling's life is no more than a fleeting star."

"Yue – salt!" I commanded.

I didn't see Yue move, but I didn't expect to. Between one moment and the next, Yue disappeared and then reappeared in front of the Oujou with a barrel of salt in her hands. There was another flash and then the Oujou had raised her right arm to try and block the salt Yue was launching at her. After that split second had passed there was salt everywhere, but more importantly the Oujou was staggering backwards, looking unsteady. When I focused in to see her composition, I could tell immediately that bits of her form were flaking off. The salt was working, but it wasn't enough. The Oujou particles that had been hit directly were affected – mainly the arm she had held outstretched – but the whole of her was still strong.

"Hotaru!" I called her name as a signal for her to do her part and create water on the Oujou, in order to hopefully speed up the disintegration process, but I should have been more specific.

Hotaru surged forward, but instead of creating water like I wanted her to, she manifested her two swords – one short and one long – and made to attack the Oujou physically. I knew immediately physical attacks were not the answer here, despite Hotaru's blades being made of water and ice, their effect on the Oujou – who was made up entirely of individual particles – would be minimal. The Oujou could control her form at will, forming it and reforming it as necessary, so unless we were able to fight the particles like I had with the salt water in the bodies of my patients, we would be hard pressed to stop the Oujou from doing as she liked. Right now, what she wanted appeared to be Prince Narlhep, dead or alive.

Hotaru slashed at the Oujou with her swords, first the longer ice sword in her right hand and then the shorter blade made from water in her left. The ice sword connected across the Oujou's middle with a grating sound, sending a shower of green particles into the air. The second sword was too far behind the first and by the time it would have struck, the Oujou had already swooshed into a multitude of particles without visible form. My eyes were good at a distance – much better now than they used to be – but even I could not follow the Oujou particles as they whirled across the room.

"Did I get her?" Hotaru asked no one in particular.

Narlhep made to take a step forward to leave the room, intent on following after the Oujou. "No, don't," I counseled him. "She's still out there and the one she wants is you."

Out in the center chamber, the Oujou reformed herself on the first floor balcony. I noted distantly all of the other doors were shut tight and the students were nowhere to be seen. Neither was their matron; she must have made herself disappear once more.

"I can't just stand here and do nothing," Narlhep stated.

"You can stay safe, Your Highness," Rama said over his shoulder as he drew his sword and headed forward after the Oujou.

Yue had disappeared and Hotaru was already making a break toward the Oujou, so I watched as Sabien and Kaji followed after Rama to do the same. I wasn't sure if any of them were really sure what they were up against, but they were willing to try and face her just the same.

"I'll stay by your side," I told Narlhep. I could be more effective from a distance regardless, and there was little point to us all rushing forward to where the touch of her crystal particles could affect us in the manner of her choosing.

I hoped against hope they would all remain safe. It was not lost on me that although Sabien had seen the Oujou kill, I alone could truly appreciate what the true nature of the Oujou was, having seen the intelligence and perseverance of each individual particle firsthand as they attacked in the form of the 'curse' of the Sanctioned Outpost. "As a leader and a King, you'll have to get used to staying behind and giving the orders. Direct me if needed, I can support the others."

Out in the main chamber, I could see the Oujou was moving a little more jerkily than I remembered from the throne room and moments ago when she had held the crown. Was it possible the salt was beginning to take effect? The Oujou gathered herself as if to explode again, as she had when we were fleeing the throne room. No one else was near her, but if she expanded her particles she could easily reach anyone and everyone in the room. Someone had to stop her and disrupt her focus before she could attack.

I didn't hesitate; I had range and precision, and even at this distance my arrows could reach the Oujou before even Yue could get there at her top speed. I raised my arms and formed an arrow with my thoughts. I only needed one, but I charged it with power so it would explode when it struck and let it loose, centering it on the Oujou.

My blue energy arrow whizzed out the door and curved its flight unnaturally to avoid striking Rama and Sabien, before arching upwards to fly toward its intended target. Presumably due to the earlier salting, the Oujou was too focused on trying to gather control over her failing particles, so she was unable to react quickly enough to avoid my arrow or disperse her form before it connected with her. The arrow struck her right side and exploded on contact, shattering her right arm below the elbow and scattering the particles all over the balcony and below.

There was no blood or anything to indicate I had actually wounded her, since she wasn't technically a living being, but I knew at least that I had been able to distract her enough that she had to expend effort to try and reform herself, rather than attacking. I watched with grim satisfaction as the Oujou lifted the remaining stump of her arm and tried without success to summon enough of her particles to reform herself completely – I had damaged her.

The Oujou let out an enraged howl, but the sound was cut short as from out of nowhere Yue barreled into her with increased force due to her inhuman speed. I was a little surprised Yue was able to make contact with the Oujou, but whether it was the salt that was helping us against her, or if she was more corporeal than I had originally thought, the force of Yue's impact was enough to send the form of the Oujou careening backwards into the Jade wall behind her.

Meanwhile, Hotaru and Kaji, running as fast as they were able, reached the other side of the main chamber, though they were a whole floor away from reaching the balcony where Yue was facing the Oujou. In mid-stride, Hotaru leapt into the air and jets of water shot out from her hands, propelling her upwards so she could make the jump up to the next floor.

Kaji stretched out his hand as if to grab hold of Hotaru, though she was in the air and still a ways ahead of him. His hand closed onto something and he was lifted right along with the force of her jump, not slowing Hotaru down in the least. I surmised this was some sort of new power he had developed, though I wasn't exactly sure what he was doing or how.

Hotaru landed on the balcony and Kaji landed inexplicably on thin air, as if it was solid ground. He walked forward calmly to join Hotaru on the balcony as Yue, not wasting a single moment, flashed-stepped forward again to ram the Oujou further into the wall. After gaining control over herself at last, the Oujou dissolved into particles just as Yue would have slammed into her, causing Yue to impact solidly with the wall itself.

I winced in sympathy as Yue staggered and slumped to the ground, but I couldn't focus on her. Instead, I scanned the room to try and predict where the Oujou would form next.

"Where did she go?" Narlhep asked from beside me.

"I don't know–" I began and then realized I did know, or at least had a way to find out.

I closed my eyes to concentrate and sensed to feel for my earlier target, knowing I had been able to lock onto her before and so my arrows should still be able to find her. I ground my teeth together in frustration; she was technically everywhere, her particles spread about the room, and I couldn't pinpoint her. If I stayed focused like this I might be able to feel when she reformed, but by then it might have been too late.

Giving up on that method, I opened my eyes and I was surprisingly pleased to note a slight cyan glow forming in the center of the room, though it was at least twelve feet off the ground.

"There!" I called out to everyone. "In the centre – she glows!"

The Oujou reformed much more quickly this time – it seemed she was recovering somewhat – though her right arm where I had struck still stopped at the elbow. She hovered ominously in the exact centre of the main chamber at approximately the height of the first floor balcony, glaring balefully at where Kaji and Hotaru knelt by Yue's slumped form.

Sudden motion caught my eye and I noticed a sword hurtling impossibly far through the air in a straight line.

"All right, Leon!" Narlhep cheered, and I followed the line the sword had travelled to see Rama was holding his arm extended, with a look of concentration on his face. It seemed Sir Rama had a few surprises of his own.

The sword crossed the distance in a perfect line and struck the Oujou, whose form exploded outward. It was possible Rama's sword had damaged her or broken her hold over her form, or this could have been another trick of the Oujou's. No one reacted and I held my breath as we waited to see if Rama's attack had been successful or not.

Scanning the room gave me only a second's warning of what happened next. I saw Kaji's reaction as a look of horror passed over his face and he dove to cover Yue's unconscious body with his own to protect her from the Oujou's attack. There was nothing to see, but simultaneously Kaji and Hotaru cried out in sudden agony, their bodies arching, and a moment later on the ground Rama and Sabien did the same, as the crystalline particles of the Oujou presumably reached them.

On the ground level, Rama was closest to the room where Narlhep and I were, and as he fell to the ground I could see a sheen of blood coating his skin like sweat. I could tell from where we stood that his breathing was laboured as it came in short gasps, and I found myself wondering what the Oujou had done to him and the others, and if any of them were going to be okay.

While Rama and the others struggled to regain their strength, the Oujou reformed on the ground with a wicked smile contorting her face. She stalked purposefully toward the open door to the room where Narlhep and I were, and I prepared myself to defend the prince from her by drawing my canteen of salty water from my belt. I didn't have much left, but I prayed it would be enough to catch her off guard, giving myself and Narlhep a chance to defend ourselves or flee.

Rama struggled to his knees as the Oujou passed him, intent on the prince for whom she had come, and with a jerky motion he forcefully swiped his arm through the air. Responding to his command, Rama's sword scraped along the balcony, where it had landed after his first attack, and whooshed through the air at the Oujou's back.

The sword passed right through the Oujou this time; she paid it no more mind than she would a fly, but Rama was another story. With a look at Narlhep and I that clearly said she would deal with us later, she turned to face Rama.

"Yukari, do something," Narlhep pleaded, worried for his friend.

I didn't need prompting. I had already dropped my canteen to form another arrow between my hands. I let this one loose, not on the still glowing form of the Oujou, but on Rama beyond her.

The Oujou glanced over her shoulder at the last possible second to see my arrow coming straight for her, as she was between me and my target. No doubt remembering the devastating effect my last arrow had on her arm, she exploded once more into particle form to avoid my attack. This suited me just fine, since I hadn't been aiming to hit her anyway. My arrow wrapped its lengthy tail of rope around Rama's midsection and, grasping the end of the rope in my hands, I gave it a good yank. Rama slid easily along the Jade floor, thanks to the copious amount of salt coating it, and shortly, Narlhep and I were able to tug him over to relative safety.

I knelt down beside Rama and quickly began to check him over as best I could around his armour. Like Sabien, he wore no helmet, and as my hand wiped some of the blood from his brow I was able to see his wounds were miniscule but everywhere. With my enhanced vision, I could see the pinprick holes decorating his armour as well, making it seem as if he was bleeding from his very pores. I didn't know how deep the tiny wounds went, or how much damage they had actually done, but thankfully, Rama was conscious and looked likely to remain so, even though he was in a great deal of pain.

"Yukari!" Narlhep called my name sharply and I looked up as yet another chorus of screams filled the mountain.

Out in the main chamber, the Oujou had repeated her last successful attack. Thankfully, Hotaru had recovered enough that she was able to anticipate the move this time by propelling herself into the air with her water jets. She had been able to get out of the range of the Oujou's particles, which evidently had been aimed downward at her adversaries. Kaji wasn't as lucky; he hadn't moved from where he protected Yue, and I saw his back arch once more under the attack of the Oujou's particles before he, too, slumped over unconscious.

I breathed a sigh of relief when I saw that Yue, at least, had actually been protected, and was now awake and alert enough to move. She stood, scooping Kaji up into her arms and swaying slightly. After a moment to prepare herself, she ran forward and leapt from the balcony.

The fact that I could watch her run and jump told me immediately that she wasn't feeling up to her usual speed. From the last attack, I knew it took the Oujou some time to reform herself after she exploded like she did, and I counted the seconds it took for Yue to land and make her way across the room. Yue was fast even without using her powers, and she skidded to a halt beside me with Kaji in her arms before there was even the faintest hint of the cyan glow, which would warn us of the Oujou's return.

I grabbed hold of Yue's arm as she put Kaji down on the other side of me from where Rama lay. "We need water to make this work," I told her. "Please, make Hotaru see that, and if you have more salt–" She cut me off with a nod of agreement and a gesture toward Kaji.

Letting go of her, I looked down and gasped with the sudden realization that my friend wasn't breathing, and he was covered in blood more thoroughly than even Rama had been.

"Kaji–" My breath caught in my throat; it wasn't supposed to be this way.

Kaji was stronger now, we all were. We had come to this fight prepared to face the Oujou, or so we had thought. I felt tears welling up in my eyes and a tightness in my chest; he couldn't be dead – not one of us.

I fought for control over my emotions. I knew what was wrong with him, what had been done to him by the Oujou. I had seen the effects on Rama, and I just needed time to figure out what could be done about it. Placing my hands over his chest, prepared to do CPR, I leaned my ear to his heart first – yes! There was a beat, so there was still a chance.

Kaji, stay with me. We need you. I desperately willed my friend to live as I did what I had been taught to do back in Japan to get someone to breathe again. I breathed, I counted, and I applied pressure to his chest, all the while willing him to stay alive and keep fighting. *Don't give up, Kaji, please.*

I could feel I was losing him, but instead of getting more frantic, my motions became more controlled and deliberate. What was the point of having limitless power at my disposal if I couldn't use it to save someone I cared about? If Sapphiros really was a god and had invested access to his power in me, then I was going to find a way to make use of it – now, before I was too late. Sabien had warned us, but I wasn't going to let emotion get in my way.

Willing my power to manifest, I held onto that feeling of determination and, not allowing myself to doubt, I sat up straight and placed my hands over Kaji's chest.

They began to glow.

When Kaji took his first breath on his own a moment later, my relief was palpable. I didn't take my glowing hands away – if they were keeping him alive, then I would keep them in place until Kaji was well enough to tell me otherwise.

"Kaji!" Narlhep exclaimed, tearing himself away from whatever was happening out in the main chamber to look down at the two of us. "I thought for sure…"

I nodded to forestall him; I didn't want to hear what had almost been true.

"He's going to be okay," I stated with conviction. "What's going on out there?"

Narlhep swallowed visibly and I took that to mean things had not improved. "Sir Sabien tried to get her when she reformed, but it didn't do any good. Yue reached Hotaru and now there is some white stuff filling the air out there. I don't think it's salt, but I can't see a thing. I don't think the Oujou has reformed again yet either."

Kaji coughed once and then seemed to breathe a little easier. Without stopping my newfound power – I remained focused on the truth that Kaji would live through this and my hands continued to glow in response – I took the opportunity to wiggle around so I could once again see out the open door.

Narlhep was right; it was difficult to see, and it definitely wasn't salt obscuring the view, but it was also hardly the water I had asked for. The far side of the room was now blocked by a swirling thick white cloud – Hotaru had made it snow.

I assumed she had used the same power she had demonstrated during our original flight from the Roughlander Sanctioned Outpost when I had asked for a distraction, only this snowfall was in a confined space and much more concentrated. As I peered into the whiteout intently for any sign of motion, I began to notice my targeting was still in effect, so at the very center of the blizzard there was a faint, pulsing cyan light.

"She's in there," I whispered to Narlhep, "and I think she's forming in the centre if she hasn't formed already."

Narlhep nodded. "Then this is where I come in," he stated with a sudden increase in confidence. "Leon, can you still use your sword?"

Rama lifted his sword arm and held it outstretched. His sword flew to him from where it lay just outside the door to fit into his hand comfortably. With a grin in Narlhep's direction, Rama let it go once more and the sword hovered impossibly in the air next to him. "I think I can manage."

"Good. Don't attack her, but use your sword to direct the others to where she is. Yukari can tell you if she moves," Narlhep said as he looked to me for confirmation and I nodded. "We need to coordinate because individually we are getting nowhere, and she can attack all of us at once."

I smiled slightly – I knew Narlhep had it in him to be a good King; he just needed to believe in himself. Hopefully, if we could make it out of there okay, this experience would allow him to gain the confidence he needed to grow into the role since, if we had our way, after that day he would be King.

"Yue!" Narlhep called out and Yue was beside us in a flash. "Do you have any more salt?"

Yue flash-stepped to the door and placed her hands on a pile of salt on the ground, then a sizeable chunk of it disappeared at her command. "Now I do," she answered with grim determination. "Point me at her."

"That's Sir Rama's job," Narlhep informed her. "Follow the sword."

"You'll need Hotaru to make water for you," I told Yue. "Dry salt isn't working as well – she can just shake it off. It needs to be dissolved in liquid."

"Forget Hotaru," Kaji interjected from behind me and I whirled to face him, surprised to discover that not only was he talking, but struggling to his feet. "I'll get you the water you need. Just coat her with salt and don't let her get away again."

Yue nodded and with another flash-step, she was out the door once more.

"That's my cue, I believe," Rama commented and sent his sword flying out the door after her.

"Are you sure you're okay, Kaji?" I asked him quietly, getting to my feet beside him.

"Just get me closer to the door," he responded tersely.

I offered him my support and together we ambled to the door as quickly as we were able. Kaji leaned on me heavily, but I was simply glad he was awake, let alone able to move about at all.

As we reached the door, I saw that Hotaru was in no better shape than Rama, but she was determinedly holding her concentration on maintaining the snowfall before her, as she sat slumped on the Jade floor.

"Hotaru!" I called out. "Stop the snow!"

She looked in mine and Kaji's direction with a surprised and confused expression, her eyes glazed over with pain, but the distraction I had caused her was enough that the snow began slowing and the flakes still in the air began to settle.

Yue appeared once more on the second floor balcony. Rama's sword had flown into the whiteout, but with Hotaru no longer concentrating on her power, it was becoming visible – and so was the form of the Oujou.

Her expression was filled with a malevolent rage as she struggled to reform the arm I had damaged previously. It appeared she had made some progress; her arm to her wrist had mostly reformed, along with part of her hand. However, she seemed to be having trouble holding her damaged, and now sluggishly cold, particles together.

I watched Yue as she leapt into the air from above and behind the Oujou on the second floor balcony, propelled by her impressive speed. As she passed over where the Oujou stood, she summoned the salt from wherever she had put it and let it loose to rain down upon the Oujou with the last of the snow.

The Oujou did not react this time when the salt made contact. She stood glaring at us all malevolently.

"We are Oujou for we are many," the sorceress proclaimed defiantly, her voice ringing throughout the main chamber. "We are relentless. We are eternal. In this place, our temple, we are as the gods once were. What are you, when compared to the Oujou?"

"Chosen," Kaji responded simply as all around the main chamber, the partially melted snow began to move and swirl, gathering speed as it mixed with the salt coating the floor. Letting go of him, I dodged out of the way as I became aware of a crackling noise behind me. Turning my head to look, I saw the water on the floor was freezing rapidly, starting in the area around Kaji's feet and spreading quickly in the direction of the Oujou.

I looked to Kaji for the source of the power at work and his expression clearly showed his intense focus. The swirling water whooshed about the chamber, freezing in a spiral pattern as it went until it surrounded the surprised Oujou in the middle.

Her expression turned from surprise back to arrogance as she regarded the ice around her, despite the state of her arm, not believing we could truly damage her, but at the last, Kaji used the flowing ice to form a massive spike, extending thickly from the ground, right through her forehead.

An inhuman scream broke the silence as the Oujou – impaled on a spear of salty ice – exploded for the last time in a shower of inert green crystals.

Yue spun from where she had landed and in the same motion swung the bundle from her back over her shoulder – Jedeite's sword? I wondered what she was up to, as she began unwrapping the blade from the cloth bandages she had used to keep it hidden.

By the time she was done, I had helped Kaji to sit upon the ground, just outside the room on a drier patch of floor that wasn't coated in the ice he had made. Yue stood with the Jade-bladed sword I had helped her remove from the museum held aloft in her hands and a bewildered expression on her face.

"What are you doing, Yue?" I asked her. "It's over now, isn't it?"

At that, Narlhep, who was supporting Rama, came up beside Kaji and I, and Sabien reformed from a puddle near to Hotaru.

The Jade sword's blade began to glow in Yue's hands.

"It's not me doing it," Yue said, her voice sounding a little worried. "It's Jedeite…he wanted me to–" she cut off, and then continued as if she was talking to someone the rest of us couldn't hear. "Okay, already."

Yue walked slowly and uncertainly toward the spot where the Oujou had fallen, Jedeite's sword held before her. As she walked, the sword continued to glow with an inner light, which grew brighter as the particles of the defeated Oujou drifted up and were absorbed into the blade itself.

"The Oujou stole Jedeite's power and held it captive," Yue explained with a note of wonder in her voice. "The last Chosen of Jedeite grew tired of his immortality – of watching everyone around him age and die, over and over again. He was alone and desperate, and the Oujou offered him release from his never-ending torment. She took his power for herself and it changed her into what we knew her as – powerful, but not really alive." Yue struggled with the words to describe what Jedeite was telling her, "Corrupt."

The sword was glowing fiercely now – Kaji was trying in vain to shield his eyes from the magic that must have seemed so much brighter to his enhanced sight – and all the green shards were gone, leaving only the melting ice and the Jade floor beneath.

With that completed, there was a sudden, intense green flash of light, then Yue and the sword disappeared from the ground floor and shot upwards. The flash left Kaji hopelessly blinded, but I was able to watch the beam of light land on the topmost balcony above and the sword Yue had been holding reformed in the hands of the Jade statue of the Croatin-like Jedeite. There was another flash a moment later, and the sword shot off in a beam again, only this time upwards and through the roof of the Jade mountain.

The surprised silence that followed was broken by the sound of a wooden door slamming open high above. Sounds of a brief struggle ensued and I focused my eyes to better see what was happening to Yue.

I saw Viron first. He was backing toward the rail nearer to where the statue stood, trying to draw his black-bladed sword from its sheath, when all of a sudden Yue tackled him and the two were flung over the edge of the balcony.

I watched the two of them fall in a state of shock. I don't know what Yue thought she was doing, but at this rate the two of them would fall to their deaths on the unforgiving Jade floor beneath them. I couldn't let that happen, not even to the traitor Viron – and certainly not to Yue.

Determined, I formed an arrow with a trail of rope and let it fly. I didn't really know how my rope-arrows worked, but I didn't question them; I just hoped they could do what I wanted.

The arrow struck Viron – I didn't think to spare him the pain of it – and it instantly formed a net made of rope around him. The net also caught Yue, since she was still holding tightly to his back. From there the arrow did not stop, but continued on to the next target I had designated. Still trailing its rope, attached to the net itself and through Viron's armour, it wound itself tightly around the rail of the second floor balcony.

The rope held and so did the net, though not well, with the parts of it that rubbed forcefully against Viron's armour beginning to fray and snap in places, as the net came to a swaying stop no more than three or four feet from the ground.

Yue looked murderous from her position strapped unwillingly to the ex-Regent's back.

"Let me down," she insisted, struggling within the confines of my net.

Sabien drew his sword and approached the dangling net. Viron did not so much as move or protest as Sabien reached through the ropes to grab hold of Viron's sword with his free hand and pull it out of its confinement.

Watching Viron closely for any sudden movements, Sabien cut the support rope, and Viron and Yue tumbled the remaining distance to the ground. As the two of them touched ground, several things occurred simultaneously.

Viron twisted his body suddenly to reach a blade hidden in his boot and then uncoiled, sending his blade flashing after Yue, who bounded out of reach with her usual finesse. Sabien struck faster than lightning, pinning Viron's hand holding the dagger to the ground with the traitor's own sword, causing Viron to cry out in agony, as another of my nets covered him thoroughly to keep him from trying anything like that again.

Sabien knelt down, removed the dagger from Viron's limp and bloody fingers, and tossed it aside. "He will have to be searched to see if he is hiding anything else."

"Can I try first, Sabien?" Yue asked, dashing to Sabien's side.

Sabien nodded his head, but kept a close watch on Viron. Narlhep had joined us and was glaring down his former regent. I knew the prince had a number of questions for this man, who had betrayed him and tried to end his life, but I held up a hand to forestall him. I knew Yue had a better chance than any of us to get the truth of what had happened, since she could see directly into the man's mind.

Yue knelt by Viron's head and reached down to his neck, as if to feel his pulse. Viron met her eyes and glared at her, but Yue serenely ignored him, trusting in Sabien and the rest of us to ensure she did not come to any harm. Yue's eyes closed and her fingers touched his skin.

Yue's memory transfer took no time at all, as usual, but less than a second after touching Viron, her whole body went rigid and her face contorted in a grimace. When she opened her eyes she looked disgusted, and she stood abruptly, her eyes avoiding Viron's prostrated form entirely. Without even a word of explanation, she flash-stepped and was gone, though I managed to catch a hint of her here and there as she jumped from balcony to balcony, heading upward.

Sabien continued his stoic watch of the prisoner, but Narlhep looked confused. "What's going on? Where'd she go?" He turned his attention to Viron, "How do I open the door?"

Viron said nothing, but my mind wasn't on him; it was elsewhere, following Yue. What had she seen in Viron's mind that had caused her to run like that? She hadn't been fleeing; she had gone with purpose. I looked up as Yue landed again on the topmost balcony and saw she was going to wherever it was Viron had come from.

I turned myself to mist and began to drift upwards after Yue. I had no hope of catching up to her, but I followed just the same. The ornately carved wooden door beyond the statue had been left open. I floated through it and down the hall, before coming to a sharply curved stairwell and floating up that too.

I found Yue in a round room formed by the stairwell widening gradually. There was nothing in this room other than a podium at its center, where Yue stood with her hands resting upon its surface. As I drifted in, the light in the room grew and, looking upwards, I could see the ceiling was opening, revealing the sunny outdoors.

As the sun filled the room, a person who hadn't been there a moment before appeared before Yue; it was Kosetsu, but she was somewhat transparent, as if she wasn't fully present.

Yue saw Kosetsu and I noted tears filling her eyes.

"But…you're dead, aren't you?" Yue asked her and I realized what it was Yue had likely seen in Viron's memories.

The ghost of Kosetsu – for that's what it was – nodded slowly with a sad smile.

"It was because you wouldn't fire the weapon, wasn't it?" Yue asked and Kosetsu nodded again, placing her hands over her heart. "You cared about us?"

I floated over to Yue and landed to reform beside her on the platform. "It was Narlhep. They're in love. She couldn't obey her father's command to fire on him."

"But he killed her for it," Yue said, crying freely now. "Her own father…"

An immense sadness filled Kosetsu's expression as she slowly began to fade. As the strange visitation came to an end, a grinding noise began and the platform Yue and I were standing on started to rise.

The platform rose one level at a time, creating a flight of steps all the way around where we stood in the center. The rising continued until Yue and I were standing on the very tip of the mountain and looking out over the fields of Taiyou below. There was a trail of green light trailing off to the south, visible in the ordinarily empty sky.

"Okay," Yue said with a nod, "I'll find them for you."

I gathered she wasn't speaking to me, but I waited patiently for her to explain, taking this peaceful moment to look out over the beauty of lush, green Taiyou, and to grieve for Narlhep and the loss of his Kosetsu.

Yue took a deep breath. "His power is free now. Jedeite wants me to find his Chosen and bring them to Taiyou."

I nodded slowly, but said nothing. Until today, I hadn't really thought of the concept that the gem gods would interfere or speak to us – or even that they really existed. Now I had to believe – it was either that, or my longtime friend was now hearing voices.

"Do you want to go down?" I asked her. "I'm not sure if they've managed to get the doors open, but I can get us out from here."

Yue nodded and I took her hand, turning us both to mist. Together we drifted down the side of the mountain to land in front of the temple doors below.

The doors were open; Narlhep had succeeded, but as I reformed Yue and I next to the others, I realized not all was as it should be.

Sabien, Rama, Narlhep, Hotaru, and Kaji each had the same stricken expression as they looked out upon the lands surrounding the temple. There were trees uprooted, gouges in the land, and bodies strewn everywhere – some only in pieces.

The cries of the wounded and dying filled the air, and the smells of blood and fire assaulted our nostrils. I took in a ragged gasp of air, my eyes frantically scanning the devastating scene. I saw Roughlanders, men of the Lion Brigade, and fallen Knights – people I knew, people I had travelled here with – strewn about as if in a refuse pile.

What lay before me what the most shocking and horrible thing I had ever seen, so much so I couldn't begin to process it. There was only one thought in my mind that floated clearly to the surface – Masaru – and look as hard as I might, I didn't see him anywhere.

Chapter 14 – Remembrance

Sabien was the first of us to break the tableau. He took off down the stairs like a shot fired after Ris, whose battered form I could see from here. One of her wings was bent backwards and stuck upwards, where it flapped listlessly in the wind.

Just as Sabien needed to go to Ris, I needed to find Masaru. I had to know first and foremost if he had survived this – whatever this was – and to do that, I needed higher ground.

I took off, soaring upwards into the air. I was well above the carnage and circling slightly to the right to angle for a better view when I realized I wasn't travelling as mist. Over my left shoulder I caught sight of a glowing blue feathered wingtip – wings?

I was too overcome with distress to wonder at how it was possible or what I had done; I needed to be in the air and my power had provided for me. I suddenly spotted Masaru below and without any conscious direction I started to glide downward through the air toward him.

He was on his knees and being held upright by two Roughlanders, one on either side of him. The one on the left was Razor, I noted distantly; the other was one of the aged women, altered forever by the Oujou's curse. The white shirt I had cleaned for him was torn, bloody, and covered with dirt. The rest of him was not much better, but as I landed he raised his head and saw me, and I realized, belatedly, he was still alive.

Tears blurred my vision and my legs were unsteady. I tried to take a step toward him, but I wasn't capable of it – my legs wobbled and faltered beneath me. I tried again, holding my hand out to him, just wanting to confirm what my eyes had seen and convince myself he was really there.

I stumbled again and I felt myself begin to fall, when I was caught by steady hands and a familiar scent. I looked up into Masaru's blue eyes – somehow, despite his injuries, he had managed to cross the distance between us in the space of a heartbeat – and he tightened his arms around me in an embrace.

I held onto him tightly. He was alive and I hadn't left him out here to die without ever knowing how I felt about him. I sent a silent thanks to Sapphiros, not knowing whether he had had anything to do with protecting Masaru or not – or whether the distant gem god even cared. He wasn't dead, so I wasn't too late.

"I was so worried about ye," Masaru whispered into my ear as he held me close.

"Worried about me?" I questioned, not understanding.

"Aye," he answered, "you were all stuck in there with the doors sealed shut and we didn't know what was happenin' to ye."

"Oh," I commented, deflated, and loosened my hold on him somewhat. He had been worried about all of us in the temple because of the Oujou and Viron – it hadn't been me he was thinking of. "But out here…we knew you were in danger because of Sabien's connection with Ris, but – what happened?"

Masaru opened his mouth to answer me, when he was interrupted by someone calling his name, "Masaru!"

I turned my head sharply to see who was calling him and Masaru did the same. It was a Roughlander I didn't know, but evidently Masaru did. The man was cradling his left arm, but gesturing wildly with his right in the direction of the trees just beyond him. "It's Lady Sirrah, she's hurt real bad!"

"Where is she?" I asked, leaning past Masaru.

"This way," the Roughlander answered, starting back the way he had come.

I let go of Masaru to follow after the man to Sirrah. It was time I started using the medic kit I had been given. I could be of help in this situation if I could keep control of my emotions enough to stay focused. I expected Masaru to accompany me, since it was him the man had actually requested, but when after a few steps I realized he wasn't following me, I looked back.

Masaru was down on one knee and gripping his left side with a pained expression.

"Go on, don't worry about me," he said through gritted teeth. "I'll be along in a minute."

I rushed back to him, despite the frantic Roughlander's impatience at the delay. "What do you mean? You're clearly hurt." I removed his hand and felt along his chest on the left side. "You have at least one broken rib."

"Aye and there are others who need you more – go on."

"I got him," Razor, who looked relatively unharmed, said as he came up behind Masaru and put a hand on his shoulder.

Masaru shot daggers out of his eyes at Razor, but I figured if he was well enough to do that, then I should see to Sirrah and whoever else I could actually be of use to.

"Thank you, Razor," I nodded to him and scurried after the Roughlander who was waiting for me.

I wasn't sure if Sirrah could be considered lucky or unlucky to still be alive. Most of her left leg had been removed at the thigh and she was losing blood at an alarming rate. The ground around her was soaked already, but since there were a few dead Roughlanders around her, I couldn't be sure how much of the blood was hers. As I arrived, one of the surviving Roughlanders tending to her was doing the sensible thing and fastening one of his belts around what was left of her leg to cinch the wound and try to stop the bleeding. I was astounded and impressed once again at Roughlander ingenuity, and it struck me this was likely only one of the many uses for the belts they wore, which I had always thought of as unnecessary adornments.

Borrowing the man's canteen, I flushed out Sirrah's wound with water and got a better look at it. The cut was cleanly made – it looked too perfect to be made by even the sharpest sword blade – even the bone itself was sliced cleanly through. As I put on the gloves from my medic kit and prepared a needle with thread, I wondered what could have done this.

"Can anyone tell me what happened?"

Surprisingly, it was Sirrah who answered me; I had been so preoccupied with her wound that I hadn't even noticed she was still awake. I realized how distant I felt from reality and I forced myself to listen to her, using her words to distract me just enough from the horror of what I was doing and why I was doing it, but still holding me to the present so I could function. But Sirrah's words told of a different horror – one was just as vivid.

"I didn't see what they looked like; there was only a hooded figure in a long blue cloak…

Lady Sirrah stood with Razor and a cluster of other Roughlanders.

"What do you think is taking them so long?" Sirrah asked no one in particular. "I mean, they just have to put an end to that wretched excuse for a Regent and be done with it, right?"

"I'm sure it's not half so simple," Razor answered with a lopsided grin, "it never is. But they'll be out when they're good and ready. There's no sense worrying about it."

"Better them than us in there. I saw all that green stone when the doors were open," Sirrah noted. "I think I've seen enough green now to last me a lifetime – not that out here's any better."

"What's that?" Razor asked suddenly, narrowing his eyes against the sun's glare and peering forward past the view of the mountain.

There was a lone figure in a floor-length cloak with the hood pulled forward to hide any facial features. The figure stood perfectly still, back to the sun, looking over the loose crowd of people gathered around the Jade mountain.

The figure didn't move from the spot where it stood, but it raised its arms, one outstretched and the other one held back in what appeared to be some kind of arcane motion. Something on the figure's wrists glinted in the sunlight, as the cloak drew back to reveal hands with fingers held curved like claws.

Blackness darker than a shadow formed in the figure's hands and was pulled back above the figure's head, and then flung forward like a black whip. The black tendril sliced through the air, ribboning this way and that, and then the air was filled with the screams of the dying.

"I fell," Sirrah said, her voice rough. "I didn't even see it coming for me, but it must have been that black whip that did it."

"Shh," I hushed her, "I'm almost done here and we'll get you bandaged up. You'll be okay." They were empty words – Sirrah had lost her leg – but I had to say something.

Leaving what bandages I had to the thoughtful Roughlander with the belt, I stood shakily and looked about. Immediately, I wished I hadn't. There were so many people hurt. Being brought suddenly back to reality by the conclusion of Sirrah's tale made the sounds of people suffering so much more acute, and now that I had been made aware of it, I couldn't shut them out.

"Do you know where the pallet of supplies ended up?" I asked the Roughlander who had led me to Sirrah, forcing myself to stay focused – there would be time enough to come to terms with events later. "Can you take me there?"

The supplies were undamaged, though the contents of the pallet had been strewn about. It was there that I found Jeth looking more concerned than I had ever seen him.

"Are you all right, Jeth?" I asked him, rummaging through the supplies looking for my crate of bandages and the small box of Flaqqers Rama had gifted to me.

"Me, I'm fine – she didn't lay a finger on me," Jeth answered, sounding perturbed, "but I can't find Adel or Aysel."

"When did you last see them?" I asked. It wasn't like Adel to be missing when she was needed and Aysel would have been a help with the wounded, unless of course either, or both, of them were hurt as well.

"Well, Adel ordered the Knights to protect everyone else when we saw her coming…

"Form a line," Adel commanded. "We don't let her through, and if she attacks or advances we rush her, understood?"

"Do ye think she intends to attack all of us, then?" Masaru asked.

"I wouldn't underestimate her," Jeth said. "There's something familiar about her, only I can't place it."

"Like she's been around for over eight hundred years, ye mean?" Masaru questioned, awestruck.

"Yeah, could be," Jeth replied. "Just keep on your toes, okay?"

Her first attack ignored the assembled Knights completely and soared over them to cut down the Roughlanders beyond. Before she could prepare a second strike, the Knights were upon her.

Jeth made to strike her middle, which she avoided along with each slash of Masaru's two knives coming for her right side. Adel swooped in with her mace to strike at her hooded head, but she ducked out of the way, the motion not upsetting her stride in the least, but being enough to cause the hood to fall from her face.

She was serenely beautiful, with long, straight, deep blue hair, unruffled by the motions of dodging, framing an elegant, oval face, and narrow eyes with bottomless black pupils. Her expression was as unruffled as her perfect hair, as she weaved and dodged the various efforts of the Knights, her gold earrings and bracelets chiming gently with each movement; it was like a dance, only performed by the greatest dancer the world had ever seen.

Jeth stopped to stand back and watch a moment, confused by this woman, and a little frustrated at not being able to make contact with her. Using momentum, the blue-haired woman was able to put Masaru off balance and get him out of the fray temporarily. In that momentary opening, the woman gathered yet another whip of black energy and tossed it around her head toward Adel, who – if it mattered to this woman at all – may have been the greatest threat.

At the last possible second, Aysel dodged in between her sister and the blow meant for her, blocking it with her shield. The shield deflected the greater part of the attack, but it did not withstand the damage and a sizable part of it was sliced cleanly off. Pressing what small advantage she had, Aysel drove the shield toward the woman and brought her sword up over her shoulder for an attack.

Mid-swing, Aysel froze through no fault of her own. She was held in stasis by her foe and was slowly lifted into the air, with no more than the direction of the blue-haired woman's hand. Aysel's sword arm fell limply to her side, the blade dropping from her slackened grasp, before she convulsed in sudden pain and went rigid, her arms pinned to her sides and her legs together.

The blue-haired woman made a crushing motion with her fist and Aysel's screams combined with the sounds of tearing metal.

With the woman's focus completely bent on Aysel's torment, she didn't see Jeth's fist before it collided with her face. Adel caught Aysel's limp form as she fell, rolling with her sister to get a safer distance away from the blue-haired woman. Jeth pressed his advantage and traded blows with the woman while she was disoriented, driving her back and giving Adel a chance to get away.

"I don't know where she went after that," Jeth finished. "Maybe she's hiding with Aysel, but I'm worried about her."

"Well, I'm sure there are a lot of people in disarray right now, Jeth. The best thing to do right now would be to get those who can walk to organize those that can't. See if you can get people to bring the wounded that can be moved closer to the temple and I'll see about organizing the healers.

"We'll find them," I reassured him. "Organizing people is the best way to start, and then we can range out further and find anyone who's missing. Can you do that for me?"

"Yeah," Jeth answered. "I'm on it. Just let me know if you find them, okay?"

I nodded and started back toward the temple stairs with my finds from the supplies. On the way there, I repeated the instructions I had given Jeth to any able-bodied persons I found, and I stopped to treat some of the more serious injuries I came across, or at least offered bandages or a Flaqqer to those who looked competent enough with healing.

I found Kaji with Narlhep and the still imprisoned Viron near the temple doors. The former two were speaking animatedly with the matronly sorceress from earlier in the temple. Her poise and self-confidence were back, and she was hovering her customary couple of inches off the ground with a controlled expression on her face.

"Of course we have healers," the sorceress was saying, "but they do not leave the school. If you would like them to see to your wounded, you'll have to bring them inside."

"You will send out your healers to help those they can," Narlhep decreed authoritatively, "and you will also help with the wounded – I won't accept any more excuses."

The matronly sorceress nodded, looking taken aback.

"I've begun instructing people to bring those who can be moved closer to the temple," I informed Kaji and Narlhep as I reached the top of the stairs. "The healers will have to go to the ones that can't, but I have Jeth and a few others out searching for them."

The sorceress left, entering the temple once more to presumably go about the task she had been given, and Narlhep turned to Kaji. "Kaji, would you be able to find Sir Rama for me? I'm sick of looking at Viron after what he's done–" Narlhep faltered and I realized that somehow he also knew the extent of Viron's crimes and was trying to do his best to cope, at least for the present. "I can't risk leaving him unguarded."

"Certainly, Your Majesty," Kaji replied with a wink, before suddenly splashing to the ground in a puddle of water.

"Don't worry," I told Narlhep, in an attempt at being light hearted – we were all trying to cope. "It just means he had another one somewhere else. He does that."

"Having you four around is going to take some getting used to," Narlhep admitted. "Your powers are like nothing I've ever seen."

"So does that mean you accept our help?" I asked, referring to the alliance we had been trying for since our arrival in Taiyou.

Despite everything, Narlhep smiled slightly. "I'd be a fool not to. You've helped me so much already and you're right, things are not necessarily always what they seem. There's so much I don't know – so much I was deliberately kept in the dark about." He spared a slight glance over his shoulder at the still smoldering Viron trapped in my net. "It's possible I will need you again to help me keep Taiyou safe."

I nodded, satisfied. "And we will be there."

Rama arrived shortly after and I left Narlhep with his friend, making my way back out to the field where I could be of use. I was needed, but besides that, I didn't want to stop working for fear the reality of our losses would set back in and I would be forced to face them. Wounded men and women had been arranged in a semblance of rows a little ways out from the base of the temple stairs. Thinking I would be of the most use where people could find me, I began helping those gathered there because they needed medical attention.

"I'm fine, I'll keep a while – go ahead and look after someone else."

The man was one of Rama's Lion Brigade: his arm, still encased in his armour, was mangled beyond belief and he held it cradled close to his body.

"I can look at you now, that's what I'm here for," I told the man, somewhat impatiently.

"There are people worse off than me. How about that person?" the soldier said as he indicated an injured Roughlander a row over.

"Fine," I replied, not wanting to waste time arguing, "but since I'll be nearby, in the meantime, you can tell me what happened to everyone. I heard about the blue-haired woman attacking the Knights, but how did everyone else get hurt? Did she bring troops with her?"

"No," the man answered as I began inspecting the Roughlander he had indicated. "It was just her…it was all her…

The Roughlanders readied their weapons – most of them had something they called a carbine rifle, a long distance bolt thrower with quite a bit of power behind it. As a group they formed up and took aim, launching everything they had at the cloaked woman as soon as the Knights were clear.

The woman reacted as if the bolts were no more than skipping stones travelling across water. She moved and weaved those parts of her body necessary to avoid impact with the projectiles and even went so far as to bat one or two away with the bracelets on her arms. She didn't take a single hit, and when the bolts were clear of her she faced the Roughlanders, drawing her hood back up to cover her face from the sun.

Meanwhile, the Lion Brigade had formed up at their captain's orders – minus the scouts who had ranged out around the mountain and had no clue there was one woman who had gotten past them to terrorize the rest. The Lion Brigade charged with swords drawn, but their advance was not enough to intimidate, or even distract the woman, as she gathered yet another black whip of energy and decimated those Roughlanders who had gathered to try and stop her.

The Lion Brigade engaged their target and one by one they were defeated, as the woman danced between their blades and shields, avoiding harm to her person and causing death and dismemberment to the armoured men facing her. The lucky ones she outright killed or just knocked aside; those that weren't so lucky, she lifted into the air and crushed them with the force of her will, before leaving them where they fell and going on to the next.

"One woman did all of this?" I asked, incredulous and worried. "Is she dead? What happened to her?"

"I don't know," the soldier answered as he indicated his mangled arm, "I was a little distracted."

"Here, let me see that," I said, finishing up with the Roughlander I had been bandaging.

"No really, I'm good," he protested, "help the others first. You can come back to me later."

"Yukari!" Hotaru called my name, suddenly reforming from a puddle next to me. "It's Aysel! I found her and Adel, but…" Hotaru looked pale and worried, so I gathered whatever state Aysel was in, it wasn't good.

I spared one last glance for the soldier with the mangled arm. "I'm coming back for you. Hotaru," I addressed her, "show me where she is."

Hotaru turned herself back into water; I figured it was easier for her to travel that way right then because of the weakened state she was in after withstanding the Oujou's attacks. I followed the puddle as it danced ahead of me anxiously and led me into a copse of trees. The trees, and even the ground itself, were cut through with a swath of destruction and I began to seriously worry about what I would find at the end of it.

At first Adel was all I could see, which appeared to be how she wanted it. Adel sat hunched over with her shield out before her, covering the majority of her sister's body from view and therefore, from harm. Her eyes were red and not from crying, though there was a hint of that as well. Her pupils glowed with an unnatural red light and she gripped her mace tightly in her right hand, the end of it glowing faintly red to match her eyes.

"Adel?" I asked cautiously, approaching from the side instead of head on where her mace was pointed. I didn't think Adel would attack me, but with the murderous expression on her face, I didn't think it wise to take any chances. She didn't answer me at first; it seemed her mind was somewhere else entirely, her thoughts filled with a rage I didn't understand. "Adel, can I look at her, please?"

Adel blinked and her eyes dulled to a more natural-looking red, though they still were a far cry from her usual blue. With stiff and cautious motions, Adel lifted her shield enough to move it to the side and allow me access to Aysel's inert form. Taking a deep breath to steady myself, I moved into Adel's reach and squatted down on the far side of Aysel. Hotaru reformed on the other side of Adel, but thankfully did not say anything to upset her.

Aysel's armour was in a much worse state than the soldier I had just left, though their injuries were similar. Detaching myself from who it was I was looking at, I was able to take full account of the state her body was in. Firstly, she was still breathing, though she was without a doubt unconscious. For now, I thought that was for the best, given her extensive injuries and the amount of pain they must be causing her.

From the state of her armour, Aysel looked as if someone had squeezed the right side of her body like an open bottle of toothpaste. Looking at her, I wanted nothing more than to begin to pry open the armour and attempt to salvage the flesh beneath, but I knew at that point the crushed armour was likely the only thing keeping her from bleeding out and dying immediately. There was no hope for her right arm – I could see that clearly. It would have to be removed, as not even Ris could regrow limbs.

Ris! I abruptly remembered the Kumori with her miraculous healing abilities and wondered why I hadn't thought of her sooner, given all of the injuries I had seen. Then I recalled she had been the first wounded being I had noticed upon exiting the temple. Was she okay? Had Sabien found a healer to look after her yet?

I looked over at Adel, who was watching me carefully with her sister. Nodding to her, I placed my hands over Aysel's chest and did what I had done for Kaji inside the temple; I willed her to continue living and to get stronger. I didn't know if my power would be enough or if it would help her, but Aysel would need every drop of strength anyone could give her to live through the operation that would have to occur to get her out of her suit of armour.

My hands glowed with a cyan light as I faced Adel. "She's going to live," I said with conviction and tears filled Adel's eyes in sudden relief. Hotaru caught the Knight as the tension bled out of her and she sagged limply.

"The woman who did this – is she dead?" I asked Adel.

Adel shook her head. "I don't know," she answered brokenly. "She could be, but I do not think it likely, even though I saw most of it from here."

"Tell me."

The ground opened up at the woman's feet. Startled, she hopped backwards to avoid the gaping pit widening before her when from behind her a sand shark – like the ones from out in the desert – formed impossibly out of the very rock and dirt of Taiyou, biting down on her midsection and dragging her down with it into the depths.

A scuffle ensued beneath the ground, a fin or hand surfacing from the hole now and again when Masaru – back on his feet now – summoned his blue energy knives and dove into the pit after them.

"I assume the sand shark was his creation," Adel commented drily. "He has developed an interesting power."

Masaru managed to damage her where others had failed, but it was still she who emerged from the hole victorious. Seeing there were still people to destroy, she raised her hands again and curved her fingers like claws grasping at air. This time, before the deadly black energy could form in her hands once more, something entirely different struck her. Thin, yellow-green streams of energy shot through the air in an arc directed by the Second Spawn Croatin, Pine, and slicing off three of her fingers.

The woman screamed and clutched at her hand in sudden agony, but it wasn't long before her screams subsided to heavy panting and she lowered her cowled head to focus her gaze on her hand. After a moment, the shadow formed by her hood wafted downwards corporeally toward her fingers and slowly reformed them as perfect as they had been before the attack.

There was a sudden flash of red light as Adel directed a blast of power through her mace to strike the blue-haired murderess. The backlash pushed Adel and Aysel back through the trees, but the blast itself stuck the woman as not much else had and sent her flying, putting more distance between the woman and her victims.

"I don't know what happened after that," Adel finished.

I nodded. "I'm going to go find Ris. I'm not going to risk Aysel by trying to work on her alone. Will you be all right here until I come back?"

"You've told me Aysel is going to live and I believe you," Adel answered. "Go and come back quickly."

I left Hotaru with Adel and Aysel, and hurried over to where I had last seen Ris. She wasn't there, but I did find Yue with the Second Spawn Croatin, Pine.

Pine was almost unrecognizable without his cloak, as I had never seen him with so much as his hood down. The Second Spawn looked very different from the other Croatins I had seen; he was small, for one, and slight of build. His wiry frame was covered in lime green skin with purple markings and without his cloak he wore only a folded loincloth, like a Sumo wrestler might. His features were sinuous like a snake, his eyes and nostrils no more than slits and his hands looked almost human – not like Ticket or Stephen's suction-cup fingertips.

Pine was lost in a powerful wave of emotion, which, other than his odd appearance, was what caused me to stop and stare a moment. He was wailing, his heartfelt cries of loss the most human thing about him, despite their inhuman sound. His hands were curled into fists and leaked a sticky yellow substance – I could only assume to be his blood – as he rammed them repeatedly on a large rock before him, shaking with sobs and unwilling, or unable, to control himself.

Yue was much nearer to him than I was and I watched as she – despite her warnings of the touch of a Second Spawn Croatin being poisonous – placed her hands upon his shoulders and gave them a slight squeeze.

Pine's eyes opened wide with sudden shock and his screams cut off abruptly, his entire form freezing. He slowly turned to face Yue and with tears in her own eyes, she pulled the Croatin in for an embrace.

Feeling uncomfortable at witnessing this display, I looked away and continued on toward the temple stairs, hoping Ris had been well enough to move over to where the rest of the wounded were being gathered.

I found Ris, not with the other wounded, but a little ways away from the hustle and bustle at the base of the mountain. Sabien was by her side, and by the look of his reddened eyes and the way he grasped her limp hand, he had not left her. It was a heartbreaking scene.

Unlike most of the others I had seen, Ris did not have any limbs missing or any cuts on her body. She was not crushed in any way; she simply looked battered and broken, like she had perhaps fallen from a great height and tried to roll unsuccessfully with the impact. She was unconscious and her breathing was shallow. Sabien was the only one with her and I wondered briefly why he hadn't thought to get me or one of the healers who had finally come out of the temple to help thanks to Narlhep's request.

"Sabien," I addressed him, perhaps a tad sharply, "if I'm going to look at her, I'm going to need you to move."

Sabien's head snapped up to face me and I noted his eyes were largely unseeing, as I had suspected they might be. Sabien was in a state of shock, which explained why he'd been near to useless at getting help for Ris. I felt sorry for him, but right then I needed him out of the way so I could see what could be done for Ris.

"Sabien – go get Yue," I ordered him, regretting the necessity of doing so. "Tell her I need her help with Ris. Do you understand?"

Sabien nodded, but it was another moment before he could tear himself away from the sight of Ris and do as I had commanded him. I ignored him and turned my attention to Ris, who needed me more.

I inspected her wing first, which was the most obvious problem, being bent back upon itself. I didn't know too much about the biological make-up of a Kumori – in fact I knew nothing, save what I could tell by looking at her – but from what I could tell, the break on her wing was a clean one; provided I could set it properly, it should heal.

As I followed the wing down with my fingertips, I noticed though the break in the wing might be the most obvious injury, it certainly was not the most serious. I couldn't be sure, but it seemed that the angle the wing had bent had shoved it into Ris' shoulder. It was deeper set than the other one, and I could tell just by looking at it and feeling the damaged tissue around the joint that it wasn't natural.

There were other bruises and strained muscles, and her left shoulder was dislocated, but that wing seemed to be the worst of it. I was just completing my initial inspection when Yue arrived, her eyes and face blotchy, but otherwise composed. Sabien seemed to have also recovered himself somewhat and took a position a little ways away to let us work.

Yue placed a hand over Ris' heart and closed her eyes.

"The wing bone is…fractured? Is that the word for it?" Yue said after a moment, her eyes still closed as she concentrated. "It's jabbing into her lung and there is blood everywhere where it shouldn't be. The wing itself is also broken, like you said. And her left arm is not attached right.

"It's not like I can see it," she tried to explain. "It's more that I can sense what is wrong. It'd be better if you could look for yourself, but it's the best I can do."

"No, that's helpful. I was wondering how extensive the damage was," I replied, awed at Yue's ability. "So we need to extract the wing bone, but if we do it'll likely bleed more and leave a hole in her lung?"

Yue nodded, looking perturbed; I supposed it was one thing to sense what was wrong and a wholly different thing to discuss it in clinical terms. I had to remember that although I had read extensively about medicine and biology, and now had had some experience dealing with broken bones and gaping wounds, Yue had never been more than an indifferent student at best.

"Wouldn't that be bad, though?" Yue whispered with a furtive look over her shoulder at Sabien. "I mean, internal bleeding?"

I nodded, considering the situation. "She's bleeding internally now and her lung is already punctured. I don't see that we have any other choice." I didn't like the odds, but I was right in saying we couldn't just leave her as she was – Ris wasn't going to get better on her own.

As Yue and I were deliberating, Masaru hobbled over to where we were. "Did the two of ye need any help?"

Yue and I looked up at Masaru and then back at each other – the answer was suddenly obvious to us both. "Flaqqers!"

"Aye, I think I have one here, there's not much left of it, though," Masaru said, removing the Flaqqer from the belt at his waist and holding out to us.

"I have some as well," I said, taking the Flaqqer from Masaru. "I took the remaining ones from the supplies, but I didn't even think of using them."

"Why ever not?" he asked. "There's a whole lot of people who could use 'em out there."

I felt my face flush with shame. I hadn't even thought of the Flaqqers as a viable solution to most of the injuries I had come across, not because I didn't have access to them, but because I didn't like the thought of little baby sand crawlers infesting the people I treated. My squeamishness was not an excuse to ignore a medical miracle when it could save lives and limbs.

"They can save Ris," Yue stated. "If reset the wing, maybe the Flaqqer will be enough to fix her lung before the bleeding gets too much worse."

I nodded in agreement and said, "They're the best chance we have."

Though Masaru looked weak and tired, we had him help us by holding Ris down in case the amount of pain we were going to cause her would send her into convulsions. We didn't warn Sabien about what we intended to do because we knew there were great risks involved, but it was obvious we needed to try before she got any worse.

Yue was stronger than I, so I directed her on which direction to pull to reset the wing bone, and I hoped I was right. Yue gave a sharp yank on Ris' wing and I jabbed the Flaqqer into her flesh as near as I could get to the injury, as Masaru had taught me. We did the same for the break in the wing and the dislocated arm, and then sat back to wait and see if the Flaqqer was enough to save her.

As the process was completed, Sabien moved back to his position holding onto Ris' hand tightly. Masaru, optimistic of Ris' chances because of the Flaqqer, leaned up against the base of the mountain and closed his eyes to rest a little. Anxious about Ris and needing to keep my mind off of the horrors of the present, I asked Yue to tell me what had happened to make Pine so upset.

"Dudgi is dead," she stated simply. "He and Pine are both of the Second Spawn and they got special permission to come with us to Taiyou because I asked for them…

"It works," Pine said to Dudgi, his whispery voice just loud enough to be heard from the cowl of his cloak. "The beams work and no doubt our touch will work just as well on her if we can get close enough."

Dudgi nodded to Pine's words and responded, whispering in kind, "I won't let you down."

Pine placed his hand on the younger Croatin's shoulder. "I know you won't."

They stripped down to the bare necessities, removing the cloaks that protected them from the harsh sun and the stares of those who did not approve of Croatins, and together the two Second Spawn bounded forward in the direction their target had been sent by the inexplicable red beam of light. When they found her, she had their Seventh Spawn brother, Stephen, held aloft by the neck. He was struggling and kicking feebly, but to no effect.

The blue-haired human was regarding Stephen with curiosity, her hood still back and her head tilted to one side, watching him as he ran out of air and his strength bled from him. There was no malice in her expression, until she caught sight of the Second Spawns approaching and her calm expression contorted into a grimace of displeasure.

Pine swiped at her for the second time with his finger-beams, but this time she moved easily out of the way, expecting this form of attack. Her hold on Stephen did not loosen as, held in her outstretched arm, he was forced to move with her.

Dudgi and Pine separated to either side, running to surround her in hopes it would be enough to divide her attention and allow one of them to get in close enough to take her down.

Pine leapt first, hands outstretched, but the human woman anticipated that too and moved Stephen's body before her to block the attack. Pine hesitated, held back by years of training and conditioning himself to avoid touching another Croatin, lest they die by his poisonous grasp.

Satisfied Pine's attack had been avoided, the woman spun to face the direction Dudgi had been advancing from, when something struck her on the head and she froze in surprise. Stephen used this opportunity to fish a second krevel out from his belt pouch and launch it, too, at her face. "That's what you get, lady!"

The human's face contorted once again, but this time with rage. Without hesitation, she snapped Stephen's neck and let his corpse fall to the ground, but the moment she had wasted killing the Seventh Spawn had been enough to allow Dudgi to get in close.

The Second Spawn's yellow hands closed around the human woman's head and she faltered, suddenly feeling the effects of the Croatin's poisoned touch. Any normal human would have fallen to the ground dead, or at the very least unconscious, but this woman only staggered before gathering enough of her power to lift Dudgi off of her and levitate him in the air.

Pine sliced at her with his finger-beams from behind, but it was too late. Dudgi was crushed by their opponent's will and left as no more than a lump of mangled yellow flesh and blood.

Yue's story of Pine's loss left me reeling, but more so for the loss of Stephen whom I actually had known, though only briefly. I was touched by his noble sacrifice and his moment of bravery, and I regretted his loss. It was not much of a consolation, but at least he had accomplished his family's mission and made it into Taiyou. Without our help, he might have died before getting a chance to even board the ferry.

"I think she's going to be okay." Yue's words startled me out of my reflection, and I noticed she had her eyes closed and was checking on Ris again. "The Flaqqers are working quickly on her lung and they've slowed the bleeding quite a bit already. The wing looks like it's where it's supposed to be. I think we did it."

I let out a relieved sigh.

"That's good news," Masaru commented, "I'm glad to hear it."

Again, simultaneously, Yue and I looked in Masaru's direction and at the broken rib he was still holding in place on his left side before meeting each other's eyes.

"Hold still Masaru," I warned him.

"What, I–" Masaru began to protest, but before he could even string a sentence together, Yue and I had tackled him, and I made sure his rib bone was aligned correctly as Yue Flaqqered him. "Aahhh!"

Masaru glowered as the pain subsided from the Flaqqer, but he couldn't legitimately protest us helping him to recover. After a little while Yue wandered off, but I lingered a bit longer, resting with my back to the mountain side and taking comfort from the sound of Ris' lungs getting stronger with each intake of breath.

"Razor saved my life," Masaru said after a moment, his voice subdued.

I stayed quiet, hoping Masaru might open up to me and explain the enmity that existed between him and Razor.

"He put himself in danger to save me," he continued, "which is something I never thought he'd do…

The Croatins had done their best, but two of them had already been killed and the other was lost in grief and rage, when Masaru finally tracked down where the blue-haired killer had landed after Adel's blast.

Masaru was in rough shape, but so was everyone else, and so he had to try to stop her before more people died at her hand. He engaged her, blue knives flashing, and though she had been made just a little bit slower by the poison of the Second Spawn Croatins, she was still just fast enough to keep out of reach and allow his knives only the barest taste of her blood.

Realizing she was losing speed and taking more and more grazes from Masaru's attacks, the woman suddenly changed tactics and allowed a knife to slash her arm, as she abruptly leapt back out of range.

Not one to be caught off guard by an enemy suddenly shifting the style of battle, Masaru threw one of his knives at her. She flipped over it athletically and landed palms down in a handstand. Darkness rippled out from where her hands made contact with the ground, and where that darkness touched, the grass itself died and turned to ash.

In no time at all, the darkness reached the body of the Croatin Stephen and reduced it to ash as well; next it incinerated the remains of Dudgi. Masaru had no more than a split second to react before the ripple reached his feet and he, too, would experience its devastating effect.

Masaru felt the wind knocked out of him as he was knocked forcefully aside; disoriented, he was rolled by the impact to land a distance away from where death had come for him.

"She got away after that, but it was Razor who saved me," Masaru finished. "Thankfully, he got us both far enough away, or it would have ended very differently."

I nodded slowly, absorbing it all, but I could say nothing. I was physically and emotionally exhausted by everything I had heard and witnessed, but there was still one very important thing I had to do, and it looked like Ris wasn't going to be in a state to help me any time soon.

I stood and stretched my tired muscles. "I have to see Aysel," I told Masaru. "I promised Adel I would come back."

Masaru nodded at my words, but seemed lost in his own thoughts. I left him with Sabien and Ris, and began the trek back through the carnage, the loss, and the pain, seeing it a little differently now that I knew all that had happened. One woman…one powerful woman had decimated all of these people for seemingly no reason at all, before leaving just as suddenly as she had come – a swath of destruction and pain in her wake.

It hadn't been the Oujou, as we had kept her occupied inside, and from the descriptions given to me, it hadn't been anyone known to any person I talked to – except for maybe Jeth. That meant it was possibly someone who had been around for eight hundred years – was she a Chosen, like us? There were supposedly five gem gods represented on this planet – was it possible we had more enemies than just the Vile Emperor to worry about?

The thought was an uncomfortable one and I pushed it from my mind – whoever that woman had been, for the time being she had left us alone and I was glad of the respite. We would have to deal with her if she came back, but for now our priority was to pick up the pieces and try to get as many of these people as we could save back to safety, however we could.

"No, no! I'm fine, don't worry about me," the soldier from Rama's Lion Brigade was protesting to one of the healers from the sorceress school who was trying to see to his arm.

"Still being stubborn?" I asked him bluntly, before commenting to the sorceress, "He said the same to me. I don't think he wants our help."

"That's not true," he responded. "I just want to make sure everyone gets the attention they need."

"Right," I commented caustically, my patience already used up for the day. "Well, right now it's your turn, so let us see it."

Together, the sorceress healer and I pried off the man's armour and did what we could for his arm. Actually, I had to admit it was better the soldier had waited for the magical healing. With the state his arm had been in, there would have been little I could have done for him, but the sorceress was able to regrow parts of his skin and knit everything together with magic.

Looking about, I counted the sorceresses. There were three Kumori, including the white one with the red markings, and one human girl other than the one I was working with. The matronly sorceress was nowhere to be seen, despite Narlhep's earlier orders that she help personally.

"I'm going to need your help with an amputation," I told the sorceress beside me. "In fact, with how seriously she was injured, the more of you who can help me, the better. Would you be able to ask the other healers if they will help?"

The sorceress nodded and did as I asked. After a few moments, the white Kumori and one of the others accompanied us into the trees, and I led them to Aysel. If I couldn't have Ris, I could at least have Kumori healers to help me do what needed to be done.

Aysel was in much the same state as she had been earlier and Adel had not moved, despite a serious leg injury I hadn't known she had. The human sorceress insisted she see to Adel's leg and did so, as the Kumori healers looked over Aysel with a practiced eye.

The white Kumori was unmoved, but the smaller one beside her seemed distressed at the sight of Aysel's crushed side and arm. The two Kumori healers seemed to deliberate silently, using hand gestures and facial expressions as they contemplated the patient before them.

"We cannot remove her armour without first sealing the wound," I informed them, "which will probably mean cauterizing it, unless you have some other way."

The white Kumori put her finger up to request me to wait a bit longer, so I took a seat on the other side of Hotaru to await the Kumori's decision. I had asked them to help, so I had to let them see what they could do.

After some time, the white Kumori nodded to me to indicate she was ready. With a series of elaborate hand gestures, the two Kumori tried to explain to me what they were going to try to do, and what help they needed from me and the other healer. I had them explain certain parts again until I was satisfied I fully understood, and then I explained to them how I could help.

"If she can do my part as well," I said, indicating the human sorceress, "I think I would be of more use lending Aysel the strength to get through this," I told them, activating my power and causing my hands to glow above Aysel's chest, doing my part to hold her to this life.

The white Kumori nodded her agreement and raised her hands like Ris would have done, threading her fingers together and then pulling them apart to create ten thin beams of red light between her hands. The Kumori healer held her power like that a moment, while the smaller Kumori summoned her power as well.

Together the Kumori raised their hands higher and were about to create the first incision as they had discussed, when as one they stopped, and the power between their hands faded.

Concerned, I glanced at their faces to see what had happened and I noticed they were looking beyond Aysel to something behind me. Turning my head over my shoulder, I saw that Ris had arrived, supported by Sabien on one side and Masaru on the other. She was shooing the other Kumori away weakly.

"Ris is willing to try," Sabien told us. "She says she has enough strength for Aysel, even if she cannot stand on her own just yet."

From where she sat on the ground with her now bandaged leg outstretched, Adel took hold of Ris's hand and gave it a slight squeeze, tears running down the proud Knight's face. "Thank you, Ris."

"Hey, there you are!" Jeth's voice spoke suddenly from behind Sabien. The Knight came into view with Yue at his side. "I've been looking everywhere for you."

Yue said nothing, but knelt down beside me and also placed her hands on Aysel. After a moment, Yue looked up and met Ris' eyes, before walking over to the Kumori. "This is the line you must follow," she whispered and placed her hand on Ris' brow to transfer the memory of what she had seen or sensed within Aysel.

Ris nodded, looking down at Aysel determinedly, before taking a deep breath to steady herself and tugging at Sabien and Masaru to move her closer to Aysel. I wriggled out of her way, so I was sitting by Aysel's head, and did my part by keeping up my glowing cyan hands.

Ris bowed her head and brought her hands together, pulling her power through her fingers and encasing Aysel in her signature blue bubble of healing energy. Despite sagging in Sabien and Masaru's arms, Ris still did not pause as she formed the beams of blue light like the white Kumori had done and proceeded to direct her power like a blue laser beam, cutting along the mangled portion of Aysel's body and removing the damaged part from the rest of her, sealing the skin with her magic as she went.

It was a miracle in progress.

Aysel remained unconscious throughout the process, and if her sleeping form was anything to go by, she felt no pain. Even though Aysel's arm was lost, the rest of her would be saved, thanks to the power of Sapphiros and the dedication of his Knights.

When Ris was done, she swooned into Sabien's arms and Adel gripped her sister's form tightly with relief. I watched Jeth clap a worried-looking Kaji on the back and I wondered when he had gotten there. I was distracted from the thought by Hotaru, who pulled Yue and I both into a grateful hug for helping, and my eyes met Masaru's across the small crowd as he, too, smiled at Ris' success.

Aysel was going to be okay.

The group of us – not just Kaji, Hotaru, Yue, and I – but the Knights as well, had come a long way to make it to Taiyou. Together and apart, we had braved many dangers across the Sand Lakes, the outposts, and the deceptively peaceful countryside, and today we had lost so much, but there was also much we had managed to save as well.

If there was anything I had learned since coming here, it was that this world was a dangerous place and it was far from perfect. We had arrived with no clue as to why we were there or where we were, but since then we had struggled every step of the way to get to this day, this point in time, where we finally had a small foothold in this place and had taken the first steps to finding a way we could belong here.

I looked out over the faces of the others. The ten of us, bound by friendship and duty, were still together, and despite the sadness I felt at the horrors of the day and the losses we had all suffered, I smiled, feeling thankful I didn't have to face them alone.

I had arrived in the sand with nothing, thinking I had lost everything, only to learn that the things that truly mattered I had taken with me, and there were things on this world that called to me more strongly than anything on Earth ever had.

As harsh, brutal and vivid as this world was – and no matter the circumstances under which I had arrived here – I wasn't sure anymore if I even wanted to leave it.

…unfortunately, only time would tell whether or not I could survive it.

End of Volume 1

To Be Continued in Vol. 2,

Lands of Jade

About the Author

Justine Alley Dowsett is the author of nine novels and counting, and one of the founders of Mirror World Publishing. Her books, which she often co-writes with her sister, Murandy Damodred, range from young adult science fiction to dark fantasy/romance. She earned a BA in Drama from the University of Windsor, honed her skills as an entrepreneur by tackling video game production, and now she dedicates her time to writing, publishing, and occasionally role-playing.

To learn more about our authors and our current projects visit: www.mirrorworldpublishing.com, follow @MirrorWorldPub or like us at www.facebook.com/mirrorworldpublishing

To learn more about our authors and our current projects visit: www.mirrorworldpublishing.com, follow @MirrorWorldPub or like us at www.facebook.com/mirrorworldpublishing

We appreciate every like, tweet, facebook post and review and we love to hear from you. Please consider leaving us a review online or sending your thoughts and comments to info@mirrorworldpublishing.com

Thank you.